Fred Mather

Men I Have Fished With

Sketches of characters and incidents with rod and gun, from childhood to manhood, from the killing of little fishes and birds to a buffalo hunt

Fred Mather

Men I Have Fished With

Sketches of characters and incidents with rod and gun, from childhood to manhood, from the killing of little fishes and birds to a buffalo hunt

ISBN/EAN: 9783337045739

Printed in Europe, USA, Canada, Australia, Japan

Cover: Foto ©Andreas Hilbeck / pixelio.de

More available books at **www.hansebooks.com**

CONTENTS.

PORTRAITS.

A WORD WITH THE READER.

THESE sketches originally appeared in the *Forest and Stream.* Read between the lines, and at times in them, will be found the wanderings of a boy who had no further object in view than to be in the woods and on the waters, and who had no taste for anything like the harness of civilization.

During the years of vagabondizing many things occurred which at the time seemed to deserve little notice, but subsequently grew into pleasant memories; and I began to write them up, naturally expecting that my immediate relatives and personal friends would read them with some interest. I was surprised and gratified to find how many strangers said pleasant things of them, and to know that there was a demand for them in book form.

The present volume comprises the twenty-four chapters which appeared between July 11 and Dec. 26, 1896. Other sketches of "Men I Have Fished With" have been printed since, and at this writing, in October, 1897, the series is in progress.

I have aimed to make a sketch of the boy or man of whom I wrote, so that the reader, gentle or otherwise, would know him, as I thought I did, and I find myself telling how to bob for eels, camp out and sleep in barns, kill deer with wooden plugs, taking my first trout on a worm, hunting turtles with Colonel Raymond in boyhood and reviewing his famous setters in after years, shooting turkeys, spearing eels through ice, and many other things too numerous to mention, up to the time when I was glad to get back home.

My lesson had been learned in that dearest of schools, but it took more years than with apter scholars.   Yet I have never regretted the cost of the education.

The earlier incidents recorded took place in Greenbush, N. Y., and on the Popskinny Creek. I have outlived them both.   The creek was merely an arm of the Hudson reaching behind an island, and water no longer flows through it.   I tried to get at its correct name, but failed. Mr. A. C. Stott, of Stottville, N. Y., writes that on a 1777 map it is spelled "Popscheny," and that older writers give "Palp-Sikenekoitas," while O'Callaghan, in his "History of the New Netherlands," speaks of the "Papsknee." Colonel David A. Teller, whose family has owned a farm on its banks for over a century, gives me other spellings, and I've seen it as "Popsquinea," therefore I have fallen into the habit of spelling it as we boys pronounced it.   It makes no difference now, it does not exist.

Greenbush is dead in name only.   It is now a city of the Empire State, having been consolidated with East Albany, Bath and other places, under the name of Rensselaer—confound the vandals who had no regard for the historic name honored in history by Fort Crailo, which is the oldest building now standing in America, and by Washington's headquarters on the McCulloch farm, on the heights above the village.

So, one by one, the columns supporting the arches of our memories are swept away by a younger generation, which cares nothing for them.   They are falling fast. Men who are now reckless boys will live to realize this. A year ago I made a pilgrimage to the old scenes, and I regret it.

I was a stranger in a strange land.   The tan-yard was gone; the nut orchard was filled with cottages, and the trees had gone where good trees go.   No one likes to outlive his cherished world or wants to know the holder of his birthplace and the intruders in the haunts of his boyhood. I will go there no more; I prefer to have my memories left undisturbed. The "City of Rensselaer" may grow and prosper, but Greenbush has passed away.

I hope the reader may find as much pleasure in these memories of boyhood as I did in writing them.

F. M.

REUBEN WOOD.

THIS noted sportsman, who for nearly half a century made his home in Syracuse, N. Y., was well known throughout the State, and it was my good fortune to have him as an instructor in the art of angling in earliest boyhood. We were born in the then small village of Greenbush (opposite Albany), he in December, 1822, and I eleven years later.

Almost every man who has passed the half-century milestone on life's journey loves to imitate Lot's wife and look over his shoulder, and usually the retrospect is pleasant because we do not remember clearly; we conjure up the roses in the pathway, and the small thorns are indistinct in the distance; a faint humming of the bees whose honey we stole brings no remembrance of the penalty paid for it; the wound of the sting is cured by the honey—in memory, at least. Poor indeed is the man of fifty who has no wealth of retrospect and who thinks the punishment of Lot's wife was fitted to the crime! It was cruelly unjust, and in compensation at this late day she should be sainted perhaps with the name and title of Saint Salina. Here I pause to ask if there is really any such thing as an occult cerebration which caused my pen to turn to thoughts of Lot's wife while writing an apology for looking back at the boyhood of a citizen of Syracuse, N. Y., the great salt-producing city of the State?

There are men who never could have been boys—engaged in boyish sports and had a boy's thoughts. Every one has known such men. Men who must have been at least fifty years old when they were born—if that event ever happened to them—and have no sort of sympathy for a boy nor his ways; crusty old curmudgeons who never burned their fingers with a firecracker or played hookey from school to go a-fishing. They may be very endurable in a business way, but are of no possible use as fishing companions. I speak by the card, for I've been in the woods with them.

Reuben Wood was a boy, and was one to me as long as he lived. We were boys together, he being a big boy when I was but a little one; he was at our house a great deal, and is among the earliest of memories. He was "Reub" all through life to all his familiars, and they were many.

It was a summer day, and I was some six or eight summers old, when Reub came down the street with some fish that he had caught in a stream then the northern boundary of the village, but now in it and fishless. After much solicitation he agreed to let me in the party next day—Bruin and me. Now, Bruin was a big Newfoundland dog belonging to my father which Reub had taught to pick me up whenever he said, "Bruin, go fetch Fred," no matter what screams, kicks and protests his burden made, and this was one of Reub's jokes which I failed to appreciate. We started, Bruin and I, in high glee. Reub cut some poles, rigged the lines, floats and hooks and put on the worms, and he soon had a perch, a monster it seemed then and does yet, while the sunfish that tried to run away with my float and which Reub helped to land probably weighed more than the grocer's scales could tell; it must have been as big as 100 modern ones, and Reub said "it was as big as a piece of chalk." Such was my first experience in angling, as clear in memory as if only a week ago.

A little pond turtle stuck his head up near the float,

looked at it and us, and paddled to the bottom in the funniest way.   Reub called it a "skillypot," but he had funny names for everything.   Then I caught a perch, actually bigger than the sunfish, and a new world seemed to open; but the spines of the fish cut my hand and the world was not so bright.   Five fish came to my lot in all, but Reub had about twenty—some perch, sunfish, two bullheads and an eel.   He said that I let the fish eat the worms off. I saw a turtle climb on a log while Reub was up the bank after more worms, and I went out on the log to get it, but the turtle slid into the water, and so did I.   A scream brought Reub, who whistled for Bruin and ordered him to "Fetch Fred," and he did.   Oh, the dripping of clothes and the splashing of shoes as we went home, and the fearful tale of a turtle who wouldn't wait to be caught!   This last seemed the greatest cause of grief and afforded Reub and other boys a text for teasing, which they worked to an annoying extent, and it was long before he would take me fishing again, saying, "No, you'll go diving for turtles."   This occurred about 1840, and Reub referred to it the last time I saw him, in 1883.

At this time Greenbush was a very quaint little village on the upper Hudson, whose connection with the outside world was by the Albany stage to Boston and by ferry to Albany.   No railroad entered it, and in fact the only one at that time in the whole State of New York ran from Albany to Schenectady, and hauled its cars to the top of the hill by a stationary engine before hooking on the light locomotive.   The place was favorable for the development of character, unhampered by the conventionalities which come from contact with outside people, and Reuben grew to manhood there and retained a quaint simplicity all his life, a rugged, honest nature, whom it was refreshing to know, and was a lovable man to meet.   If, as a boy, he ever indulged in forays on the fruit and melon patches of the farmers, the fact is unknown to me. That I did is certain, but the disparity of years forbade comradeship in such nocturnal pleasures. He was large, strong and heavy of movement, with a deep chest voice, even when a boy, that was remarkable. His brother Ira, nearer my age, resembled him in this and other particulars, and in both there was an air of honesty and truthfulness, not so frequent in boys, which was fully borne out in their characters as men.

In after years I had a joke on Reub which was originally on me as a boy, but later knowledge reversed it. With some other boys I had been fishing away up the hill in the pond of the locally famous "red mill," and had seen a pair of wood ducks alight upon a tree. We somehow knew that they were wild ducks, but had no idea that the term included more than one kind, for at that day we only knew one sort of tame ducks. To see a duck alight on a tree was strange, and I told Reub of it; and he spread the incredible story, for he knew nothing of wood ducks, and the laugh was on me. "Seen any ducks lightin' on trees lately?" was a common and annoying salutation, and years later the question was turned on Reub. I fished with him many times as a boy, never after he left Greenbush for Syracuse, in 1852; but we met occasionally after 1876, when thrown together at fairs and fly-casting tournaments, and he seemed to be the same boy that somehow had gray hair.

The picture of him gives an excellent idea of his manly face, but the cigar I do not recognize. This is not remarkable, because he used from a dozen to twenty each day, and there are people who might not recognize his picture without a cigar of some kind. The badge upon his corduroy coat is a certificate that he is a member of the Onondaga Fishing Club, of Syracuse, which was always represented at the State Sportsmen's tournaments. Take a good look at him! That kind, honest face would be a passport anywhere. To me he was always the same lovable boy to whom I looked up as guide, philosopher and friend on my first fishing trip away back in the forties. I think I am a better man for knowing Reub Wood when he was a big boy and I a child. From him I learned that the world was round—"rounder than a marble," he said— and I saw that the sky was the upper half and that we were inside the world; if he knew better he never explained the matter.

Reuben's humor was manifested in the use of strange words, which he probably manufactured, as I never heard them from any other person. A bad knot in a fish line was a "wrinkle-hawk," an excellent thing was "just exebogenus," a big fish was "an old codwalloper," and a long-stemmed pipe was "a flugemocker." What a blank page is a boy's memory that such things written on it remain indelible for over half a century when more important ones have faded! The name of Reub Wood conjures up these trifling things, which, if heard ten years ago, would have been forgotten. But he had such a strong individuality that a person who only met him for ten minutes would be impressed by it, and would know him in after years; what wonder that he should carve his personality on the mind of a child? Impressions of other men and boys in that small village are also quite distinct, and, as is usual in such places, there is more profanity and obscenity heard by a boy than in cities, for the tough boy in small places excels in such things, and it seems to me that he was worse then than now. But the worst that I ever heard Reub say was "Gosh hang it," under the provocation of having to cut a fish hook out of his thumb.

His mind was as pure as his life, and that is more than can be said of many who live straight enough, but have to resist temptation frequently.   A man is not so much to be judged by his actions as by his thoughts, if you only knew them, and Reub's thoughts were his spoken words.

In Greenbush he was employed in the bakery of Jonas Whiting, where he learned the mysteries of bread and cakes, and when he went to Syracuse he blossomed out as a caterer for balls and parties, and then established a business in fishing tackle, now carried on under the name of "Reuben Wood's Sons."   His old cash book is still extant, and was not only what its name implied, but was day book, journal and ledger all in one, with a margin for a weather record which contained such items as "Gone hunting," "Went after ducks," "Gone a-fishing," etc. This is indefinite, and one wonders what the result may have been until we strike the entry: "Wood returned from Piseco with 250 lbs. of trout."

In that early day, in the fifties, Onondaga Lake abounded in pickerel and eels, and Reub and his companions often made a night of it, taking them with torch and spear, as was the custom of the time, and the catch went to their friends and the poor.   When this mode of fishing became unpopular and unlawful, in later years, Reuben was one of the foremost in suppressing all kinds of fishing that the law forbade; but at the time of which we speak there was neither law on the subject nor public sentiment against spearing.   He followed the custom of the day, merely drawing the line at fishing on Sunday.

A chum of Reub's was Mr. Charles Wells, of Wells, Fargo & Co.'s Express, and they went shooting and fishing when the spirit moved.   Mr. Wells had not only all the railroad transportation necessary, but could have trains stopped anywhere in the woods if necessary, night

REUBEN WOOD.

or day, by flag or fire signal. This brings a sigh, not of envy, but merely a wish that such conditions existed to-day and I was "in it," as the saying goes.

One day in the fall of 1857 a report came to Mr. Wells that there were "rafts of ducks" on Cayuga Lake, one of those numerous large lakes of Western New York lying some thirty miles west of Syracuse, and a famous one for ducks. He told Reub just in time for him to gather his muzzle-loader and ammunition and get the next train going to Cayuga, at the foot of the lake via the "old road" of the New York Central R. R., a road then so slow that it took the best part of a day to get there. Wells had his camping outfit, and they camped for the night. As Reub told me the story years afterward, daylight found him in an old dugout, the only semblance of a boat at hand, while Wells had a good place on the shore. The ducks were flying down the lake and Wells had killed several, and was signaling him to come and pick them up, when a great flock of bluebills came up the stream and turned directly over Reub's head. As he let both barrels go the dugout somehow let him go into ice-cold water, but he hung on to his gun and got ashore chilled to the bone, and took the first train for Syracuse, where he traded his gun and equipments for a Knight's Templar badge and other things, and from that day foreswore the gun and devoted his energies to wielding the rod.

About this time Mr. Wells learned to fish with the fly and taught Reuben the art, to which he became devoted. It was long after this that I met Reuben, the occasion being the tournaments of the New York State Association for the Protection of Fish and Game, where he was a frequent competitor in the fly-casting tournaments, but never would allow himself or his brother Ira to win first prize because of a chivalric idea that another competitor—

to whom he always deferred—should not be beaten. Either of them could outcast the other man, whose hoggish nature never allowed him to acknowledge the knightly courtesy—if he had the capacity to appreciate the sacrifice. Not until the State Association held its tournament at Brighton Beach, Coney Island, in June, 1881, did Reuben Wood ever have a chance to cast unhampered by his sentiment. Here he had a new competitor with a great local reputation, who had never cast in a State tournament before. This was in the two-handed salmon rod contest, and Reuben won the first prize, valued at $50, with a cast of 110ft. His brother Ira came second, with 101ft. Harry Prichard cast 91ft., and F. P. Dennison 94ft. All but Prichard were members of the Onondaga Fishing Club, of Syracuse, and cast with the same rod—a split-bamboo, won by Reuben in the tournament at Buffalo in 1878; length, 17ft. 1 in. As there was an allowance of 5ft. for every foot of rod in length, Mr. Prichard was allowed 9ft. 10 in. because his greenheart rod (made by himself) was 1ft. 10in. shorter than the one used by the others; hence his amended record of 91ft. had an allowance of 9ft. 10in., making it 100ft. 10in., giving him third prize over Dennison.

In 1883 Prof. Spencer F. Baird appointed Reuben to take charge of the angling department of the American display at the International Fisheries Exposition in London, an appointment of which he was justly proud, as he wrote me in a farewell letter, and on June 11 he took part in the English fly-casting tournament at the Welch Harp, where he won first in salmon casting with an 18ft. split-bamboo rod, scoring 108ft., Mr. Mallock casting 105ft. with an 18ft. greenheart rod. In the single-handed trout contest he won first with 82½ft. over four competitors. In a contest with two-handed trout rods, a thing unknown in America, Mr. Mallock won first with 105ft., and Mr. Wood took second prize with 102ft. 9in. His many trophies in the tournaments in Central Park, New York City, are familiar to readers of *Forest and Stream.*

He died at his home in Syracuse on Feb. 16, 1884, in his sixty-second year. Mr. R. B. Marston, editor of the English *Fishing Gazette,* said of him: "I know many an angler in this country will feel sad at hearing genial, jolly, lovable 'Uncle Reub' has gone to his long rest. During his stay in this country he never failed to make friends of all who came in contact with him. I shall never forget the enthusiasm and almost boy-like glee with which he enjoyed a fishing trip with me to the Kennet, at Hungerford. He would stand for hours on the old bridge watching the trout and marveling at their cuteness. The system of dry fly-fishing pleased and astonished him greatly, and he told me he meant to try it on some wary old American trout he was acquainted with. Then he would show us some of his long casting with a split-cane rod. If we in this country, who only knew him so short a time, feel his loss so keenly, what must those home friends of his feel—his family and that wide circle of acquaintances who were proud to call him friend?"

His death was very sudden—he fell dead while entering his dining room. In addition to his love of the rod he was for many years an active member of the Syracuse Citizens' Corps, and later of the Sumner Corps, two well-known military organizations. He was also a member of the Baptist Church, and his name was a synonym for all that was honest and manly. The last time I met him he referred to our first fishing experience by saying, "Fred, are you catching many turtles now?" And the answer was, "No, Reub, it keeps me busy watching wood ducks light upon the trees."

BILLY BISHOP.

BOBBING FOR EELS.

I F these hills should come together where would I be?"
asked Billy when he found himself alone in Quackendary Hollow, where he had been sent to cut cord-
wood. This was his excuse for returning from a lonesome spot which his superstitious mind peopled with all
kinds of creatures, which might even draw the hills together and crush him, as they had done on many occasions, he said, in Holland, where his grandparents came
from. The scarcity of hills in that country may not have
been known to Billy, but that was a matter of no importance to him.

The hollow lay half a mile above the village of Greenbush, and was then well timbered and uninhabited.
Twenty years later it had quite a settlement, and was often
called "Nigger Hollow." But Billy Bishop was fonder of
the society of man than of those weird inhabitants who
worked evil in the dark forests by day or in open fields by
night. On the hill above the railroad was a field which
formed part of the farm of Mr. Frederick Aiken, and a
dilapidated barn in it was prominent in the sky-line from
the river road above the first creek. This was the "spook-
house lot" and the "spook-house barn," the house which
gave the name having burned before my recollection.
Billy told me that spooks danced in the barn on certain
nights, and that in the shape of stumps of trees a dozen of
them had chased him down the hill one night; but before
daylight they changed into bats and flew back. This was
certified to by John Pulver and Jakey Van Hoesen, chums

of Billy and rivals in doing odd jobs about Isaac Fryer's tavern when thirsty and time was plenty. The weight of evidence was convincing. These things happened in 1841, the date being fixed by the death of President Harrison and the fact that Billy said: "Ef I'd 'a' knowed he was a-goin' to die so soon I'd never 'a' woted fur him."

At this time Billy may have been forty years old, may, have been sixty; it was all the same thing to me—he was old. All men over thirty were old, and ten to thirty years more made no difference.

"Ef you got a lantern I want to borry it to-night to get some worms outen yer garden," said Billy; and it was a revelation to me to see him pick up a quart of big "night walkers" in a short time.

"What are you going to do with the big worms, Billy?"

"Bobbin' fer eels; don't yer want to go, to-morrer night?"

"Yes, if mother will let me; come around till I ask her."

"Well," said mother, "he may go with you, Mr. Bishop, if you will take care that he doesn't fall overboard and you don't keep him out too late at night."

"All right, ma'am; we can't stay late, because I'm only goin' here in the crik beginnin' about sundown, and eels don't bite at a bob much a'ter ten o'clock, nur, fur that matter, much a'ter nine. I'll take keer of him all right, an' mebbe I'll have some eels to skin fur yer bre'kfas', ma'am."

The worms had been put in a keg with plenty of earth and set in a cool place. I was home from school early in the afternoon, for the mystery of bobbing for eels was to be unfolded to me by a master of the art. Billy was on hand an hour before sundown, and getting a few yards of stout linen thread and a knitting needle from my mother, we started for the woodshed to arrange something, but just what it was to be was a mystery. First Billy cut off about six feet of thread and fastened it to the middle of the knitting needle by a knot and two half-hitches, two young eyes watching every move. Next he threaded a big worm straight through from one end to the other, ran it the whole length of the thread and fastened it so that it would not slip off. This was repeated until the thread was full and was six feet of living worms; then he wound the string around the fingers of his left hand until the upper end was reached, when he cut off the knitting needle, took the coil from his hand and laid it on a piece of fish line, which he doubled over and tied hard and fast, cutting through to the threads and leaving a number of worm-covered loops at each side, and the "bob" was made. The fact that it was a dirty job did not disturb Billy nor me; in fact, we boys made many of them afterward, and neither dirt nor the possible suffering of the worms were ever given a thought; and at this ripe age it seems to be no worse than the ordinary baiting of a hook with "our mutual friend," as a late writer called that humble beast which we have termed a "barnyard hackle" and scientists have dignified with the title of *Lumbricus terrestris*, to signify his ownership or occupancy of the soil. It simply seemed a trifle worse because the labor of impalement and the consequent dirt came all at once. These things are a matter of taste and temperament, nothing more.

With the boat at anchor in the little creek, just below Hiram Drum's slaughter house, which was about as far up as a boat could go at ordinary times, Billy told me how to proceed.

"In swifter water we'd had to use sinkers to get the

bobs straight down," said he; "but we won't need 'em here.   You see, you want to let your bob down till it touches the bottom and then raise it a couple of inches, for eels they swim near the bottom and hit the bob just right."

"But you didn't put any hooks in my bob, Billy; how can I catch 'em when they bite?"

His back was to me and he was looking upward.   He smacked his lips, put something in his pocket, and said: "I have to take a little sassferiller fer my lungs, the doctor told me.   Oh, no! we don't want no hooks; the eels just gets their teeth tangled in the threads and comes up, if you bring 'em easy, then when they are just up to the surface of the water lift 'em quick and gentle inter the boat and they drop off theirselves; but if you jerk 'em they're gone, er ef you hit the side of the boat with 'em they're gone.   Drop yer bob over easy, so," and he lowered his bob in the water without a splash.   Soon I felt a jig, jig, very sharp, and said to Billy, "I've got a bite." "Pull up!" said he; "never let 'em more'n touch it," and he landed an eel in the boat.   I tried it, but Billy said I was too quick, for the eel left.   He took several before I boated one, for what with jerking the line and slapping them against the side of the boat they dropped back into the water, if they even got fairly started on the way up.

It was easy after once getting the hang of the thing, and it soon came natural to haul up slowly to the surface and then swing them into the boat.   Good fun this is in shallow water, when no better fishing offers, and many a night have I rowed from Albany down the Hudson to Van Wie's Point—some six miles below Albany, more or less—with a friend or two and spent a pleasant evening, in later years, fishing behind the dyke and just above Van Wie's light, and then rowed back to the city about midnight with a bushel of eels, weighing from nothing up to two pounds or more, for the larger eels are not so easily captured in this way, their weight tearing them loose in the air.

The night was clear and starlit; bats circled about picking up insects here and there. Billy told me that they could be caught if I threw up my cap and said, "Bat, bat, come into my hat and I'll give you a pound of cheese." There was no room in the boat to do this, but I tried it afterward and didn't get any bats. A large bird flew just over our heads with slow and noiseless flaps, and Billy said something in Dutch. "What was that?" I asked. "They're bad, them things that fly at night a-making no noise, an' I doan' like 'em," and he took a little medicine for his lungs. The moon, a few days past the full, came up slowly just south of the spook-house barn, and Billy said if a bat flew across its face I must say:

> "Hookum skookum,
> Rollicum kookum,
>   Holliche Bolliche,
> Baniche spookum."

"Ef you don't," said he, "you'll go blind on the side next the moon." No bat crossed the moon that night to my knowledge, nor do I ever remember seeing one cross it; but the charm has been remembered and held in reserve should such a thing happen, for no man cares to lose an eye when it can be so easily avoided by simply following the directions of a man so skilled in spook lore as Billy Bishop.

This night we had fair success, and when Billy put me ashore he saw me safely home, only a few doors below, and said that he would send us up a lot of dressed eels for breakfast; and he did. During the fishing Billy faithfully followed the directions of Dr. Getty and took his medicine frequently, as I could testify; but he did not seem to be as disgusted with it as I was when the same doctor prescribed his great tablespoonful doses for me. I mentioned this fact to mother, and she said that Mr. Bishop was older and more accustomed to medicine, and knew the importance of following the doctor's orders better than I. No doubt mother was right, but I can't help thinking that what Dr. Getty gave Billy must have tasted better to him than what he gave me; but I was young.

Several times afterward Billy Bishop took me with him when he went eeling. Mr. John Ruyter, the tanner, said it was because Billy was afraid to go alone, but it is possible that a luncheon which mother left on the table for us on our return may have had its influence. Father said that Billy was not good company for a boy, and besides that, "It would be better for Fred to stay at home and read or study instead of being out bobbing for eels; his mind runs too much on such foolishness." But mother argued that a boy must have some fun and could not study all the time, and Billy Bishop was a kind-hearted man who had never done anything wrong, and the result was that we had eels for breakfast many times.

Billy occasionally played the fiddle for dances, not for the balls and parties of the more fashionable sort, but just dances, where the musician did not become wealthy all at once. I was too young to know much of this, but once he told me in a low voice, while putting on a fresh bob when the water was warm and the old one was spoiled, that he had played for a dance a few nights before, and the big boys had been "pizen mean. They asked me out for 'freshments an' I laid down my fiddle an' bow, an' when I come back they'd sawed that bow 'cross a candle an' it was that greasy that it sp'iled the strings, an' I was done fur the night. Who done it I do'no, but there was Bill Fairchild, John Stranahan, Pole Sherwood an' a lot on 'em there, an' they made out like they was awful sorry."

Poor Bill Fairchild in after years died of burns received while rescuing the books from the burning freight house of the B. & A. R. R., for which he was a book-keeper; the others have gone to rest with old Billy, and no more will they grease his bow nor pour water in his fiddle when he goes out for " 'freshments;" but I was told that Billy learned to take his fiddle and bow with him when called from labor. The humor of these things did not strike Billy in the least. This was evident when he asked me: "Now, what fun was ther' in that? They hed to pay me fur the evenin', and it stopped the dancin'. I tell ye there was folks there that was mad, but, bless ye, they couldn't find out who done it. No one done it. It done itself! They tried to make me believe it was spooks, but spooks don't come to dances where folks is; they catches you all alone, in the dark."

Some years later, probably about 1845, when a large country store was kept in the brick building on the corner of Columbia street and Broadway, and in great letters announced "I. Fly, Headquarters," there was a large shad seine being knit in the hotel of Isaac Fryer, just above. About a dozen men had an interest in it, and they knit away every evening, Billy Bishop and Jakey Van Hoesen being busy filling the needles with twine. I somehow used to drop in there and knit a little early in the evening, but the men stayed late. No one went down Broadway except Billy, and Mr. Fly would have a man or two in waiting to scare him. Sometimes a few stones rolled after him would be enough to start him on a run; at others "spooks" would spring at him from the churchyard, and although the victim may have been well fortified with

Fryer's "Hollands," his starting for home required the courage of a Tam o' Shanter, which he did not possess. He would go up street with friends and around the back way until his tormentors found it out, and in despair Billy told the story of his persecutions, when he was furnished with an escort and saw no more spooks.

Once he confided to me a great secret: "If the eels don't bite good," said he, "just go to a stable and look over the horses' legs. You'll find a scab on the inside of every leg, and when this is big and comes off easy just take it and put it in your bob and the eels 'll come a long way to get at it; it is powerful strong, an' they can smell it for miles."

"Why don't we use it in our bobs?"

"We don't need it; they bite well enough as it is; we don't want all the eels in the river; what could we do with so many?"

That was sufficient, and if the thing was ever tried I do not know. Perhaps the idea originated in Billy's brain or was told to him by some joker, yet it is possible that the very powerful odor of that gland would either attract or repel the fish in a decided manner. Let some eel bobber try it and report to *Forest and Stream.* My time for bobbing passed years ago, but if opportunity offers I will try it tentatively in the interest of knowledge.

Once the shad seiners of the village had arranged to make some hauls at the lower end of the island which lies opposite Albany, and Billy had brought up his little boat the night before and left it at the ferry where "Old Josey," the ferryman, kept his skiff for late night service after the steamboat had finished the day and the horse-boat had carried the early night passengers. The fact became known to "Pop" Huyler, the blacksmith; Charley Bradbury, the livery man, and Steve Miles, the carpenter.

After some deliberation and discussion of the case they decided that a short piece of board, fastened edgewise to the under side of the keel and at an angle of about forty-five degrees to its length, would be about the best thing that could be done at the time. Bradbury finished the board and Miles affixed it, and the boat was placed in the water with the improved combination centreboard and rudder.   The big scow came up the river bearing the great seine on a platform over its stern, and four stalwart oarsmen made her stem the current past the ferry.   A crowd had assembled when Billy appeared with a pair of oars on his shoulder, and casting loose the painter shoved off his boat, put the oars in position and began to row. The boat seemed bewitched, for it kept going round in a circle, no matter how the oarsman tried to keep it straight, and Billy, pale as a ghost, dropped his oars and was evidently praying in Dutch.   The boat drifted near the dock below, when Pop Huyler kindly called to the old man to throw him the rope; he did so, and Billy was safe, but weak and faint.

"Must ha' been spooks in the boat last night, Billy," said Pop.

"Yes," he replied, "I 'spect so; might a know'd there'd be bad luck, fur a hen crowed yestidy an' the fust man I see this mornin' was cross-eyed."

"Sure," said Charley Bradbury, "that's enough to bring bad luck; but, Billy, come up to Brockway's tavern and take something, and say that Dutch prayer once more, and that'll fix 'em all right."

While Billy was repeating the exorcising words Miles got help and pulled the boat on the dock and ripped off the board, launched the boat, and then, after much persuasion, Billy tried it again; and behold! the spell of the witches, spooks and other evil-doers was broken, and

Billy, with great good humor, joined the party just in time to help haul on the line as the seine boat reached the shore, fully convinced that, while spooks might temporarily annoy him, he could triumph over them in the end. Old Vose, who played the clarionette in the band on top of Fly's "headquarters," heard of it, and got Billy to repeat the verse which could so undo the work of witches; and as neither Billy nor he could write, Bill Fairchild volunteered to act as amanuensis, and what he wrote no man knows, for when Vose asked his landlady to read it for him she became angry and burned the paper. No doubt but her method was a good one, for no one ever heard that Billy's boat was ever bewitched again.

Poor old Billy! He died after I left the place, and is remembered by very few. Spooks can no longer chase him at night, grease his fiddle-bow, nor obstruct his boat. The hills have at last come together above him, but he is safe.

JOHN ATWOOD.

FIRST NIGHT IN CAMP.

L OOKED at from later years John was not a bad
boy, neither was he a good boy, but just one of
those ne'er-do-wells that could not be kept in
school nor out of the woods. He was long of leg and
could tell where most of the birds' nests were within a
circle of two miles, with the schoolhouse as a centre. His
acquirements at school dwarfed beside his knowledge of
the best "fishin' holes," and some parents I knew did not
look upon John as a desirable companion for a younger
boy. He was some three years my senior, and his knowledge of the country roads, and of the birds, beasts and
fishes made him easily a leader of boys who had a taste
for such things.

It was long after Reuben Wood had shown me how
to fish that I sat on the railroad dock fishing with a pole
and float, for the Albany & Boston Railroad had invaded
the village, coming down between the present site of the
Episcopal Church and the district school to where the
lower bridge to Albany now spans the Hudson, and it
made a good fishing place for boys. John Atwood came
there that Saturday morning and sneered at my tackle.

"Yes," said he, "that's the way Reub Wood fishes, but
there ain't no fun in it, for you h'ist 'em out too quick
with a pole; throw that away and take off yer float, rig
yer sinker below the hooks, and when you get a fish haul
him in hand under hand and feel him wiggle all the way
in—that's sport!" John's advice was followed and ap-
proved, the heavy sinker, with two or three hooks pendant

above it, was swung around two or three times, and away it went with a plunk, and a new style of fishing was acquired, much to Reuben's disgust; but the majority of the boys about Greenbush seemed to prefer this mode. The fish that we took in the Hudson then were white and yellow perch, bullheads, shiners, eels, spawn-eaters (which were small minnows), and an occasional sucker; but John knew of the mud creek and the dead creek, a couple of miles down the river, where the fish were larger and more plentiful. The "dead creek" was a short inlet from the river running only a few hundred yards into the island, but the "mud creek," as we boys called it, was some five miles long and formed the island; this was the bayou which we knew later as the "Popskinny."

One Friday morning, while on the way to school, John was met. Two boys were with him, and they were on the way to the mud creek with all equipments. It was in the spring of the year, and John said:

"Come along and have some good fishin'; I wouldn't go to school when the fish are biting as they are now. We are going to stay till Sunday night, and have three days' fishin' and birds'-nestin'. Come along; you're a fool if you don't."

"Where will you sleep?"

"In Rivenburg's barn, in the hay; it's good and warm, and we got lots o' grub an' lines."

Here was temptation in very strong shape, but the consequences loomed up. His mother was a widow, mine was not. I could square it with mother, but——. After some debate the books were left at the schoolhouse, a hasty note written to mother, saying that I would be home Sunday night, and we went.

Such fun! John cooked fish over coals of fire, we covered ourselves in the hay at night, and the crickets

sang weird songs, the bats flapped about, the frogs sung
and the owls hooted. Surely this beat Robinson Crusoe
all hollow, for he was all alone for a while. This was life
of an ideal kind. Sunday night, when a reckoning might
be made, seemed too far off for consideration. The present life was perfect!

We made explorations across the bottom lands and up
the wooded hills, saw wild pigeons, and John wished for
a gun; chipmunks, squirrels, birds of kinds new to most
of us, but which John could name, and a rabbit! Here
was big game indeed, and when John oracularly said,
"School is a fool to this place," there was no dissenting
voice, and all regretted when the time came to depart.
We had more fish than we could carry, and only took the
freshest and best, and toiled wearily homeward, one in
the party at least dreading the arrival. What mother said
over the torn clothes and spoiled shoes we will not repeat,
but when father invited me to a conference in the woodshed she said: "Joseph, I have punished him severely, and
he has promised never to go off again without permission;
and he should not be punished twice for the same offence." A look of disappointment crossed father's face;
he evidently missed something that he had mentally
promised himself and me, but, as I told John Atwood
next day: "Mother spanked hard with her slipper, but it
was nothing to what she saved me from;" and John agreed
that it happened just right. "But," said he, "we are going
there next Friday for three days more of it; will you go?"

"No, I can't; I must go to school."

"Ask yer mother; she'll let you."

"Not now; father would object; wait a little later, and
I'll join you there on some Saturday." And I often did.

As near as memory serves, I was about eleven years
old when John proposed that I join him and another boy

in the purchase of a gun, which could be bought for $1.50. It was an old flintlock musket that had been altered to percussion, and we bought it. A grand hunt was arranged, and off we went. By drawing lots it was decided that I was the first to carry the gun until game was shot at, and then it was to be passed to the next. No knight who, after watching his armor alone all night, girded it on for the first time to engage in tournament or battle, was prouder than I at shouldering the musket after John had loaded it; nor did Natty Bumpo ever scan the distance for sign of Mingo keener than my eyes penetrated each bush and thicket for game. At last I saw it! We were in a road between two rail fences, and the game was in plain sight a few feet beyond a fence. Slowly I crept up after John had cocked the gun until the fence offered a rest, and the game appeared unconscious—a tribute to my cautious approach. Surely I was destined to be a mighty hunter! Be still, my heart, your beating may destroy my aim! The game was fully ten feet from the muzzle and deliberation was necessary. A long sighting of the gun, and the trigger was pulled. "Hurrah! I killed him! I killed him!" and jumping the fence I picked up what had been a beautiful little summer yellowbird which had been picking the seed from a thistle-top, wholly unconscious of danger, but now a stringy mass of flesh, bone and feathers. Reviewing this feat in more mature life, it looks this way: "If some kind-hearted man had then appeared and taken that gun and broken it on the fence, and then whaled me with the ramrod, he might have taught me that the life of that little bird was as valuable to him, and perhaps to the world, as my own, and it had been killed to serve no useful purpose. Oh! ye unthinking fathers who use guns for what we call legitimate sport, do not give your boy a gun. A boy is a savage.

I was one—an unthinking savage, who would take life without other reason than the pleasure of taking it. Remember this: You can carry a gun all day without shooting anything except what you consider game; but a boy is bloodthirsty, and his desire to kill is at once intensified when the means are at hand. As a boy I did my share of killing every living thing I saw, whether of use to me or not, and most boys will do the same. Once I wrote: "Don't give a boy a gun until he is ninety years old, and then fit him out and tell him to shoot at every swallow, bat or chipmunk that he may meet." Bless me, how I have preached over that little yellowbird!

John could build bird cages, and in the spring we would wade through the wet grass of the meadows to trap bobolinks, which we sold. He was most successful in rearing robins, thrushes and other young birds taken from the nest, while most boys lost theirs. Later we used to shoot wild pigeons in the spring and fall flights, and with our old musket would bring back from a dozen to a hundred birds in a day, with an occasional snipe, squirrel or rabbit. In winter we set spring poles and box traps for rabbits, and within four years from our first fishing scrape we knew the whole country within a radius of ten miles from Greenbush on the east side of the river. My father was a stern, strict business man, at that time part owner in, and Albany agent of, the Eckford line of towboats, having three steamboats and many barges plying to New York, for then the canal boats came no further east than Albany. Thirty years later, when John Atwood was dead, father told me that he once put John in charge of one of his barges; but he would not attend to business, and he had to discharge him and then give him a subordinate place. "Confound him," said father, "he has no sense of responsibility; he is sober and capable, but would just as soon be a deckhand as to be captain." He had John's measure to the fraction of an inch. John worked because he was forced to do it; if by diligently applying himself for a year he could attain a competency, he would have said, "I would rather go a-fishin'."

I have said that John was a long-legged boy. He was also a very quiet fellow—never in any boyish fights or troubles. These qualities commended him to Mr. Charles Crouch, a harness-maker and superintendent of the Methodist Sunday-school, and John was in demand for the May anniversary to carry the centre pole of the banner, while two shorter boys steadied the corners with cord and tassel. "Jine the Sunday-school," said John to me; "I'll get you to hold a corner of the banner, and we will get the first whack at the refreshments when we stop in Albany." I "jined," and at the first meeting there was a pathetic appeal for funds for missionaries, and I chipped in the only sixpence I had, and which John and I had figured to spend in this way: six fish-hooks at Coshy Lansing's, 2 cents; ten knots of blue-fish line at Tom Simmond's, 2 cents; lead at Pop Huyler's blacksmith shop, 2 cents. "And you went and threw that to the heathen," said John. "Who are the heathen?" he asked. "What do you care about the heathen that you give 'em your last cent? I thought you had some sense! Now we've got to make a raise to get some fishin' tackle in the mornin' just because you are a blamed fool! I only go to Sunday-school just before anniversary so as to get in on the refreshments; they don't get no sixpence out of me. Why, them heathen is all right; they're satisfied to be heathen, an' I'm willin'." I had done wrong and felt abashed in the presence of a superior mind, and to-day I regret the donation of that coin, for John's closing argument is good.

The "nut orchard" lay just out of the village and consisted of something like a hundred trees of shell-bark hickory, straight of stem and tall. It belonged to Glen Van Rensselaer, a man of middle age then, who watched it as well as he could in the nut season; but we boys always had a sentinel out when foraging, and his shabby old silk hat in the distance was a signal to gather the plunder and leave, in order to avoid confiscation of the results of our labor. There had not been frost enough to drop the nuts, and several of us who were strong and active climbed the trees and shook the limbs while smaller boys gathered the nuts. A sentinel had just called, "Here comes Glen!" when there was a scream and a thud, and a poor little Irish boy, named Ryan, was lying on his back. We were crying around him when Mr. Van Rensselaer arrived on a run to catch us. The boy's head was bleeding and his brain protruding, but he breathed. We gave him water, and a passing hand-car on the railroad took him down to John Morris' rope-walk, where his people lived. He died next day. Most of the boys were shy of the nut orchard that fall. The place is now filled with cottages, but the name is retained. The "Indian orchard" is also gone, and not an apple tree is left to hold the nest of a flying-squirrel or a woodpecker.

West of the nut orchard some acres of pasture were plentifully sprinkled with hawthorn bushes, which, by the way, were called "thorn-apple bushes," and among these were many of the big paper nests of the bald-faced hornet. What fun it was, with John as the leader, to advance in line, a cedar bush in the left elbow and as many stones as the forearm would hold against the body and a big stone in the right hand. "Fire!" cried John, and the stones flew in rapid succession; and when all were gone the enemy was upon us. Then how we retreated, swinging the bushes about our heads, and how an occasional yell would announce the wounded! Fun? It was the very height of fun, with its spice of danger, without which some one has said there is no sport. Those who know the bald-faced hornet know that he is as swift as a humming-bird and carries a poniard that for penetration and venom discounts a bumblebee or any other stinger with wings, and this reminds me: John Atwood and I had been away beyond Bath after berries, when we passed a house that stood only a few feet from the road. In front, just inside the picket fence, stood a tall pear tree, well loaded. "Them's nice pears," said John, disdaining all grammatical rules; "le's have some." A study of the situation showed that I could easily mount the tree, shake it, and drop about ten feet in the road, and if the people in the house were aroused John would be off with what pears he could get outside the fence. I shook. Hard, burning things struck my face, and I saw the nest of a colony of bald-faced hornets within a foot of my head. Something dropped—it was I, and I dropped running. Oh, the agony of eleven stings on head, face and neck, and the swollen face of a boy whom his mother did not know an hour later! Days in bed and a doctor seem a trifle now. The pears were not good and John Atwood did not get a sting. To-day, in 1896, it seems as if it was my mission to volunteer if there were hard knocks to be got, while some other fellow got the pears. But this is a most common case, and we see that same sort of a fellow every day; and in the economy of nature he is a necessity to the fellow who gets the pears without the stings.

John taught me how to snare the brook suckers with a noose of copper wire on the end of a pole. Brass wire was too stiff, he said, and horsehair was not stiff enough. We would get above the fish and drift the open loop so as to inclose him, and when it was about his middle a smart jerk landed him on the bank. If the current took the snare one side and the fish was not disturbed we would try it over.

Once we walked down the track of the Boston Railroad to Kinderhook Lake to fish for pickerel through the ice, after planning the campaign for weeks, and we carried knapsacks filled with camping goods of more or less utility. We got a fish, and took a rabbit and three grouse from the snares of some poacher, and had a good time, all of which was written up for *Forest and Stream* of January 3, 1889, as a "Christmas Reminiscence." The great wonder to me then and now was where John learned all the mysteries which he unfolded to me. He never told this, and perhaps his air of mystery helped to magnify his knowledge.   He did not consort with Port Tyler, the local Natty Bumpo, who lived by rod, gun and traps; for Port was a solitary man, and later, when I was taken as an occasional companion by Port, he once said: "John Atwood can't stick to one thing nor one place long enough to do anything at hunting; he runs all over, and, durn him! he spoiled some good pa'tridge ground for me once." This remark was a little foggy, but the impression was that John had interfered with some fences and snares that Porter had set; but it was only an impression, for no more was said. Perhaps the snares that we took the grouse from were Port's! Port's remark fitted John in other respects than hunting. A job in John Ruyter's tannery, grinding bark, in Ring's "white mill," or in Herrick's distillery, feeding cattle, was not kept long. My father's estimate of him was a just one, but of the boys that I knew in youth few have a warmer spot in my memory than John Atwood.

Among the boys of Greenbush was one named Philip Spencer, who came from Hudson, and at one time was a schoolmate of my oldest brother, Harleigh. His father was the Secretary of War in President Tyler's Cabinet in 1841. Young Spencer had a copy of "The Pirates' Own Book," and left it with one of the village boys with the remark, "Keep this until you hear that I am a pirate;" and through his father he was appointed midshipman in the Navy in November, 1841. He planned a mutiny on the U. S. brig Somers, was discovered, and with two others was tried by summary court-martial and hanged at the yardarm on December 1, 1842. This book passed around among the boys of the village for years, until John Atwood loaned it to me. It had pictures of heroic pirates, with belts well stuffed with pistols, boarding merchantmen and putting the crew to the sword or making them walk the plank, and it had in it Spencer's autograph and newspaper slips of his execution. My mother found it in my trunk, and after making me tell where I got it, took it to Mrs. Atwood with the request that no more books of that character be loaned to her son. John said: "It was a fool book, anyway, and there was no fun in sinking ships and killing people." And here again we can agree with John.

An old darkey who had been a cook for my father in his young days, when he was a sloop captain on the Hudson, had smallpox, and father fitted up a room for him in the barn, and John Atwood volunteered to attend him, and stayed by him until he was out of danger. As I have said, John may not have been a good boy, but he was not a bad one. Idle, shiftless and lazy? Yes, if you will, but that is a combination to get much out of life, in a way. John may have been "shiftless," but legs that followed him on a day's tramp would deny the charge of laziness. It would be fairer to say that he could only apply himself to things which interested him. That is my latter-day summing up of his character. Men who think that the accumulation of money by continuous industry is the main thing in life have always decried those who did not follow their precepts and examples, but there are other standards of life than those of old Ben Franklin, who thought that a boy or man should work like Gehenna and never spend a cent. John Atwood followed the bent of his inclination, and was happy when he did not have to work at uncongenial labor; yet who could be more energetic at removing a stone heap and digging out a rabbit?

As he approached manhood the necessity of labor that was more remunerative gradually pressed upon him, and the day came when John had to leave the birds and the fish in their haunts and take a place as fireman on a railroad locomotive. The engine which startled the wood duck from the lily pads had to be fed with great pieces of wood, and the puffing monster drowned the song of the bobolink and the whistle of the quail. John never could have loved such a noisy, obnoxious thing. One winter day about thirty years ago his engine stood at a side track at Poughkeepsie; the boiler burst, and the mangled body of John Atwood was thrown far out upon the ice of the river. As I read the account of it in a distant land the thought came: Who will say to the boys, "A flock of geese went north yesterday and the fish ought to bite good now," or "The bluebirds are building in our pear tree an' it's time to go in a-swimmin'"? Who, indeed?

The geese have gone north many times since, and the bluebirds nested in their old home until the aged tree broke and left only a stump, which I saw last year when on a pilgrimage to the place; but the poor, torn and shapeless thing which the Coroner took from the ice no longer notes the seasons by the coming and the nesting of the birds.

PORTER TYLER.

A T first Old Port Tyler was a far-off and almost mythical person. He appeared vaguely in the stories of older boys who had really seen him, always in connection with fish and game. Garry Van O'Linda had seen him cross the ferry to Albany with a lot of rabbits and partridges, and Charley Melius saw him with a great load of wild pigeons; but to me he was a mysterious person who lived by fishing, shooting and trapping. A man rowed a light boat around Dow's Point and John Atwood said: "That's Old Port; he's been down the dead crick after snipe," and here was the real live man at last, but his mysterious and poetical life seemed as far off as ever. A most ideal life to me, and he was at once enthroned among my collection of idols, which then included Davy Crockett, Daniel Boone, Baron Trenck, Natty Bumpo and Charles XII. of Sweden. These men I had not seen, but Port Tyler had passed Dow's Point before my eyes, and his boat may have contained untold numbers of snipe and countless fish.

Gradually it was learned that he was a bachelor and lived alone near the red mill—"Mechanic street" they call it now; then it was "up by Fred Aiken's woods," and they said that he had huts and caves all over the country and lived in them when he pleased. These stories, and the fact that a lunatic named Asher Cone had a hut back of Harrowgate Spring and chased the boys with a club when he saw them, added mystery and perhaps a bit of awe to the personality of Old Port. In my own case this was true, and at the age of twelve I never even hoped for personal acquaintance with a man whom I placed higher than the rulers of kingdoms—for he was my ideal of the highest form of manhood.   I may as well say right here that this was my ideal fifteen years later, and was lived up to as closely as possible; personal freedom from dictation by others, a love of nature, and, above all, a sense of perfect independence, caused me to cast civilization aside, and—whisper it—after six years return, not a prodigal, but, like him, with a flag of truce in the rear, which the small boy terms "a letter in the post-office."

The pigeons were flying well one October day, and I had about twenty.   They were in scattered flocks seeking mast, and my neck was stiff from looking upward for them.   Often a dozen would start from a tree where none was seen, and a wing shot was not possible, if I had been capable of it.   Resting on a log and watching the open for a flight to come, and, like Irving's skipper, who guided his craft up the Hudson, "thinking of nothing in the past, the present or the future," I suddenly became aware that a man stood beside me.   The leaves were damp from a two days' rain, a high-hole was drumming away on an old stub near by, and a couple of bluejays were scolding about something—perhaps about men—and, being intent on watching for pigeons to come my way, the whole combination favored a silent approach that a falling shadow was the first intimation of.   The stranger said:

"There's a big flock feedin' on beechnuts over there in Teller's woods, an' they may come this way; there's somebody just south of 'em, 'cause the crows all left there a-hollerin'."

He was a small man, rather thin, but wiry, clothing not noticeable except a little faded, a keen gray eye and a light double gun were the first impressions made by the speaker.   For young men it might be well to say that all guns in those days were muzzle-loaders, and that the use of single-barrelled guns was so common that the exception was a matter of remark; therefore the fact that he carried a "double-barrelled gun" was duly noted. I told him that I had been through Teller's woods an hour before, but only found a few pigeons there and got but three of them.

"The big flock was down to the crick for water, then," said he, "and I saw 'em rise and go into the woods, about three or four hundred of 'em in the flock; and they haven't left yet. You can stay here and get a few shots if they come this way, as they will be likely to if that man over south of 'em gets among 'em. I'll work off to the east'ard and get beyond 'em if that man don't start 'em first," and he moved off and was soon lost in the underbrush. He was a man I had never seen before, and the incident was only called to mind when, out after rabbits in the winter, on Crehan's farm above the mill-pond, in jumping a little stream I landed near a man who was skinning a mink. It was the stranger of the pigeon hunt, and instinctively came the knowledge that this was the mysterious woodsman of whom so much had been heard. To my surprise he knew who I was, and said: "Oh, yes, I've often seen you down the crick and in the woods, and when I saw the gun you carried I knew it belonged to your brother Harleigh, for he told me that you had it most ev'ry day when you were out of school."

This was the first mink I had ever seen, and I watched the skinning, which went very well until the tail was reached, and this could not be skinned far because the skin was so tight. We talked until he had finished, set his steel trap and gathered his skins, and went on with the hides of two minks and six muskrats—a very good morning's work. Truly he was not now "mysterious;" he was no longer a half mythical person, but a real, live man, and to me a most interesting one, whom I hoped to know much better.

In the spring, perhaps of 1848 or '49, just after the ice had left the river and the creeks, a party of us boys went down the island creek, as we called it, Popskinny, or Popsquinea, as it appears on maps, to fish. It was merely an arm of the river which crooked out and in again, making an island some four or five miles long, beginning a couple of miles below Greenbush. The water was cold yet, but the hardy yellow perch were astir and the creek was full of them. A railroad has filled the creek in where it crosses and the water is shallow to-day, and but few fish go in it now. There had been a few perch and bullheads taken when Old Port came rowing a light scow down the creek. Some one said that he had gill nets for herring set further down, and this was a way of taking fish that I wanted to see; so, when he stopped to ask, "What luck?" I got permission to get in his boat and go with him. Two nets, each about one hundred feet long and four feet deep, were stretched across the creek, and had been there all night. I helped raise them, and it was such fun! To-day it would not be fun; we take such different views of a thing at different times of life. He took perhaps a bushel of perch, half as many suckers and some 200 "herrin'," as the alewife is called up the Hudson. "The perch an' suckers ain't worth much," said he; "about ten cents a string of a dozen or fifteen, accordin' to size; but the herrin' fetches $2 per 100 as early as this; when they begin to catch 'em in the river they drop to half that price, and by May 1 they are so plenty and cheap that I don't bother with 'em. At this time, you see, the people want to eat 'em fresh, and they're fine; but later they are spawning, and are only fit for saltin' down." This was the financial part of Port's herring fishing. I went in his boat with him to the nets many times, even as late as 1868, when he was a man of fifty-eight and I of thirty-five, for he asked me to his house and I became intimate with him from that first trip to the nets.

"It's a cur'us thing," he said on one of these trips, "to know how the herrin' get past these gill nets that reach from shore to shore and from top to bottom; but they do. Last night I set my two about one hundred yards above two of Cutty Carson's, and when I got through settin' them there was Lon Crandell settin' his above mine; but I'll get about as many herrin' as they will, yet I can't see how the fish get past the first net. They don't jump 'em, for I have watched all night to see if they jump the cork-line. As far as that is concerned, I'd just as soon have my nets in the middle as anywhere else." This is a puzzle—a greater one even than how the shad get up the Hudson past drifting gill nets and staked ones, to be caught by the seiners of the upper river; but these do not reach from bank to bank and from surface to bottom, as the nets in the Popsquinea did.

He it was who first attracted my attention to the breeding habits of fish. We were trolling minnows for pike down this creek; the water had fallen and left strings of perch eggs hanging to the bushes above the water. "Porter," said I, for the days were getting long and permitted the occasional use of his proper name, "there must be millions of perch eggs left to die that way every year; I should suppose instinct would teach the fish not to spawn high up during a freshet."

"Well, a yellow perch is a dull kind of a fish, and don't know as much as a herrin'. When a flood comes and covers all these bottom lands the herrin' go all over them, but the minute the water begins to fall they scoot for the creek and seem to find the ditches leading to it; and they don't spawn on the flats, but among drift stuff; their eggs are separate, and stick fast to what they touch. These strings of perch eggs are not fast to the limbs, but are just hung over 'em with both ends down. I have put lots of 'em back in the water. Maybe it's of no use, for there's plenty of 'em and they ain't o' much account. It's cur'us, though, to watch 'em spawn. I've seen 'em spawn in my nets when I've been watching at night with a lantern. When they are first laid they come out small, and there's nothin' in 'em until the he one goes over 'em, and then they swell up as big a mass as the fish that laid 'em."

When we came to his net he showed me perch nearly ripe, and stripped a ripe male. I took perch eggs that day—in 1867—and hatched them in the State Geological rooms on State street, Albany, by permission of Dr. Hall, the curator, and through my intimacy with this observant field naturalist I became a fishculturist and made it a life work.

There was a gap of some nine years in my intercourse with Porter, as I spent the years 1854-60 in the West and parts of 1862-65 in the army; but the old man gave me a warm welcome, "For," said he, "I liked you because you took so much interest in all the live things, even if they were no-account things." I never saw him after 1868. He died at his home, which he owned, in 1882, aged seventy-two years. Some of the Albany shooting men thought him an old poacher because he sold much of his game, and they said that he snared partridges (ruffed grouse); and it may be that he did; I can't say; but to me he was a kind friend and instructor of my boyhood in things of interest, if not of usefulness. He was one of those real outdoor observers, and the kind of naturalist with whom the modes of feeding and habits of birds, beasts and fishes take the first place, while of their structure he knew little more than an outside view of fur, fin and feather gave him; yet his knowledge of many things was far beyond what a scientific education could have given him. Not that I wish to underrate such an education, or to speak slightingly of it, for it is of very great value; but it is a fact that with most of our biologists structure and comparative anatomy are the beginning and end of their knowledge of animal life, and a day spent with Port Tyler would have opened up a new chapter to them. Such a day might also have been of use to that class of sportsmen who are mere butchers and measure the pleasures of an outing by the amount of slaughter they have done, and whose only knowledge of nature is where certain kinds of game could be found at certain seasons.

A man who, when out shooting, would stop, lean his gun against a tree and spend half an hour watching a little chipmunk dig his hole, has higher tastes than a mere game butcher, and Port Tyler did that one day when I ran across him in the Indian Orchard. "It's cur'us how he does it," he remarked, "and because you don't find the dirt piled up about the hole they say he begins to dig at the bottom; your brother Harleigh told me that, but I think he was joking." This last by way of apology, for his sense of humor was not keen, and he did not always realize the fact that some people would trifle with such questions, and that his innocent and unsuspecting nature invited just such remarks as the above. "That little cuss is cute," he said; "he leaves a clean hole between two roots, with no sign that he has been diggin'. But Harleigh is wrong; he begins at the top and carries the dirt away in his cheeks, and drops it when he gets far enough so that it won't attract attention. Maybe when he gets down he can pack it one side into some hollow and save labor. He ran off when you came, and there he is on

that fence there by Cassin's house, jerkin' his tail because
he is mad at you for coming here to stop his work."　He
knew that the little ground squirrel was a "chipmunk"
and stored its food under the protecting roots of trees, and
by observation had learned how it dug a hole without
leaving outside evidence of it, even though he knew nothing of its anatomy.

Port's great fur harvest sometimes came in midwinter,
but always in early spring, by a "January thaw," and
surely in April.　The ice never melts in the Hudson about
Albany, but is broken up by floods when the snow melts
in the upper country or in the Mohawk Valley, and often
goes out in great fields, nearly two feet thick, which crowd
on top of each other and break by the overhanging
weight.　Grounding on shallows just above Castleton,
which bar in the river the Dutch knew as the "Over-
slaugh," the water is dammed and floods the lower parts
of Albany so that boats can often float up Broadway as
far as State street, and all the flats and bottom lands on
both sides of the river are several feet under water, often
for weeks or until the ice dam breaks.　The muskrats of
that region have been so accustomed to this state of
things that they rarely build houses, as in other parts of
the country, although I have seen an occasional house
there; but houses being of no use in such events, the instinct to build has been nearly lost.　When the freshet
comes the musquash is drowned out of the holes in the
bank and seeks the piles of flotsam to hide among.　Every
gun in Greenbush and on the hills below is brought out,
and everything in the shape of a boat that can be had is
put into commission for the slaughter, and the roar of
successive guns reminds a veteran of a skirmish line.
Many men are shooting for profit, Old Port among them,
but a larger number are out for fun and pile the rodents

in their boat to give to some one who will want them.   In
the early '50's there would be found a number who were
shooting for fun and saving the animals for Porter.
Among these were Colonel David A. Teller, James Miller, Reuben and Ira Wood, Harleigh Mather, Godfrey
Rhodes, Bill Fairchild, myself and about a dozen others.
The result was that Port had to hire help to skin the animals while he would stretch the hides.

At this late day, with a memory hardly worth a hill of
beans, it is not safe to make an estimate of the slaughter
of muskrats during a freshet on the eastern shore of the
Hudson River, between Dow's Point, which is less than
two miles below Albany, and Castleton, which is nearly
ten miles from the city.   I had to go to school, sure, for
my father knew well that only an iron hand could keep
me there, and he had it; but two days in the week I
claimed for rest and recreation.   The latter I had, while
the former was not needed.   It was poor shooting when
I did not pick up thirty muskrats in a day during a freshet,
and men have killed as high as 200 in a day.   Perhaps
with about fifty gunners there was an average of thirty
musquash each, which would count up to over 10,000 in a
week!   It seems too big a figure for eight miles on one
side of a river, but the flats or bottoms were from a half
to three-quarters of a mile wide, rich with alluvial deposit
from each overflow and rank with vegetation along the
river, the island creek and the ditches which drained the
bottoms into the creek; also our sociable little mammal is
largely a vegetable feeder.   With donations from his
friends, in addition to his own gun, Port Tyler one year
marketed over 2,000 muskrat skins, a few obtained by
winter trapping, but mainly shot during the freshets. Just
what these were worth at that time is forgotten; all were
not "prime" because of the shot holes, but they brought

enough to keep this man of simple tastes until the fall season, even if the spring run of "herring" were not considered, and in addition to the winter's fur there was always a few mink and other skins, for he was not above taking in a prowling cat, as he said: "A common cat skin is not worth much, but when I've killed her the skin might as well be saved; and I kill 'em on principle, for they kill nesting partridges, rabbits, and every young song bird they can get hold of."

Port once said to me that a game dealer, hotel keeper, or some other man, wanted him to shoot reedbirds in the fall. "Now, what do you suppose he called reedbirds?" he asked. "They're bobolinks in their fall gray coat— and that's goin' too far. I've shot blackbirds and snow-birds for market, and while I was a-shootin' 'em I thought it was small business compared to shootin' quail, pa'tridge an' rabbits; but when it comes to shootin' bobolinks, which makes the medders ring with song in the spring, I'll be durned ef I'll do it! You've offen seen a he bobo-link fly toward his mate an' then set his wings all a-trem-ble as he told her that she was the best she bobolink he ever see—and the music! I've offen sot and listened to him when I ought to be goin' on to my herrin' nets in the spring. Of course the bobolink gets gray in the fall, an' he looks just like a she one, but that's his natur', an' I ain't a-goin' to shoot him for market. I'd rather hear him sing, an', besides, he's too small to eat."

I have always held this opinion, that it is a sin to kill this songster for the morsel of meat it has, and have consistently refused to touch "reedbirds" when they have been served at dinners. The bird is nearly extinct in the meadows which it once enlivened, and during a life of thirteen years on Long Island I have not seen a bobolink. Guns, guns, guns! I sometimes think it would be well if gunpowder had never been made. The true game birds hold their own in many places fairly well—only men of intelligence can find them—but in the older settled regions the redheaded woodpecker has gone and the brown thrasher and bobolink have almost disappeared. The reason is a combination of gun and boy.

Game that Port didn't sell he cooked for small parties at his house. He was a good cook, and when it was known that he had a few ruffed grouse on hand a supper party would be organized at once, and he would furnish everything but the liquors. He was a very temperate man and seldom used either wines or stronger stuff, and said that he did not care to sell it even if he had license to do so; but the jolly old cocks who were fond of his game suppers did not allow themselves to suffer on this account. I attended only one of these affairs, as I was rather young for that sort of thing; but I had been out after grouse and had three, which I gave to Porter, whom I met near home. The cause of this generosity was because I did not dare to take them home, having surreptitiously borrowed a fine double gun from my father which I was forbidden to take or handle; but, as he never used it, he often loaned it to me without his knowledge. Under these conditions Porter got the birds and I was invited to the feast. General Martin Miller, of the State militia, presided; in times when Greenbush was at peace with all foreign countries he kept a grocery store and was commonly known as Mat. Miller; Tobias Teller, Bill Fairchild, Godfrey Rhodes, Port and I—fourteen of us in all, six men and eight grouse. After the last bone had been polished Bill Fairchild was thoughtful, and as he was sucking away on the backbone of a grouse, trying to extract the very last of the bitter that is so dear to the lover of all kinds of grouse, he asked:

"Porter, did you ever eat a muskrat?"

"Yes, I've eat 'em many times, an' they're right good, too, if you know how to dress an' cook 'em, an' I'll tell you what else is good, but you may not believe it; that's young quawks; the old ones are fishy, but the young ones are not, though they are fed on fish, an' I'll get you up a——"

"But about the muskrat, Porter; I've eaten him, and I don't want any more."

"Wa'n't it good?"

"I'll tell you," said Bill; "you know old Dandaraw, the Canuck Frenchman who keeps the little drunkery just north of the B. & A. passenger houses? Of course you do. Well, after the spring freshet I dropped into Dandaraw's, and we were talking about shooting muskrats. Dandaraw said: 'You shoot-a da mus'rat, hey, Bill?' 'Oh, yes,' said I; 'sometimes, just for fun, and I give 'em to Port Tyler, and he skins 'em for market.'

" 'You doan eat-a da mus'rat, hey, Bill?'

" 'No, I don't eat 'em; they smell a little too musky for me.'

" 'Oh, Bill, you mus' eat a-heem; you doan' know how good-a he ees.'

"I asked him how he cooked 'em, just for curiosity, for I had no idea that the things were eatable, and I only wanted to hear him chirp. He said:

" 'First you skeen da mus'rat an' clean him fine; den you bile him a leetle; den you fry him an' you eat him, an' (smack) o-o-o!'

"Well," said Bill, "I skeen-a da mus'rat an' I clean him fine; den I bile him a leetle; den I fry him an' I eat him. I could do the whole trick except the (smack) an' the o-o-o. I could eat a muskrat on a pinch, but for choice would prefer one of these partridges that Port serves up so good."

Port thought that he could serve up some nice fat young muskrats so they would fill Dandaraw's description, and even Bill Fairchild would smack his lips loudly and say "O-o-o," and it was agreed to try it a few weeks later; but I missed the feast.

Tyler was the only man I ever knew who could successfully hunt woodcock without a dog. He seemed to know just where to look for them and how to find them, and said that he did not want to be bothered with a dog. An English gunner and dog fancier lived in that lower end of Albany called Bethlehem—perhaps the same district now known as Kenwood. They called him Ken King, his front name being Kenneth, and I bought a bitch puppy from him, the mother being a pointer of famous stock and the father the then celebrated setter Dash, the crack setter of the time, owned by Mr. James Bleecker. By the way, this Nell of mine never showed the slightest trace of setter blood, and she went to Michigan afterward, and was the mother of many good pointers with never a sign of setter blood.

This was in 1853, and my people having moved to Albany there was no place for Nell, and Port agreed to take care of her. I wanted him to work her on snipe and woodcock, but he said: "A dog is all right for men who can't find birds without one, but they are little use to me; I like to find 'em myself, and on the old grounds that I've hunted for years I know the best feedin' spots in every marsh or cornfield, and if the birds are there they'll not be far from these spots." This is a strange statement, but the fact that this man lived up to it and shot both snipe and woodcock for market without a dog can be attested by men now living in Albany and Greenbush. Surely a most strange and interesting character was Old Port Tyler.

GEORGE DAWSON.

MY FIRST TROUT.

ABOUT 1850 my people moved across the river into Albany, and I was a student in the "Classical Institute" of Professor Charles H. Anthony, on Eagle street. Among the scholars was George S. Dawson, eldest son of George Dawson, who at that time was assistant editor of the Albany *Evening Journal.* Young George told his father that I knew of a good trout stream down near Kinderhook lake, and it led to an interview. Mr. Dawson wanted to go, and we would take an early train for Kinderhook station, on the B. & A. R. R., and if the distance was too far to the brook he would hire a horse to take the three near the stream, for George S. would go. This seemed a reckless bit of extravagance to a boy whose whole expenditures for fishing had been a few pennies for hooks and lines and of leg muscle to get to the fishing places.

The only thing that serves to fix the time of year is the memory that pond lilies were in bloom; the cat-tails were just pushing up their curious blooms, and had not burst to scatter their seeds, and the black-cap raspberries were ripe. It must have been early in July, for the swallows were skimming the meadows and had not begun to congregate on the telegraph wires. These things are recalled by Mr. Dawson's wish to take home the pond lilies, our picking berries near the railroad station, and young Dawson's doubt of my statement that swallows could gather on wires charged with electricity. What a thing is man's memory, and by how slight a cord is it tied to the past!   The exact year is forgotten, but it was before 1854, probably three years before.   Mr. Dawson carried a short, hand-made rod of some kind of wood, with ring guides, the first thing of the kind I had seen, and that gave me an impression that he must be a very superior angler, especially as he said that his father had brought expensive rods for trout fishing from Scotland, but they had been lost.   This was a revelation!   "Expensive rods"—he called them "rods"—and the idea of paying money for such things when we could cut an alder pole and thought it expensive to buy fish hooks and lines; but, like the Irishman's owl which he had bought for a parrot, I said nothing, "but kept up a devil of a thinking."   If money had been more plentiful in boyish pockets it is doubtful if its expenditure would have been in the direction of "fish poles," which could be cut anywhere and thrown away after use.   This was a bit of dilettanteism in angling that hardly seemed consistent with our primitive ideas of using only those things which nature furnished, always excepting hooks and lines.   His hooks were also a revelation. We used only Limericks of large size, and boys usually prefer big hooks because they look so strong, and they fear that a big fish may break a small hook.   Mr. Dawson's hooks were small and the wire was slim, but they were long in the shank, something like the hook now known as the "New York trout," if not the same, and the most wonderful thing about them was that they were neatly put on gut snells—another new thing.   He rigged my line with one of the smallest hooks and discarded the sinker, which before seemed to be an indispensable part of a fishing outfit, and he showed us how to fish down stream and how we must keep a good distance apart.   We fished with worms, and the slim, long-shanked hooks were perfect, because they did not break a small worm and allowed the use of a generous bait on the long wire. How I treasured a dozen of these hooks which he gave me, and how some boys looked at them with envy and others sneered at them, saying, "A big fish would bite 'em in two," are things well remembered.

The stream was small; in places one could jump across it; then it would widen out, sometimes in deep holes and at others in shallow riffles, through meadows most of the way and often fringed with alders, which troubled the angler to use his rod. In the latter case trout would be hauled in as on a hand line. There was no landing net in the party. At this time the existence of such an implement was unknown to us boys; we hauled in a fish, unhooked it, and either strung it on a twig and carried the string or let the fish hang in the water to keep alive. This day the latter mode was not practicable. The trout in this stream did not run very large, perhaps from four to six ounces; but the new kind of hooks, the absence of a sinker and the consequent ability of the fish to fight, made it the grandest event in all my fishing, and one ever to be remembered. The day was perfect: a light breeze, the sun not too bright, and the fish taking the bait freely. Crawling through the brush or skipping the places where it was too thick to get a short rod and line in the water, we worked slowly down stream. I had let my hook drift under a log in a hole on the other side of the stream, when a trout struck it hard. We had not arrived at that point in fine angling when reels were used, and the strike caught me with my tip lowered, and there was a struggle which soon ended in the line being fast to some immovable thing, and a strong pull parted it, and for the first time the biggest got away. This has happened to others.

Surely it is hard to tell, at this late day, whether grief

GEO. DAWSON.

over the loss of a big fish overtopped the grief of losing
one of those marvelous hooks; but that grief in solid
chunks was abundant in a little clump of swamp willows
is certain.　The gut snell was frayed and had parted in
the middle, as if chafed over something rough; and after
bending on a new hook I came upon young George near
a little foot-bridge, on which most of his clothing lay in a
wet state.

"What's the matter, George?"

"Fell in.　How many you got?"

"Nine, nice ones; but I just lost an old whopper and
one of those hooks your father gave me.　How many
have you got, and how did you fall in?"

"I only caught three; the fish get scared as soon as
they see you and scoot away.　I was after one that started
down stream, and stepped on a slippery stone and just
plunked in, that's all."

After pointing out to him that trout must not be
chased in order to make them take the hook, he was reminded of what his father had told him about not letting
the fish see him, but in his anxiety to get a worm under a
trout's nose all rules had been forgotten.　The morning's
work had brought on a first-class appetite on my schoolmate as well as on me, and Mr. Dawson had the material
to alleviate and cure that gnawing sensation if he could
be found.　Leaving all my traps and fish at the foot-
bridge, I started down stream to find Mr. Dawson.　Soon
he hove in sight, coming up stream, and he had a string
of about twenty fine trout.　"It's getting near midday and
the fish are not biting well, so we might as well rest and
eat a bite," said he, "and then by the time we are through
and walk back to the station the freight train will be along
and we will go back in the caboose, as the agent said, for
if we wait here for more fishing we will not get home to-

night, as the fish will not be on the feed again before an hour or two of sundown."

———

George Dawson, while a trenchant political writer, was also fond of depicting life in the woods and on the streams.   With pleasure I renewed my acquaintance with him in later years, when peace reigned in the land, and by invitation accompanied him to the Adirondacks when both were familiar with the use of the fly in luring the trout.   He was born in Falkirk, Scotland, in 1813, and came with his parents to America five years later.   He had no early schooling, but learned the printers' trade before he was thirteen, and educated himself.   Then he went to Rochester and worked for Thurlow Weed, editor of an anti-Masonic paper, and in 1836 Dawson became editor of the Rochester *Democrat*.   Weed was afterward editor of the Albany *Evening Journal*, and in 1846 Dawson joined him as assistant editor.   Weed retired in the stirring days of 1862, and Mr. Dawson took his place as editor and proprietor of the *Journal*, then as now one of the leading papers of the State of New York; and it soon became known that the pen of the new man was a most vigorous one.   His love of nature was a most prominent trait, and fishing was his favorite means of enjoying this love.   Once, while on the way to the Adirondacks with him, I remarked: "The woods to me is a place to loaf." If I had read Whitman then I would have added, "and invite my soul," but only added, "A couple of hours' fishing morning and evening is all I want; if the fish bite good it is well; if not, the trying for them suffices."

"My boy," he replied, "that is just exactly my own notion, and I have a dislike for the companionship of the bustling, busy angler, who fishes as long as he can see to do it, morn, noon and dewy eve, in the hope of getting the last trout in the water. Such a man makes a labor of fishing; I go to the woods for rest and other attractions purer, higher and more ennobling than the mere act of taking fish."

He put these same words down in a notebook, and while in camp wrote an account of the trip to the *Journal* and used them in its columns in June, 1873, now before me.

Once, in writing of "how really garrulous are the silent men of meditative mood," and relating how, when in the woods, their faces would be illuminated by the passing thoughts while they were really communing with distant friends, and their silence was only seeming, and musing in an abstracted way was a rare and pleasant gift, he said: "It is not so with the chronically absent-minded, who may be heavy-browed, but are vinegar-visaged and constitutionally morbid, and would no sooner think of angling than of robbing the exchequer of the realm. An editor's life is neither the best nor the worst in which to cultivate this rare gift. There are those in the profession who can so concentrate their thoughts that the pertinacious pleadings of a score of office-seekers cannot tangle the thread of their meditations. And sometimes even the least abstracted among us have to throw off sentences amid such persistent din that bedlam itself would blush at the clatter. What little of the art came to me by nature and compulsory practice has been strengthened by the opportunities for silent meditation afforded by the habit of angling." Thus spoke the weary political editor, and we read between the lines his disgust with the horde of office-seekers, who, under the ante-civil-service laws, rendered miserable the life of every man who had "inflooence" in the smallest degree; but the deduction which he draws—that the practice of angling conduces to deliberate thought—is one that should commend its practise to parents as the best of all sports for their sons. The murdering instincts of a boy are often satisfied with the death of a low form of animal life which cannot suffer as much pain as mammals or birds, under any circumstances, because their nervous organizations are lower. Shakespeare was greatly in error when he wrote, in effect, that: "The poor beetle that we tread upon in corporal sufferance finds a pang as great as when giant dies." Suffering is entirely a matter of nerves. A worm which can be cut in two and go on living, and perhaps grow into two worms, cannot suffer much. Pull a lobster's claw from its body and a new one grows; pull a limb from a mouse and the animal dies.

Under date of July 3, 1878, Mr. Dawson wrote me: "No pastime is so attractive to me as angling, and when not at it I greatly like to talk and write about it, ethically, not scientifically, for I have never been able to master an 'ology' of any kind," and then he goes on to ask about the details of grayling fishing. Some time before this I called on him and enlarged on the pleasures of a trip to the Au Sable River, Michigan, with Mr. Daniel H. Fitzhugh, of Bay City, and of the capture of the gentle grayling. He listened a while and then asked:

"How large do grayling grow?"

"Those we took were fish that would weigh from three-quarters to one and a half pounds, but some have been taken that would weigh as much as two pounds."

"My boy"—he seemed to be fond of addressing me in this way, perhaps because of the fact of the great disparity of years when we first fished together back of Kinderhook Landing, or because his son, George S., was my schoolmate—"you talk enthusiastically about this new fish, which never exceeds two pounds in weight; did you ever take a salmon?"

"No, but——"

"Well, I have, and the grayling may be a good little fish for those who have never hooked bigger game; but it seems rather small to one who has taken a salmon."

This was a setback from an enthusiastic angler, and, after pulling myself together, I ventured to suggest that his angling literature, as far as I had read it, rather placed the weight and number of fish in the background, and that, as the originator of the saying that "it is not all of fishing to fish," I had thought that the newly discovered grayling might interest him. He saw the point at once, became interested in the fish and went to Michigan to take them, an account of which can be found in his "Angling Talks," published by *Forest and Stream* in 1883—a most interesting little work, full of flavor of the woods and waters.

Mr. Dawson died February 17, 1883, after a few days' illness, aged seventy years. His life had been such an active one, and as a political leader he was so prominent, that his death produced a profound sensation. The Albany *Argus*, politically opposed to Mr. Dawson, said of him: "To journalism this man bore no undistinguished relation. He was a ready, wise, dangerous writer. He was a Greek to be feared when he came bearing presents. * * * He was very able in stating a case for a party; he was even abler in stating a case against a party. He was ablest in giving a man either a fatal defence or a fatal attack. His genius ran to combat; battle was his element. Routine tired him. Peace gave him a sense of *ennui*."

About five months before his death he retired from his

editorial labors, although his well-knit frame and compact form showed no more sign of weariness than did his mind.   The *Argus* said: "Pneumonia wrestled the life out of this Scot, they say.   Doubtless it did; 'twas pneumonia of which he died.   But how came his constitution to take it?   Through cold?   Why, he had summered for years in water knee-high, or waist-high, putting up jobs on fish.   Why, he had repeatedly slept on the floor of lumber cabins o' winter nights, his feet to a fire and his head under an open window, in the Michigan woods.   He had the conquering will that defied wet and blasts.   Did his prolonged labors undermine his constitution?   Emphatically no!   He was ever strongest in harness.   When he went to press every day he went to bed every night to sleep the easy-breathing, refreshing sleep of a boy. Knocking off work unsettled this man's strength.   Labor was a tonic to him.   He would have lived through sheer love of labor had he remained a scalp-taker every day, armed with his keen pen and keener thought.   None can be blamed.   He quitted work because he said he wanted to quit it.   He thought that lessening the tension would enable him to play in the youth of old age.   And he loved to play.   But work was his best play.   Then he played with thunder."

Only once did Mr. Dawson hold public office.   He was postmaster of Albany from 1861 to 1867, at a time when his pen was most actively engaged in the patriotic work of upholding the integrity of the Union.   But he did not stop at writing editorials and equipping his eldest son for the army.   He publicly announced that he would pay to the families of any six printers who would volunteer $4 per week during the time they remained in the United States service, and he did it.   One of the six, Charles Van Allen, of Bethlehem, Albany county, went out with my regiment in August, 1862, and died in Andersonville prison September 18, 1864.   His wife received the pay for nearly a year after he died, or for the full term of his enlistment, some $624, all to one family.

George Dawson was a member of the Baptist Church, a Sunday-school teacher and lay preacher.   A noble man and a most charming one to be in camp with.   Entirely without ostentation, his acts of charity were known to but few, and if within his power his pencil would be drawn through most of these lines, written by one who is proud to have known him and to have called him friend.

MAJOR GEORGE S. DAWSON.

CAPTAIN GEORGE S. DAWSON, Second New York Heavy Artillery, my schoolmate and fishing companion on the one trip which has been related, was stationed in the defences of Washington, near Alexandria, in 1863, and came to visit me when my regiment, the Seventh New York Heavy Artillery, occupied the forts from Tennallytown, on the Harper's Ferry road, to Fort De Russy, near the Seventh street road, and we had a grand review of the schoolboy days and of the only fishing trip that we ever had together. Said he: "That day will ever be remembered, for in my case it filled the proverbial measure of fisherman's luck; and that lunch! Did you ever strike anything so fine?" His regiment, in June, 1864, was in the Second Brigade, First Division, Second Corps, Army of the Potomac; while mine was in the Fourth Brigade of the same division and corps. While we lay in the trenches at Cold Harbor I sent him a note asking if he was catching many trout now, and he answered, in effect, that his regiment caught something else in the charge on June 3, and to the best of his knowledge the Seventh Artillery had some of the same brimstone. The official records show that the Second lost 215 officers and men killed, wounded and missing in that terrible assault on the impregnable works at Cold Harbor, mainly in the charge on the morning of June 3, 1864. My message had the desired effect; it showed that my schoolmate had lived through the storm and was still on duty. Twelve days later our brigades were halted near each other, preparatory to forming for the battle which

MAJOR GEO. S. DAWSON.

took place next day, and he sought me out. In the few minutes' chat he ran over several incidents of school days, and referred to good old Professor Anthony and our trouting. That day's fishing was firmly fixed in his mind. I never fished with him again, and do not know that he ever went fishing after that time. In later years, while fishing with his father, we often talked of the Major, and he was a favorite subject with the elder George, but no reference to his fishing, except on that one occasion, was ever made.

A bugle call broke our conference, and with a hurried grip of the hand Captain Dawson said: "I think we will intrench here and besiege Petersburg, and then we can visit often. Good-by."

There was a siege of Petersburg after the assault on the enemy's works on June 16, but Captain Dawson took no part in it. A rifle-shot just above the left knee, which he thought only a flesh wound and which the surgeon termed "a thirty-days' scratch"—meaning a furlough for that length of time—took him off the field; and twenty-four hours later, while on his way to the Second Corps hospital at City Point, he was strong enough to hold in his lap the head of a poor fellow whose leg had been amputated. Whether the wound was more serious than was at first supposed, or because of the jolting in the ambulance, his leg was amputated shortly after reaching the hospital, and he was sent by steamer to Washington, where he remained four months before he was allowed to be taken home. Shortly after reaching Washington his commission as major was received. "That's good," said he; "when my leg gets a little better I'll be mustered in as major, and then I can join my regiment as a mounted officer; for a fellow with one leg is of no use in the line, and I want to see this war fought to the end." Poor fellow! he died on December 6, nearly four months after receiving his wound, aged twenty-six and a half years.

The post-mortem showed that the bone was injured above the amputation, and in army parlance he is still "awaiting muster." As a schoolboy he was very bright and studious, and although several years my junior he helped me out in my studies and "exams." many times. After leaving school he entered the service of Weed, Parsons & Co., publishers, and was a member of the Tenth Regiment, New York Militia, before the war. Early in the war he offered his services as a private, but was rejected because of a defect in one eye from an accident in childhood; but he was bound to go in some capacity, and after the Second Artillery left Albany there was a vacant first lieutenantcy, and he got the appointment and joined the command at Staten Island, before it left the State, and was afterward made captain. No less a poet than Alfred B. Street wrote quite a long poem on "George Seward Dawson, Major Second New York Artillery, died from wounds received before Petersburg, June 16, 1864." After his death the Governor of the State forwarded to the bereaved father a brevet commission for his son (in memoriam) of lieutenant-colonel, "for gallant and meritorious conduct before Petersburg, Va." His regimental comrades bore witness to his soldierly qualities in a set of resolutions sent to his father, and Post No. 63, Department of New York, Grand Army of the Republic, of Albany, is named "George S. Dawson," after the young soldier whose life of promised usefulness was, like so many others, brought to a sudden end, but cannot be considered wasted.

GEORGE W. SIMPKINS.

IF I was ever a good boy my mother never told me of it. Hundreds of times, when I would come home from a nutting expedition with trousers torn by shag-bark hickory, she has said, while viewing the breaches in the breeches, "I declare, Fred, I think you are the worst boy in the world." As this was often repeated when my shoes were ruined by being in mud and water all day, I accepted it as a correct estimate of my rating. But, I ask you, how is a boy to get the first whack at the shellbarks before they drop unless he climbs the trees? How can he wade a stream without wetting his shoes, unless he takes them off? The fact was apparent to me that my mother knew little about a boy's needs, and therefore was not competent to criticise a boy's actions. You've got to shin up a tree to get the nuts if the frost has not opened the shucks and the tree is too tall to use sticks and stones on with good effect. That's a plain statement of fact, and it can't be disputed; but somehow mothers fail to see these things in the proper light.

"When vacation time comes," said my mother, "if you are a good boy and go to school regularly, don't ruin your shoes in the swamps nor tear your clothes in the nut trees, you may go and visit with Mr. Simpkins, where you will have all the fishing and shooting that you want. He writes that he would like you to spend your vacation with him, and perhaps you may see a deer, for they are plentiful near his place. It all depends, however, on the way you behave between now and then."

"Who is Mr. Simpkins, mother, and where does he live?"

"He is a farmer who lives up in Warren county, on the border of the great woods. His farm is on the Schroon River, where there are plenty of fish, and the woods are full of game of all kinds. He married a distant relative of mine whom you never met, but who spent some months with us before you can remember."

Here was a prospect of fun! Fishing and shooting, with the chance of seeing a real live deer! There was a stuffed buck in the State Geological Hall in Albany, but it appeared to be ridiculously small to my notion, for I had read that "A monstrous buck came crashing through the underbrush," while the little animal, a trifle moth-eaten, that stood, stuffed and looking unhappy, was not as big as our brindle cow.

This was in the spring of 1849—recalled by one of mother's letters now before me—and I would be sixteen years old when August came. From a public library Cooper's "Deerslayer" was borrowed, and John Atwood and I studied it carefully. It was excitingly interesting, and we held our breath when the cap was lifted from the old pirate, Hutter, in his ark, and he was found to be scalped when they thought he was only drunk, and the whole story of Indian fighting, capture and escape from torture so took possession of us that the book was finished before it occurred to John to say: "It's a mighty good story, but I'll be durned if it tells much about killin' deer. I thought it was a-goin' to tell a feller how to find 'em, an' how to shoot 'em, an' it's all about killin' Injens. I don't want to kill any Injens—they never hurt me none—but I would like to get a crack at a deer. You got to have a good rifle an' take 'em jes back of the fore shoulder, right in the heart, or they'll run off an' die. You couldn't kill a deer! You'd git scared if you saw one. I don't believe Ole Port Tyler could kill a deer, 'less the deer stood still, for they jump a hundred feet at a lick, an' lightnin' 'd have a hard time to ketch 'em."

The days were filled with talk of the coming expedition into a land where the deer had not only lived, but had been seen feeding among the cows; and the nights were filled with visions of deer whose horns were as high and branching as an oak, and the squirrels were leaping from tine to tine, disturbing the partridges which were nesting in the antlers. Even dreams have ends to them, whether of sport, fame or wealth. The long-looked-for day came, and the start was made. At this day all is blank until Glens Falls was reached, and whether we started from Albany by rail, canal or stage is uncertain. The ecstatic pleasure of at last really going to this promised land of fish and game obliterated all such purely mechanical ideas as the ways to get there. But Glens Falls was a place to be looked out for with open eyes. Here was the cave in which Hawk-Eye and Uncas stood off the Mingoes! Here was the precipice from which Uncas killed the Mingo who fell from an overhanging tree, and Uncas was chided by the scout for hitting him some "two inches below" the painted belt line, as memory recalls the story.

Mother went up with me. She was entirely ignorant of the history of that terrible night in the cavern when the screams of the tortured horses directed the rescuers to the cave, and actually seemed indifferent about visiting places which to me were not only historic, but sacred.

Here I must pause and look back. At that time the difference between history and fiction was not a strictly defined line. My ideas of such things were crude. To-day, forty-seven years later, when one should be able to discriminate between fact and fancy in what passes for history, that line seems as misty as ever. Prescott's "Conquest of Mexico" is grand, but we do not find the evidence

of an advanced civilization before the conquest of that
country.   The great temples have not a stone left.   There
is not a trace of an aboriginal, intelligent people, while at
Glens Falls the cave of Uncas is there, in part.   The great
cliff, where the Mingo was shot by Uncas, is being torn
down, and a few years ago I was there with a Fish Com-
missioner who had no poetry in his soul, and who actually
suggested cutting away a portion of the celebrated cave of
Uncas to make a fishway!

I have strayed from my text, but let us hope that the
people of Glens Falls or of the State of New York will
preserve this cave, as all other historic places are preserved; for if the cave is not a part of real history, it should
be made so by law.

———

It was evening when Mr. Simpkins met us at the hotel
in Warrensburgh with his team.   He was a stalwart
farmer, whose appearance, from team to person, denoted
thrift, and his cordial reception soon made us friends.   A
drive of three or four miles northward brought us to his
farm, a welcome from Mrs. Simpkins and supper.   The
house was at the foot of a mountain, up which ran a road,
and most of the farm was in a deep bend of the Schroon
River, where the soil was very rich and from which a crop
of grain had been taken.   It was too late in the day to fish
or shoot, but my fishing tackle was laid out and inspected
and we talked of field sports until bedtime, when a tired
boy turned and caught enormous fish which unhooked
themselves and either walked back into the water on their
tails or vanished into air.   A squirrel which I had killed
turned into a live bear and was charging me when Mrs.
Simpkins called me to breakfast, and the real world came
suddenly back.   If the shade of Shakespeare could have

spent the night with me he would have amended his saying: "Dreams are the children of an idle brain." Mine was busy.

Bait had been provided and the river was reached. Mr. Simpkins had often fished before, but it was evident that my schooling under Reuben Wood and John Atwood rendered me competent to show him how to rig his lines, select his poles, and how to properly impale a worm. He chose a low point of land where there was a high bank and a deep hole on the opposite side, in the bend, and we fished. At that early day there were no black bass in either Schroon Lake or the river, and we took a fine lot of perch and a few other fishes. He was an observant man and showed me where kingfishers had nested in a hole in the bank, under a stump, and we dug out the nest and a lot of fish bones, and the nesting habits of this bird were learned.

Gray squirrels were plenty; they could be seen and heard in all directions from the house, and as this kind of game was rare about Greenbush, where the little chickaree, or red squirrel, was abundant, there was every morning either fishing or squirrel shooting, and in the evening a shot or two at the great northern hare, a new animal to me, which they said was white in winter. Mother went home after a week, saying that she had eaten fish and game enough to last for some time, and I went up the mountain the day before she left and brought her five ruffed grouse (we called them "pa'tridges") to take home to the family. I made the usual promise which a mother always expects, to be a good boy; no hard matter, with no schoolmaster near and all the time to do as I pleased.

One day we were fishing in the river, taking an occasional fish and watching the little rafts of boards float by, when one with a man on it came in sight. He was steering it with a pole and starting any others that had lodged along the banks; when he saw us he pushed up ashore, and, after the usual greeting, said: "Simpkins, we are going to have a deer hunt day after to-morrow; will you go?"

"Yes; where are you going to make the drive?"

"Over on the West River, where we went last year. Our boys haven't had a bite of venison this summer, and they think it about time for it; we'll look for you, sure," and he poled his raft into the stream and was soon lost to sight.

The "West River" was a local term for the Hudson, the Schroon being the "East River." I had heard that Simpkins was a mighty hunter, especially good at still-hunting. He said that the season was too early for the latter sport, because the trees and underbrush were in full leaf. He brought out his favorite gun, oiled the locks and cleaned the barrels. It was a double gun, one barrel a rifle and the other a smooth-bore, quite heavy and handsomely finished. I had been using a single-barreled shot-gun on the grouse and squirrels, and had not seen this one. Old Gunner, his hound, had an eye on the gun, and it might have been hard to say whose excitement was greatest, his or mine. There was this difference between us: Gunner was asking and expecting to go, and I would not ask and did not expect to be invited to join in a hunt with men who might not like the intrusion; but you have no idea how much I would have liked an invitation!

"Ever shoot a rifle?" Simpkins asked.

"No; but I've seen a man shoot at a mark lots of times, and have often sighted it on his targets, and I know how to load one." All this to show that I thought I could be trusted with a rifle if he'd only ask me to go. Oh, if he only would! "I know you put the bullet on your flat hand and pour on powder enough to cover it, and that's the proper load. Then you put the powder in the rifle and lay a greased patch over the muzzle, put the bullet on the patch and force it down, way down, until it is home and the ramrod bounds on it. The rod won't bounce if the bullet isn't home." This was to give him further proof that I knew enough about a rifle to use one. Would he ever take the hint?

"I've killed eleven deer with this gun," said he, "and I haven't had it two years. Killed all but one with the rifle barrel. That one was close by, not over thirty yards off, and I missed it clean with the rifle; the bullet may have touched a twig and gone off somewhere else, for the deer stood broadside to and didn't see me. He jumped at the shot, but I fetched him with buckshot in the other barrel. Ever see a deer?"

"Not a live one; only stuffed ones, in the museum; but I would like to see a real live deer in the woods, jumping as they do in pictures." There! that was a distinct bid for an invitation. If it didn't come after that he was a stupid, or did not want me. He put the gun aside, filled his powder horn, spent much time with other things, and then slowly said:

"How would you like to go along?"

"Oh, Mr. Simpkins! you don't mean it! I would be in the way, I fear."

"No, you can go if you like; I'll go up the hill to Kellam's and borrow a rifle for you; he has three, and you can practise with it this afternoon, and we'll get an early start in the morning."

My rifle shooting that afternoon did not break all records, unless for bad off-hand shooting; but who could do good shooting when all a-tremble from head to foot? The fact that many monstrous bucks were killed in bed that night proves that I had some sleep. Otherwise I doubt if an eye was closed.

Two boys joined the party before we had gone far. They were Henry Tripp and my later army comrade, Colonel M. N. Dickinson, both living in Warrensburgh to-day. Ben Kellam and another man made up the party of six, and there were about as many hounds.

A man took all the dogs and put them out singly as he found a deer track, while the rest went on to take stands on the runways. I was placed in a road looking over a field to a piece of woods some two hundred yards off, and told to watch a point where a deer might come out, but not to shoot until it had jumped the rail fence, when it might stop to look up and down the road if not frightened, and so a good shot could be had. It seemed many hours —it may have been half of one—when a hound that had been baying for some time in the distance was evidently getting nearer; still he was afar off. A farm wagon came rattling up the road with three men in it. When opposite me, as I turned to look at them, one arose and yelled: "See that deer!" I looked back and saw something like a small calf turn and re-enter the woods. So that little thing was a deer! Where was the hound? In the pictures the hounds were pressing the deer hard, some of them tearing at his flanks. More time passed; such long hours I never did see; the sun was not yet at meridian, and the hound kept slowly approaching—oh, so slow!—and finally old Gunner came out of that bit of wood, giving tongue at intervals, and after slowly getting to the place where I first saw the deer he turned and followed its track, making a V out into the field. I had at last seen a real live deer! That was a thing to tell John Atwood and Port Tyler, and to brag about.

Young Tripp, who had been stationed next to me,

came running down to learn if the deer had crossed. The driver soon appeared and said that it was an old runway that was seldom used, and none of the party wanted it. "Yet," said he, "the first deer of the season took it, and you'd have got a shot only for that wagon."

Perhaps it was well that it turned out so, for, as he spoke, a rifle shot was heard off to the left, where the deer went, and we learned afterward that Dickinson stopped my deer a mile above, and it was a fair-sized doe, in good condition.

So far there was a lack of excitement in hounding deer. The long, solitary waits, not long in reality, but intolerably so to a boy whose gun was ready, and, as he fixed himself on the runway, mentally said: "Now bring on your deer!"

The patience of the fisherman somehow was mislaid. The case was different. Of course you must wait in the quiet of a mill-pond for a fish to come to sample your bait, but here was a noisy, bell-mouthed hound proclaiming his every move, bringing to you a new game of great size, which tested your marksmanship to its utmost. He would not swallow your hook and be pulled in by main strength, oh, no! Here I give up the comparison. We all know just how it is. I've tried to tell how I think it is, but give it up. Can't do it.

Ben Kellam took me over to the river, and put me on a runway there, and left. He said that the other hounds were off, some out of hearing, but they might bring a deer this way. I was on a high bank on an outside bend of the river, and could see down to the next bend, about one hundred yards, and there was a shallow riffle that a deer could walk from opposite my station to the point below, on my side. I ate my lunch. Squirrels jumped about and a partridge alighted on a nearby limb. Temptation is one of the hardest things to resist, and I have not always been equal to the task; but this day I simply took good aim at them and thought. It had been impressed upon me that I must not shoot except at a deer—that a shot from me would testify that a deer had come my way and would confuse others. Hounds were tonguing in several directions. I had about lost interest in this stupid work when, "flecked with leafy light and shadow," a buck walked down the opposite slope into the river! It must be a dream! There were no hounds after him that could be seen, and it seemed as if I was choking. He drank, looked around and drank again. I must shoot him! That fact came slowly to me, but I was all a-tremble. He walked diagonally across the river. I aimed and fired. He floundered in the water. Surely he was hit, but might escape! Never thinking to load and shoot again, I left the rifle, and with bare hands started for the buck to take him by the horns and drown him. I slipped on the slimy stones and fell twice, but the buck was slipping and falling also. I was within twenty feet of him when a rifle shot dropped him. It was Simpkins, who had hurried forward at the sound of my shot, and just in time to save the day. Unless a scratch on top of his neck was made by my bullet, I missed him. The slippery stones threw the buck when he tried to run, and to my statement that I intended to take him by the horns and drown him Simpkins said: "You durned fool, he'd 'a' ripped all the clothes offen you with his forefeet, and might 'a' taken your bowels out at the same time. Don't you ever go to foolin' with a deer that has got fight left in him, or you won't have any left in you." The shots brought Dickinson and Tripp, and the buck was soon skinned and cut up for transportation. Although the horns were in the velvet and said to be of no use, I insisted on saving them as a trophy of my "first deer," for, like Falstaff over the dead body of Hotspur, I intended to "swear I killed him myself." So the trophy was preserved and taken to Albany, and for many years I did more lying about killing that buck than a dealer in garden seeds does in his spring catalogue.

Simpkins said: "A little lie like that never hurts anybody. Most all young hunters lie a little about their game." At first it hurt me to lie about it—especially to Old Port Tyler, who wanted all the details—but the story soon assumed the veracity of history. In later life I killed many deer, but they somehow never assumed the importance of the only one I ever lied about. I wrote John Atwood about it, quoting from "As You Like It:" "Which is he that killed the deer?" and winding up by telling him that he didn't know a thing about the jump of the deer, for they couldn't make over fifteen feet at a jump.

A quarter of the doe which Dickinson killed was given me to carry. I was put on the road home, while the rest went another way. Stopping at Kellam's about sundown, his wife gave me supper; and, leaving the rifle, I took a shotgun and shouldered the venison for home, down the mountain. An unearthly scream came from a distance, and my pace quickened. Again the horrible scream was given closer by, and with an open pocket knife and a cocked gun I jumped down the hill, leaving tracks that surprised men who saw them next day. Getting over a rail fence near the house the knife pricked my wrist, and it seemed as if the animal had me. I was faint with fright, and it was some time before Mrs. Simpkins could learn the cause. Her husband came about midnight and heard her story as he was about to get in bed. He dressed, called Gunner, took his rifle and started up the hill. Kellam and he put the dog out, but old Gunner soon came back, cried, got between his master's legs and could not be made to stir.   A puppy went on and put up something, but they could not follow it.

A panther had been about the locality, and shortly after I left Mr. Simpkins killed a large one.   A Mr. Beadenell said it was a bluejay that screamed and scared me, but when I told this to my friend he said: "Bluejays don't scream after dark," and that settled the jay question.

At this time Simpkins was perhaps thirty-five years old.   He had not lived near Warrensburgh long, and moved West a few years later, and I lost track of him. Memory recalls him as an intelligent farmer, a good hunter, an indifferent fisherman, and a good friend who helped me lie about that deer, for which let us hope that both he and I have been forgiven, and that the recording angel, as in the case of "Uncle Toby," after recording the sin dropped a tear upon the page and blotted it out forever.

COLONEL CHARLES H. RAYMOND.

TURTLES, SETTERS AND DUCKS.

THE only fishing companion of earliest boyhood with whom I have kept in touch throughout life, and who is living to-day, is the subject of this sketch.   He was born in Albany, N. Y., in January, 1834, and is near my own age.   He frequently visited me across the river, and we hunted turtles in the creeks from the red mill to Quackendary Hollow—pond turtles, snapping turtles and box turtles—and the point was to collect as many as possible and try to train them to race.   We fished a little once in a while, but to Raymond it was too slow and lacked the excitement of grabbing turtles; and this was characteristic of his life throughout.   As a fisherman pure and simple he would never have achieved fame.   He lacked that quality of patience which is not strained, but droppeth like the gentle worm overboard when it is the last in the bait box.   I cared little to fish with him because of this lack of patience.   He was of the class who say, "Yes, I like to fish if they bite fast."   But he was a born hunter, wing, rifle shot and "bird-dog" man, and took to setters as ducks go to a mill-pond.

We would watch old John Chase lift his fyke nets in the creek, and he would give us the turtles that he caught. We would stroll down the Greenbush bank, past old Fort Crailo, where I went to school, and watch the sturgeon jump in the river.   Then a big one would jump every few minutes; now there are few, if any, in the Hudson.   We went back of the nut orchard and drank the strong sulphur water from Harrowgate Spring, which we often talk of to-day.   It is singular that we never went shooting together, perhaps because his ideas of sportsmanship were higher than mine, and he could go to more distant and better places than I; but, whatever the reason, we often talked of shooting, but never shot in company; yet I kept track of him and of his shooting trips in various parts of the country.

While still a small boy—too small to carry the smallest arms—he followed afield such sportsmen as the late Dr. Judson and his pupil, Alexander Bullock, of West Sand-lake, Rensselaer county, N. Y., in admiration of their skillful handling of the Doctor's slashing English setters, of which I heard much at that time. The masterful way in which those adepts in the art of wing shooting grassed the plump brown woodcock, which they flushed in front of their dogs in the rich coverts that lined the banks of the Wynantskill, taught him lessons in that "deliberate promptitude," so dear to Frank Forrester, that have never been forgotten. As he grew older he was permitted to accompany these sportsmen and shoot with them, and I heard a great deal of these trips after I became his school-mate at Professor Anthony's, with the late Major George S. Dawson, the subject of a sketch in this series.

The first field dog that young Raymond owned was a setter bred by Doctor Judson, called Prince, a very good dog for a boy, because he knew the ways of birds, and, as I remember, had a way as well as a will of his own. His next—and a rare good one it grew to be—was a pointer from my Nell, who was described in the article on Port Tyler as a pointer whose father was a setter. She was stolen from me and recovered by my father after I left Albany, and he bred her to a liver-colored pointer owned by Mr. Sawyer, of Albany, and gave the choice of the litter to his nephew, young Raymond, who named him Don and trained him to a perfection that was rare in those

Colonel CHAS. H. RAYMOND.

days, took him to Michigan and shot over him, to the surprise of the shooters there, who had never seen a field dog work on feathered game and had no experience of wing shooting. These things to hear I, like Desdemona, would seriously incline in after years, and the fame of my Nell and her progeny seemed partly mine. Young Raymond gave Don to his friend, Harry Palmer, in 1856, and shot over him again two years later. After Mr. Palmer's death Don was sold at auction for $50, a very high price for a bird dog in Michigan at that time. I had given Nell such training as she had. My boyish knowledge of dog training must have been crude, although I did not suspect it at the time, for I had read Youatt, Frank Forrester and other authors, and had seen some bird dogs work, and thought, boylike, that I knew it all; but Nell was not broken to suit the fastidious taste of Master Raymond. He next bred her to the famous Pumpelly pointer, and then to a club-tailed pointer owned by a man named Maguire, and one of the litter was a beautifully coated liver-colored setter, the first one in four litters that showed the blood of her sire, James Bleecker's well-known setter. This puppy, Fifine, Mr. Raymond gave to Monsieur Pierre Delpit, his fencing master, in 1859.

It was in Jackson county, Michigan, where Mr. Raymond and Don surprised the natives, and the woodcock and game of all kinds abounded there. Mr. R. learned to track the deer amid the oak openings, through the mossy swamps around Vineyard Lake and along the windings of Raisin River. Here the early lessons of old "Uncle Henry" Harris, the famous hunter of Lake George, who taught the boy to "shute rifil," found their academy of graduation, and thereafter, so long as eyes held their own, Charles could look with confidence along the sights of a rifle at moving game. We had drifted far apart until

my return in 1860 from a six years' tramp, and we no
more lured the sunfish from the creeks, nor held disputes
over the species, age or other things appertaining to turtles and tortoises.   We left the frogs to be stoned by
younger boys, and contented ourselves with reminis-
cences of our mighty deeds, the only difference of opinion, then and to-day, being the question which of us it
was that attempted to jump a stream and changed his
mind when half way across and stuck in the mud.   I still
believe it was Charles.

In the meantime he had undertaken long journeyings
abroad, and save a chamois hunt in Switzerland, with its
climbing, sliding, crevasse leaping and glacier scram-
bling, there was no shooting for two years.   After wandering through Germany and Italy, living on foot for
months along the valleys and on the mountains of Switzerland, he went back to France and made his home in the
Latin Quarter of Paris, along about in Trilby's time; and
if he failed to meet Little Billee, I know by what he has
told me that he must have been on friendly terms with
Zoo Zou and the Laird, for he knew all the pretty songs
mentioned or hinted at in Mr. Du Maurier's truthful re-
cital of life "in the Quarter," and from conversation with
him within the year I gained the impression that he even
knows the fourth and expurgated verse of *"Au Clair de la
Lune."*   Be that as it may, he returned to his native land
with the ripened experience of a man of the world, and a
mind well stored not only with the literature of various
countries, but enriched by that contact with the people of
those lands which only travel afoot can give.

After his return the Insurance Department of the
State of New York was being organized by the Hon.
William Barnes, superintendent.   Mr. Raymond was ap-
pointed to a clerkship in that office, from which he rose to

succeed the Hon. James W. Husted as deputy superintendent of the department. While thus engaged he became a member of the Albany Zouave Cadets, a fine body of citizen soldiers, which was afterward merged into the Tenth Regiment New York State National Guard, as Company A. Then came the war, when men left the farm, the store and the workshop to hasten to preserve the Union. The Tenth Regiment volunteered, was recruited to the full standard and mustered into the U. S. service as the 177th N. Y. Volunteers, and on its rolls was "Charles H. Raymond, first lieutenant, Company A." The regiment was assigned to the Department of the Gulf, under General N. P. Banks. Just before the siege of Port Hudson he was appointed aide-de-camp on the staff of General F. S. Nickerson, and later was made Assistant Adjutant-General on the brigade staff.

All through that weary siege, lying in the trenches in a swampy country which filled the hospitals with miasmatic patients, Colonel Raymond was at his post of duty, even when, as his comrade, Colonel David A. Teller, told me, he had been positively ordered to the hospital; and in the first assault on the works, May 27, 1863, was again at his post, although hardly able to stand. Looking over one of his war-time letters this sentence is found: "This campaigning with field men and field guns, but without field dogs, *Inter arma silent canes*, which, being interpreted, means that when men go afield to shoot each other pointers are no longer to the point, and setters get a setback. These are not the dogs of war."

While in the field Colonel Raymond could not entirely sink the sportsman in the soldier, for in writing to me of the second assault on Port Hudson he said: "You cannot think how sad and strange sounded the whistling of the quail in the fields over which our brigade charged on that fateful June 14, and how that weird whistle seemed to exult over men who, with empty guns, were rushing forward to glory and the grave." A little more than a year ago he again visited that battlefield; again heard the whistling of the merry Bob Whites, descendants of those birds of 1863, and received from the proprietor of the plantation—the son of the owner at the time of the battle—a cordial invitation to come down when the season opened and shoot in peace over the field where his men had shot in war some thirty years before. Verily the whirligig of time brings wondrous changes, as well as revenges!

With the return of peace the Colonel went back to his former position in the Insurance Department of the State, and to the dogs. He bred a good and serviceable line of setters from the native strains of Mr. Truax, of Albany, N. Y., and of General William J. Sewell, of Cape May, Colonel E. M. Quimby, of Morristown, and Mr. Theodore Morford, of Newton, all in the sporting State of New Jersey. With these dogs he established the kennels of Fox Farm, near Morristown, N. J.

In the early '70s Mr. Raymond entered into partnership with Mr. John A. Little, the general agent of the Mutual Life Insurance Company for New York City. Later on, when Mr. Little retired from business, Mr. R. assumed sole charge of the Mutual Life's metropolitan agency, which includes Long Island and Staten Island, a position which he retains to-day. In 1890 he was elected to the presidency of the National Association of Life Underwriters, and few men are wider known or have more warm personal friends than the genial and cultured gentleman who is the subject of this sketch, of whom a writer once said: "The fine and distinctive personality of Mr. Raymond is what makes him what he is. We might sweep away all business details, and all that men know and value in him would remain ineradicably stamped upon the memory and embalmed in the affections of those who call him friend. A joyous temperament, luminous intellect, almost inerrant sagacity, forceful initiative, womanly tenderness, brilliancy, wit, courage and generosity were blended in the alembic from which his nature was evolved. Learned in the literature of books and in the lore of field sports and the natural kingdom; a poet, a sportsman, a soldier and a mathematician; suggestive, inventive, steadfast and true, such is the man as he is known to the editor of this journal and to those who know him better." As the editor of the *Insurance Times* has described Colonel Raymond so much better than I could, and in fewer words, I am content to quote him and not to attempt to improve on his concise and truthful description.

In 1874 Mr. Edward Laverack, of Shropshire, England, offered for sale two of his most famous setters, Pride of the Border and Fairy. These were sought for by several sportsmen both here and abroad, and after some correspondence their breeder decided to sell them to Colonel Raymond, who at once arranged for their importation and transportation to Fox Farm. This was the first pair of that renowned and highly-bred strain of setters sent from Mr. Laverack's kennels to America, and their presence in this country excited much attention among sportsmen and in the sportsmen's press, both here and abroad, in England and on the Continent. Fairy was a great beauty and a natural fielder, staunch on the point and at backing, with great pace, fine nose and grand staying qualities. Pride of the Border at first seemed puzzled at both the scent and the habits of our quail and ruffed grouse, but after a short experience on both he showed extraordinary intelligence and brain power in working on his birds, and was a most admirable and satisfactory field dog, working on game as closely and knowingly as a man could do if he had a dog's form and faculties. Neither of these Laverack setters retrieved game, but they made a rattling brace on a snipe meadow, backing on sight at any distance, absolutely staunch on point and dropping in good old-fashioned style to wing or shot. They still live in loving memory of many human hearts, and their strain, crossed with the Morford stock, is still carefully bred; its inherited physical and mental qualities and capabilities, the resultants of generations of selection, training and association, making these canines as thorough workers in the field as they are affectionate and intelligent friends and companions at home. They are so human that it is often said of them, "They think themselves folks," and the best in the house, be it window-seat, lounge or hearth-rug, is never too good, in their own way of taking it, for these two comprehensive and comprehending members of the family. Nevertheless, unlike Squire Kayse's famous pointer Lee, of Sussex county, N. J., these setters can't catch fish with hook and line, and if they have occupied much space in this narrative it is because they deserve it. No sketch of Colonel Raymond would be complete without an extended notice of this importation of some of the best blooded setters of England, and of their having been bred to some of the native stock, for which American lovers of high-class setters will ever be under obligations to Colonel Charles H. Raymond.

During the period that the Fox Farm Kennels were in existence it was my fortune to be a guest of the proprietor and to talk bird dog as well as turtles with him, while picking the wing of a partridge at his table. I have long since forgiven him for saying that Nell was imperfectly broken and would not "back a point." Of course she would not back, because she never hunted with another dog until he had her. How could she? That is not just what troubled me. There was an insinuation that at eighteen years old I could not train a bird dog to perfection. That thing tasted sour forty years ago, but to-day it looks as if my cousin Charles may have been right.

It is many years since I have cared to shoot anything except ducks, which come to hand dead. I have grown tender-hearted, and say, with Iago, "Though in the trade of war I have slain men," yet I have cried over a doe whose fore-shoulders I had broken, and refused to shoot more when my retriever brought a live quail to be killed by hand. Therefore fishing came to be the more enjoyable sport, because there was no regret when the lower form of life was taken, no keen suffering, because of a lower nervous system; but there is always a latent interest in any kind of sport in which a man has once engaged. To prove this it is only necessary to point to the fact that Colonel Raymond still has a faint liking for fishing. Not for the kind which we had in boyhood, for it is possible that a pond full of painted and spotted tortoises, or a pool full of frogs with an assortment of stones at hand, would hardly be attractive to him to-day. He is blasé on turtles, frogs and sunfish, and needs more exciting game and a broader field. He fishes occasionally, incidentally, as it were, when nothing better offers in the way of sport. Every June he visits, as a guest, Camp Albany on the Restigouche River, and there he occasionally casts for, and even occasionally lands, a fine salmon; but I fancy he does this in a perfunctory way, because there is nothing else to be done. How I would like to stand on the bank and criticise his fly-casting, and thereby get revenge for his remarks on the training of Nell!

The owners of Camp Albany are Messrs. Dudley Olcutt and Abram Lansing, of Albany, N. Y., two skilled and accomplished salmon anglers, learned in all the intricate lore of that grand art; but it can hardly be possible that Colonel Raymond, lacking, as he is, in that virtue of patience which alone bears good results to the angler, can profit by their precepts and example; yet he occasionally sends a fine salmon to a friend, and as Colonel Olcutt and Mr. Lansing both say that he actually catches them, I am certain that he does; and the fact that there are no bullet holes in them proves that his Jock-Scott, silver-doctor, or other combination of hair, fur, feathers and steel can be cast by my friend with occasional effect.

Later, in November, and on the ducking shore, it is different. Then the gallant Colonel is himself again, and no doubt returns the compliment to his friends of Camp Albany and sets them a pace which may worry them to follow. Shooting from a blind, over decoys—that truly Presidential sport, the great delight of the sportsman of or past middle age, when the long tramp over hill and through marsh after pointer or setter seems now to require more exertion than it did in youth—has a fascination for Mr. Raymond, and a better appointed shooting-box than his at San Domingo, on the Gunpowder River, I fancy would be hard to find; and few, indeed, are the places where better sport has been found. But duck shooting, like all other earthly joys, must have its day and fade away. Each year the ducks are fewer and their flights further between, so that ere many more years in their turn shall have flown the canvasbacks and redheads will have gone to join the once countless flocks of passenger pigeons and the innumerable caravans of the bisons, "and the places that knew them," throughout our broad land, from Alaska to Florida, "shall know them no more forever."

THE BROCKWAY BOYS.

THERE seemed to be no end to them. The woods were literally full of them—of Brockway boys, I mean. Boys, and girls also, from babies to men and women, they were everywhere I went. This ceased to be surprising after my uncle, Erastus Brockway, had driven mother and me from Monroe to his home at East Ogden, in Lenawee county, Mich., and after crossing the county line pointed out each house for miles as being owned by one of his numerous kinsmen, until it seemed to my boyish fancy that all Michigan must be peopled by Brockways.

The fact is that mother's two brothers, older than she, had emigrated to Michigan in the early thirties, while it was yet a territory; each had a large family, and at this time they had grandsons older than I, for their many sons had followed the parental example in the matter of replenishing the earth.

Mother was an invalid, and the journey from Albany to Buffalo was made by canal, and from the latter place to Monroe by steamer. The packets which carried passengers on the canal had been about killed off by the railroad, and we had good quarters in a large freight boat, the captain giving up his cabin to us and a woman with two boys. It was an ideal trip. In 1875 I had frequent occasion to go from Lynchburg to Lexington, Va., up the James River and Kenawha Canal, and it is my mature opinion that traveling by canal is the very poetry of traveling; it is the ideal mode of getting about.   This statement is often met with ridicule—"it is too slow."   My friend, listen: You who say this know little of the pleasure of travel for itself.   You wish to annihilate space in a business-like way; you want to go from New York to Chicago, and consult the time-tables for the train which will land you there an hour sooner than another, and you take a "sleeper"—that abomination rendered necessary by merciless business!—and you go that way even on your wedding trip! Go to! The mad American train-catching spirit has possessed you, and, like my friend, Col. Raymond, of my last sketch, you "can fish if they bite fast."   The pleasures of that week on the Erie Canal often arise as I whirl over the route in late years.   Little Falls!   There we boys jumped ashore and stole apples and caught the boat at the locks.   Weedsport!   Here we got off on the "heel-path" side and ran into the outlying edge of Montezuma Swamp and had to swim the canal, when I was the only good swimmer, and, after carrying all the clothes across and safely landing the smallest boy, was forced to lick the older one in the water to keep him from drowning me. His story to his mother conflicted with mine; his blackened eyes and swollen nose seemed to prove his claim to have been beaten without provocation, but mothers will be mothers, you know, and there was a drop in the social mercury.

Pardon me; the canal took me off into the swamp, miles away from the Brock-way.   I will try to get back to the Brockway boys, as I knew my cousins and sons of cousins away back in Michigan in the long ago.

Jim was a big boy—nearly a man.   He could not only smoke a cigar, but could also empty a clay pipe without any visible protest from his stomach.   He was big and strong, and could beat us all at jumping, and was one of the younger sons of the oldest of the brothers, Eusebius, or Uncle Sebe, as he was called—a man who, at sixty-nine years of age, was entered for a foot-race the first day I saw him. Martin and Oliver were smaller boys, sons of Erastus, who, by the way, was many years younger than his brother, physically much weaker, but intellectually stronger. Jim could throw me by sheer weight and strength; Clark or the others of his age could not, for wrestling and boxing had been my study as well as play. This put me on a good square footing with my backwoods cousins, who had little respect for my soft hands and city ways. They had small facilities for schooling, but great opportunities for clearing land for the plough, chopping trees that had been deadened by the girdle, piling great logs for burning that a few years later would have been worth more than the land originally cost. Harvesting the hard-earned crops had given them a rude strength that made it seem incomprehensible how a city boy, who couldn't pitch a fork full of hay into the mow, could lay them on their backs. From a subject for ridicule this city boy came to be respected, especially when they found that he could turn a back somersault from the floor and alight on his feet. They had seen pictures of such things, but to find an ordinary boy outside a circus turn a flip-flap was a thing that made him a hero. My city manners and fine fishing tackle were all forgotten, and the Brockway boys from far and near were invited to come and see their cousin, who in a few hours had overcome all prejudice and was voted to be a really decent fellow.

Said Jim: "Let's go a-fishin'; what yer say? We'll take a team and wagon and go over to the River Raisin and have a good time—yes?" And we went, about six of us. There was William, twenty-eight years old, a hunter of deer and turkeys, who owned a rifle that became mine some years later; Jim, Martin, Oliver, Mathew and others whose names are forgotten, but all brothers, cousins or uncles to each other, and a jolly party they were. Harvest was over, and threshing, corn-husking and such work had not begun; just the time for a fishing trip. An early start and a drive of ten miles behind a good team brought us to the house of another relative—for, as before said, the woods were full of Brockways. The team was cared for, and a walk of half an hour brought us to the river. They cut poles and rigged up their lines with float and sinker and with worms for bait. They had said that the river contained pickerel, and I tied on some very small hooks and with a little switch caught several minnows while they were taking a few catfish, sunfish and others. Grins went around, and Martin asked: "Is that the kind o' fishin' you do down in York State?"

"Yes, sometimes."

"It 'pears like small kind o' fishin'," said Jim; "don't ye ever ketch bigger fish 'n that when you go a-fishin' 'bout Albany?"

"Yes, sometimes."

"Mighty small eatin', them things," said another; "guess you've got to get yer specs on to see 'em when they're cooked. I wouldn't take 'em home if you'd gi' me a cartload. Here, take my pole an' fish for fish that's worth having."

By this time there were half a dozen live minnows in the little water-hole scooped in the bank, and, reaching for my pole, I bent on about twenty feet of line a fair-sized hook with a gimp snell—another new thing to the boys— and hooking a minnow through the lips I cast and skittered it, a trick learned from Old Port Tyler on the Popskinny in the spring before. All except William, the oldest "boy," haw-hawed out loud; he simply watched the curious performance. Cast after cast was made, when a garfish took the lure and was landed—a strange fish to me, but no stranger to the others, who with one accord voted him "no good." They had all stopped to watch this way of fishing, which now was proved capable of taking a gar at least, but when a pickerel of about eighteen inches long came in it was my moment of triumph. If this (to them) crazy mode of fishing had not been a success that morning ridicule would have been my portion. I had known that from the remarks at the beginning, so, turning around, I said: "Yes, Jim, we often catch bigger fish than that when we go a-fishin' about Albany;" and William, who had said nothing, borrowed a hook on gimp and arranged to skitter, while Martin and Jim went catching minnows for the same purpose. When you beat a man or boy at a game he thinks peculiarly his own, he suddenly develops a respect for your abilities—perhaps beyond their real deserts.

William and others took some good fish by skittering, and altogether we had a fine lot, something like two hundred pounds of fish, many strange kinds to me, including pickerel (pike, we call them now), suckers, a strange green sunfish, a strange catfish, as well as the familiar bullhead and the common yellow perch. There was also a "dogfish," strange in that day, and, stranger still, this last-named fish and the gars were said to be uneatable. I had supposed that all fresh-water fishes were eatable, even the suckers in winter, only, like the beer story, "some's better 'n others." We were all learning. When the whole catch was collected it was divided into as many parts as there were houses to be passed on the road home, some fifteen or twenty, and strings arranged to be left at each, with a special one containing choice kinds for a widow, and we rattled home in short time under a full moon.

Going among people whose whole life, training and mode of thought is different from my own has not been an uncommon thing, but this first experience was new, and at times annoying. I felt as a dime museum freak must feel, if he does feel. Interest in such things as changing autumn foliage, the form of a passing flock of wild geese or the strange appearance of clouds, seemed to my backwoods cousins to be silly; these things had never occurred to them as worthy of thought because they were every-day affairs, and to-day I know that a boy who has to turn out at five o'clock in the morning, milk the cows, feed the horses and pigs, and get ready to hoe corn after breakfast has no eye for the beauty of a sunrise any more than he has for a glorious sunset after a hard day's ploughing, when the horses have to be cared for, and all those things which a farmer calls "chores"—not work, by any means—have to be done before he eats his supper and crawls to bed, only to be awakened before nature tells him that he has slept enough. Yes, to-day it is plain why the city boy was a "freak." He had no "chores" to do at home. He could breakfast at eight, go to school at nine, and after four o'clock he had leisure to observe the change of foliage, the flight of wild geese and the colors of the sky at sunset. On Saturdays he could shoot and fish, and there was a six weeks' vacation when the only things he had to obey were his instincts.

Lenawee county was marshy in many places. It was the source of water flowing east into Lake Erie, west into Lake Michigan, and south into Ohio. The country was heavily timbered, and the phlebotomizing mosquito was abroad in the land. We boys slept in the barn to avoid them. Boys came from nearby houses for the frolic in the hay, old and young boys, sometimes a dozen or more. Uncle Erastus did not object to their sleeping there, but did forbid card playing; whether he objected to cards at all times or only to the lights necessary to their use among his hay we did not know. One day, after a little talk leading that way as we sat in the house, he said: "I suppose the boys have a game of cards once in a while in the barn?" this in an inquiring sort of way.

"They couldn't play cards in the dark," I answered; "they'd have to have lights for that. There! What was that big bird that passed the window?" and I ran out to see.

The next day mother said: "Fred, did you find out what kind of a bird it was passed the window when your uncle asked you about playing cards in the barn?"

"No, ma'am; it was gone——"

"Yes, it was probably gone before you saw it; but I'm glad that you did not tell on the boys nor lie to your uncle. Do they play cards there nights?"

"Yes'm, but William said not to tell uncle, and Jim threatened to lick me if I did, and I hope he won't ask me any more. I'll lie to him if he does."

"No, you mustn't lie to any one, and I am glad you told the truth to me. I knew they played cards and had candles there, for I saw the light through a crack that their blankets did not cover, as I walked out last evening."

Oliver had heard this and said afterward: "Golly! but you got out of that scrape nicely; if you had told your mother the boys didn't play cards in the barn she'd 'a' had you, sure."

"Well, Oliver, I was in a corner, but I never tell mother a thing that is not so, nor father either, and I try to be truthful all the time, but it's hard work sometimes. There was no other way to dodge your father than to see a big bird and run out, but before that I fear that what I said was almost a fib, but I wouldn't tell on the boys."

"That's all right. Martin wants to know when you want to go after the blind snipe we started the other day. What was it you called 'em?"

"Woodcock; say to-morrow."

"O. K.; there's a spaniel over at Uncle Sebe's that William trees pa'tridges with; don't know how he'll do on these birds; nobody shoots 'em here. I never saw more'n three or four in my life, and never thought they were plenty."

The spaniel was not a promising dog for the work, but we started. In the talk about woodcock shooting something was said about shooting them on the wing, and Martin almost shouted: "What! You don't mean to say you shoot 'em a-flyin'?" And here again was a surprise; but the success of skittering for pickerel was in mind, and there was no ridicule, but an amount of curiosity to see the thing done. Such a thing had never been heard of, and on a small scale it resembled the experience of Colonel Raymond in an adjoining county a year or two later. I had William's light double gun, and Clark carried a single one, while Oliver was to look after the dog. When we reached the bog where we had kicked up a bird before when crossing it, Oliver started with the dog to try and quarter the ground somehow, as I had explained to him; but it was queer work, for Dick had no idea of woodcock, and being used to ranging out of sight for ruffed grouse, and barking to call his master when he found one, we had hard work to keep him in sight. Martin kicked up a bird, and I fired and missed it; but as it dropped behind some bushes he insisted that it dropped dead. He had a long cord in his pocket, and proposed to tie Dick and keep him with us, and as Oliver was bringing the dog he flushed one that came our way and I killed it. The boys thought this wonderful and the bird the strangest they had ever seen.

"What's his eyes doin' in the back of his head?" asked Oliver.

"That's so's to see who's a-comin' after him when he's feedin'," explained Clark; "and he can see good, too, and don't scare up till he thinks you're going to step on him. Say, I'll tell what let's do. Let's all three and the dog walk abreast an' kick 'em up. What d'ye say?"

This seemed to be a good proposition, for the dog was of no use, and we tried it with better result than I expected, for we succeeded in putting up eleven birds that morning, of which I killed five, Oliver retrieving them almost as soon as they were down, with the help of Dick, for the dog soon learned what we were after and was a fair retriever. The boys told of that morning's work with great pride, never failing to add: "An' he killed 'em all a-flyin'."

On the way home one of the boys shot a big blue heron which was standing in meditation by a marshy brook, and wing-tipped it. Oliver proposed to capture it alive and we surrounded the bird, which had no idea of allowing us to catch it. Standing with head drawn for a stroke and with defiance in its eye, now ablaze with fight, and facing the one who came nearest, it was a most heroic figure, worthy of study by an artist. The spaniel essayed a hand in the fight, and then tried four spry legs on the homestretch after the heron stuck his spear-like bill in the dog's back.

"You make a dive for him," said Oliver to us, "and while he is facing you, I'll get him by the legs and neck." He tried it, and the bird wheeled like a flash and struck the boy a blow on the back of the hand that rendered it useless for months.   Martin then tried to stun him by a blow on the head with a stick, but the heron met him with a jump and a stroke at his face that luckily missed, or he might have been killed or lost an eye.   We learned something of the fighting qualities of a blue heron that was new to us all.   I had not been as rash as the others, for Port Tyler had told me how one had made a dent in the stock of his gun; and after seeing what Oliver and the dog got I had great respect for a wounded heron, which, by the way, the boys called a "crane" as they took him to the house dead.

We made several trips to the river and each time had fine sport.   Martin once had a big turtle on his hook, which fortunately was strong, and the turtle was landed. But it was a singular beast.   In the last story it is related how the collecting of turtles was a fad of early boyhood, and I thought I knew them all, yet here was one with a soft, flat shell which felt like wet sole leather, a snout like a pig's, and a temper as savage as that of a snapping turtle.   Verily Michigan had singular fishes and turtles, but no unfamiliar bird had been seen so far; but that was to come, and in a way to be remembered.

"Ever shoot a wild turkey?" asked Jim.

"No, never saw one; we don't have 'em about Albany."

"I'll get you a shot at one if you'll come over to my house," said he, "and you won't have to go far for it.   I know where it feeds every day."

If I had known the whole story, or how it was going to turn out, perhaps the turkey might have lived longer; but Jim had an idea of getting some fun out of either me, the turkey or some other thing.   It happened that a neighbor of his had a flock of white turkeys which ranged the woods, and a stray young wild turkey fed with the tame birds, meeting them in the morning and leaving them in the evening, when they went home. A boy about Jim's age, whose people owned the flock of white turkeys, knew of this wild one, and had marked it for his meat later on. Jim went with me and posted me behind a fallen log, and I killed the turkey and started for the road to find Jim, when a big boy appeared and claimed the bird. Now the killing of that turkey had not a bit of sportsmanship in it and was nothing to be proud of, but it was a wild turkey and mine. I refused to give up my game.

"This is not one of your turkeys; yours are white."

"I say it's mine, and I'm going to have it. That sneakin' Jim Brockway sot you up to kill my turkey; he dassn't kill it himself, but I'll have it."

"You won't get it. Jim Brockway is down in the road yonder, an' if you call him a sneak he'll lick you."

"Jim Brockway can't lick one side o' me, nur you an' him together. Gi' me that turkey," and he pushed me. I set the gun back against a log and tossed the turkey behind it. He was bigger and stronger than I, but lessons from Shel. Hitchcock, Albany's teacher of sparring, gave me confidence, if he could be kept from a "catch-as-catch-can" hold. He struck an awkward swinging blow and got a stinger on the ear. He was astonished, but made a rush, which was avoided, and took one on the nose, which, as Professor Sheldon Hitchcock would have said, "brought the claret." So far I was unharmed except for my right hand, which has never been equal to the biceps which drove it, and I had only learned to use the left as a guard. He gathered himself and struck straight this time, but I dodged and upper-cut him on the jaw, and, in the language of the Professor, "he grassed." By this time Jim appeared. He had seen it all, but affected surprise.

"Hello!" said he, "what's this all about?"

The fellow picked himself up and said: "You know what it's all about, Jim Brockway, and I'll get square on you for it some day, you mind."

"Why don't you get square with this boy?" said Jim, in a tantalizing manner. "You seem to have had some trouble with him. I don't know what it's about."

"I'll tell you, Jim," said I; "I killed a turkey and he claims it; there it is, a wild one, and everybody knows that all the tame turkeys about here are white, so't they can tell 'em from wild ones. Come on, Jim; he don't want that turkey now, 'cause he said he was goin' to take it, but he didn't."

On returning to the house of Uncle Erastus with the turkey, which was doubly mine now, first by right of having reduced it to possession and again by the gauge of battle, mother at once saw the condition of my hand, now painfully swollen, and, mother-like, wanted to know what had happened. I answered: "Mother, if I should try to tell you just how I injured my hand in shooting a wild turkey the story might get twisted, and I was excited so much that I might be mistaken. Jim will be over to-night. He was there and knows all about it; let him tell it." This must have made her curiosity almost boil over, for there was a mystery, but she was one of those stoical people whose faces never give an indication of either curiosity, pleasure or pain, so she said: "Very well," and waited. After hearing Jim's version of the turkey hunt she never referred to it afterward. She may have detailed the whole affair to father, but when I said, one day after getting home: "Father, I killed a wild turkey out in Michigan," he only asked: "How much did it weigh?"

My cousin, Mrs. Gilleland, of Adrian, Mich., wrote me a year ago: "William H. is now living at Somerset

Center; Jim died in '67.   Of my brothers, Clark died
when twenty-four years old; Oliver died in Andersonville prison; Mathew lost a leg at Vicksburg; Alonzo was
in the army, but came out comparatively well; Martin B.
was in Andersonville twenty-one months, and is now living at Petersburg, Mich."

I do not know what became of the fellow who claimed
the turkey.   I knew his name at the time, but I remember
that he didn't get the bird.

CAPTAIN IRA WOOD.

I KNEW him better in after years, for he was only a child when he left Greenbush, and while his older brother, Reuben, oversaw the capture of my first fish, as before recorded, it was some years later before I had the pleasure of fishing with Ira. Along in the early '50's, perhaps in 1852 or '53, he came from his home in Syracuse to Albany and called on me. He was then a young man of medium height, closely knit, muscular, and the owner of a deep chest voice, which was pleasant and melodious. He had been an actor, and had an engagement in the theatre at Albany to play old men's or other parts, and next week I was to go with him to the theatre to his dressing-room. Like many other young fellows, I had thought the stage a most desirable place to strut a brief hour, although my choice did not lay in his direction. Stars did not travel with their own companies then, but depended for support on the stock companies, and as they usually had two or three different plays each week the members of the company had to study hard, and there was always an after-piece. But this was a rare treat for me. I knew Charley Kane, the low comedian, who also tortured the bass drum in Johnny Cooke's brass band, and Shel. Hitchcock, my sparring tutor, who raised the curtain; but this did not give me the privilege of the stage door. Ira did.

The week opened with Mr. Eddy as the star. Ira

played Brabantio to his Othello, but who the Iago was is forgotten. For a boy of eighteen or nineteen Ira's make-up as the "reverend signior" was excellent, and he filled the dignified part well, as many said. Eddy was an actor of the robust school of Forrest and not unlike him in manner, and would bear nothing that would even slightly mar one of his scenes. Ira also played with Mr. Eddy in "Richard III." that week, and afterward with Couldock and other stars of those days. I do not remember seeing him in comedy except once, and that was as Sir Anthony Absolute, in "The Rivals," with Mrs. John Drew as Mrs. Malaprop, with her "derangement of epitaphs," but forget who played Bob Acres and Sir Lucius O'Trigger.

One day Ira wanted to go fishing, said he had only some four hours after the morning rehearsal, and did not want to put in all his time in going and coming to the fishing grounds and back. Evidently the Popskinny was too far on the east side of the river, and the Normanskill equally so on the Albany side. Fishing off the dock for such strays as might pass had ceased to be attractive as manhood approached, and after a moment of hesitation I said: "Have you ever fished for striped bass in the river here?"

"No," said he, "the only fishing I have ever done is on the inland streams and on Onondaga Lake. I don't know what a striped bass is like. If they are near here and there is a chance to get one or two let's try it. How big are they?"

"Down in salt water they grow big. Up here they run up to half a pound. Meet me at the State Street Bridge at any hour you name and I will be ready with everything that we need." Naturally all these conversations in the long ago are reproduced in substance in the words that memory suggests as she recalls the facts; no stenographer was present. When Ira came he found a boat hired from old John Cassidy, who had a fleet to let, and it was provided with long ropes and anchors at each end—one of those wide, flat-bottomed scows, built like the Dutchman's wife, who said: "She vas so besser built for sittin' down as for runnin' "—and we rowed out of the basin under the Hamilton Street Bridge, for there was a bridge to the pier in those days, and out into the river opposite the foot of Dallius Street, which bears another name now. We dropped anchor just on the eastern edge of the channel; I knew the ranges well in those days, before bridges over the river were built, and their piers had changed the currents and filled in the creek behind the island opposite the city, where we boys fished and swam.

After dropping one anchor, we brought the boat across the current and dropped the other. There is a tide at Albany except when the great freshets come down. The water in those days at ordinary stages varied from one to two feet at high and low tides, but even on flood tides there was always a current down stream, weak or strong, as the tide might be flood or ebb. Therefore we could fish from the lower side of the boat, no matter how the tide was. I opened a two-quart tin pail. "What's that stuff?" asked Ira.

"That's sturgeon spawn, for bait." He made no reply, but watched the production of some linen thread, and a lot of white mosquito netting, which was cut into four-inch squares. Then I rigged him a hand line with sinker, about two feet above which was a hook on a one-foot snell. Above the hook was tied one foot of linen thread, and, putting a quantity of sturgeon eggs in a square of netting, it was fastened about the hook by the thread and cast far out down stream. I had learned this mode of fishing from my brother Harleigh, who, with Uncle John

Wilson, the ship carpenter, and John Ruyter, the tanner, were the only ones who practised it about Albany. It was an art. The fly-fisher may curl his lip if he pleases, but I am a fly-fisher to-day, and will say that to take small striped bass by this mode is more difficult than to take a trout on an artificial fly, after the novice has learned the trick of casting.

In order to explain this mode of fishing I will tell it as I probably did to Ira, premising that the mode is obsolete because the sturgeon in the Hudson are nearly obsolete; or, if not, their eggs, instead of being thrown away, as in the "good old days," are now made into caviare, which men otherwise truthful have said was a delicacy, and the Albany angler no longer fishes in this way. Perhaps the young striped bass, which only ascended the river to feed on the spawn of the shad and the sturgeon, may also be obsolete in these waters.

"Now, Ira," said I, in obedience to instructions under Harleigh, "hold your line taut. When you feel the lightest touch give a twitch as though you didn't want a fish to have a taste of your bait. A bass will quickly follow the hook and you will feel it again. Keep this up, hand under hand, until you either feel them wiggle on the hook or they abandon it. In either case haul in, for the bait is gone or the fish is hooked. Don't allow a bit of nibbling or the bait is lost. Snatch it from them as if you did not want them to have it, until in despair they make a rush and take hook and all. Allow no sampling and sifting of the eggs through the netting."

After a while he got the hang of it, losing much bait in the meantime, and we took quite a number of small striped bass in the only mode of taking this fish near Albany, where they were rarely found outside the channel of the river, that I knew. Fish of half a pound were con-

sidered big ones, but Captain John Hitchcock, a retired
river man, who fished from the steamboat landing almost
daily, once caught one of two pounds weight. While we
were fishing we saw young shad, perhaps two or three
inches long, rising near the boat, apparently after such
loose sturgeon eggs as might escape through the netting
or were dropped from the boat. With destructive man
in addition to all these eaters of sturgeon eggs it is no
wonder that "Albany beef" is no longer found in the mar-
kets of that city. The great fish held its own for un-
counted centuries against all these enemies, the greatest
of which was the eel, but man upset the balance that
nature had kept and the sturgeon has nearly followed the
buffalo, the wild pigeon and other beasts and birds which
man has pursued for market, and has not been saved from
extinction by artificial propagation, as he has saved the
shad and some other fishes. We did not philosophize on
these things then. We were boys and life was before us.
The future of the sturgeon troubled us as little as the
precession of the equinoxes or the differential calculus.
Boylike, our mental vision was bounded by the year, and
a year was a long time then. It was so long from one
Christmas to another. A man of thirty had lived a great
while, we thought, and the disrespectful boys of Greenbush prefixed "old" to the name of every man over fifty.
This reminiscence is brought up by Ira's questions.

"Does old Hogeboom let the boys go in swimmin' off
the dock now?"

The man referred to was a justice of the peace, an office
which he held for years, but from my earliest recollection
I never heard him called anything but "old" Hogeboom.
Once my mother expressed surprise that I had returned
from a swimming trip in the island creek so soon.
"Yes'm," said I, "we on'y just got nicely in when ole

Morris came down and drove us out." She said: "Don't let me ever hear you call Mr. Morris 'old Morris;' you should have said: 'Mr. John Morris drove us out.'" Therefore I said to Ira:

"No, Squire Hogeboom," with emphasis on the Squire, "doesn't allow us to go in off the village dock, but there's good swimmin' off the rafts over there by the island."

He thought a moment and said: "There's one thing sure, I've got to quit the theatre or begin a course of study that I never thought of. I must learn dancing, fencing, music and a whole mess of things if I continue in it. I thought that a little knowledge of elocution was all that was needed, and I got a little of that and went ahead. It is all up-hill work, and I think it is best to quit. Reub says that old Genet gives fencing lessons yet, if he's living; is he alive?"

With mother's lesson in mind I answered: "Yes, General Genet is alive," again with emphasis on the title for Ira's benefit, "and he is the same skillful swordsman that he always was, and as he is still going around selling building lots in Greenbush, with no buyers, the chances are that he will be glad to give you lessons." If Ira was beside me now he would be reminded of his irreverence and told, what he may have learned in after years, that his fencing master was a son of the illustrious "Citizen" Genet who figured in our Revolutionary times. In after years Ira had the reputation of being a good swordsman, and while he was learning I picked up a point or two which was of service in garrison when the neck of a champagne bottle was to be severed at a clean stroke, "but I anticipate" you may be told of this when ex-President Arthur is under the searchlight.

After all his lessons in fencing, and his studies in other

directions, Ira shook the dust of the stage from his feet, left Thespis, Melpomene and other more or less reputable goddesses behind him and sought other fields. We did not meet again for many years. Boys do not care for each other as men do, if they take the trouble to care for any one except their royal selves, and we went our ways, but somehow we were thrown together again; perhaps by some occult fatalism of which we then, and I now, know nothing, for on a review of life to-day no man is recalled whose early ideas so fully accorded with my own. He never thought of accumulating wealth. A powerful physique enabled him to disregard all thoughts of health and a romantic disposition led him to seek adventure. Without consultation we both went away in the same year, he to the army and I to try a different but equally adventurous life.

Ira Wood enlisted February 18, 1854, in the Engineer Corps, U. S. A., at Boston, Mass., for five years. He was under instruction at West Point for a while and was then employed on Fort Sumter, at Charleston; Fort Taylor, at Key West, and was discharged Feb. 18, 1859, at Fort Cascade, Washington Territory, by reason of expiration of his term of service as an artificer of Company A, First Lieutenant James C. Duane commanding. He had made application for examination for promotion to a lieutenantcy, but no examination was held between the time of application and his discharge.

At the call for volunteers after Fort Sumter was fired upon, and the regiments of State militia were found insufficient, Ira Wood raised the first company for the first regiment of volunteers that was organized in the State of New York; but by some delay at Albany other organizations were numbered ahead of it, and the regiment left the State as the Twelfth New York Volunteer Infantry, with Ira as first lieutenant of Company A. He was mustered into the United States service on May 13, 1861. During that year he participated in the battles at Blackburn's Ford, Bull Run and Upton's Hill, all in Virginia. He was promoted to captain, and mustered as such, to date October 29, 1861. He was engaged in the following battles while a captain: Near Big Bethel, siege of Yorktown, Hanover Court House, Seven Days' battle, Gaines' Mills, Malvern Hill, Malvern Cliff, second Bull Run, Antietam and near Shepardstown. He was honorably discharged on tender of his resignation by special order, War Department, October 14, 1862. He resigned to become a field officer in a new regiment, but owing to the clamor of politicians for places for their favorites he did not get the appointment. While with the Twelfth a friend writes me: "The regiment was for a good part of the time commanded by Captain Wood, the senior captain, and he was the only company commander who was present at every engagement up to the time he resigned. At Antietam he made a record with his color guard, when ordered to retreat, by backing off the field as much as possible, declaring that he preferred to take the bullets in front."

On leaving the army he was for a few years in the employ of the American Express Company, and while living in Buffalo became a captain in the Seventy-fourth New York State National Guard. He then went back to Syracuse and for four and a half years was chief of the fire department of that city, resigning the position in October, 1881, to travel for an Eastern manufactory of fire hose. Upon his resignation as chief the Board of Fire Commissioners tried to induce him to remain, and passed resolutions of regret. Steamer No. 1 and the Hook and Ladder Company presented him with an elegant desk clock,

with an inscription commending his mode of handling
fires. The leading citizens and merchants of Syracuse
presented him with a costly watch in recognition of his
efficient service.

In 1867 Ira married Miss Brinckerhoff, of Albany,
who, with one son, Frederic K. Wood, survives him. He
was born in Greenbush, N. Y., May 18, 1834, and died
at Albany, N. Y., April 6, 1886, after an illness of only
three days, caused by some bladder trouble. He was an
enthusiastic Mason and Grand Army man. He attained
the thirty-second degree of the Scottish Rite in Masonry,
and was Adjutant of George S. Dawson Post, G. A. R., of
Albany. He was buried with services of the G. A. R.
and with those of the Knights Templar, these organizations attending in uniform. It was also my privilege to
witness the last sad rites over the friend of a lifetime, one
of the bravest, truest and gentlest men that ever trod the
earth.

Ira went to Albany in 1883 as head of a branch of the
house of Pierce, Butler & Pierce, of Syracuse. Long before this his fame as a fly-caster and winner of prizes at
tournaments of the State Association for Protection of
Game, held at Rochester, Buffalo and Syracuse, had
drifted eastward, but not until the tournament of the
State Association was held at Coney Island in June, 1881,
when I superintended the fly-casting contests, did we
clasp hands since we parted in Albany, some twenty-seven
years before.

"Why, you old duffer! You have been in a flour mill!
Your hair is all white! Take off your hat and I'll dust
you off!"

"Yes, that'll all come off, but your head is mildewed,
and you'll have to bleach it in the sun to kill the mould."

His record in that tournament was 101 feet with a

two-handed salmon rod, a full account of which appears
in the sketch of his brother Reuben. In the class for
single-handed rods Reub and Ira entered. Ira had not
got out all the line he could handle, and Frank Endicott
said that, as his brother Reuben cast before Ira and took
first with 75 feet, he withdrew for fear of beating his
brother. This was probably the fact, because I had attended a State tournament after this where the contestants were Seth Green, Reuben and Ira Wood. Seth had
a wonderful reputation as a fly-caster, and they used
to report his casts without strict measurements, because
his only contestants up the State were Reub and Ira, and
Reub would not beat Seth under any circumstances; nor
would he allow Ira to beat Seth. Once I stood on the
casting platform. Seth had cast, and Reub had re-
strained himself and was restraining Ira.

"Don't you do it, Ira," said Reub; "hold it, don't beat
the old man, it will break his heart. There now! That's
far enough."

"Go in, Ira," said I; "go in and win," for I never loved
Seth as Reub did; "don't let Reub hold you back; this is
a fair open contest, and you should win if you can."

He didn't win; could, but wouldn't. He listened to
his brother, and if the little fly-casting tournaments of the
State Association had been kept up the same old farce of
"don't you do it, Ira," would have continued. After the
Coney Island tournament was over "The National Rod
and Reel Association" was organized, with Francis Endi-
cott as president, and yearly tournaments were held on
Harlem Mere, Central Park, New York City. Here both
Reuben and Ira were freed from Reuben's worship of
Green, who never cared to meet Hawes, Leonard,
Prichard and the other great fly-casters, and the scores
of the Wood brothers are familiar to readers of *Forest and*

Stream. After these meetings, when Ira and I got to talking over old times and swapping army experiences, something always happened to interrupt, and the loss cannot be repaired.

At the tournaments in Central Park it was a common remark how Ira was always on the casting platform untangling the lines, tying on flies and helping the men who were in the contest against him; a course so opposite to that of the "mug hunters," which the lax rules of the Association encouraged to enter the lists, that it could not have passed unnoticed.   Unconsciously the subject of this sketch was exposing himself and his great, kind heart to the public, and, worst of all, to one who in later years chose to write him up and show him by lime-light on the great curtain of *Forest and Stream.*

In 1885, after I had begun the stocking of the Hudson River with salmon, Ira organized the Eastern New York Fish and Game Protective Association, which still exists. Under date of November 18, 1885, he wrote me: "I have set on foot a plan for forming a club or society, to be composed of the best men in this city (Albany), to care for the salmon which you have planted in the Hudson, and also to protect all other fish and game in this region."

In this imperfect sketch I have been greatly assisted by Mr. William Allen Butler, of Syracuse, N. Y., in gathering facts concerning Ira's life in that city.   He tells me that "Captain Wood came of good old New England stock, being a descendant of Dr. Samuel Wood, who came from England in 1684, and was one of the first settlers of Danbury, Conn., in 1696.   His mother was a Breed, and her father, with three brothers and their father, fought in the battle of Bunker Hill on their own farm; their ancestor, Allan Breed, having emigrated from England in 1630 with Governor Winthrop and the Puritans."

IRA WOOD.

As a boy, Mr. Butler was one of Ira's pupils in fly-casting, and speaks with great enthusiasm of his teacher when he relates their trips to the Adirondacks.

About a week before his death Captain Wood opened a store in Albany, at 15 Green Street, for the sale of fishing tackle and general sporting goods, with every prospect of success. Cut down by the reaper before he was fully ripe, those whose good fortune it was to know him intimately can say with Marc Antony:

> "His life was gentle; and the elements
> So mix'd in him that Nature might stand up
> And say to all the world, 'This was a man!'"

GENERAL MARTIN MILLER.

WITH clothing torn and bloody, his face bruised and cut, one eye blackened and swollen shut, Mat Miller came down the main street in Greenbush one day. Beside him walked a giant negro, like Eugene Aram, "with gyves upon his wrists," and in a condition like Mat's as to face and clothing. This sight so impressed me that it always came up whenever I heard of or saw Mr. Miller. We little boys had never seen such a sight, and when we learned that the colored desperado had been a terror to the country for miles around, and was a burglar, and that Constable Miller, having learned that he was sleeping in the old spook-house barn, had attacked him alone and captured him after a long and fierce fight, he was our hero. We learned in later years that this genial, fine-looking athlete was the champion wrestler of Rensselaer County, and at "collar and elbow" or "square hold" could lay the local wrestlers on their backs. But this capture of the powerful burglar overtopped his other feats.

Some time after this event Herr Driesbach, the great animal trainer, wintered his menagerie in Greenbush, in the stables of Bill Gaines, the local racing man, on Broadway, just below Columbia Street, back of Fly's brick store, which still stands there. In those days the circus and the menagerie were two distinct things. The circus had no animals, while the menagerie had a ring in which dogs and monkeys rode on ponies and appealed to that portion of the public which objected to men and women in tights. In early days, when my father's barges brought emigrants up the river to Albany, Jake Driesbach was an emigrant runner for a line of canal boats which took them to Buffalo. He then went to Germany, and returned as "Herr Driesbach, the world-renowned lion tamer." Boys were not wanted in the stables, but as father's business froze up when the river did, and Driesbach came to our house in the long evenings to play chess with father, I had the run of the show, to the envy of the other boys, who could not get in unless I chose to take them. To be on intimate terms with so great a man—for a lion tamer is the biggest kind of a man to a small boy—was indeed a pleasure unknown to men who were never boys. By that I mean those old fellows who were born "young men" and never had any fun.

The privilege of seeing these animals at all times was something, but to witness the rehearsals that were necessary to keep both men and animals in readiness for the opening performance in the spring was a thing that a real live, full-blooded boy would naturally class as but little below paradise, if he didn't consider it a dozen miles above. As the village constable, Mat Miller walked in the menagerie when he pleased. In fact any reputable citizen could; the line was drawn at boys, who might get hurt or into mischief. There was no steam-heating apparatus in those days, and the two elephants, the giraffe (the first one ever in America), the monkeys and other inhabitants of warm countries were in the end where the great stoves were. One day a chained elephant became scared at something; Driesbach said the animal saw a mouse and feared it would go up its trunk. The cage containing the royal Bengal tiger was overturned, and pandemonium, or the Cooper Union after an Anarchist meeting, was a Quaker assembly compared to it. The elephants trumpeted, lions roared, hyenas howled, monkeys screamed and what the cockatoo said is lost. "Mat" was there, and so was Driesbach and the writer. The constable jumped, grabbed the cage by the top and forced it back to its place at the expense of a coat and a torn shoulder from the tiger's claws. Driesbach was astounded at the quickness and strength of this unassuming man, and offered him a lucrative position to travel with him, which was declined. Me? Oh, yes! After it was all over "Dandy" Nesbitt, the jockey, Tom Scribner and I were found safe under the wagon where the trick bear had his residence.

Up to about 1845 there was lots of fun every year at "general training." This was an assembling of the uniformed and the ununiformed militia for several days or a week's drill in camp, as required by law. The ununiformed militia consisted of every man between certain ages, not specially exempted, who could, I think, escape by paying a certain sum. It was a grand spree for some and the guard-house was always well filled with drunks. When in garrison in later years this gang was known as Company Q.

Martin Miller was a general of militia, but of what rank I never knew; in fact, rank was unknown to us boys beyond the fact that there were officers and privates. It was my fortune to see two "general trainin's," one on the farm of John Morris, above the village, and the other at Clinton Heights. Then I think the law was changed and they were abolished, perhaps before 1845, for I was then old enough to remember more than two such rackets. It was a great event. Drums, flags, the squads of farmers' boys who couldn't keep step to the drum, the neat uniforms of some of the companies, the usual crowd of bumpkins, yokels, three-card-monte men, thimble-riggers, sweat boards, chuck-luck and other gamblers, peanuts, gingerbread and, above all, General Martin Miller resplendent in *chapeau bras*, epaulet, sword and sash, mounted on a white horse, trying to bring order out of chaos. If all these things did not make soldiers for the State out of the rawest kind of material it certainly made a very large day for the small boy.

If any one trait was more prominent than another in the mental make-up of General Miller it was his love of boys and his desire to see them have fun. Having no children of his own at that time, he was fond of those of his neighbors. Things were getting along in shape and the gamblers were reaping a harvest, when the General invited a crowd of boys to follow him if they wanted to see some fun. Every sweat board and chuck-luck table had piles of coin of all sizes and values piled up to show their ability to pay bets, and as the General came alongside of one he would wheel his horse suddenly, clap the spurs to him, and that gambler's coin was scattered far and wide, a harvest for those who could reap. Somehow the gamblers did not appear to like this, judging from their remarks.

Years after this the General became a grocer, and in that very democratic community subsided into plain, every-day Mat Miller, so called by every man, woman and child in the village.

We were in his store one day talking of going down to the Popskinny for a couple of days' fishing and to camp in Rivenburg's barn in the hay.

"What do you boys do down there at night?" he asked. "Perhaps you raid Teller's potato patch and roast his potatoes with his fence rails. I think I'll go along to keep you straight."

"Come along," said Billy Shaw, "we'll let you gather

drift-wood, and then you'll know whether we use fence rails or not."

"Yes," chipped in John Atwood, "and you can hook the potatoes, too, if you want 'em. We never trouble the farmers and they don't trouble us. We take our grub along and just cook a few fish."

Billy Atwood, a boy who seldom said anything, remarked: "Mat might go and milk some of Rivenburg's cows if he wants to eat his fish in milk," a reference to a man who was said to have tried this dish on recommendation of one Harleigh Mather, whose humor lay in such things. This man was known as "Suckers and Milk" until life became a burden to him and he moved away. This same irreverent joker in after years replied to a clergyman who wished to know how to cook frogs: "Oh, we stew them just as we do bats." I do not approve of this sort of thing except when I do it myself.

Rivenburg's barn was only used to store hay in until it could be pressed into bales and sent off, therefore it was empty most of the year, but there was always enough loose hay left to sleep in. It was one of the finest barns you ever saw, for ventilation. The doors were off the hinges and were propped up by poles. We did not disturb them, but walked in from whichever side was convenient. The double doors were, if I remember, a trifle larger than the other holes.

John Atwood had brought the worms for bait in some old mustard boxes, and we assured Mat that they were not brought in the coffee-pot because that had been kept hidden in the barn as part of our permanent outfit, along with the frying-pan and tin cups. Hot coffee, fried sausages and other things saw us comfortably fed by sundown. Great clouds came up and the wind shook the barn and we hurried to the tightest corner as the storm suddenly broke over us. The thunder made the barn shake and it could not have rained harder. Flash after flash came so fast, and the thunder followed so quickly that one could hardly note the interval. Heaven's artillery opened right over us, and every fellow was doing his own thinking and keeping it to himself. Billy Shaw was the exception. He ventured to remark: "Maybe you fellows like this, but I wish I was home!" That broke the spell, and he was nearly smothered in the hay which they piled on him. During this smothering of Shaw I saw, or believe I saw, a flash of lightning shoot up from the ground. It was so close to the barn that it seemed as if a man had shot a gun in the air. Two boards were off that side and there was no man there. If such a thing ever occurs, I saw an instance of it; if it does not I was deceived. No hole in the ground was visible in the morning, but half a century has not dimmed the picture.

Such a rain never lasts long, and soon the stars were shining, and we rebuilt the little fire, and with dry material from the barn for seats were enjoying life, when the sound of oars was heard, and soon the lapping of the water under the bottom of a little scow told that a boat was near.

"Halt! Who comes there?" was the challenge of the General.

Bill Atwood, John's younger brother, who had already shown symptoms of nautical bacteria which eventually dragged him to a sailor's life, hailed the coming craft with: "Aboard the scow! Pull on yer starb'd oar or you'll foul our coffee-pot!"

A few more strokes and the boat was beached and out stepped the old trapper, Port Tyler. "Where's that coffee-pot?" said he. "I'm wet an' cold, and some hot coffee is just what I want. No, thanks, nothing to eat; I've got lots. Why, Mat Miller! What you doin' here campin' out with these boys? I see ye all go by when I was hid in the lilypads around the bend yonder watchin' for wood ducks, an' I knowed the hull lot on'y Mat, an' I'd a knowed him ef I'd a-suspected he'd come a-campin' with you boys. What're ye up to, Mat? Burglars or thieves been on the island, or are ye on'y lookin' up the boys that's just come of age and just goin' to vote for the first time this fall?"

"Sit down here," said the General; "get outside of this warm coffee. I'm not looking for you, but there's a widow up there at John Morris' rope-walk that is, and she'll get you, too, if you don't look out."

This was a clean knock-out, for if ever there was a man who was shy of a woman it was that confirmed old bachelor, Port Tyler.

The stars twinkled. Venus, just about to disrobe and retire for the night, winked at Polaris, the night clerk, and hid herself behind Bethlehem woods. A night heron said "quawk" in a derisive tone, and even the little barn owl seemed unduly hilarious as it alighted on the gable of the barn with a field-mouse. Then there was a vast wave of silence that rose like the battle waves of Ossian and overflowed the lands on either side of the historic Popskinny. Miller's shot struck home, and the bashful trapper took it in silence. Not a leaf stirred. Billy Shaw finally ventured to ask, "What kind o' game are you after, Port?"

"Oh, just lookin' for yellow-legs and shore birds. I've got three young quawks* in the boat, and nobody

---

*This is the way we called this night heron, *Nycticorax.* The common name is sometimes spelled "squawk," while some naturalists call it "the qua bird." If you take my spelling and add "quock" to it, and then divide the sum total by two, you will get very near to the bird's own pronunciation of its name; and who should know better than he?

GENERAL MARTIN MILLER.

about here eats 'em but me; so I can't sell 'em, an' if you'll eat 'em I'll cook 'em."

By unanimous consent it was voted "a go," or words to that effect. Billy Shaw, who had no fear of thunder now that it was not in his immediate front, said that we were down for fun and might as well have it. "If you are not hungry now," said he, "you will be by the time old Port gets these song birds dressed and cooked."

John Atwood and I took Port's boat and put out his set lines for eels, in order to have fish for breakfast. These lines were of quarter-inch cord, reaching from bank to bank. At every two feet was a one-foot snood tied with a "bow-timber hitch," dropping only one foot below. This enabled the fisher to snatch a snood loose and drop it in the boat, eel or no eel; but the beauty of Tyler's rig was the eyed hooks with a knot above and one below, which prevented an eel from unlaying the snood and breaking it strand by strand, merely turning the hook as if on a swivel. There is no patent on it.

The quawks were roasted when we returned after putting out the eel lines in several places, and the fact that we had eaten one supper did not prevent us from eating of the strange birds, and they were not a bit fishy, as one would suppose, but were tender and good. Port had set up a wind break and heat reflector by the fire and hung the birds on strings, so that they kept twisting round. When we came to crawl into the hay for the night Billy Shaw seemed a bit nervous and inquired if there might be rats about, and that started stories of enormous rats that lived along the creek and in the barns, all for his benefit. The little owl would whinny not unlike a horse, and Billy was evidently uneasy until Miller ran a stick in a wiggling way into the hay and said something about snakes. Then Billy vowed that he would go home.   The General owned up and persuaded him to lie down, and the next we knew the night had gone.

We had eels enough for breakfast on the first line, and then Port took up the others and left us.   We fished until near noon, when the fish took a rest, and we gathered at the barn, each with several strings of perch, bullheads and rock bass.   John Atwood had a strange fish, one that none of the party had ever seen before. We learned that it was a black bass, a Western fish that had come into the Hudson by way of the Erie Canal, so Harleigh said, and he was the village authority on fish and fishing.   Just why the bass have not become more plenty in the upper river is a problem.   Down about Newburgh, where the water is often somewhat brackish, they seem to be more plentiful.   A little more fishing in the afternoon, and we went home after sundown.   The General declared it was a pleasant trip, but I never knew him to fish before or after this once.

Back of Ruyter & Van Valkenburg's tannery there was a great heap of spent tanbark to tumble in, and Jimmy Brown and I practised somersaults there; the other boys merely jumped.   This interested the General, and he would help us in a whirl with his strong arm, which landed us on our feet.   This was a special help in the back flop.   Poor Jimmy Brown!   We used to play the banjo for each other's jigs on the sanded floor until he was burned up on the steamer Reindeer in the summer of 1850.   General Miller also taught us to wrestle in the "collar-and-elbow" and "square hold" styles, and always impressed his correction of a fault upon us by taking hold himself and making the faulty one put his foot or his weight in the wrong position and then quickly laid him on his back.   There were many fair wrestlers then among the boys of Greenbush.

One winter, when the ice was exceptionally good, he proposed a skating party to Hudson, some twenty-eight miles down the river. We had an ice boat that some of the boys built, and this was to go along to pick up stragglers and to return on. Cub Wilson sailed the boat. A Greenbush boy of those days had little reverence and less respect in his composition, and nicknames were common. Wilson was then about twenty-five years old, fat and unwieldy, and had been called Cub from boyhood and didn't mind it. He may have had a given name, and no doubt his mother called him by it. The party consisted of John Atwood, John and Hiram Stranahan, Jerry Van Beuren, James Miles, Isaac Polhemus, John Phillips, General Miller and myself, the youngest in the party. We started in the morning about eight. A light south wind was in our faces, and coats and overcoats were soon piled on the ice boat. In places the ice was too rough to skate, and once we took off the skates and walked about half a mile. Phillips and the Stranahans were the best skaters, and took the lead and kept it, reaching Hudson some time ahead of us. Atwood, Van Beuren and I brought up the rear. We did the stretch in four and a half hours—some claimed less time—pretty well tired and with numb feet. We all wore high boots. The skates, with great turned-over prows ending in brass acorns, were guttered in the bottoms, and strapped so tightly over the foot that the blood could not circulate. We did not think skating possible under any other conditions. When the strap would not take up another hole we drove wooden wedges between the strap and the boot to make it tighter. A few years ago I tried on the old style of skate and could get around a little, but could do nothing with those of the present model.

At Hudson General Miller took us to a hotel and we

had a good dinner. We had a strong wind from the west on the homestretch and the ice boat did not have to tack once, and we were not long on the way. Skipper Wilson remarked: "You boys beat me when I had to tack against a head wind, but you couldn't do it now." On telling the story the General said: "The boys are all good skaters, but you should see 'em eat! They cleaned up everything in that hotel, and if they ever go to Hudson again that landlord will close his house when he sees 'em coming."

> "Hans Breitman's gife a barty—
>   Where ish dat barty now?
> Where ish de lofely golden cloud
>   Dat float on de moundain's prow?
> Where ish de himmel strahlende stern—
>   De shtar of de shpirit's light?
> All goned afay mit de lager beer—
>   Afay in de ewigkeit!"

This philosophical verse of Leland's comes up when that day is recalled, for all except the writer have passed into the *ewigkeit* of the Plattdeutsche, or *evigkeit* of the German. Five died peacefully. John Atwood was killed by a boiler explosion, Van Beuren was drowned in California, and Phillips was killed by interlocking his "turn-over" skate with that of another boy, and his skull was broken on the ice. Surely I may ask: Where is that party now? And *ewigkeit*, or eternity, as you choose, is the only answer.

I learn from one of boyhood's companions who has not yet crossed the Styx that General Martin Miller was born on May 12, 1816; was Doorkeeper of the State Senate in 1845-46; was member of Assembly in 1858, and died in the summer of 1882. The General married and died in the summer of 1882. The General married a sister of my friend, Garrett M. Van Olinda, who is now in business at 18 Harrison street, New York, and one son survives him.

For a few days during the time of the Mexican war the sleepy little village of Greenbush was disturbed over a very small word and argument ran high. Abram Van Olinda, brother to the General's wife, had raised a company of volunteers for the war, and the citizens of Greenbush purchased a sword to be presented to the Captain; but it must have an inscription of some kind to tell who presented it and also who it was presented to. A few had agreed that the blade should be inscribed: "Presented by the citizens of Greenbush to Captain Abram Van Olinda, and never to be sheathed but with honor." This was the sentiment of Volkert P. Douw, Squire Hogeboom and John L. Van Valkenburgh. Isaac Fryer moved to strike out the word "but" and insert "except," and Thomas Miles and others backed him. The inscription hung fire, and the women of the village took it up and hot arguments were held as to which of the two words was the best to use in the inscription. A meeting of all who had subscribed for the sword was called at Fryer's tavern, and after much argument from each side "Mat" Miller was asked to give his view of how the inscription should read. He rose and said: " 'Never to be sheathed but with honor' is good; we all know what it means. We also know what it means if we say, 'Never to be sheathed except with honor,' and it's only a choice of words, and 'but' is Dutch." That settled it. The Douws, Van Valkenburghs and Hogebooms were defeated by this thrust. Captain Van Olinda was killed while leading his men at the charge on the heights of Chapultepec, on September 13, 1847. The result of which was sent home, and is still in the possession of his family.

Mat Miller—I love to think of him as "Mat"—was a warm friend to boys. Perhaps he liked some boys better than others, but he was always my friend, and he was the manly sort of man that I could look up to with confidence. He was a man when I was a boy. When I was fourteen he was thirty-one, but he was always one of us on such frolics as have been related, and never seemed to know of that gulf which separates the fun-loving boy from the money-grubbing man which some men develop into.

General "Mat" Miller! You covered yourself all over with glory when you attacked a desperate burglar, who outclassed you in weight, alone and single-handed in the old "spook-house" barn and brought him to justice. May you be crowned with glory now, as the reward of an honest life, is the prayer of your boyish friend.

GARRETT VAN HOESEN.

THE village boys called him Garry Van Hooser, and I am not sure but the whole family pronounced it in that way; but Garry could write, and he spelled the name as it is given above. He had been a clerk in the grocery of Thomas B. Simmonds since my earliest memory, and had none of the Dutch accent common to his people, for at this late day the descendants of the original settlers of the Upper Hudson often spoke Dutch, and their English had an accent which Garry had lost by frequent contact with other people. He was older than I by some six to ten years, and was a shy young man, who never seemed to have any companions, and often went fishing and shooting alone or with his spaniel Coody, which was a good retriever. He told me where he got the dog, but where its name came from even he did not know. He said: "Oh, I do' know; he had to have a name, and I just called him Coody."

That settled the matter to the satisfaction of Garry, the dog seemed to be pleased with the name, and who could object?

One day in '48, after the election of General Taylor as President, when the ice was just thick enough for skating, I had been told to stop at the grocery for something when I came home to supper, and Garry said: "I am going up to the mill pond in the morning to spear eels. How would you like to go with me?"

"First-rate; what must I take along?"

"Nothing but a pair of woolen mittens; your hands will freeze without them. I'll put up all the grub we want.   Meet me here about nine in the morning and we'll start."

During the night about two inches of snow fell. The morning was still and clear, and the snow was soft and dry.   Garry carried the basket and axe, while I shouldered the long spear up past schoolhouse and along the railroad, which then came down to the lower ferry, to the mill pond away up by the red mill. The snow was blinding as we faced the morning sun, and it also reflected every sound. The far-off crows seemed close at hand, a little sapsucker pecking on a tree made a great rapping, and we could hear what the men were saying down at the mill.   "Why is it so still after a fall of snow?" I asked.

It's always that way after a snowstorm," he answered, and I went along not entirely satisfied with his laconic answer, but accepted his statement of fact.   Some philosophers give us equally lucid explanations and take a whole volume to do it in.

"A week from now the ice will be too thick to spear eels," he said, "and it would take half an hour to cut a hole.   It's just right now, nearly four inches, and no one has been spearing here this year.   Down yonder, in the bend, is where they bed; the water is deep there."

All eels bed in the mud in cold weather, and an eel spear for soft bottom has a stout central tine barbed on both sides; then come flexible tines, about five on each side, with barbs on the inside only.   The tines are nearly a foot in length, and radiate from the pole-stock in a flat plane, which is some 10 inches wide at the lower end. Rigged with a light pole, twenty feet or more long, the mud is sounded in a regular manner in a circle of perhaps thirty feet in diameter. When an eel is struck the spear does not pierce it, but holds it by the spring of the tines, which open and clasp it. It was soon apparent why woolen mittens were an essential part of the outfit. As they became wet they were warm, even with ice on the outside of them, just as a boy's foot will be warm after the first chill when his boot is full of ice water if his stocking is of wool. But continual freezing to an icy spear handle is hard on a mitten.

I watched Garry begin sounding under the hole and then increase the circle until the spear handle was at an acute angle with the ice, throwing the spear strongly into the mud and then withdrawing it. He brought up sticks, brush and an occasional eel, which soon stiffened on the snow. "How can you tell whether it's an eel or a stick?"

"That's easy enough; try it."

He chopped me a new hole and I made a thrust. "Harder," said he; "shove it hard or the barbs won't snap on 'em," and I sent the spear into the mud. An eel? No, a stick! After landing several sticks something was struck that wiggled and sent little thrilling pulsations up the staff, and then I knew all that is to be known about spearing eels through the ice. It is not a high class sport, but it gives a boy an excuse for an outing in winter and is a healthful exercise. This thing of exercise is better understood to-day than when I was a boy, and men who go out with rod and gun are not thought to be idle, good-for-nothing fellows, as they were thought to be half a century ago. Not that I was not an "idle, good-for-nothing fellow," who preferred a day's shooting or fishing to a week's confinement in school, but I am speaking in a general way, excepting "present company."

About noon Garry flung the spear in the snow and said: "I'm hungry; what do you say?"

Now that the matter was mentioned, there did seem to be something lacking, and without giving it that profound consideration which Garry gave to questions, I answered him in his own simple style: "So'm I." All the morning I had been as silent as he; in fact, when a fellow gets shut up with such short answers as are here recorded there is nothing for him to do but to shut up. But how I did want to talk about the habits of eels, what they found to eat in the mud and other things. Away up the pond, a quarter of a mile away, a man was chopping wood. The sound of his stroke did not reach us until his axe was raised again. I asked father about this when I got home, but I did not intrude the question on Garry. He did not then encourage talk.

We went ashore by a spring and made a fire. Garry opened the basket and brought out bread, butter and sausages. Just how he could cook the last was a mystery, and they could not be eaten raw. Bolognas were unknown then, as this was before the German invasion and the era of limburger, schweizerkäse, bolognas, pretzels and lager beer. I gathered dry fire wood and watched. He dragged two longs limbs and rested one end of each upon a low stump. This was table and chairs. Then he took birch twigs and ran them lengthwise through the sausages and stuck them up before the fire. The ground being frozen, he held them nearly erect by pieces of wood, and there they fried in their own fat, the birch twigs imparting no bad flavor. A tin cup of water from the spring served for both, and if a hungry boy astride a branch of a tree with a big birch chip for a plate did not do full justice to his appetite then he never did.

Many a dinner did I eat after that one, but this was so exceptionally good that it stands out in bold relief. During weary months in military prisons the odor of those sausages came in hungry dreams. The white bread from Jonas Whiting's bakery and the butter from Dennison's farm were often remembered in days when such remembrance was more substantial than anything in sight.

That dinner is memorable for another thing. It opened up a human mind. John Atwood had said: "Garry Van Hooser never talks because he doesn't know anything to talk about. He just knows enough to weigh a pound of tea and say, 'Yes'm, fifty cents.'" When I told John a little of this trip he was incredulous. The eels were in evidence, however; he couldn't deny them.

After we had destroyed the dinner and Garry had lighted his pipe, he remarked between puffs: "When spring comes we will go down in the dead creek and shoot ducks. I often go there alone, but have felt that I wanted some one to be with me, some one to talk to at times. I went down there once with John Atwood, but he talked all the time and scared the ducks away. Now you don't break in when a man is thinking, and we've had a good time. I don't know what you were thinking about when we were spearing, but I thought that if it is true that this world is round and turns over every day, how is it that the water does not spill out of the holes we cut in the ice, and why the weight of the trees does not pull 'em out of the ground when they're upside down. I don't say that I don't believe it, but I can't understand it; and men that know more than I seem to believe it, but they can't tell just how it is. I never had much schooling, and this thing has bothered me for years. It keeps me awake nights and bothers me daytimes.   If I ask about it they make fun of me.   Now you've had a good education and I want to know what you think about this thing, and if you don't know how it is don't tell that I asked about it; for there's a lot o' fools that don't know the first thing about this business, and don't care, that are always ready to make fun of a fellow who does want to know."

This was the longest speech that I had ever heard Garry make up to that time.   I explained the rotation of the earth as well as I understood it, and afterward gave him what literature bearing on the subject I could find, and his reserve was thrown off.   He was a different man to me, and I soon liked his simple, honest ways, his studious mode of looking into things and his philosophical conclusions.   Every man's mind is a study, a curiosity, if you will, if you have time and inclination to look into it.   It is curious because it differs from yours.

After his long speech, delivered between puffs on his pipe, and my explanations, there was a period of silence. Then he asked: "Did you ever trap any rabbits?"

"No; I've shot a few, but never trapped any.   Why?"

"What time do your folks have breakfast?"

Without seeing any intimate connection between the trapping of rabbits and the hour when our family broke their fast, I replied: "In summer at seven and in winter at eight.   What's that got to do with catching rabbits?"

"I was thinking that you'd have time to tend the traps if you could get up about six o'clock.   Then you'd be back in time to get breakfast and go to school.   There's lots o' rabbits up in the woods back o' the rye field, and I've got six box traps in the old barn there.   If you'll see to 'em every morning we'll go over there now and set the traps before we go home.   What d' you say?"

"Tell me all about it, and I'll do it. It must be heaps o' fun. Come on."

We crossed over to the rye field—a field as well known to every boy as the ball ground, where no one drove us off, but which had been a pasture since my recollection—and carried the traps into the woods. Garry had got some sweet apples, and we set a trap here and there where rabbit signs were thickest.

"When you come to a trap in the morning," said he, "if it is still set you want to see that the bait is there and the cord or the spindle is not frozen so that it can't work. If it has been sprung you want to go slow and find out what's in it. If it's a skunk he'll let you know when you touch it with your boot, and then you want to tie a long string to the cover and let him walk out. If it's a rabbit, put in your hand and take it out."

"Won't it bite?"

"No, they never bite. The best way to kill them is to hold their hindlegs in your left hand, and hit 'em with a stick in the back of the neck."

"I don't believe I could do it. I can shoot one, but I know I could never do that."

"Yes, you could; it's easy enough. But if you are afraid to do it that way, take a bag, put the mouth of it over the trap, dump them into it, and bring them down to me."

That seemed the best way. I was not afraid to kill a rabbit by shooting it—Garry did not understand me— but the bag scheme let me out and it was settled in that way. We went back to the mill pond, gathered our basket of eels and went home. I promised to let Garry know how many rabbits I had and to let him do the killing.

Next morning I was up very early. There had been

a light, drizzling rain during the night, and now there was a hard crust on the snow which crunched under foot and made a great noise. The first trap was approached with a quickening pulse, and my heart was beating high as it was neared. Alas! it was unsprung and the cord was frozen fast. The crust did not tell if the trap had been visited, but the apple was untouched. All the traps were in the same condition, but I fixed them so that they would spring, and on the way home reported the facts to Garry.

"You needn't have gone to them this morning," said he, "for you might have known that a rabbit would not go out and get all covered with ice in a rain like that one last night."

I might have known, but with a head filled with the excitement of a first visit to rabbit traps, with the expectation that at least one rabbit might be found in each, I never thought that they might prefer dry hides to my traps.

The next night was clear and crisp, and, oh, how cold that morning was! The stars seemed to echo my tread on the crackling crust as I trudged along. The first trap was unsprung, and my faith in taking rabbits in box traps was shaken. Old tracks, made before the crust was formed, were abundant, and there was "sign" on the crust where no tracks could be seen. Surely there were rabbits there, if they could only be caught. These were the thoughts when the second trap was sighted. It was sprung! The rapid puffing of an early freight train on the railroad below did not exceed the beating of my heart. Cold as it was, a perspiration broke out all over me. Pshaw! Perhaps the string had broken or the trigger had slipped from the notch!

I stood for a moment like one in a dream. Could it

be that the trap actually held a rabbit? I went up to it
and kicked it lightly with my boot. There was no indication of an "essence peddler" in the air and I peeped in.
There was the game crouched in the far end. I let the
trap down, and for a few moments enjoyed my triumph.
I was a mighty trapper! Me!

This was long before the deer episode, and a rabbit
was the largest game that I aspired to. Heart never
beat faster over a first grizzly or bighorn than mine did
then. As I have said, I had shot an occasional rabbit;
but this early morning tramp over crusted snow seemed
somehow to make the event seem like the life of a real
woodsman. A great part of Greenbush was asleep, and
here was I in the forest with its largest game in my
power!

I carefully adjusted the bag over the trap and then
opened it. There was a thud in the bottom of the bag,
and then a glimpse of something gray and a sound of
"zip, zip," and if that was really a rabbit it was gone.
The unexpected had happened. That was all I knew,
and there was a period of depression such as always follows intoxication. After pulling my scattered senses together, I reset the trap and went on. The third trap,
held a rabbit, and with the last failure in mind great care
was exercised in arranging the bag. No mistake this
time! I knew how to hold him. I knew how, but somehow the same thing happened again. The second time
the unexpected occurred, and some old philosopher has
said that this is the only thing that ever does occur. I
was despondent and demoralized, especially when the
next two traps were found empty. As the sixth and last
trap was sighted, the fact that it was sprung started no
heart pumping. I was cooler now that I had seen just
where the last rabbit got out. The bag had been tight

around the trap until the trap was opened; the top and front end were nailed together, and the bag left a hole on each side when the trap was opened. Twice was enough. The mistake should not occur again. Remembering what Garry had said about a rabbit not biting, I put in a hand and brought the trembling animal out in some way, either by the ears or the hindlegs; memory fails to recall how, but it does bring back the pitiful cries that rang through the woods. This troubled me, but I hardened my heart and dropped the game in the bag, and started for home with my prize, in triumph not unmixed with other feelings.

With bag on shoulder I stopped at the foot of the hill to drink the strong sulphur water of Harrowgate Spring, of which Colonel Raymond and I were so fond in boyhood. Here the events of the morning were reviewed in cold blood. Hardly two hours had passed, but the crowded events made it seem ten times as long. The little creature was still now, probably wondering what would come next. After pondering for a while on the escape of the two rabbits and taking another swig of Harrowgate, the recollection of those pitiful cries came up in full force. Then I seemed to realize that they came from a poor, terrified and harmless thing that I was taking to be killed without the excitement of the hunt. I peeped into the bag. Two large eyes and a trembling form were in the corner. Somehow the grip on the mouth of the bag was loosened, the bottom was turned up and a white lump of cotton in a field of gray went bobbing off into the brush.

When I entered Tom Simmonds' store I said to Garry: "Here's your bag; I haven't got any rabbits and don't want any. I'll go up and spring the traps after school; it's time for breakfast now."

It was months afterward before I told him the whole story, and he said: "Well, I don't know as I'd like to kill a rabbit if it cried like that. The fact is I built the traps some two years ago, and after some such scrape as yours I left them in the barn. Some boys like to trap rabbits, but I don't care anything about it; I only thought you might like it."

I am not so chicken-hearted as this story makes me out. I have been a trapper for fur; will tell you about this later, and I never had the slightest feeling of pity for a bloodthirsty mink, marten or other animal of that class. I have killed them in steel traps, found them frozen to death in them, and have seen where they left a leg behind, and never felt more pity for these merciless brutes than I do for an oyster when I eat it alive. Somehow the very helplessness of a rabbit appeals to a fellow, and its plaintive cries--I give it up! I let that rabbit go that morning by the waters of Harrowgate, and that is all there is of it. I have tried to make a story of it and failed.

Once or twice after the eel spearing scrape Garry asked me to fish with him, and the other boys wondered at it. Some years later we shot ducks, yellow-legs and rail along the dead creek, an inlet on the island below Douw's Point, and above the hilly dwelling of "der Yaw-cum Stawts wot lives on de Hokleberic."*

This creek is now filled up, and is known no more except as a low, marshy spot. We had a good day once; two mallards, a wood duck and some half a dozen rail. A very good day it was, for ducks were wild and not

*This is a phonetic spelling, as the Albany Dutch spoke it when they referred to Joachim Staats, who lived on the Hogleberg, or "hog's back," the only hill on the island, just back of the landing known as Staats' dock.

plenty, when Garry crawled up to a flock and got three. Coody retrieved them, but unfortunately they proved to be tame ducks, and the owner came down on Garry. I was below and kept still, hoping for a shot if anything came my way. After waiting a while a mud hen got up below me, flying low, and I shot. I missed the mud hen, but hit Garry in the back of the leg, and he promptly yelled. He had paid the man for his ducks and then went around back of me, hidden by the brush, and was just in time to intercept a few shot that the mud hen failed to get because of its haste. The shots, some half a dozen, were only under the skin in the calf of his leg, and I had no trouble in taking them out with a pocket knife.

Said Garry: "It's lucky that I was below the bird, or your lead would have gone in deeper."

"What were you doing down below me and how did you get there? I didn't see you. I thought you were up above squaring it with the man for his tame ducks. I suppose he wanted twice what they were worth."

"No," said Garry, "he won't charge much; he trades with us, and will bring me the ducks and settle to-morrow. I wouldn't like to take up a lot of tame ducks; the boys would laugh. Now, see here! If you promise never to tell that I shot into a flock of tame ducks I'll give you my word that I won't say a word about your shooting me in the leg. Is it a go?"

"It's a go!" Garry is dead and it's a long time ago. As both stories are told now for the first time, I don't see that any harm is done to him. Neither of us meant to do it, and after all the intention, in a shooting case, is always carefully considered by a jury.

Garry was short and stout, wore his face without hair, and his teeth were stained by tobacco. I should think he might have been born about 1825, but while I knew of his death and attended his funeral, I have pressed every button in memory for an approximate date, but the wires seem to be crossed. Mr. Garrett M. Van Olinda thinks he died in 1861, and that seems likely.

I only know that he married about three weeks before he died. It was like this: I was in Greenbush one day and he invited me into the back room.

"I want your advice," said he, "and I ask it because I am only a raw countryman and you have more knowledge of the world than I have."

This almost took my breath. If he was contemplating the opening of a grocery in opposition to Tom Simmonds and Mat Miller it was useless to consult one like me, whose only object in life so far had been to get what fun he could out of it, and whose knowledge of business was *nil.* Of course I did not formulate all this then—I was merely surprised and asked: "What's up, Garry?" ·

He thought a moment and then said: "I am thinking about getting married, and am in doubt whether it is the best thing to do or not. What do you think?"

If memory reflects my mind at that time, I did not think. Here was a man who was shy of men and boys, one whose business compelled him to talk to women and girls, but whose shyness cut the conversation to the strictest business limits. I was astounded. Pulling my scattered wits together, I said: "Why, Garry, I never heard of your keeping company with a girl; who is she?"

He told me, but it was no one that I had ever heard of. Said he: "She is the nicest girl I ever saw, and she comes to the store every day and I can talk to her by the hour. She is not a bit like the other girls that come in. I wish you could see her."

That settled the marriage question.   Of course, I had nothing to say, and he didn't expect I would have, but he was compelled to confide his secret to a human being of some kind, and the one before him served his purpose.

In after years whenever a box trap was stumbled on in the woods it brought up the picture of Garry Van Hoesen, the shy, sensitive fellow who longed for human sympathy, but from a lack of aggressiveness or an excess of diffidence, self-consciousness or whatever you please to call it, seemed lonesome in this great bustling world.   If I'd brought him that rabbit he would not have killed it.

In after years I fished with men of all conditions in life, men of high character and men of no character worth mentioning, men of education and intelligence and those who had neither, but among them all I have a warm spot in my memory for simple, honest Garry Van Hoesen.

STEPHEN MARTIN.

STEVE was a different sort of fellow from any of the boys of whom I have written.   He came into our boyish set after we went across the river to live, and I naturally dropped into Scott's occasionally by day, but frequently in the evenings.   W. J. & R. H. Scott made, sold and repaired guns on Beaver street, between Broadway and Green street, and after their rival—poor Steve Van Valkenburgh—died, theirs was the only place of the kind in Albany.   Gunners of all kinds had business there, and every evening a few could be found in the salesroom discussing all kinds of questions pertaining to guns, their proper loads and powers, as well as telling their personal experiences while trying to conceal the exact location of a bit of snipe bog or partridge cover.

We boys soon got acquainted—it never takes boys long to do that, especially if they have a common interest in anything.   Martin was one that dropped in there, and as he was about the age of our party he went with us on a fishing trip to Normanskill, a brook which rises somewhere off toward the Helderbergs and enters the Hudson a few miles below Albany.   We called it the Normanskill Creek in ignorance that "kill" was Dutch for creek, and that the added word was a repetition, but then what would you do with Kaaterskill, anglicized into

Catskill as the name of a village, a range of mountains and a stream? And then the word creek is used in New York for a bayou or arm of a river which forms an island, like the Popscheny, and also for a brook or even rivers like the East and West Canadas, which form the great Mohawk.   All this has nothing whatever to do with Steve Martin, the subject now under the scalpel and microscope. A cog slipped and some ink went astray—only this and nothing more.

The day was quite young when we reached the stream near its mouth and some distance below the first dam.   George Scott was going to try a new bait, and had brought a lot of fresh-water mussels—*Unio*—"for," said he, "if these things aren't good for bait, what good are they? What do they have shells on 'em for if it is not to keep the fish from eating 'em?"

"Lemme smell 'em," said Steve, and he took a sniff and with a look of disgust said: "George, a fish couldn't eat that thing; you can't eat it, and it's my opinion that nothing will eat it. What do you think of it, Fred?"

"I dunno; the only way to find out is to try 'em. Old John Chase has used 'em for bait in his eel pots, and he wouldn't fool his time with the things if they are no good. I've seen him pick up a peck on the flats at low tide. Hogs eat them, and Port Tyler said that some kinds of wild ducks eat the little ones. I don't see why they shouldn't be as good as clams or oysters; they live like them."

"Oysters!" yelled Steve, "I'll bet you daren't taste of one.   Nobody eats them, and I believe they're poison."

"I'll eat one if you will."

"That's fair," said George Scott.

Pete Loeser remarked: "I dink Stefe he vas scart to

eat von of dose muschels, he don'd got some pepper-
sauce. Oh, Stefe, you vas scart und you pack oud!"

The question had assumed a personal form, and Steve
was getting warm. The reflection on his courage braced
him up, and after giving Pete a look which might have
meant that he would like to cut him up for fish bait, he
asked, "Where is the pepper and salt?" These things
put before him, he selected a mussel of medium size,
groped about until he found one to match it in size and
shape, and with one in each hand he offered me the
choice in the courtly manner that duellists are reported
to do upon the field of honor. My careless challenge
might have been passed by if only Martin and I had been
present, but the comment of Loeser settled it. A contest
was unavoidable. A choice was made, and each opened
his mollusk, salted and peppered it with deliberation.
Then, eye to eye, we raised the shells and took in the
contents.

Charley Scott, brother to George and the firm of gun-
smiths, watched the faces of the contestants closely, and
after the last morsel was swallowed by each said: "Well,
if mussels ain't good to eat, you fellows lie. I've been
a-waitin' to see one of you weaken on 'em, but you only
looked at each other as if you were chewin' oysters."

The truth is that we afterward acknowledged to each
other that fresh-water mussels might be good for fish
bait, but we had no very great desire to eat any more.
There is a remembrance of a combination of toughness,
sweetness and sliminess which did not provoke an appetite for more. We put on a bold front and challenged
the other boys to try them. Martin even went so far as
to say that they were as good as oysters. This statement was received with some doubt, and Charley Scott
suggested that if Steve thought so he could save money

by using them in place of the salt-water product. George offered to eat one if we would each eat another, but the German was mean enough to ask: "Oof Stefe dinks dose dings was so goot we oysders, vy don'd he ede 'em some more?" A yell turned the conversation; George had thrown his line back in the wrong direction, and the hook took Loeser in the ear, and tore a hole big enough to let it be taken out easily. Years afterward, at a dinner of the Ichthyophagous Club, we had a bisque or some other preparation of *Unios* fixed up by the *chef* of one of New York's crack hotels, and I tasted it, with a thought running back to an early day on the Normanskill. After tasting it I looked around to see how the rest enjoyed it. Frank Endicott made a show of taking frequent spoonfuls, but his plate seemed as full as ever. Mr. E. G. Blackford tasted it and said: "That is very fine," but somehow let it go at that; and when the waiter removed his plate you could not miss what had been eaten. No doubt the mussels are good, but you've got to learn to like 'em. I never persevered in this direction. As bait that day they took a few fish, but the verdict of the boys was that they preferred the old reliable angle worm.

Down in the lower end of Albany is a portion called Bethlehem, and on the river road was the Abbey, a noted road-house a couple of miles below the city. An English sportsman named Kenneth King lived in Bethlehem, and the Abbey was kept by another English shooting man named Sheldrick, who got up pigeon shoots, and we boys used to attend them. At these affairs we used to make matches to shoot at ten birds each, the loser to pay for and the winner to have them. One day after the shooting was done Martin said to me: "We are not going to shoot any more because there are not enough pigeons for a match, but as your gun is loaded and there

STEPHEN MARTIN.

are a few pigeons left, I'll shoot you a match of two each. We want to shoot off our guns, any way. What d'ye say?"

I had left my gun standing in the corner while I had gone on the front porch for something, and had just returned when Steve made this proposal. "All right," said . I, "we might as well shoot at a couple more and empty our guns before going home." He picked up his gun, and as I reached for mine Ken King quickly passed me his and with a wink said: "Take mine."

Without thought I went to the score after Steve had killed one of his birds and missed the other, and killed both of mine. The boys laughed, and Steve looked surprised as I hastily walked back and put up King's gun. While they were talking things over outside King asked me: "Do you know why I gave you my gun to shoot?"

"No, but you gave me a wink and I asked no questions. Why did you do it?"

"When you went out on the front porch Steve drew the wads and took the shot out of both barrels of your gun. See the joke? They're talking about it now."

I went out and took my three birds; Steve paid for four and merely remarked: "Well, you beat me this time; we'll have to try it over again next Saturday."

As we got ready to start I stepped back and shot off both barrels, and Steve asked: "What gun did you kill the pigeons with? I thought it was your own."

"No, I used Ken King's to see how it shoots, as we may want to trade. It shot very well; couldn't have done better. When I shot off my gun just now it made a light report; perhaps I forgot to put shot in it."

Steve made no reply, but Pete Loeser said: "I kess, Stefe, he dinks dere vas no shot dere; hey, Stefe?"

The laugh was on Stephen, and the boys guyed him so that he had to own up, but after that event we each kept our guns in sight at pigeon matches.

It was after this that I bought the pointer Nell from Ken King, the one referred to in former sketches, and King showed us the woodcock grounds on the Albany side of the river, and we shot with him over his dogs and Nell. Sometimes when he was not with us we consulted Mrs. Sheldrick, who was well posted on these matters, and far more communicative than her husband. In her vocabulary "birds" meant woodcock only; all others were spoken of by name. For instance, she would say: "Well, boys, you won't find many birds in the swamps this morning; you might get an odd one up in the corn-field after the rain last night, but you can find plenty o' pigeons in yon wood, an' mebbe some plover on the hill or a few yellow-legs along shore. But birds 'll be scarce to-day."

Steve was wonderfully good on woodcock, and usually beat us all in bringing down that bird of erratic flight. He used a short gun of twelve-gauge. Just how short the barrels were is more than I would like to say now—perhaps twenty inches—while my gun was an extra long one of twelve inches more. I once saw him drop five "birds" in succession in a swampy thicket where this swift, dazzling bird would drop out of sight within twenty yards, and this was not an exceptional case. Those who have shot this quick, zigzagging bird in close thickets are the only ones who know just how quick and unruffled a shooter has to be to get a fair proportion of the birds he flushes. They had all learned from Ken King the lesson which I had been taught by Port Tyler in former years, to use small shot in small quantity, with a very light charge of powder, for this kind of shooting at close quarters, in order not to mutilate this royal game bird.

Steve went with us on several fishing trips, but never in the open season for game; fishing amused him when there was nothing else to do; it was fun, but hardly sport to him. He cared little for camping out, or for the fields and streams outside of the fact that game abounded in one and fish in the other; hence I said at the beginning of this article that he differed from any of those of whom I have written. He was impatient of any delay, and eager to be stirring; hence some of the ingredients of a good fisherman had been left out of his mental make-up.

In the early '50's there was an epidemic of rifle shooting in the State of New York. Not shooting at game— that is one of our steady and never-decreasing infirmities; but this prevalent disorder took the form of long-distance target shooting. Heavy rifles were shot on bench rests at six hundred yards, mainly in winter on the ice below the city. They had "patent muzzles," a detached piece with pins to set over the true muzzle while seating the bullet in order to leave the muzzle perfectly square, the enlargement necessary to start the bullet in the way it should go being entirely in the false muzzle. These guns were all hand-made. If there were machine-made rifles in those days I never heard of them. All rifles were hand-made. Soldiers did not use them; their muskets were smooth-bores, and it was believed that rifling was a principle that would work well up to a certain calibre, but was only practicable for guns which were shot from the shoulder. For field pieces which threw a six-pound shot it was believed to be useless, because it was thought that the weight of the projectile would prevent it from following the twisted groove. To-day they rifle not only the largest cannon, but even mortars. In the '60's

I handled rifled guns up to those known as one hundred-pound "Parrots," but now such a gun is only a toy, and our ten-inch seacoast mortars with their smooth bores are obsolete. This digression is not for the benefit of the old fellows who know all this, but is intended for the boys of to-day who have the cartridges for their breech-loading shotguns filled for them before they go afield, and whose machine-made magazine rifles are wonderful pieces of mechanism. Remember, boys, in my shooting days we went afield with powder flask on one shoulder, shot pouch on the other, cap box and either cut wads or newspapers for wadding in the pockets. If we shot the rifle we moulded our own bullets, measured our powder and carried greased linen patches to envelop the bullet, a ramrod and box of caps. Such a thing as buying prepared ammunition was not dreamed of.

There was a little squad of rifle shooters from both sides of the river which met in contests on the ice. There was Billy Wish, the ferryboat engineer; William Tallman, Sr., a machinist; Steve Martin, and John Clark, a printer, who, in spite of having but little color in his eyes, was the best shot of all. It has been said that gray-eyed men make the best rifle shots, but Clark's eyes were lighter than gray.

The shooting was counted by string measure, and the targets were displayed nightly at Scott's. Such discussions over the wind in explanation of a bad shot, and such arguments over the merits of rifle makers, would fill volumes of *Forest and Stream.* The merits of Lewis and James as makers of rifles was the main point. One lived in Troy and the other in Syracuse, and they were always going to shoot a match with rifles of their own makes, but like some gladiators of to-day it ended in talk. Billinghurst, of Rochester, was another famous maker;

I remember him because he made the first open reel for fishermen. Scott made a rifle for Martin, and he induced me to join the shooting and use his gun. There was no betting, just pure sport, and I tried it. The rifle was sighted long and deliberately, then a rest of the eye and it was gone over again until the shooter had it as fine as he knew how. Then the flags were watched, with the eyes off the rifle, until the long strings of muslin hanging from the poles placed at intervals showed the wind to be right, and the hair trigger was touched.

I never made much of a shooter of this kind; my eyes blurred at one hundred yards then and they do at twenty feet to-day, although I read and write without glasses at sixty-three. Black-eyed Steve Martin was a fair shot, but that did not satisfy him; he always had an excuse for not being first—the powder was not as good, the patch was too thick or too thin, a puff of wind came just as he pulled the trigger, etc.

Pete Loeser once said: "Stefe he shoot pooty goot, but never so besser as he can; dere vas alvays sometings dot spile his string. Oof dot clout had not come der sun between ven he make der sixt shot he peat Shon Glark all hollow. I dink he makes besser string in te efening by Scott's stofe, by shimminy!"

To this George Scott replied: "Pete, if you could make half as good a score as Steve you might be proud. There are his targets, look at 'em; they show a splendid average, and one hard to beat. It's not a good one for two or three days and then a durned bad one, but a steady, good lot of shooting day by day."

"Dot's all ride," said Pete; "but he alvays got some oxcuse for de one shot wot makes de oder nine figger oop big on de averich."

Just then Steve came in and George said: "Steve, you

are just in time.   Pete says you can't hit a pancake if it's tied over the muzzle of your gun."

"That may be so, but I'll tell you what I'll do, Pete. If you'll stand one thousand yards down on the ice and let me shoot a pipe out of your mouth, I'll buy you a new hat if I don't break the pipe."

Another way in which Steve Martin differed from my other fishing companions was that he was a practical joker.   Now, fun is one thing and "practical joking" is another.   In the mind of the p. j. they are the same thing, but no other human being agrees with him because the fun is all on his side, and the misery of others is his joy. Therefore he is a selfish mortal and that settles him.   We were once rowing round Douw's Point against a stiff current, just all that two pairs of oars could do to make a bit of way at the extreme point.   The scow had a plugged hole in the bottom to let out water without tipping her over when beached.   As we were near the shore Steve said: "I guess I'll lighten the boat," and jumped ashore, taking the plug with him.   The water was up and wet our feet before we noticed it, and we were only saved from a ducking by promptly beaching the little scow.   The author of the mischief was up the bank and off.   A new plug was whittled out and we went our way scolding, not so much at what had happened as at what might have occurred.

Of course he was forgiven, although he never asked to be, but for a time he was made to feel that his fun was not appreciated by the boys that were in the boat. We often shot together over Nell at woodcock, snipe, golden plover and shore birds.   He sometimes took her out alone, and when I learned that he was trying to make her retrieve I protested.   Steve insisted that a pointer could be taught to retrieve as well as a setter, and instanced one that we both knew, but I still objected. She was lost for about a month before I went West in '54, but Steve found her after I had gone, and so she came into possession of my father, as mentioned in a former sketch.

When I returned, over five years later, my old chums were looked up. Steve had grown into a strong man, Pete Loeser had gone West, George Scott had accidentally killed himself while pulling a loaded gun from a bed, and quite a number of changes had taken place. I did but little at fishing or shooting for a year, and then the war broke out. Some time in July, 1861, Steve told me about the scheme of Colonel Hiram Berdan to recruit a company of sharpshooters, every man of which must be able to make a string of ten shots at a certain distance whose united measurements from the centre of the target should not exceed a certain number of inches. I forget the figures, but they were not in excess of the scores usually made by the riflemen on the ice.

"Now," said Steve, "you can pass this test; it is not a severe one—merely intended to get men who are fair shots, and know how to use and care for a rifle. After enlistment and muster every man will be given the rank and pay of a second lieutenant, and will have a darkey to carry his rifle and equipments. I've heard you say you'd like to go, and here is your chance. I'll go if you will."

"Steve," said I, "there is much doubt if my score would pass; you know that I do not see well at a distance, and besides this my family affairs forbid my going. That's a queer story about the enlisted men ranking as commissioned officers; where did you get that?"

"Why, that's the arrangement between Colonel Berdan and the War Department; the men will all be commissioned after they are mustered into the United States service; at least that is what they tell me."

While it was out of the question for me to think of going at that time, and as there was then no doubt but the trouble would be all over in a few months and my services would not be needed, still this story of the rank of enlisted men seemed strange. I knew little of military matters, but I had friends who were well posted. I met Colonel Michael K. Bryan, of the Twenty-fifth State Militia, afterward Colonel One Hundred and Seventy-fifth New York Volunteers, who was killed at Port Hudson on June 14, 1863, and sez I to Colonel Mike, sez I: "Colonel Bryan, our friend, Steve Martin, tells me that in the regiment of sharpshooters which Colonel Berdan is raising every enlisted man will be a second lieutenant after his muster into the United States service. How is this?"

"Steve proposed to you to enlist?"

"Yes; said he would if I would."

Then Colonel Mike sez he to me, sez he: "That's a beautiful bit of gossamer from Steve's workshop, spun to catch such green bottles as you. A regiment of second lieutenants! I suppose the corporals must be captains and the sergeants field officers, and just how they would find rank enough for the drum major only Steve could tell. Did he tell you that he had authority to raise a company for this regiment and already had his commission as captain?"

"No, that's all news to me. Is it so?"

"Yes, he has the company partly filled and his commission has been issued."

"Thank you very much, Colonel; I think I understand the situation now. Good morning."

This was some time in late July, and I talked with Steve often and he appeared anxious to enlist if I would. Nearly six years among men who were simple in their ways had shown its effect. I was very green! The fact was painfully evident, and after a month or more of listening to Steve and doing a little thinking, I said: "I heard yesterday that the Governor had given you a captain's commission in Berdan's sharpshooters."

"Yes, I got it last week. You see, I had been at work for the regiment because I was bound to go out with it, and my friends told this to the Governor, and he said that I deserved a captaincy and issued the commission at once. Now I'm in a position to make you a definite proposition. The other company officers have not been appointed, and will not be until the company is full, and if you will enlist with me I will have you appointed first lieutenant before we leave the State."

"Thank you very much, Steve, old boy! I'll think it over. Somehow it doesn't seem much to be a first lieutenant in a regiment wholly composed of second lieutenants; but you know that I know nothing of these things, and if I should decide to go with you of course I trust all this detail to you as an old chum, for I am ignorant of all that pertains to soldiering."

"Very well! If you will go with me I'll fix you all right and look after your interests as I would my own. That story about the privates being all second lieutenants is not true; it came from some fellow in the Adjutant-General's office, but that's all right between us. I'll fix it right for you."

I went home that night and in a dream John Atwood and I were snaring suckers with a fine copper wire on the end of a pole. We were landing them bravely for a while, and then things got into one of those queer mixtures that dreams are only capable of and which never untangle. John Atwood disappeared and Steve Martin stood where he had been, and as he lifted an unusually large sucker to the bank I felt that I was being choked—and awoke.

The rush of awakening thoughts brought Longfellow's lines:

" 'Twas but a dream; let it pass, let it vanish like so many others!
What I thought was a flower is only a weed, and is worthless."

And then the reply of Clarence to Brakenbury came up:

"Oh! I have pass'd a miserable night,
So full of fearful dreams, of ugly sights,
That, as I am a Christian faithful man,
I would not spend another such a night,
Though 'twere to buy a world of happy days."

After this I never heard of Stephen. I looked for him in the army, but never could find any who knew him. When we lay in the trenches of Cold Harbor for ten days within one hundred yards of the enemy a detachment of Berdan's sharpshooters was our picket as well as skirmish line, and as they could not leave their pits in daytime and live, I used to ask after Steve when a man came over to our works at night for rations or ammunition, but none of them knew him. After the war none of the boys seemed to know what "got" Steve. Phisterer's "New York in the Rebellion," p. 517, says of this regiment: "Company B, Captain Stephen Martin, * * * was organized at Albany, and mustered into the United States service for three years, November 29, 1861." The official register of volunteer officers gives his resignation as November 15, 1861. Therefore I am not now surprised that I could not find him in the field, when he resigned his commission fourteen days before his company was mustered into the service.

Looking all this over in the light of riper years, I

have been impressed with the high-minded and honorable way in which John Atwood snared suckers. There was no false pretence by John. He did not take the sucker into his confidence. Not he! The loop was lowered in plain sight, drifted down behind his gills in broad daylight—the pole jerked, and there is your fish.

As I recall the things which happened years ago I have great respect for John's honest, straightforward methods.

GEORGE RAYNOR.

THE time came when school was left and business began. The happy days were in the past. No more Saturday holiday, and the grind of recording shipping marks, weighing goods and signing receipts, when ducks were flying down the river and carloads of venison were coming in, was getting too much to bear. In that vast and vague country called the West there was freedom—and game. Finding opposition useless, father sent to Michigan for his rifle, the one that William and Joe Brockway had used for years, and gave it to me when I left.

Said he, "You may have this rifle, if you are bound to go, and the only thing I ask of you is never to join any expedition that goes out to murder poor Indians."

That was an easy thing to promise because there had never been such a thought or desire. I was twenty-one and bound for the great West, with no definite idea what part of it would be best to go to or just what was to be done when the journey ended. Pete Loeser, the German boy mentioned in the last history, wanted to go to some relatives in Wisconsin, and he went along. At Chicago we could decide what would be best to do, and there we stuck.

One day while fishing in the lake off the breakwater an old gentleman of eighty years named George Raynor, who had frequently fished with us, told me this story: "At the massacre of Wyoming, in 1778, my old parents were killed, and I, a boy of about four years old, was taken by the Seneca Indians and then sent to Canada by a British officer, where I lived with a farmer until I ran away and shipped on a vessel that went to England. There I worked in a cutler's shop and learned the trade. How many years passed I don't know, but the desire to get back to America grew strong, and I went to Liverpool and shipped for New York. By this time I was a young man, and I worked at my trade until I saved money enough to try to seek my relatives, if I had any. I remembered a sister, Susan, and a brother, John, both older than I, and I longed to see them. I had forgotten the name of the place where the massacre occurred, and I did not know in what State it happened. There was an indistinct recollection of an alarm at night, a hurrying to arms, and the burning of buildings and killing of people. I had kept a little picture book with my name in it. One day a lady came in the New York shop, and bought some cutlery to be shipped to some point in Luzerne County, Pa. The name of the place seemed familiar, and I talked with her. She knew of my people, and the result was that I went there and afterward married her daughter—— That's what we call an eel-pout that Pete's got. The fish is not eatable. Excuse me, where was I? Oh, yes; we prospered, and all went well until our eldest boy was killed in the Mexican war and our daughter was burned to death in a fire that destroyed my business a year later, and with my wife and only boy I left New York for this place in 1848. In a railroad accident my wife was killed and injuries about my head hurt my eyes, so that it was uphill work to make a living until my boy William helped out by singing in the church choir. Now that I am nearly blind he is my sole support. You've heard his wonderful tenor voice in

Warner's Hall, on Randolph street, where he now sings with 'Northrup's Metropolitan Minstrels.'"

During this tale the fish had taken my bait unnoticed, although Pete had attended to business and taken several fish. The story as told by the old man had made me wish he would stop, for there was no fun in the way he told it, and it had started a leak in my eyes. But down the breakwater—an old one, not in existence now—came the sprightly young tenor, who put his arms around the old man's neck and kissed him, saying: "Well, father, what luck to-day?"

"Billy," said the old man, "I fear I have not fish enough for breakfast; I have been telling your friend the family history because he seemed to take an interest in it, and I forgot to put my line out. Here is the hook and the bait by my side now. My old eyes do not see well enough to tell if a hook is baited or not, and certainly cannot see if the line is in the water or is coiled up at my feet. Now, Fred, don't you honestly think that an old man who has lived his life and can't see——"

"Here, father, stop that. You must meet the infirmities of age and accident in a philosophical manner. I can and will care for you while I have life and strength, and I don't want to hear any more of that talk."

The young man baited his father's line and we fished on. This eel-pout, as he called it, was a new fish to me then, and its long, flattened head and eel-like fins made it an object to be remembered. This specimen was twenty inches long. Pete said: "Py chimminy! he's cot a whisker on his chin, so like a pullhead, on'y de pullhead he cot fife oder six." And this was a wonder to us, for there were no fish with barbels where we had fished except the bullhead or catfish. We found the fish quite common in the lake. In other parts it is called "lawyer," "ling," and has several names besides that of *Lota*, which the scientists have taught us to believe is its true name Twirling the sinkers vertically, and letting go at the proper time, we cast our bait as far as possible from the breakwater and hauled in hand under hand, and a good-sized pike perch or a big eel-pout made quite a fight at the end of a long line. Even the common yellow perch ran larger than we were accustomed to see them, and we green Eastern boys voted it the finest fishing we ever had.

Mr. Raynor told me that there was very good fishing in the South Branch of the Chicago River near where he lived on Van Beuren street. Those who only know the Chicago River as it is now may doubt this statement, for in its black and ill-smelling water a self-respecting mud turtle would decline to live. Yet I ask to be believed when I say that many good fish were taken from the docks in the South Branch by myself and others forty-four years ago. As a rule, the fish were not as large as those taken in the lake, and just what kinds they were is partly forgotten, but yellow perch were plenty, and so were small dogfish—*Amia*. These latter even the omnivorous Pete could not eat, although he pronounced the eel-pout "Pooty goot."

The old gentleman was greatly pleased when I called at his house for him to go and fish. He said: "It is very good of you to come for me; very few care to bother with a man when he is no longer young and is nearly blind. I often think I've stayed here too long, and only for Billy——"

I interrupted with: "Yes, Billy is a good boy, one in a thousand, and you may be proud of such a devoted son." Then he was led from that depressing line of thought by a story of a deer hunt in northern New York, and of jolly times in camp with Port Tyler, until he forgot his infirmities and told stories of fishing in salt water and of shooting bay birds on Long Island, which were unknown sports to me.   He became enthusiastic and finally said: "I'll sing you a hunting song which I learned in England," and after crooning for the key sang in a rich baritone, a little shaky with age, the following, which I never heard before nor since:

> Some love to roam over the dark sea's foam,
>   Where the shrill wind whistles free.
> But a chosen band, in a mountain land,
>   Oh, a life in the woods for me.
> The deer we mark thro' the forest dark,
>   And the prowling wolf we track,
> Our right good cheer is the wild boar, here;
>   Then why should the hunter lack?

Billy Raynor, the exquisite tenor, came honestly by his voice, that was certain, and I induced the old gentleman to sing it until both words and tune are as familiar to-day as then.   A tolerably musical ear told me long ago that if I ever attempted to sing the police would pull the house on the suspicion that there was a dog fight in the back room, and therefore whenever asked if I can sing I quote the Hon. Bardwell Slote and reply: "Those who have heard me say I can't."   But in my house is a young lady and a piano, and on the wall of my den hangs a banjo of the vintage of 1860, and its strings seem to have treasured up the air of that hunting song so that the piano sympathizes with it, and the young lady sings the words occasionally to the accompaniment of the aforesaid implement of torture.   There was a sort of "yo, ho" chorus which is forgotten.   The second verse ran:

When the morning gleams o'er the mountain streams
  Then merrily forth we go,
To follow the stag o'er the slippery crag
  And chase the bounding doe.
For with steady aim at the bounding game,
  And a heart that fears no foe;
Thro' the darksome glade in the forest shade,
  Oh, merrily forth we go!

The little we know of it serves to bring up the memory of the dear old singer who sang it amid the unpoetic surroundings of the Chicago River one day when his poor heart was lighter than usual.

One day he said: "Billy is going to have a week off, the hall is to be renovated, and he will spend his vacation down at Kankakee shooting ducks, and last night he said that he would like to have you go with him if you could get off. Poor boy! he needs a week off if anyone does; working in the office of the grain warehouse all day and singing at the minstrels six nights and in the church choir twice on Sundays keeps him so busy that he never has an hour to himself. Only for me he would not have to work so hard, and I sometimes think——"

"Now see here, Mr. Raynor, this is only an idle fancy of yours. Billy is a busy boy, to be sure, but he likes it, and his main delight is to see you happy. You are not a burden to him, but it is his pleasure to see you made comfortable. He has no bad or expensive habits, and I know that his first thought is about you. Drop the idea that he would be better off without you. I believe that I know him better than you do."

"It seems good to hear you say so," said he, "and it is no doubt true; but my mind has outlived my body, and at times I feel morbid, blue, or whatever you may call it. If you will go down there with Billy I will know that you and he will look out for each other. I will take a vacation if I know that you two boys are together taking one. Will you go?"

"I will find out. Like Billy, I must consult others. To-morrow night you will know, but it might be well to have the invitation from Billy. Surely, he cannot expect me to go with him without a direct invitation; I was with him last night and he did not mention it."

"Not to you, but he first consulted me as one whose approval of a companion for a week seemed to him to be necessary. No matter how much Billy might think of you he would want his father to know the kind of company he was in and have my approval. His business associates are not always his social ones, and like the wise boy that he is he separates them. He doesn't care to ask your companion, Pete, to go because he overheard him say something about his kissing me. Billy was brought up that way, and doesn't like any comment on his kissing his father. We are all there is left of the family, and our customs are our own."

A ten-gauge gun was hired, and we went down some fifty miles south of Chicago to the great ducking grounds of the Kankakee, of which I had heard so much. Even the preparation for the start was a revelation to one whose idea of duck shooting about Albany had been that it was a large day if he got ten shots and four ducks. Then one pound of powder and four pounds of shot was a great allowance, and more than half of it was lugged home at night unless it was expended on blackbirds, rail or other small game. Therefore, when we talked over the trip and came to the detail of ammunition I was astounded when Billy said: "Let's see, six days; well, say twelve pounds of powder, fifty pounds of shot—ounce and a quarter to each load—that's fifteen ounces of shot for a dozen charges, say a pound for a dozen loads and a hundred shots per day; yes, fifty pounds will do to start with, and we can get more down there if we need it, but these things can be bought cheaper here."

There was a belief which I cherished that I had done some shooting, and had on one occasion loaded up with two pounds of powder and eight pounds of shot for a week's sport, but Billy's figures staggered me—metaphorically speaking, "they took my breath away." As soon as I could come up to the surface I ventured to ask: "Have you ever shot down there at Kankakee?"

"Oh, yes; I go down there in spring and fall; the ducks are plenty, I assure you. Did you think that I didn't know anything about the place?"

"No, I only asked for information because the amount of ammunition seemed somewhat larger than I have been accustomed to use, but if you think it is what we will need it's all right; you know best."

"You'll need it all. Have everything packed for the eleven P. M. train Sunday night, and I'll meet you at the station and we'll have a good time for a week."

Such flights of ducks! Such flocks of ducks! The sky, the lower air and the water was full of them. As Billy rowed our little boat along the marshes in a small stream it seemed to me that he was wasting time and missing shots, but when he pulled up on a dry point of land and we hauled the boat ashore and propped it on edge, the reeds and rushes with which we covered it made a splendid blind to shoot from. No decoys were necessary; the ducks were uneducated in the matter of artificial blinds, and came past ours without a thought of danger. We two were not up to the modern plan of having several guns, or the slaughter might have been greater. Where I had shot, along the Popskinny, a half dozen ducks was a large day's shooting and one was not considered bad. Day after day no duck was bagged, and a few rail and blackbirds were accepted as better than nothing—with the hope of better luck next time. On those trips mud hens and hell-divers, or even a sheldrake, was counted as a duck, and it was a new sensation to be told: "Don't shoot; they're only sawbills."

Accustomed to taking in everything which came within range, this was something new. The fact that a gunner could sit down in cold blood and select the kind of waterfowl on which to expend ammunition was a novelty. Instead of wishing for any sort of duck to come within shooting range, here we were refusing shots to all except a favored (?) few.

It was cruel shooting—cruel because it was wasteful We shifted our blind so that we shot against the wind as it changed, and the dead ducks drifted to us. A cripple that escaped the first fire could not be chased, for we had only one boat, and if not killed before it got out of range it crept into the marsh to be eaten by mink, gulls or hawks. A philosopher might ask what difference all this made to the duck: whether the mink or the birds got him, or whether his carcass passed into the hands of a hotel *chef* and was served to a convivial party, with the accompaniment of celery and juice of the vine?

We shot only at mallards, pintails, widgeon and teal, letting all other fowl pass. At night we counted out 153 ducks of these species—the number is remembered because it was the most wonderful duck shooting for two guns that I had ever dreamed of—and we could have taken in a number of butterballs, whistlers and other ducks if we had wished to kill them, but Billy said they were not worth wasting powder on.

Heretofore there had never been more game than

could be taken care of and consumed at home or given to friends, and the presence of about 350 pounds of ducks in the boat and the prospect of five days' more shooting presented a problem. What could we do with this mass of game? We could not eat much of it and we had but few local friends. In the excitement of shooting these questions had not obtruded themselves as they did now. Pondering on these things, I asked: "Billy, what will we do with all the ducks?"

"They are all right; there'll be a man at the landing to meet us who will take care of them; there he stands now waiting for us. He will send them to market every day, and on Saturday we will keep out what we want to take home."

The man took the game and put it in his wagon and drove off to the railway station, and after supper he came in and settled up, paying us $15.30 for our ducks, or about what it had cost for the expenses for ammunition and travel. This was certainly paying expenses, and just what I had hoped for in going West, but somehow it was not satisfactory. It brought into the transaction a mercenary spirit which had never before been connected with my sport. At first the feeling of dissatisfaction was vague and without shape. We divided the money and talked it over. The expedition was more than successful from a financial point, but there was something in my manner which caused my companion to say:

"You don't seem as enthusiastic as you did. What's the matter? Don't you like the table they set here, or did something happen down in the marsh which displeased you? Be frank with me, and spit it out if anything has gone wrong; don't sulk, fire it out."

Up to this point I really did not know the cause of a

change of demeanor which had been noticed.   There was only a dim consciousness of something unpleasant.

"Billy," said I, "if I have appeared to be depressed it is because our ducks were carted off by an unknown man to be sold to unknown consumers in the market.   Every duck, pigeon or rabbit that I ever killed before to-day was either eaten by my own family or given to a friend.   Part of the triumph of the hunt lay in the bringing of the game to the table, and as my friends enjoyed the treat I also enjoyed being the treater.   If I was at the feast every mouthful eaten by each individual was enjoyed by me as a contributor, whose hard work on shore or upland was rewarded by the knowledge that others were enjoying the fruits of my skill and——"

"That you are a blooming egotist whose personality enters into every duck or other game.   Is that what you mean?"

"Billy, you have put it into words which are strictly true, but were in a nebulous condition in my brain.   You have summed up the case in a masterly way.   Never before did I measure the value of game of any kind in money, although I have had a desire to turn my love of field sports into a way of making a living.   This desire was in a crude form before this, but now that the man has carted off my game to be eaten by men who do not thank me for it, do not know me, and may be drunk when they eat it, I wish I had my ducks and he had his money——"

"Well, you'll go out in the morning and shoot some more, won't you?"

"Yes, but I'll build a blind and use the boat to chase cripples.   I don't like to see a wounded duck go off into the marsh to die or to be eaten by minks or gulls.   It isn't right."

"All right," said he; "anything to keep peace in the family, but down here ducks are too plenty to go chasing cripples. The gunners here will think you are crazy to waste your time in that way and scare off a flock to get a cripple. Go ahead, though; I don't care."

I tried it, but it did keep flocks from coming our way. Some gunners one hundred yards below protested, and the chasing of cripples was stopped.

We shot six days. The first day more than paid all expenses of the trip, and there was a good balance in our favor as well as thirty ducks among our plunder on our return Saturday night. The ducks we gave to friends, and when Pete Loeser received a pair and heard the story he said: "Py shimminy, de air must pe so full mit ducks dere vos no room for shot to co between dem ven dey fly. I never dinks dere vos so many."

I had an invitation to dine with Mr. Raynor and his son next day, and the old gentleman was very jolly and sang the hunter's song and that sweetest of old English ballads, "Sally in Our Alley," while the son, who, like all professional singers, usually declined to sing on social occasions, at the earnest request of the ladies gave us "Mary of Argyle" and several other songs. When the others had retired Mr. Raynor beat me at two games of chess, the clock struck midnight and the vacation week ended.

The winter closed in and before spring I could now and then checkmate my elderly friend, and when that happened he would explain how it could not have been done if he had not made a certain move some ten moves back of the finish. He was a delightful old man when his mind was off his physical troubles, and he and his son were devoted to each other. As soon as the ice was out of the river he sent me word to come up and fish with him the first moment possible. His bodily infirmities had increased, and he had now but one eye that was of service, and that was very poor. I baited his hooks and threw out his line, and when he pulled in a fish saw that the hooks did not enter his hands. He was quite despondent one day. Said he: "Freddy, my boy, I wonder that the good Lord doesn't take me. Many a time I've asked Him to call me, but for some reason He does not do it. I am only a burden on Billy, and the pains in my head from that railroad accident are more than I can bear. Billy has a severe cold, and has been laid off several days; if anything should happen to him I——"

Things were getting uncomfortable, and to turn the tide I ventured to say: "Don't worry about Billy; we all have colds and get over them; of course, he couldn't sing in his present state, but he'll be all right next week. There! That fish is off and your bait is all right again."

Billy's cold did not get better, and I was called to sit up with him. Pneumonia developed and the old man had to be removed from his room. Pete had gone to Wisconsin, and the minstrel boys and the church choir sent watchers in such numbers that they could not be used.

It was my duty to superintend the watchers and comfort the father, but the end came in a few days. Relatives from Boston came to the funeral, but Mr. Raynor clung to me and insisted on my being with him at the last sad rites.

The next day, while walking up Market street, I heard a little girl say: "They've found a drowned man in the river; come on, Maggie, let's go down and see him." I followed along in idle curiosity and saw the man. It was the body of an old man, and I gave his name to the coroner.

CHARLES GUYON.

THE little mining town of Potosi lies in the south-west corner of Wisconsin. It has three streets in the only possible places for streets; the three narrow valleys which meet in the centre of the village afford outlets for travel. Some two miles to the west one valley leads to the Grant River, near its mouth, and here a Mississippi steamer came for freight occasionally. A stage came from Galena down another valley, and thus Potosi was connected with the outside world. Here I drifted in the spring, and found good fishing and shooting. My friend Loeser had gone a few miles further north to Fennimore Grove, near Lancaster, where he settled down into a farmer's life.

Charles Guyon was one of the French-Canadian colony which formed the largest portion of the village. There was a settlement of Cornish miners in one of the outskirts called British Hollow, but the two peoples mixed very little except in the way of trade and in the gambling rooms, which were then run wide open. Charley was a strong young fellow about my age, and he proposed that we should go jacking for fish some night.

"I don't know the first thing about jacking, Charley. I'll go and try it. Tell me all about it."

"Well, it's this way," said he (very few of the French-Canadians spoke anything like a dialect). "We have a jack light on one side of the bow and it hangs over the water, so that no fire drops into the boat.   One man paddles and the other stands in the bow, and when he sees a fish he gigs it."

The jack was a cresset made of strap iron—a twelve-inch ring to which half a dozen strips were riveted to form the bowl, which was fastened to an iron staff long enough to bring the bowl above a man's eyes as he stood in the boat.   Charley had gathered a lot of bark from the shell-bark hickory, which he said made the best of all lights, and we got a ride to the landing with our traps. The "gig" was a spear of some six or eight prongs, with a wooden handle about eight feet long, to which a small cord was attached to the upper end to recover it by.

As soon as it was dark enough we lighted the jack and started.   The boat was a light-bottomed scow and I used the paddle.   Guyon stood in the bow and gave orders; he did not use nautical terms, but said "right" or "left" as he required the boat to go.   Soon he said, "Steady, left, hold up," and then after a pause, "Go on slow; there's a big pike about here, but he was shy and I couldn't get a crack at him.   Hold on, right a little," and he poised his gig and sent it buzzing into the water. "A clean miss.   I didn't strike low enough.   Go toward that tree top up there; there may be some buffalo near it."

Surely I must have misunderstood; he could not mean that buffalo might be grazing in that tree top, but I was in a strange land, and my new friend might be having a little fun at my expense, so I kept still.   Soon the orders came, and as the spear left his hand it struck and gave a little tremble, and my companion yelled out: "I got him!" and taking hold of the string, which was tied to the gunwale, he pulled the gig staff to him, and then landed in the boat a huge fish of about twenty pounds—huge to me. "There's your buffalo," said he. I looked at the great, ungainly fish, with a hump on its back and a mouth like a sucker, and asked if it was good to eat.

"Oh, yes; it's better than red-horse, but not as good as bass and pike. Here, you take the gig and I'll paddle. Now you've got to put the gig into the fish, and not in the place he looks to be at. If he's nearly under you throw right at him, always with the gig across his body and not in line with him. The further he is away the more you must throw under him, because he's deeper than he looks to be. You know how a board appears to be bent when half of it is in the water; the lower end seems to be higher than it is. Well, it's just so with a fish; unless he's right under you he's deeper than he looks, and the further off he is the deeper under him you must strike."

I took the gig, with some doubt of my ability to gauge the depth of a fish and judge his true position, for I knew what Guyon said was true, only I had never thought of it before. I did think of his names of fishes; we had a buffalo and he spoke of red-horse. I had seen dogfish and catfish, but where was this kind of nomenclature to end? Soon I saw several large fish. There had been plenty of small ones seen, but with a twenty-pound fish in the boat as a pattern my ideas were no doubt enlarged. Soon I said: "Steady, stop!" and plunge went the gig and missed.

"I knew you wouldn't touch that fish," said Guyon; "you threw too far from the boat, and it went clean over him by two feet. Next time aim two feet below where he looks to be at and you may get him. It's very seldom that a man throws the gig under a fish that lies ten feet away from the boat. Try it again."

At the next chance I was bound to miss the fish by throwing under it, if I missed it at all, and I plunged the gig in the water at what seemed an absurd low point and struck a pike of some five pounds.

"There," said the man at the paddle, "I knew you could do it if you could only believe the fish was a foot or two below where he looked to be at."   This use of the word "at" was new to me then, but I found it common in the West and South.   Lately it has had attention called to it by its use in Congress.   It sounds odd to those who hear it for the first time.

And so we passed the first half of the night, and returned to the warehouse and slept in it, for Charley had the key; but we took the precaution to take our fish inside, too, for he said: "The moon will be up in an hour and she'll spoil the fish, and then we don't want minks and wildcats carryin' 'em off or chewing them up.   We'll get a ride up in the morning, for Joe Hall's going to bring down some potatoes and there'll be teams down with lead."

Morning came and we went back with the first empty wagon, taking over two hundred pounds of fish—bass, pike, buffalo and big red-finned suckers, which proved to be the "red-horse;" and I had been initiated into the mysteries of jacking for fish, handling a gig, had received a lesson in practical optics, and knew positively that a fish in the water was not always in the place which it appeared to be "at."

Somewhere in an omnivorous course of reading I remember a statement that "Man shall not live by bread alone," and in the practical every-day life it began to be painfully evident that no matter how desirable it might be to hunt and fish forever, there were needs other than what the chase afforded.   There was a man who really demanded pay for letting me live in his house. Of course the house was built, and I did not hurt it by living in it; but he had put a man out because he did not pay. Then there came a day when a really serious bit of thinking over the sordid spirit of man had been indulged in for fully ten minutes, when Charley Guyon came along.

"Say," he began, "you ain't doin' anything, an' I want a pardner to sink a shaft. I think I know where we can make a strike, an' I've got all the tools. What d'ye say, will you jine me?"

"Well, Charley, I was just thinking that it was about time that I went at something; but I don't know the first thing about lead mining. Tell me all about it; how do you do it?"

"It's just like this: A man owns a piece of land, and he throws it open for mining or he keeps it for other purposes. Suppose he throws it open; then any one can dig, and he takes one-tenth of the mineral for rent. A windlass, rope, bucket, pick and spade are all the tools we use. Mineral may be struck at ten feet, or it may be at sixty; but we go down until we come to hard pan; it never lies below that. You may get some "drift" that will pay or may not; it's all chance. You may work a week and not get a dollar, and you may strike a lead*; and then you drift in and follow it. You see, there are lots of abandoned shafts which were sunk ten years ago, when mineral was worth ten dollars per thousand. Now it is worth thirty dollars, and two men can make wages if they get a thousand pounds per week."

"And a fellow has to work down there under ground like a mole to do this?"

---

*This is pronounced leed in the mines, and is a corruption of lode.

"Yes, but pardners take turns, one in the shaft and one at the windlass, and of a hot day you'll prefer to be below. There's men here who hire other men to 'tend windlass, and they take the chances—make it all if they strike it big, or lose their time and the man's wages. It's all chance, just the same as when you go into Coons' and sit in a keno game; you may win or you may not. But all business is chance anyway, just like gambling; the only man who's got a sure thing is the man who works for wages, and he gets left sometimes."

Behold the mighty hunter, with a band and candle socket on his hat, grubbing away like a well-digger, and assorting an occasional lump of "drift," with its white coating, from the earth and clay, and depositing it in a "hen's nest" until there was a bucketful—always hoping that the next stroke of the pick would cut into a bright bit of galena; or at the windlass waiting for the word "up," and dumping the earth on the down-hill side and keeping an eye out for stray bits which had escaped the eyes below. So passed the summer, with occasional fishing trips with Henry Neaville and his brother Frank, for Guyon cared little for the 'sportsmanlike methods of fishing; gigging and netting them in quantities was his delight, yet the fun of it was ever uppermost in his mind. He thought fishing with a hook and line was too slow work; his mind was active and required more exciting sport.

In considering what constitutes sport, a question on which the doctors disagree, it might be well to allow a little latitude for individual notions; I was about to say idiosyncrasies, but if Guyon read this he would ask: "What's them?" and so we will let it go at "notions." Please remember that this was forty years ago, and none of us had given thought to the possible exhaustion of a source of fish supply which seemed only to invite the slayer by appearing next year in undiminished numbers. This is the only excuse I have to offer for our destruction of life in those days of its plenty, and an excuse seems necessary to-day. If it is sufficient, well and good; it is all I have, and I throw myself on the mercy of the court. We all needed education in the matter of fish and game preservation in those days, and I hope that I have atoned for the misdeeds of my youth by both precept and example in later years.

In sketching Charles Guyon, who was an honest, sturdy fellow, not averse to a fight if it was forced upon him, but not a quarrelsome man, it is only fair to him to say that, having been reared in a mining town, gambling came as a natural thing, just as luck in mining did, and if his week had been successful Saturday night found him at the keno table staking the last sovereign that he had earned. The smelters sent wagons to weigh and gather the mineral every Saturday afternoon, and the pay was in British sovereigns, which passed for $5, for no miner would accept paper money for his mineral, although he sometimes did in exchange for his gold.

Saturday nights the gambling places and the drunkeries kept open until morning, and the Cornish miners from British Hollow rested from their labors by drinking, gambling and fighting. These were the highest forms of sport known to them, and in fact to the majority of men who work underground all the week in all parts of the world. One night I dropped into Sam Coons' to look on. Here I want to say that I have never won or lost one dollar in any form of gambling except at the house of a gentleman in Germany, where a small stake was the custom, and there was no escape. I don't claim any special credit for this because I never had a desire to

gamble—was too cowardly to risk my wealth, if you wish
to put it in that way.   Plenty of good men gamble, and
I have other faults, but am not one of those who, as
Butler ("Hudibras") says:

> "Compound for sins they are inclined to
> By damning those they have no mind to."

I have occasionally played cards in a perfunctory
way, without caring for them, and have engaged in
games to decide who should pay for oysters, cigars and
such other goods as an army sutler possessed, but a book
always suited me better.   Speaking of games in connection with Potosi wakes me up.   In the sketch of General
Martin Miller the fact was recorded that Herr Driesbach, the great lion tamer, used to come to my father's
house to play chess, and to my great surprise Bill Patterson pointed out a finely-built, powerful man whom
we had just passed and said: "That's Driesbach, the lion
tamer."   I hurried after him, and the result was that I
often went out to his farm of an evening and had a game
of chess, the only game that I ever thought worth the
candle.   Chess players were very scarce in Potosi, and
Driesbach and I were out of practice, but if I won one
game out of five it was sufficient.

One evening he said: "You aren't one-half the man
your father was; he must have been over six feet."

"Yes; six feet two inches, and no spare meat."

"Well, I remember once when we crossed the river
to Albany in a small boat, and a 'longshoreman was
smoking a pipe in the faces of two ladies who sat in the
stern, your father spoke to him about it and got an
impudent reply, and he then jerked the pipe from the
fellow's mouth and threw it overboard.   Then threats of
vengeance came when we should get on shore.   Your

father hurried up, and ran up the steps to the dock and waited. Then he said: 'My friend, you were going to lick me when you got on shore. I'm in a hurry to go to business and have only got a few minutes to spare, and I would like you to do it now.' The man looked him over and said: 'Be jabers, it isn't worth while for the likes of us to be foighten' about an ould pipe.' Now, Fred, that 'longshoreman would have cleaned you up in about two seconds. Why, you ain't a bit like the old man." I learn from my old friend, Hon. J. W. Seaton, who still lives in Potosi, that Driesbach died something like fifteen years ago, and the vest made from a pet leopard skin was given by Driesbach to Judge Seaton, who has it now.

When we went to work in the woods near the river I took my rifle as soon as September 1 came around and it was lawful to use it. This was the one that father gave me. I only remember that the barrel was half round and half octagon, an unusual departure from the general make of rifles, which were generally all octagon, and were stocked to the muzzle, although short stocks were coming into fashion. Calibre was a word little used in connection with hunting rifles, but we reckoned them by the number of round bullets to the pound. Squirrel rifles ran as small as 120 to the pound; mine was thirty to the pound, and that was considered very large. I never used any long bullets in it—"slugs" we called them—for the theory was that they were only good in the open country, and that contact with a twig would deflect them more than it would round bullets. A modern rifleman would not know how to tell the calibre of a rifle by our measure, and I can't inform him. I only know that with such guns, and many smaller, the old-time hunters killed the biggest animals on the continent, often when the first shot must disable a grizzly or a panther, for it took time to measure powder and reload.

I had to go to the village for something, and left the rifle loaded, also the powder horn and box of caps. The bullets and patches were in a leather box in my belt, which I wore. On returning I heard several shots some distance from our shaft. Guyon and the rifle were gone. The shots kept up, and I started at a lively gait until I came in view of the shooting match. There was Guyon in among the branches of a fallen tree; crack went the rifle, and a big buck charged into the branches, but could not reach him. His back was toward me, and I hailed: "Hello, Charley! What are you doin' to that deer?"

He turned and said: "You are a great fellow to go off with all the bullets. Got any with you? If you have, throw me one. Don't come in here too close or that deer will kill you; he's fightin' mad now."

I did go in on a run and got into the tree top just in time to avoid the charge of the buck, and handed Guyon a bullet, which he rammed down without a patch, and planted it in the deer's frontal bone and dropped him.

Such a looking deer I never did see. Guyon's only bullet had broken one antler close to the head and angered him. The tree top was fortunately at hand and made a natural abattis, behind which the man could carry on the offensive and shift to avoid the enemy as occasion required. But the deer! His head was literally skinned all around his eyes, and from his forehead to his nose.

Charles said: "When he came for me and I was safe in this treetop I whittled green plugs for bullets, and thought if one took him in the eye it would drop him. Every time a plug hit him he would snort, shake his head and come at me. See how he has wet me. I think

I shot more than twenty plugs at him, and I don't know how I would have got out of this brush if you hadn't come."

The story was too good to keep. He didn't hear the last of it for some time.

Bill Patterson said: "Charley, that venison was very good, but there was a taste of wood about it. How do you suppose it got that flavor?"

Joe Hall hailed him with: "Hey, Charley! That venison tasted as if he had broken into Darcy's shop and had eaten his shoe pegs. What d' ye s'pose he'd been feedin' on?"

The multitude of islands between Wisconsin and Iowa at this point renders it difficult to tell where Grant River ends or loses itself in the Father of Waters. It is several miles from shore to shore, and channels of many depths and widths separate the islands. These waterways, the "kills" of New York and the "bayous" of the lower Mississippi, are here called sloughs, pronounced sloo. One of the beauties of our language is that this word may be pronounced sluff, slouw or sloo, each having a different meaning. In a recent letter from Mr. Seaton he says, in reply to a question: "The inland island waters, most of which go dry in summer, I think, are properly called sloughs, and the name is not a provincialism peculiar to this part of the Mississippi valley. Webster gives the pronunciation 'slou,' and here it is spelled sloo, and means a sink or depression in the islands in which the water gathers and in some cases remains all the time, and in others it signifies channels or sluiceways in which part of the waters pass from one stream to the other, *i. e.*, the over-swollen Mississippi to the depressed Grant River and *vice versa*; hence we have 'Swift sloo,' 'Hay sloo' and several others known to the fishers and hunters.   They are the natural habitat and breeding places for frogs, reptiles and mosquitoes, as well as a great resort for ducks in the spring and fall.   During the spring freshets the fish gather in them in large quantities and are entrapped when the water falls, which is usually in August and September.   This year a large number of German carp and black bass were taken in willow woven nets by the boys, although this is prohibited by law.   The upper waters of the Mississippi were stocked a few years ago with these fish by the Government.   It is in April and May, when the 'spring rise' overflows the banks and spreads over the bottoms, that the fat catfish, buffalo and other fishes are found out of the channels and main streams feeding in the grassy bottoms.   Then the boys wade in and have their fun catching them.   Sloughs are creations of the great river and are part of it."

The domesticated hog ran wild on these islands, and once a man said to me: "Now, you will want some pork, and you ought to buy a claim of hogs.   I've got five marked sows on the islands, and I'll sell you a claim in 'em fur a dollar."

On inquiry Charley said: "That's all right.   There's about ten claims o' hogs on the islands.   It's this a-way: a man turns out a sow with certain ear marks, and all the pigs found with her in the fall are hers if there's a hundred.   Give him a dollar and you can kill all the pigs you want, only don't kill an old one with marks in its ears."   I bought in, and was part owner of, all pork on the hoof that had two V's in the right ear and a round hole in the left.

Guyon, Bill Patterson, Henry Neaville and I went for pork about the middle of September.   Charley and Bill skinned theirs, and this was the usual custom; but I agree with Neaville that a properly dressed pig looked best,

but "How can we dress them on these islands?" I asked.
Henry said, "I'll show you," and we pulled the scow up
high and dry, filled it with water, made a roaring fire and
heated a lot of stones which had been brought to the isl-
and for the purpose, and boiled the water to scald the
pigs. How easy it is to do things if you know how!
Fresh pork was cheap in those days, and I have seen
where a hog had been killed and only one ham taken
and the rest left in the woods, perhaps by some fellow
who never paid his $1 to "buy into a claim o' hogs."

Once, while alone going down to the marshes with
my rifle to get a duck or two for dinner, for it was the
only gun I owned, I went a little way up the side of the
bluff to get a view of the overflowed lands, and make a
reconnoissance of the flocks of ducks and of such cover
as might conceal an approach to them. I sat on a log
to view the scene and recover some lost breath. It was
early in the afternoon, and the log was so comfortable
that I sat some time. Four half-grown foxes were playing in the leaves like kittens, and a move would have
spoiled the show. Suddenly there was a shot close by
and the foxes vanished; a pig squealed, an old hog
grunted and a boy screamed. I jumped at the shot and
started slowly to see who was shooting, but ran when I
heard the boy. There he was on his back, and a big
sow chewing his arm. Quicker than I can tell it I shot,
and fortunately hit the hog in the eye and she dropped
dead. Then I became excited at what might have happened if I had missed the hog or killed the boy. He had
fainted, and, having no water, I fanned him until he came
to. His arm was badly torn, but no bones were broken,
and the doctor soon had him repaired. A hog will
charge a man any time if he makes a pig squeal, and then
they are dangerous animals. On telling this pig scrape

to Charley he showed me some great scars on his legs where he was bitten under similar circumstances, only that he seized a hanging limb and drew himself into a tree, and fortunately some strangers heard his yell and came to his rescue, or he would have bled to death.

Charley Guyon inherited the taste of his countrymen for the violin, and he and another noted fiddler named Montpleasure had played with a travelling minstrel troupe which went up through Wisconsin and Iowa, and some of his experiences were laughable. Said he: "We struck a little town in northern Iowa just in time for a late supper and to get to the hall. The box of burnt cork couldn't be found, and there wasn't corks enough in the single hotel to make 'paste' for the troupe of ten. Yes, we had ten, all good men, too, if we did take in small towns; but what was to be done? The hall was filling, and we had small boys out looking for corks and coming back saying, 'Mother says she ain't got no corks,' or 'Pap says he'll get you a cork ef you'll give him six tickets.' The hall was full and the people began to get uneasy, when in came the landlord to the dressing-room with four boxes of shoeblacking and asked if that wouldn't do. Charley French thought it would, and we wet it up, and used it and rushed on the stage. The overture went off well, and the opening chorus was half way through when the boys began to feel uncomfortable. The stuff had stiffened and we felt as if we were varnished, and soon it began to peel off. Such looking niggers you never did see. We got laughing and the audience roared; our tenor tried to sing 'Swanee River,' but it was uphill work; he looked like a darkey with the smallpox; we shook our sides, and the people screamed until he got mad and left the stage. It was well for us that it hit the audience as being funny, but we got through somehow, and as they wanted to dance we played for them until morning, after we washed up. They had never had such dance music, and they wanted us to promise to come again, which we did, and had a grand reception."

Once when we were discussing the chances of sinking a shaft in a new place he burst out laughing. I waited to hear what the cause of this hilarity was, and as soon as he could pull himself together he tried to say, between shrieks: "Bones asked why this troupe of minstrels was like a gang of burglars which had been discovered. Ha, ha! ho, ho!—Oh, I can't tell it. But the answer was because we—he, he! Oh, my!—because—because we're spotted!" And then he couldn't stop. A roll on the ground and a kicking of heels was the only sedative, and it always got in its quieting work if no one started a laugh; if they did it took longer.

I think Charley never tired of this yarn, for he would laugh all the time until he cried; it was the great event in his uneventful life.

He was as happy as that happy race, the French-Canadian, usually is—happy if it rained or if the day was bright; happy in luck of any kind, if he had strings for his fiddle and rheumatism and the toothache kept away. In my sketch in *Forest and Stream* I presumed that he was dead. Judge Seaton has written me that Charley is still fiddling away in Highland, Iowa County, Wis., "happy as ever and vigorous." As this goes to the printer I am waiting for an answer from my old-time, honest and cheerful companion in the lead mines.

CORPORAL HENRY R. NEAVILLE.

HENRY had the taste for observing the habits of beasts, birds and fishes which leads a man to study them, a taste which may, if not checked, cause him to count the fin-rays of a fish or the scales on the tarsus of a bird, and then inflict his fellow man with a monograph on fin-rays and scales. Henry never reached that stage, but loved the woods and waters just the same, and was a very quiet, companionable fellow of my own age. His father kept the only hotel in Potosi at that time, and Henry and his younger brother Frank were kept by the hotel. Few things troubled Henry; with him it was "always afternoon," and pleasant visions floated in his mind; yet he was not indifferent to the passage of time if aroused by something which interested him. In still-hunting deer he was tireless, and no amount of fatigue dulled his ardor. If, however, wood was to be cut for the house, Henry somehow never took an absorbing interest in it, and it soon turned out that Henry and I had many traits in common.

We fished for crappies, another fish new to me, and one which I considered the best pan fish in the Mississippi. This is the fish, or brother of the one, called "strawberry bass" in western New York, and if my youthful judgment was correct it is a fish worthy of more attention from fish-culturists than it gets. There is a chance that my more mature palate would confirm the verdict of forty years ago, for I never did care to eat a black bass if perch could be had, and residence by salt water has intensified this preference. My friend, Professor Jordan, says the crappie should be called *Pomoxys*, and in his "Manual of Vertebrates" gives what he thinks the word means in Greek; but I guess the name comes from the Latin *Pomum*, fruit, for the crappie is, in the argot of the day, "a peach;" a few years ago it would have been "a daisy," and so in the process of evolution the fruit succeeds the flower. Darwin, "thou reasonest well!"

A tree top was a favorite place to find the crappie and incidentally to lose fish-hooks. We used short rods, cut in the woods, but not over seven feet long, for fishing in the tree tops, and the crappies were flat as a pancake and sometimes a foot long. In a tree top if one of them was allowed a bit of line the angler was lucky if he saved the hook. They fought fairly well, too; of course, not to be compared to the fight of a black bass nor of some perch, but it was sport to take them. We strung the fish through the gills, and hung them in the water to keep alive. Once while pulling in my string to add another it pulled heavily, and a catfish, which looked to weigh ten pounds, came to the surface. It had swallowed one crappie, but let go when it saw us. Soon after this Henry put his hand in the water, and a big catfish seized it and tore the skin badly, causing him to make remarks calculated to hurt the feelings of all catfish which heard them.

As my mining partner, Charley Guyon, never objected to having a holiday, it happened that Henry and I fished frequently in the summer, and hunted for ducks, deer and other game in spring and fall. Shortly after Guyon's adventure with the buck Henry and I were following deer up the Grant River, and I saw three of them

cross to my side within easy shot.   There was a buck and
two does.   As they came out of the water I dropped the
buck, and like an echo of my shot one of the does fell.
Henry took off his clothes, and swam over and found me
talking with a man about fifty years old, who had killed
the doe.   He proved to be a French-Canadian named
Antoine Gardapee, with whom I struck up a friendship
which will be related "in our next."   He was a trapper,
and like my old friend, Port Tyler, was a "character."
We dressed our deer, and Henry and I swam the river
with it and took turns with the heavy saddle wrapped in
the skin and the lighter forequarters.

Gardapee came to town with us and sold his venison.   In those days many men threw away the forequarters of a deer.   I asked Antoine to come to my
house for dinner and he did, but he insisted that a rib
chop out of a fat deer was the best portion, and we had
them broiled.   He was right, and to-day I follow his advice when venison is in season and buy rib chops.   He
took a fancy to me because our tastes were in common
and I had education enough to write his letters to his
friends, and would talk to him on subjects in which he
was interested.   I looked up to him as a combined Port
Tyler and Natty Bumpo rolled into one.   It was a sort
of love at first sight, or like that of Desdemona for
Othello, of which he says:

> "She lov'd me for the dangers I had pass'd;
> And I lov'd her that she did pity them."

Henry had that sense of humor which often accom-
panies a poetic temperament and permits one to both
enjoy a sentiment and to burlesque it at the same time.
This is a possibility unknown to solemn souls who think
burlesque or travesty irreverent or disrespectful, which

it is not always intended to be. Byron had this faculty in perfection, and lets you down from a poetic flight with a d. s. thud. Shakespeare turns from heroic Hotspur to fat Jack Falstaff—and Henry Neaville, who had a considerable knowledge of Shakespeare, often paraphrased him. This is what called up the above quotation. Henry once said:

> "She lov'd me for the fishes that I caught,
> And I lov'd her that she did pickle them."

Frank Neaville, Henry and I one summer day went fishing, and we rowed up against the current of Swift Sloo and around into more quiet waters, made fast to a tree top and dropped our lines. Tree tops in these waters were abundant where the freshets had washed the soil from the roots, and the tree toppled into the water, usually kept on growing, or at least in full leaf during the season, and afforded a good place to tie a boat and fish either among the branches or further out. A queer tapping noise came from the boat's bottom. I suspected Frank of making it, because he was full of tricks of that kind, but it kept up and he did not seem to be the cause. "Are there spirits among us seeking communication with mortals?" I asked.

"Yes," said Henry, "and I'll try to call that particular spirit from the vasty deep, and find out why he knocks on our boat."

"He wants to come in," Frank explained, "and he's too polite to do it without knocking first."

Henry put on a plump worm, took the little bullet which served for a sinker and let his line drift under the boat. In a short time it was evident that something was tugging at his line, and his little rod bent as the spirit, or whatever it was, struggled to get loose. Soon a large fish was pulled from under the boat, and made several kicks and splashes before it was flopping at our feet, showering water and scales. It was a "red-horse," and would weigh about two pounds, guess-weight.

"Is that the cause of the spirit-like raps on our boat?"

"Yes; he was sucking off snails and water worms. Did you never see 'em do it?"

"No; never heard of such a thing before."

"Here's another at it now; come over this side and you can see it. Come still, and don't rock the boat or you'll scare it."

I went and saw about half of the fish extending beyond the boat. It was on its back, and its red fins looked bright against its white belly and straw-colored sides. At every tap on the boat a slight contraction of the body was observed as he sucked his food from the boards. Frank thought he could capture the fish with his hands and tried it, but had to fish his hat from the water instead. "Golly," said he, "that fish was quick. He jumped when I touched him, and slipped through my hand like an eel." After this the drumming of the red-horse was often heard, not only on the boat, but upon logs that were several feet from us. This sucker is the "mullet" or "red mullet" of western New York. It is eatable in cold weather if it is the best you can get.

Henry threw the fish overboard, saying: "Might as well let it go; we never eat 'em in summer. I only hooked it for fun and to show you what made the tappings on the boat. Don't you have red-horse where you've fished? There! Look over on the bank of the sloo. Keep still, Frank; sh!"

A queer-looking object was rolling about on the shore in a singular manner. It grew large and then small. Sometimes it was the size of a small cat, and then would increase until as big as an old Thomas. It twisted, rolled sideways and back until it reached the water, where it kicked up a great bobbery.

"I'm durned if I know what that is," said Henry; "I never saw such an animal before. What do you think it is?"

"It's a 'coon rolling in the dirt and then washing himself off," said Frank.

Henry sneeringly replied: " 'Coon! yer granny! A 'coon's got a big, bushy tail and is gray. Frank, you don't know a 'coon from Driesbach's pet leopard."

By this time the splashing ceased, and one animal crawled out of the sloo dragging another. Henry and I said in chorus: "It's a mink!" So it was, but he had a muskrat with him, and musky was dead. Our exclamation startled the mink, and it jumped into the grass with its prey. I said to Henry: "That sight is worth more than all the fish we have caught and all the mineral Charley Guyon and I might have dug to-day, or for a week. I knew that mink were fond of muskrat meat, but a fellow might fish for a lifetime and never see a mink kill one."

"What made the mink hurry off so?" asked Frank; "he wasn't in any hurry about killing the muskrat. I'd like to have seen him eat it."

"Frank," said Henry, "that mink had several good reasons for hurrying off. It was dinner time, and Mrs. Mink and all the little minks were wondering why papa didn't come home from market with the dinner. Then Mr. Mink may have thought his family might mistrust that he was lingering at Sam Coons' bar, and would forget to bring the dinner at all; but the chances are that when we spoke he looked over at us and thought: 'It's best to hurry home before that durned fool, Frank Neaville, asks me a whole mess of questions.' That's the reason he went off so suddenly.   Frank, he took one look at you, and saw your mouth wide open, ready to ask him a question, and he sneaked."

Frank looked at me and said: "Henry knows a heap o' things, but somehow nobody seems to realize it but himself.   He knows just why that mink hurried off as well as I do, but he won't tell the truth.   Now, I'll tell you why he skipped out.   The mink was so interested in his fight that he did not notice us until Henry called out.   Then he looked over here and said to himself: 'There's that mean Henry Neaville, and he'll take my musquash if I don't get out.   That fellow is mean enough to take acorns from a blind sow.'   And so that mink, which would have been delighted to have eaten his dinner in decent company, sneaked off with it into the woods for fear he would be robbed."

I had taken my rifle along because the boys thought it would be well to kill a pig on our return, and, as I had "bought into a claim o' hogs," we went ashore, and after some work among these very wild animals I got a shot and dropped a "likely shoat" that would dress about sixty pounds.   After skinning the pig we laid it across the bow, and rowed around into Swift Sloo about sundown.   The strong current was taking us along toward home, when Frank saw a wounded pelican near the shore, and grabbed a tree top to hold the boat.   Quicker than it can be told the sudden check in the swift current filled the boat, and it left us in the water.   Henry was in the stern steering with one oar, and fortunately grabbed the painter and held on.   Frank and I got out from the tree top and struck for the nearest shore.   A bend hid the boat and Henry from sight by the time we landed, and then Frank began to cry: "Henry is drowned; I know he is, and all on account of my foolishness!"

I consoled him as well as possible by saying that his brother was a good swimmer and must be on land below the bend, and then we heard his yell: "Yee-e-e hoo-ooo," and answered it. We went down to him, and found that the boat and one oar was all there was left, except the three strings of fish which were tied to the gunwale.

"Well, we might as well go on home," said Frank.

I thought a moment and said: "You boys can go if you like, but my rifle is in the sloo near the tree top, and I'm goin' to stay on this island and try to get it when morning comes."

The boys decided to remain after I produced a little bottle of matches—a trick learned from my old preceptor, Port Tyler. Said Port: "You don't never want to go a-shootin' nur a-fishin' with yer matches loose in yer pocket, nur in one o' them metal match boxes; they leak, an' if ye get caught in a rain or tumble in the crick yer matches are all wet when ye want 'em most." The lesson had been firmly implanted by a neglect to follow it on one occasion, and here was proof of the wisdom of the old woodsman. At such a time, when wet, cold and hungry, one good match was worth a king's ransom, and I had it. Dead wood was plenty, and the little breeze which kept the mosquitoes from the open sloo was not felt in the underbrush. Before the fire we stripped and spread our clothing on poles cut for the purpose, and then—there is a dim remembrance of three fellows trying to keep their bodies in the smoke and their eyes out of it.

This was a mosquito paradise—for them. For us the term might be reversed, and it would require the pen of Dante to describe the place. Still, most readers of

Forest and Stream have sat in smudges, and have wondered whether it were nobler in the mind to suffer the stings and poisons of tormenting 'skeeters or by smudging end them. "Smoke follows beauty," is the adage; but when sitting in a smudge of dry fungus we old campaigners know that we are not beautiful because the smoke dodges us. Sometimes it is a question whether the insects are not to be preferred to smarting eyes, but eventually the ayes have it, and more smudge is made.

Our lunch was saved, and there was plenty of it—but the bread was soaked too much to use, the pies which Mrs. Neaville had put in the basket had disintegrated, and the ham and chicken had been eaten. We slapped mosquitoes and roasted fish and shifted to keep in the smoke. When the fish were cooked we ate supper.

"Where's the salt?" asked Frank.

Henry looked up and quietly said: "Frank, look in the basket; you'll find the salt tied up in a rag; bring us some;" and he never cracked a smile while his brother held up the soaked rag, looked at it and threw it down. "I never like salt on fish," said Henry; "it makes me think they're not fresh." Frank and I ate fresh fish and made no comment. After dinner Henry took his felt hat, and went to the sloo and brought it up full of water. Said he: "I always want a drink after a fish dinner, and of all drinks in this world there's nothing like Mississippi River water; it's rich—food and drink, too—and there's no better place to get it than from Swift Sloo. Boys, here's fun!"

It was desirable to get our clothes on at the earliest moment, so that there would be a minimum of cuticle exposed to the enemy, and after dressing we could dry the garments from the inside as well as by the fire; so we dressed and dragged the boat ashore, turned it over and slept the sleep of the just under it, leaving the hordes of mosquitoes to sing us a lullaby on the outside, while only a few of them found entrance from the ground.

Frank said: "I've had enough of this, and I'm going to get up!" And it was morning—broad daylight. The dawn had been obscured by the heavy timber and the overturned boat. A breakfast which somehow was much like the supper, in the presence of fresh fish and the absence of salt and everything else, was satisfactory to all but Frank. He said: "If I only had a cup of coffee I wouldn't care."

"Frank," I replied, "you are not an epicure. There is no more delicious breakfast known than roasted crappie cooked without salt and washed down with water from Swift Sloo. Your palate is not educated; coffee just now—hot coffee, I mean—would spoil the combination; you don't want coffee, nor anything else."

"Coffee!" exclaimed Henry, "why, coffee would spoil the taste of those delicate crappies, which all epicures eat without salt." And then he added: "Coffee would queer the whole show," a remark which made me ask if he had gone off with Charley Guyon, Montpleasure and the others on their trip into Iowa, and he admitted that he had been the treasurer of the troupe. How little things serve to show what will "queer" a larger thing! I asked: "Henry, what was it that 'queered' our trip?" And he simply answered: "Frank."

Don't think that Frank was any sort of a "hoodoo" because we guyed him in this way. He was a good, honest boy, but had no taste for camp life—hunting, fishing and mosquitoes. He afforded plenty of sport to his brother and I because he was green at these things. He wanted to know what there was interesting in seeing a mink kill a muskrat.

Henry replied: "Why, you bloomin' idiot, you might live in the woods for fifty years and never see such a thing but once."

"Well," drawled Frank, "after you've seen it what does it amount to? You knew that mink killed musk-rats, and what more is there to it?"

Henry was dazed at this practical question, and no one replied to Frank. What could you say? If a man has no liking for a thing, what can be said to prove that he ought to like it? We could only feel sorry for a fellow who had no care to observe animals in a state of nature when they were unaware of the presence of man. If a man doesn't care for literature, science or art, there's no use talking to him about them. This may be illustrated by the following story: Two fellows had journeyed from New York to see Niagara Falls, of which they had heard much. As they came in sight of the mighty cataract one said: "There, Jim! them's the falls!" The other asked: "Is them the falls?" and added: "Them's nice falls; now let's go and get some beer." That, I think, puts the case fairly—perhaps as strongly as that of "casting pearls before swine," but not in such an offensive manner. If Henry Neaville was alive to-day he would spend a week to see that solitary animal—a mink —capture and kill his prey in the manner one did when we were fishing near Swift Sloo. Frank had no interest in such things.

We cut a stiff pole, and with our remaining oar poled and paddled back to the tree top where Frank capsized the boat in order to look at the wounded pelican. After a survey of the bottom we found the spot where the rifle lay, and I undressed and brought it up at the first dive, for the water was not more than six feet deep; there was no mud to cover the gun in the swift water, and it lay within three feet of where the boat upset. We then saw where a board had lodged in the last freshet, and as our loose seats were gone I proposed to replace them with the board.

"But you have no saw. How are you going to cut that board to make two seats?" asked Frank.

I showed him how to cut a board off square with a pocket knife by taking the measure and following the mark with the point of the knife. Then slightly bending the board at the mark and drawing the knife in the cut, taking care not to bend it too much, the fibres separated with a snap under the point of the knife, and we had two seats with ends as square as if sawed. It was done so quickly that he was surprised, and I showed him how a small tree could be cut by a sharp-pointed knife if the tree could be bent so as to strain the fibres, and he very ungrammatically remarked: "Well, I'm be blowed!"

Henry Neaville was one of those rare fellows who are charming companions in camp—one of those cheerful men who never grumble, no matter what happens. It might rain, and wet him to the skin when there was no chance to make a fire; he might lose his fishing tackle when no more could be had, and he would joke about it. He would be happy when it was a choice between being eaten alive by mosquitoes or being smothered and blinded by smoke. Mark Tapley could not have been jollier under adverse circumstances than was Henry Neaville. I was with him a year and a half later in camp in northern Minnesota with a surveying party, and saw him come in with both feet frozen so badly that I feared amputation might be necessary, and as I dressed his feet afterward, when they were swollen almost to bursting, he said: "If you should have to cut these feet off just box 'em up, and send 'em back to Potosi and write father to tell the girls that I'm not dancing this winter." That I loved such a cheerful companion is not strange; any sportsman would have taken him to his heart, for if there is a disagreeable quality in a man it will show itself in camp. If he is cranky, cross or grumbly it will come out in time, and if he is a hog who will take the choice corner of the tent every time, or the best fish in pan, it is soon known, and right here let me say I have met many such men who seemed to think that no one was wet and cold but themselves, nobody tired and hungry except their own carcasses; one trip with them is always enough. They are the fellows who will shoot across you at your birds, throw out their lines alongside yours if they see you have a nibble, and in many ways, beside bragging of their personal prowess, make themselves disagreeable. You've all met 'em and dropped 'em. I will tell you more about Henry later.

We drifted down Swift Sloo, and poled and paddled to the landing, made the boat fast, and marched through the partly deserted villages of Lafayette and Van Buren to picturesque Potosi. Mr. Kaltenbach, who had been postmaster for some twenty years then and who recently died in office, the oldest postmaster known to the service, hailed us with: "Hello, boys! Did you get so many fish that you couldn't carry 'em?" But Henry told him that several wagons were on the way with our catch. John Nicholas and Bill Patterson wanted to know if we forgot to spit on our bait, but they got no reply. We had enjoyed the trip—that is, Henry and I did—it was not certain about Frank, and it was useless to try to explain it to people who measure your fun by the amount of game brought back—a most false measure, and one that should come under the supervision of the State "sealer of weights and measures."

In the fall Pete Loeser, who, you will remember, came from Albany with me, sent an invitation to go up some fifteen miles to Fenimore Grove and shoot prairie chickens. Henry went along, and was enthusiastic about the sport, which could not be had in the heavily timbered district near Potosi. We met Pete and he said: "The tay vos yust ride, und dere was t'ousands of bra'rie shickens in de wheat stubble und de cornfields." We were elated.

We had no dog, but we spread out at proper distances to take in cross shots without interference, and walked the birds up. The ease with which they were dropped surprised me after being wrought up by Henry's extravagant talk. On our return with big bags of this fine bird, Henry asked what I thought of the sport, and I summed it up in about this style: "Henry, the prairie chicken is a fine large bird and a good game bird, but as a bird to shoot it is easier than the little quail; it flies in the open, and in such a way that a duffer could hardly miss it if within range. It doesn't compare with woodcock shooting in a thicket as a test of skill, and as for partridge, I tell you that there is a feeling of triumph in downing a wary old bird, which starts like a rocket and puts a tree between you and himself before he has gone ten feet, if the tree is there, that the killing of one hundred prairie chickens cannot equal. Come with me some day and try them back of the river bluffs toward Cassville, and if you don't agree with me when we return I'll eat my hat."

Since that day I have shot prairie chickens in Kansas and in other States, and still adhere to my opinion concerning the merits of the two birds from the standpoint of a sportsman whose object is to bag a difficult bird regardless of whether he gets two or twenty. For the table I prefer the dark-meated prairie fowl, but that is another question. Also I would say that up to that time I had never seen nor heard of the practice of treeing partridges with a dog. It is only in sparsely settled districts where this can be done, and it was many years after that I had practical knowledge of this method of shooting. About the thickly settled districts of New York, where I learned to shoot, the ruffed grouse would never take to a tree for a yelping spaniel; they crouched for a spring at the approach of a man or dog, and often the thunder of their wings was the first intimation the gunner had of their presence, and he was lucky if he could flesh his shot before the swift bird had put a tree between them. It was largely snap shooting, and, as I have said, the feeling of triumph in dropping one under such conditions was great, and there were men in that day and there are men to-day who will agree to every word of this. At the risk of calling down a host of antagonists who will go for my scalp, I will say that the grandest game bird of America is the ruffed grouse, called "partridge" in New York and New England, and "pheasant" in Pennsylvania and the South. The wild turkey is a wary bird, and carries more meat about his person; but an experience in shooting both makes me put the turkey in the second place.

This talk has led me from Henry Neaville, whom I wanted you to know, but a vagabond pen wandered from the subject. I will tell you something of him later on, for he and I joined a party of Government surveyors a year later that explored a portion of northern Minnesota; but before we get to that I must, in the natural order of events, tell you about a winter spent in trapping for fur with Antoine Gardapee, whom you met in the first part of this article. Henry was my intimate companion on the surveying trip and afterward; we had so much in common that we could not keep apart if we had tried.

In gathering information about my old-time friends I was pleased to find that Hon. J. W. Seaton is still living in Potosi. During the time of which I write he published a weekly paper there, and was afterward a member of the State Senate for several terms. He writes me as follows: "Bill Patterson is living at Portland, Ore. All your other friends are dead except Thomas Davies, who went with you on the surveying trip. Henry and Frank Neaville went out with Company C, Second Wisconsin Infantry, afterward part of the famous 'Iron Brigade.' Henry was made a corporal, and Frank was first sergeant. Frank was killed at Bull Run August 28, 1862, and Henry was killed at Antietam nineteen days later."

"The neighing troop, the flashing blade,
  The bugle's stirring blast,
The charge, the dreadful cannonade,
  The din and shout are past;
Nor war's wild note, nor glory's peal,
  Shall thrill with fierce delight
Those breasts that never more may feel
  The rapture of the fight."

ANTOINE GARDAPEE.

IN THREE CANTOS.

CANTO I.—TRAPPING FUR—KILLING A WOLVERINE.

IT is possible that there may be another way to spell this name. Antoine never spelled it, but then he couldn't spell any other word; so we just take it as it sounded. After the time when he killed the doe that was with my buck we often met. Early in October I dropped into his cabin, and found him overhauling a lot of steel traps, putting in a rivet here and there, filing the catch to hold the pan stiffer, or to make it go off easier, as seemed best. His back was to the open door, and I watched him a few minutes before announcing my presence by knocking on the door frame of his little log shanty. He whirled around on the box which served as a bench and said: "Come in! You jess a man I want for see. Whar you be'n so long tam? I was go for look you up."

"I've been working hard for the past week, and have not been up the river until to-day, when my partner, Guyon, wanted a day off; so I thought I'd drift over your way and see if I couldn't get a deer, but haven't seen any fresh sign this morning. About a mile down the river a big flock of geese got up and came over my head very low, and if I had had a shotgun I might have got three or four, they were so thick; but here's one that dropped."

"You don' eat heem, he's a t'ousan' year ol'; look a

here," and he tried to tear the skin under its wing with no effect. "I'll tole you; give a-heem to ol' Miss'r Knight; he's tough, too. How much a-mineral Charley an' you clean up dis a-week?"

"Oh, we had a big week, and cleaned up about fifteen hundred. Why?"

"Yas, all drif'; nex' week you don' get noding, hey?"

"Perhaps so, but that's miner's luck; we can't expect to get as much every time. It's the biggest week we've had, and only five days at that."

"You like-a dat work—no?"

"No, I don't like it; but it helps a fellow to live."

"I tole you. You go 'long o' me dis winta an' trap. You haf good time an' make more dan dig fur de lead. I no dig fur lead."

And so it happened. He was getting ready to spend the winter in the wilds of the Bad Ax country to trap. After hearing his scheme I agreed to go with him, and we started in to get ready. He had all the steel traps necessary for small animals, and was an expert at making dead-falls for the larger ones. We drifted down to Dubuque, where we put our boat and other things on a steamer for Prairie du Chien. From that place we took a supply of provisions, mainly of flour, coffee and sugar, for Antoine said we would not need pork nor lard because we could get fat from coons, ducks and perhaps other animals. Our outfit was simple, but it loaded our boat, and two heavy tarpaulins protected the provisions. It was a hard pull up the Wisconsin River, some twenty miles, to the mouth of the Bad Ax River, but we took it easy, and the second night we camped a mile or so up the Bad Ax. This camp is memorable because of a storm which wet us to the skin, but the provisions and the ammunition were kept dry.

We went on up the little river some fifty miles, more or less, hauling over or around falls, when we hid our boat and a portion of the provisions and started on foot to some spot which Antoine seemed familiar with, for he had been over the ground before. The way he stored the provisions was curious. After dragging the boat back from the river we hung it bottom side up between two trees, and then put out lines from each side to prevent it turning over. Then we cut poles and made a shelf on the seats, covered these with a tarpaulin and stored our provisions in the boat.

"Now," said Antoine, "Miss'r Bear, Miss'r Coon and Miss'r Mouse, you doan git no flour and you doan git no sugar, an', Miss'r Rain, you doan spile noding."

We took our rifles, a frying pan, axe and some flour, coffee and salt, and started up the river into Bad Ax county, which some man with no regard for historic names has had re-christened "Vernon county," a change that destroys the individuality of the county, for there might be forty Vernon counties in the United States, but there would be only one having the old name, which savors of the settlement of the region by the whites and had the merit of being unique. I have no idea how the old name came to the river and afterward the county, but will predict that some man with a little poetry in his soul and a love for originality will arise and have the historic and beautiful—I say beautiful advisedly—name of "Bad Ax" restored to the county. I really don't know if the river has been renamed, but hope not.

We selected our camping spot some few miles above the fork of the river, on the east branch, where several small streams came in. There are, no doubt, names for all these now; we had no map and no name for anything but the main river, yet we named them for our own purposes; that was necessary in order to be understood, and I elaborated a map on my powder horn which showed all the streams, swamps and hills to the best of my ability. This horn was left in Potosi, as of no further use. Just what I would give to see it hanging on a wall of my den to-day I cannot say. We measure the things of the moment by their utility or their cash value, but those of the past which formed a part of our lives become treasures beyond price when they serve as links to connect us with a time far removed. A sword that was "held by the enemy" for over a quarter of a century is on my wall. It may be sold for old junk, but not before I am put to bed with a spade and sodded over.

Let's see; we were talking about an old powder horn. It cost only the time to bore out the tip, fit the bottom and to polish the thing—a mere nothing—but it's so easy to get off the track. I was only going to say to the boys of to-day: Never throw away anything that you can keep. A trifling thing becomes priceless after forty years have passed. That's all!

When the old trapper threw down his load and said, "We make here our house," his partner, who had begun to think that there was no end to the journey, rejoiced. On a little knoll we laid the foundation for the cabin. Antoine was one of those men who are so handy with an axe that you wouldn't be surprised to see a clock made by him with that tool alone, and he measured and notched the logs and showed me how to put the small ends, that made the sides, to the rear, and so help the slant of the roof. He split the long three-foot shingles, a few "puncheons" for part of a floor, on which we slept, and also for the door frames and the door. We chinked the logs, and plastered them with clay mixed with coarse grass, made a fireplace and stone chimney, and then

we were in a ten-by-twelve cabin, with a shed roof kept
in place by weight poles. A stone oven was made in the
fireplace, where we could not only bake bread, raised
with cream o' tartar and soda, but could also roast a
goose or a venison ham.

Not until we began to build our camp would the old
man let me kill a deer, although we saw plenty of them,
because he said that we could not carry any part of it;
so we had lived on partridges, rabbits and a coon on the
journey, and a change to venison was good. The bed
was made with hemlock boughs on the puncheons, and
covered with a tarpaulin and blankets. A swinging
shelf was made to hold the remaining provisions secure
from rats or other intruders, and we started down stream
for supplies, taking only one rifle, an axe and enough
salt, matches, etc., to last a week, for we had been three
days going up from the place where the boat was left.
After a two days' tramp we found our provisions as we
had left them, and loaded up again and started for camp.
Just how it happened, no one knows; my rifle had only
one trigger, and that could be "set" by pushing it forward, and the "set" was so light that a breath would almost let it off. Of course it could be used without the
"set," and then it took about a two-pound pull to let it go.
I had started ahead, and in my pack was the frying-pan,
which projected over my shoulder alongside my head.
Suddenly a shot startled me close to my ear, and on looking around at Antoine he said: "What for he go so easy?
I t'ought I kill one pa-tridge on de tree yonder, an' I on'y
make a hole in dat fry-pan; de t'ing go off too quick, an'
mos' kill you, hey?"

The grouse had not stirred, and I loaded the rifle,
showed Antoine how a single trigger could be set to a
"hair," and he picked the head off the partridge, saying:

"Ba gosh! he go so easy as a gun wit' two trigger; I doan on'stan dat." He learned the trick, and after beating down the edges of the hole in the frying-pan and putting in one of the trap rivets and battering it down with the poll of the axe we went on. It took four trips to get all our plunder from the boat to the camp, and the snows had fallen before the last one was made, and our snow-shoes were worn instead of being carried, for without them we would have been there until spring, for the snow was two feet deep and still falling when we reached our cabin. To our surprise there was smoke coming from the chimney, and when we opened the door there was an Indian cooking a rabbit by the fire.

He arose, shook hands with Antoine and then with me, and the Frenchman and he sat down and talked in the Ojibwa tongue for a while, and then my friend explained the matter in this way: The red man was an old acquaintance who had found our camp and entered, as was their custom; he knew Antoine's rifle, saw that the camp was new, and waited for our return. He tapped his breast and said to me, "Nidgee," which I understood to be his name, and so called him, although I afterward learned that the word meant simply "friend."

It is difficult to get at the way these Indian words should be spelt; for instance, they call themselves O-*jib*-wah, and the white man first twists it into Ojibway and then into "Chippeway." The word which I spell "Nidgee" is sometimes given as "Nitchee," and so it goes; it's a question of how it sounds and how it may be twisted at second hand. When I was among them they pronounced the tribal name with an almost imperceptible "O," and the accent on the second syllable, as given above. Our red friend came and went at intervals all winter, never saying a word at leaving and only giving a salutatory grunt on arriving. Antoine explained that his friend's name was Ah-se-bun, or Raccoon, and that he was a good man to know; I gave him a big plug of tobacco, and we were friends.

After getting the cabin well fixed for the winter we started to put out a line of traps up a branch of the little stream, which was to be my line. We were gone three days, and had good dry weather, covered about thirty miles in all—fifteen up one stream, then over a divide and down another, which came into the first one near our shanty—but we set about forty steel traps of different sizes, for otter near falls and rapids, for mink under tree roots and other covered places, and for "black cat," pine marten and ermine in their haunts. We made many dead-falls for some of these animals where it was possible to drive stakes or arrange them on stumps, and for these we carried bait of venison and fish. This was my first three days on snowshoes, and the weight of them, added to the unusual gait which they require, made some muscles that had not been used to a loping gait very sore. But the truth came out when we reached the cabin and hung the snowshoes up, for Antoine asked: "You tired, hey? I t'ink t'ree day' on snowshoe' pooty good fur fust time; he make me sore fust, but, like de skate, you git used to dat kine, an' bime-by you t'ink de snowshoe de best fur de walk. Jess so me w'en I be in de wood all winter. W'at you say, hey? S'pose we res' two, t'ree day' an' fish, den I go put my line o' trap an' you run yours; what you say, hey?"

"Well, Antoine, I do feel tired in my legs, and if you are tired, too, I'll do just as you say. We'll fish a day or two, and get a change of feed, and then you go and lay out your line and I'll run over mine."

This put it in such shape that the tired feeling was

mutual, as indeed it was, for the first skating or snow-shoeing of the season strains muscles in an unusual way. And we rested and fished. We used bits of venison for bait, and laid in a stock of trout and some other small fish, which we stored in the snow when frozen.

A portion of a deer had been hung on the north side of the cabin, and it had been torn and picked in a way that neither dogs, wolves nor bears could nor would have mutilated it, because the tearing had been done from the upper side. I called my partner's attention to it, and suggested that ravens had found us out.

He looked at the meat and said: "Miss'r Raven he doan lak come near shanty, but dem mis'able meat hawk he come an' take de meat out yo' mouf. I hate dat cuss, de meanes' bird in de wood, 'cause he no 'fraid. You keep a' eye out an' see how I fix him wid a flip."

I saw the bird the same day. It was the "Canada jay," "meat hawk," "whiskey jack," etc., a relative of our bluejay, but not so noisy. As I have since known this Northern bird on its extreme Southern limit in winter, in Michigan and Minnesota, it is of an ashy gray color, with black and white markings, and so unfamiliar with man as to be impudent, and therefore very interesting. This is all very well when a bird visits you in a winter camp where birds are scarce, and one drops down by your feet, hops around and swipes a venison chop or a fish which has been laid out ready for the pan; but when it invites all its sisters, its cousins and its aunts to a feast on a saddle of venison, which you have left out for safe-keeping entirely for your own purposes, the familiarity of the bird breeds a feeling which differs from contempt. Somewhere back in memory the word "flip" seemed connected with some sort of a beverage, and I imagined that Antoine intended to give "whiskey jack" a drink that would paralyze him; that was a natural conclusion, although we had no whiskey.

"I tell you; come see me fix de flip; he come here for heat my meat an' he'll get de flip; I fix him." He removed the chinking from between the logs for a foot, and ran out a long shingle and put a piece of meat on the outer end. Soon the enemy alighted on the shingle, when down came the axe on its inside end, and a dead "meat hawk" was tossed in the air. "I tole you he got de flip—he want no more, an' now all hees brudder got to get de flip, an' den we got no trouble no mo'." During our three days' rest we killed about twenty with the "flip," and went our rounds of traps knowing that there were a few less meat hawks to prey upon our stores.

I stayed in camp alone for three days after our rest, while Antoine went over his line and set his traps. The first trip was the greatest labor of all, for it involved selecting places and building dead-falls, but I was getting my tired muscles into condition by a rest which was merely a change of occupation. The rifle was to be cleaned and oiled; knives were to be sharpened; wood to be cut; bullets to be moulded from bar lead, and other things to be done, besides cooking and washing underclothing.

While fishing in the stream on the third day after Antoine left, there suddenly appeared seven Indians, in company with my friend Ah-se-bun. None of them could or would speak English, and after a repetition of the word "Tah-so-je-ge" and some gesticulation I began to understand that they were asking for Antoine. Later I learned that "je-ge" meant "he who does," and that "tah-so" referred to traps. As I gradually picked up some of their words and tried to use them, I often began a sentence to Antoine with "Nidgee Tah-so-je-ge, would you like fish or venison?" etc. That day when I was round fishing my red friend had named me "Kego-e-kay," or he who fishes, and I arranged with Antoine to always use the native tongue when possible; and before spring it was our common camp talk, he helping me over the hummocks. I entertained our red friends as well as possible, and their appetites were enormous. Antoine had fully informed me on all the points of Ojibway etiquette, and when I offered tobacco the exact amount was cut off and handed to each individual, or he would have considered that the whole plug was given him; and the same circumspection was necessary when a loaf of bread was cut.

I tried to get our visitors to follow Antoine's trail and meet him, as the prospect of feeding eight hungry Indians was not pleasant, but they waited. I had two loaves of bread; one for me to take next morning when I ran my line, and one for supper when Antoine came. A venison ham was boiling in the fireplace to have for supper and breakfast, and to keep me three days if necessary; but when I got ready to set it out to our guests Antoine came in. There was a grunting salutation, and then Antoine said: "I don't bin hungry, but ba gosh if I'll bin starve; it was good I come now 'fore dey heat all dat grub we got. You don't know w'at happetite **dey** got, I'll tole you." And I certainly didn't know. **An**-toine first cut bread and meat for himself and me, and then divided the rest into eight portions, which were hardly chewed, and had disappeared before we had fairly begun.

Antoine then told me: "Dey ha'n't had half plenty, but dey all say 'nish-ish-shin;' dat means 'good.' We doan got much meat, on'y for you t'ree day, an' I doan cook no more."

A smoke followed, and then it transpired, as Antoine translated it, that one of their friends had somehow broken his leg, and they wanted him to go and set it. The distance to their camp was only five miles, and if I didn't mind he would go at once. It seems that he had a reputation for surgery among these people, and I had three good reasons for wishing him to start immediately. Of course the humanity of fixing the man's leg was one reason; keeping on good terms with men who could rob and destroy our traps and drive us out of the country was another, and I fear that the third was a desire to get rid of guests who would devour our stores and breed a famine was as strong a reason as the other two.

After the exodus I cooked a partridge and some venison chops to take on the line, baked two more loaves of bread, and had the kettle boiling to make coffee when Antoine should return. A light rain the night before had made a crust upon the snow and snowshoes were not needed. It was long after dark when his step was heard crunching in the crust, and in he walked with his rifle and a coon. I told him that it was well that he had the coon, for I had cooked all the meat in sight, and there was only enough for our supper and for me to take on my trip. There were fish enough for breakfast, and now there was coon fat enough to fry them in. In the words of that old hunting song of Mr. Raynor's: "Why should the hunter lack?"

Antoine said: "Dat make no diff'. W'en I'll got hunger I'll catch de feesh or I'll kill a deer or pa'tridge, or I'll go hunger. It makes no diff', I'll come along, you doan min' me, no."

After supper we smoked in silence. I had said all that could be said about the camp larder in order that he might not put off replenishing it before he got hungɪy, and was anxious to know all about the broken leg and why so many Indians were so close to us. Not a question would I ask of the old man. He would tell it all in his own way if left alone, and would be better satisfied to do it in that way. We sat in front of the log fire on three-legged stools which his axe had fashioned, and smoked in silence until he said: "Han' me that plug tobac." I passed him the tobacco, and he slowly sliced a pipeful, ground it in his palms, filled his pipe and lighted it with a sliver from a dry pine stick. I emptied my pipe and followed suit. As he contemplated the smoke curl up and mingle with that of the fire, he removed the pipe and said: "Dese Injun jess lak w'ite man, some smart an' some tam fool." He was thawing out, and to assist the process I kept silent and let him go on thinking until he got ready to tell as much as he wished.

After a few more puffs he said: "De big fella dat was here, hees name was 'She-kog,' an' dat mean de skunk; but he ain't got no sense like a skunk. All dese men dey go on up on a Flambeau riv', dey no stay on a Bad Ax riv, an' She-kog he go fur to break a stick an' hit O-ge-ma, the head man, an' broke his bone in his O-bwam, w'at you call dat bone here?" indicating his thigh. "Well, when I foun' ole O-ge-ma he say 'ugh'* an' I feel hees laig. Sho 'nuff she was broke. I get some wood f'um dry pine an' make splits an' tear up blanket, an' den I take hees foot in bote han's an' put ma foot in hees crotch an' I pull lak de dev' till bones slip togedder an' I feel 'em all rite. Den de woman win' hees laig in blanket, an' I put on some split wood an' more blanket an' hees laig it get all rite. Dey go 'way in mornin' an' carry O-ge-ma 'longside. Gimme dat tobac."

*This Indian salutation has been Anglicized into "how," and further polluted into "here's how."

In the morning I started to run my line. Two days would do it easily if the weather was good, but rations for three was a wise provision. A rifle and ammunition for a dozen shots was also needed. Matches in a vial, blankets, some strong twine and a belt axe completed the outfit, except the snowshoes, which were slung on the back in case of need, for the crust might soften or fresh snow might fall, and snowshoes were now in the same category as the traditional pistol in Texas. This made a fairly good load for a novice, and it was increased by several skins before noon.

Night came; and as I ate supper by a little fire and crawled under my blankets with my feet to the fire and the upper half of my body in the hollow of a big tree there came a sense of loneliness that is indescribable. Perhaps there was some fear, but as near as I can recall it the main feeling was one of helplessness. The night was still, cold and clear. The stars shone through the top of the leafless, hardwood trees. I looked over the rifle. It was a big and tolerably accurate one; the cap was sound and—"Pshaw!" I thought, "a man armed as I am is the most dangerous animal in these woods; now go to sleep." That was truly philosophical, but—philosophy and sleep are not identical. Not a twig or an acorn dropped within hearing that escaped my over-sensitive ear. The fire was replenished several times, and it seemed as if day would never come.

If I lost consciousness for a moment that night it must have been the briefest of moments. Camping out with Port Tyler and the boys was one thing, but this was another. Every owl that ventured a remark seemed to be making reference to me. If a rabbit ran on the hard snow and cracked his joints as a call or challenge I heard it—but then the fact is I was not sleepy. No man can sleep when he isn't sleepy; there's nothing queer in that. Near daylight I was startled by the tramp of some animal, and I sat up and listened. The sound came from the stream below, which glinted in the starlight, and I made out a moving form going down stream. I thought it must be a bear, and if I could kill it then life would be worth living, if only to tell of it. I stood up in the hollow of the great tree, and tried to get the rifle sights in line with the animal's forequarters, but the diffused light from snow and stars made it seem impossible to tell where the gun was sighted. The thing stopped; it had probably scented my camp, and partly at random I fired. A mingled cry and growl, a floundering in the snow and a hasty reloading of the rifle followed. On reaching the spot, not more than fifty yards distant, blood could be seen on the snow and I followed. Morning was visible in the east, and by the time the sun was up I had run down my game, which was weak from copious bleeding. It turned at bay. It was not a bear, but what could it be? It made a feeble charge on me, which I dodged, and then dropped it with a bullet in the head. Now that it was dead I had no idea what it could be. Of lions, tigers, elephants and other animals of Asia and Africa I had knowledge, but here was a beast in an American forest of which I had never heard nor read of in my school books. It was bear-like, but not a bear. Its body was heavy; its legs thick and clumsy; its tail bushy, and it had a round head with eyes wide apart. The hair was shaggy and thick, the color being almost black, with a light stripe along the sides which met at the insertion of the tail. It was about three feet long, and might have weighed 150 pounds. This is how I remember it, and under such circumstances a young fellow with tastes of the naturalist notes such things. I skinned the beast, and the smell of the meat said plainly that whatever this thing may be I would starve before I would eat it. It was an odor like that of mink, weasels and other beasts of prey, or rather, those which live on flesh exclusively— for the flesh of the bear, coon, hog and other *omnivora* has no such smell. One hindleg had been broken and the other injured—a most fortunate shot in the uncertain light, and one of pure and unadulterated luck.

After a toilet in the brook and a good breakfast— such a breakfast as only one with an appetite such as I had, after the morning's work, can appreciate—I crossed the divide, and struck the other stream, which led homeward; yes, that's the word; it was home now. Soon I came to a dead-fall which had been wrecked; the back of it had been broken into and the bait taken. I thought that some animal had approached it from the rear, and in ignorance that the other side was open and that the trigger held a hospitable log, which would induce him to remain by falling and breaking his back, had considered that the only way to get at the desired bait was to break in from the side he first came to. After finding a dozen or more dead-falls entered in the same manner I began thinking. The more I thought of the matter the further I was from any conclusion. The crust on the snow was now too hard to show any tracks except of deer, whose small hoofs cut through it and often left bloody marks where the crust had retaliated.

When I reached camp, Antoine had just finished his laundry work and was hanging it up. Here I want to tell the young boys that a trapper's life is a hard one, aside from the exposure in running lines of traps. With two it is lighter because of a division of labor, but to run a line two or three days, skin, stretch and then flesh the skins so that particles of fat do not injure them, cook for yourself and partner, wash your underclothing, mend clothes, moccasins or shoe packs and snowshoes, besides cleaning guns, running bullets and doing the hundred and one things that must be done, keeps one busy every hour of daylight and often afterward. It is an independent sort of life, free from being bossed; but it is hard work in a healthy climate, and full of adventure to one who loves it.

Antoine looked over my skins. They comprised one otter, two mink, one ermine or white weasel, one fisher or "black-cat," which he called by the Indian name of o-jig, and is a strange animal of the mink or weasel family which the naturalists know as *Mustela canadensis*, but it also called "pekan" and other names. There was also a foot and part of a leg, saved for Antoine's identification, which he called sable, an animal better known as pine marten. Then came the skin of the unknown beast. When he saw that he jumped and yelled. Then he shook hands with me and said: "You b'en done it; you killed de ole dev', old Carcajou; he break all de trap you set; he know all 'bout trap, an' he go in on hin' end and steal bait. He follow you' track to all you' trap, and w'en he fin' he break 'em, mebbe he steal 'em. Oh, he spile our trap all a time, but you got-a heem. Shake."

It was a wolverine, an animal with many names, and the worst enemy the trapper meets. The badger is also called carcajou.

A day spent in stretching and fleshing skins, and then Antoine started to run his line. Our bake oven had fallen in, and I brought better stones from the brook and built it anew in the fireplace, cooked my dinner and supper from the carcass of a deer, which Antoine had killed and dressed, sat by the fire, smoked a while and turned in and slept the sleep of the just. Tired and worn out, acorns might fall, rabbits might snap their legs and wol-verines might prowl around. I had killed a wolverine, a stealthy night prowler that from pure deviltry destroys the work of the trapper, and that was glory enough for a first trip. I have no remembrance of any dreams that night. I could have said with Sancho Panza:

"Blessings light on him who first invented sleep! It covers a man all over, thoughts and all, like a cloak; it is meat for the hungry, drink for the thirsty, heat for the cold, and cold for the hot; in short, money that buys everything; balance and weight that makes the shepherd equal to the monarch and the fool to the wise; there is only one evil in sleep, as I have heard, and it is that it resembles death, since between a dead and a sleeping man there is little difference."

The sun was high when I awoke, and by my side stood Ah-se-bun; but I'll tell you about that another time.

ANTOINE GARDAPEE.

CANTO II.—ANOTHER WOLVERINE—SNOW BLIND.

I WOULD ask all such "tenderfeet," in whose ranks I was then a recruit, although the term had not been invented, how they would feel to awake in a cabin in a forest where there was no white man within forty miles, except a partner who was off running a line of traps, and find an Indian standing silently by the bed? Just put yourself in his place.

After the choking sensation which comes with such a scare, and a partly paralyzed heart had begun its regular work, the firelight, which, by the way, the intruder had replenished, showed the features of our friend Ah-se-bun, who gave a saluting grunt and turned toward the fire, where he sat until I arose, washed and dressed and prepared to get breakfast. The door had been held shut against wind and snow by a prop, for there was no fear of animals where there was a man and a fire, and our guest had somehow removed that without disturbing my sleep, but how long he had been in the cabin was unknown. He held down a stool by the fire, while I cooked breakfast, and he sat there and ate enough for half a dozen laboring men, and drank coffee until there was none left. Antoine had taught me never to betray any curiosity, and so I handed over a pipeful of tobacco and waited. Old Raccoon looked at me inquiringly, and I at once filled my pipe, although I never could endure tobacco in the morning, and I took a few puffs and awaited his pleasure, curious to know why he had made such an unconventional call at so early an hour. He smoked his pipe out, emptied it, and sat for what seemed a long time before he spoke.

After some repetition and much gesticulation, it appeared that he had met Antoine, and that the latter had killed a bear, and I must go with him and help get it to camp, and after arranging things in the cabin, I took down my rifle to start when my guest shook his head and said, "Kowin," and I replaced it at the door. I understood then that there would be load enough without a ten-pound rifle, and we went off to bring in the bear.

Enough snow had fallen during the night to make hard travelling without snowshoes, so we tied them on and started—Ah-se-bun in the lead—up a stream on the west side where I had never been, but where my partner's line of traps began. A tramp of some five miles brought us to the place where Antoine had killed the bear, about a mile off his line. He was there cooking his breakfast when we arrived, for he had been up and had the bear skinned and dressed before he started in to cook. It happened that he had run his first line of traps some fifteen miles, and was crossing the divide to his homestretch when he found a fresh bear track in the snow, which had begun to fall late in the afternoon, and he turned and followed it. The track led him back toward camp, and he came upon bruin about sunset and killed it where we found him.

When we came up to him he said: "I t'ink you better come up and take ole Afum to camp, an' I'll go on an' run my trap, hey? What you want? Bre'kfuss? I t'ink yes."

I said to him: "I have been to breakfast, but can eat

a little more after the long tramp on snowshoes; but if you'll only let our friend the Raccoon have a fair whack at that bear the load will be lighter to carry. He's had one big breakfast—about five times as much as I could eat—but just let him fill up on bear meat, and our load home will be light."

Antoine thought a minute and replied: "I'll tole you. I'll doan lak bear leever, but a Injun he lak him bes' of all. I'll cook-a heem dat leever, an' you'll heat my col' pa'tridge w'at I roas' las' night w'en da bear was warm. I'll tole you I'll have long chase for Afum, an' I t'ink I'll loss him in a dark, but he stop to look roun' an' I get him. He good an' fat, an' w'en he freeze I lak heem jess so good as de pork, an' he make some good fat for fry de feesh an' roas' de pa'tridge."

For years the name "Afum" bothered me. The Ojibway name for the bear is muckwo, and, as the word was neither French nor Indian, it was a puzzle until in later years I learned that Western hunters call the grizzly bear "Ephraim," and this must have been the name which the trapper tried to use.

Antoine rigged a couple of light, flexible poles to a piece of bark, on which we placed the hindquarters of the animal, wrapped in its skin. A short, light rope was attached to the poles, and with the rope as a collar and a pole under each arm a man could haul quite a load over the snow where a sled would have cut in. The front edge of the bark was rolled up sled fashion, and by following the stream and trail it was mainly a down-hill haul, with the exception of a few knolls. When all was loaded Antoine went his way over his line, and I pointed to each load and then to Ah-se-bun to take his choice, the hindquarters and skin being the heaviest. Which do you think he took?

It has been said of a man who is so unfortunate as to have to carve at his own table: "If he takes the best cut for himself he's a durned hog, and if he doesn't he's a durned fool." Now, in making choice of loads—as well as in some other things—I will bear witness that my red friend was not a "durned fool." There was a sort of straightforwardness among the Indians whom I met that I've never been able to acquire. They knew what they wanted, and they went for it without being hampered by etiquette. If there was carving to be done they could never be ranked with the d. f.'s, and when the choice of loads was offered I got "the lion's share." With more experience in the ways of "Mr. Lo," he would not have been offered the choice of loads; at the the risk of being thought a d. h. I would simply pick up the poles of the lighter load, leave him to choose the other.

It was quite a pull, and our freight had to be unloaded several times to get it around the bad places on an Indian trail, for an old path ran along this stream which somehow was indistinctly visible even in winter by marks, such as fallen trees, which showed where they had been worn by being stepped upon or by having lodge poles dragged over them, clumps of bushes which had been avoided, and the many things which an observing eye notes. At times it required both of us to take hold of one load, and lift or drag it over or around an obstruction, and then do the same with the other. I gave my companion frequent opportunities to exchange, but he didn't take them. I was too polite to pick up his poles, but Antoine said afterward: "By gar! W'en you want for change load, you mus' change. He t'ink you big fool w'en he gotta da light one all a tam. Nax tam you tak-a de small load. He lak-a de big one w'en dat's w'at he got. He gotta lak heem."

When we came to the cabin the sun was well past meridian. Clocks and watches had been left far behind us. "We took no note of time save by its flight." Ah-se-bun, the Raccoon, was hungry. What does half a dozen pounds of bear's liver eaten in the morning amount to half a day later, after hauling part of a bear five miles over crusted snow that often had a sidelong slope toward the stream, and over a crooked and log-barred path? I was hungry also, but had never got into the Indian habit of eating enough in one day to last for three, and so I started in to get dinner. I plucked up courage and told Lo to go and get some dry wood. He pointed to a pile in the corner that was kept for such an emergency as severe weather, and intimated that there was plenty. I was tired, hungry and cross, and just in the humor to lay aside all notions that I must treat an Indian as a gentle-man, and I then put away the bear steak, hung up the frying-pan and merely said "Nish-ish-shin" (good) and lighted my pipe and sat down; in other words, "I struck." I thought it out something like this: Here was a lazy, gormandizing Indian who came and went at pleasure, and could eat as much as four hard-working white men and then sleep for a week after it, who would probably stay by me as long as the bear lasted and eat the greater part of it, after shirking the heaviest load on me, and now he was too lazy to get wood to cook his dinner be-cause there were a few sticks in the cabin which were kept for bad weather. After smoking a few minutes and feeling no less angry I lay down, and slept as only a tired man can sleep. A noise awoke me; it was my red friend bringing in wood. It was dark outside; he had thought the matter over, and had concluded that he wanted to get some wood, and had got it. This was comfortable to me, and I cooked a great lot of bear steaks, baked some bread and we had dinner. He cared nothing for bread unless soaked with fat, but the amount of meat he could secrete was enormous. It is surprising what an amount of animal food a white man can consume in the clear, cold winter air of the woods, whether in Wisconsin, Maine or the Adirondacks, especially if he is running a line of traps or hauling half a bear over a trail that is covered with crusted snow, but an Indian can discount him. From that time forward I had no fear of asserting myself, and of bossing the ranch when our guest and I were left alone. I dropped all my civilized notions of etiquette and got along nicely. This, of course, does not apply to Antoine, for he and I vied with each other in doing camp work, and he had all the consideration for a companion that could be expected of a man who had been reared among different surroundings; but for an Indian I began to entertain different feelings. I understood and appreciated them better afterward, but just then I was in the transition state of being disillusioned.

When Antoine came, two days later, he had some skins, and a woeful tale of broken dead-falls and of traps carried off. Ah-se-bun had gone. A wolverine had struck Antoine's line, and the old man was tired and cross. He sat with his head in his hands before the fire, while I made him some coffee and broiled him some venison chops on a grill made from some wire we had brought for tying traps or other purposes, and then I fried some fish in bear fat and set out the tin cups and plates, and we ate in silence. It was a good dinner, fit for a hard-working trapper who had come in tired and angry at having lost the fruits of his labor. I would not use the hackneyed phrase, "Fit for a king," because it was too good for most of the kings who have come to my notice—the dinner was good for Antoine and for me, two American kings of the forest, who held dominion over all the beasts and exacted tributes of fish, flesh and fur from them. And another marauding wolverine was invading our realm!

By some unwritten law my stool was always at the left of the fireplace and Antoine's on the right. The tobacco bag hung on my side, and when we were in executive session it was my duty to hand out "the weed of Ole Virginny." So after we had removed our stools from the table, which was half an oak log, with legs set in holes made by an inch auger, we sat down in our places, and I handed the old man the plug. After his pipe was filled and emptied he said: "You stop here till I keel de dev'. I go watch for heem. My trap all fix, all right—he come to-night an' I keel a-heem, he keel a-me, it make no dif'. He run my line all a-tam an' I no git heem; he break all our trap like hell a'most. Gimme some tobac."

Tobacco had a soothing effect on Antoine, as it has on many men, and a second pipe quieted his anger, but did not interfere with his determination. I filled his haversack with provisions, and with blankets and snow-shoes on back and rifle on shoulder he started on his mission of revenge. He did not say with Shylock:

> "If I can catch him once upon the hip,
> I will feed fat the ancient grudge I bear him."

He had never heard of Shylock, but he had in his heart all the revengeful feeling that the poor, persecuted Jew felt for his enemies.

It was well along toward sundown when he left, and I cleaned up our table and got in the night wood, and spent the evening in the unpoetic work of darning my woollen socks, filling the box in the stock of my rifle with greased patches of proper size, putting new strings on the ear-laps of my cap, overhauling my mittens, examining suspenders and buttons, and doing all those little things which men wholly cut off from the deft hand of woman must do for themselves in their own bungling way—or have a breakdown when there is neither time nor opportunity for repairs. It is wonderful what a man can do when thrown on his own resources, when there is the same imperative word "must" which always confronts the soldier. He must, or——

Rolling up in my blankets, I fully expected some adventure or visitation before morning, but nothing happened. Three nights passed in this way. I fished, cut firewood and busied myself with other things, but always with a thought of Antoine. He was a long time coming; perhaps he might be caught in the bear trap—there was a big one on his line—or perhaps he might be crippled by some accident and be starving! He did not come, and these thoughts by repetition became probabilities. I filled my sack with provisions and shouldered my rifle. I would meet him on the back track, and I followed his returning trail all day and crossed the divide between his two streams and crawled into his camp at night. His trail was plain, although I had never been over it before. He had rigged a sleeping place beside a huge log, and had made a shelter with poles and brush. A bed of leaves was inviting, and I rolled into my blankets and slept until morning.

He had not left the trail so far—that was plain. After breakfast I started down his line on the other stream, and after a few miles found one of his dead-falls broken. Here was the first evidence of the robber. Further on I found where Antoine had left the trail and gone off to leeward, and had made himself a sort of breastwork camp in good range of the rear of a trap, and on examining the latter there was evidence of a tussle and some blood, but about an inch of snow had fallen in the night, and the affair had occurred at least twenty-four hours before; but Antoine was still missing. I saw where he had left the trail, and where he had returned to it one hundred yards below, and again where he had stepped on the stones in the brook, which lead a long way down as well as across, and I took the trail down the valley home. He was not there, and it was nearly night of the fourth day. He had been out four nights, and I was alarmed—perhaps "scared" would express it better. Here I was hundreds of miles in the wilderness alone. The feeling was not entirely one of selfish helplessness now. I could care for myself fairly well in the woods, and did not mind the solitude; but I found that I had a feeling of love for my companion which had been latent and only brought out by his long absence, which it seemed must be caused by some accident. I ate supper and tried to sleep, but for the second time in the woods I was tired, but not sleepy.

Morning came. I cooked enough to last me several days on a trip after my companion. I would go back to the stepping stones where I had lost the trail, and find it. Dead or alive, I must know where Antoine was. He had not been hurt in a dead-fall, that was sure, for I had seen them all; but, if living, he would surely have been back before this. I slung my haversack and blankets, and started back on his outgoing trail, determined to find him if possible, and to look closer along the banks of the stream, where the new snow might have covered his track for a short distance. I had hardly got one hundred yards from the cabin when I heard Antoine call: "Hello! where you go now? Come back here; I want some grub for to heat. You run 'way w'en I come lak you doan want a see me. W'at for you go off dat a-way?"

He had come in on my branch of the stream, and if I had got out of sight or hearing before he arrived there would have been a long and useless tramp for me—and perhaps one for him to find me. Who knows but we both might still be going the rounds in the wilds of Wisconsin on each other's trails? I made him hot coffee, while he unslung his pack and washed, and then it was good to see the old man "heat." Slices of cold boiled bear ham, hot broiled venison steak, tin cups of coffee, and more bread than I dare tell, went in quantities, and it seemed a long time before he pulled his stool to the fire and said: "Gimme dat tobac'."

It took three pipefuls before he felt like talking, and then, seeing that I betrayed no curiosity, he said: "I got dat ole dev'," and then paused. I knew him too well to make any reply or ask a question. He had taken his first liking to me because I had happened to betray no curiosity, and I knew that if he was questioned he would give short answers; but if let alone he would tell it all in his own way, and be anxious to do it. His pack of skins lay on the floor unopened. I sat and looked at the fire, for I could not smoke as much as he, and when the spirit again moved him he said: "I got hees skin dere in de pack; w'en I hopen it you see heem. He make me hard run all-a night after I break his laig f'um where I hide by my trap, an' it was his front laig; so he go 'long good, an' I'll run all de night w'en I can see heem or hees track, an' I shoot-a heem t'ree time on a run an' I no hit heem. W'en day come I see da track plain, an' I stop for res' an heat my grub. Ole Carcajou he no lak-a day-tam for be hout, an' I t'ink me he fin' some hole for lay hup in. So I go 'long slow for give heem tam to fin' hole, an' he go all-a day 'way off to nor'eas' lak he go to-a Wiscons' Riv'. Nex' night I fin' hees hole, an' I make fire an' sleep by heem. Mornin' I see it was all a rock an' not hees deep hole in a groun' for to have to smoke heem hout; so I pull some rock down and see heem, an' he growl, an' I shoot. He was too much tire to go on to fin' deepes' hole. I'll tole you, hees skeen a'n't wort' much, but w'en I no getta heem we no do more trap in dis part. Dat was good hunt. W'at you say, hey?"

That was a long story for Antoine, but he felt proud that his enemy's hide was in his pack; for this wolverine, sometimes called "glutton," seems to take delight in destroying traps, or in befouling the bait if he does not care to eat it, and the trapper who finds one on his range must kill it or go elsewhere. It is very cunning and has great strength—a combination of bear and fox—and is well characterized by Antoine as "de ole dev'." The skin has some value for robes and rugs, but to the trapper whose line it has discovered its hide has a greater value than any fur dealer would give for it—a hundred times more.

When Antoine unrolled his pack he had a lot of skins, mainly from one of my lines, which he had come down. In the lot was a silver fox, the first I had ever seen, and several pelts of the white weasel, which we call "ermine." It was my turn next day, but as one of my lines had been recently run by my partner the work was light, because there were few traps to reset.

In the morning I thought to make a quick run, and, as there was only a couple of inches of snow on top of the hard crust, I left my snowshoes in the cabin, but Antoine called me back, saying: "I'll tole you, w'en I'll see da ring on da moon las' night we go gat some snow bambye, and you'll want some ah-gim for walk home. I'll tole you." So I went back, and slung my snow-shoes and started again.

About a mile from camp a fox had killed a rabbit, and left the story of the tragedy recorded in the snow. There was the track of the rabbit, with its three holes in the snow made at each jump, but as the leaps were only one and a half feet apart it was evident that it was not frightened. The ambush of the fox was plain where it had crouched in the snow, and the hole scooped out where it had struck its prey; and then the single line of footprints where it had trotted off with the rabbit, all the feet set in one straight line, fox fashion.

I amused myself in picturing the midnight scene by the evidence of the snow, and went on to the first trap. It was a strong double-spring steel trap set under a log in a place which a mink or fisher would be likely to take on its way to or from the creek. The snow had drifted lightly over the pan, concealing it, and in the trap was the foreleg of a fox and a rabbit lay near it. Here was another story of the woods, briefly told. I reset the trap, smeared rabbit blood about it, took the rabbit for bait for other traps and went on. About noon it began to snow, and I ran the rest of the line in haste, taking out a mink or a fisher, resetting traps and rebaiting some, and pushed on for my old resting place. I had improved my first night's camp with poles and bark, and now had a good, warm shelter, free from snow, which now came thick and fast. Antoine was right. If the storm kept up all night no man could move next day without ah-gim on his feet, and I thought myself in luck. The intense still-ness of a snowstorm we have all noticed. How every sound is muffled, and all Nature seems hushed by its white mantle!

> "Lo! sifted through the winds that blow,
> Down comes the soft and silent snow,
> White petals from the flowers that grow
>   In the cold atmosphere.
> These starry blossoms, pure and white,
> Soft falling, falling, through the night,
>   Have draped the woods and mere."

The night was grand for sleeping, for it is never very cold when the snow comes in big flakes, and the morn was also grand. The snow had ceased falling, and the air was bright and clear. The same silence brooded over the woods, and was only emphasized by the tapping of a woodpecker or the hoarse croak of a raven. I would cross the divide and run the line down the other stream after all, for it only meant a few more miles, and then the week's work was done. It was in heavy timber all the way; my old trail was hidden, but I knew the bearings, and had only to keep the sun on my right until I struck the stream, and then follow it eastward. After breakfast I started. The sun was bright and dazzling— too much so for comfort. The traps were under twenty inches of snow, and I dug most of them out with a snow-shoe and got a few skins and set things in shape as well as possible. When I stopped for a noon lunch my eyes were so inflamed that they were painful. My soft cap was pulled down in front, and I went on in the bright sunshine and the drip of the trees, using one eye at a time, until I could no longer see. I could not be more than two miles from home, but could not avoid logs or choose my steps, and I was in despair. I shot off my rifle and yelled. Surely Antoine should hear a shot that distance in such clear weather. I shot again and again, perhaps a dozen times, and then I heard an answering shot down the valley. My eyes were streaming, and I could not have gone a rod further. It seemed hours before I heard Antoine's inquiring yell, and then he found me.

"So you gone snow blin', hey? Why, you don' take some sof' inside bark, an' make some spectacle an' make leetly hole in him w'en de ole sun come on a snow, hey?"

"Oh, Antoine, get me into camp! My eyes are ruined, and I'll never see again! I felt 'em getting weak and sore, but never thought I'd get stone blind; but maybe if I get a chance to rest I'll come out all right."

"Yes, you com-a all right. I t'ink you was got ketch in dead-fall, or got into some hole an' break you laig w'en I hear you shoot nine or 'leven tam. Gimme you' pack an' you' gun, an' keep hol' dis string an' come 'long o' me. Dat snow blin' make no dif' w'en you keep in camp ten day. Come 'long."

And so he towed me into camp by a string, stopping and helping me over a fallen tree or other bad place, for he had bandaged my eyes and all was dark. When we reached the cabin he sat one of the wooden troughs, which his handy axe had made, by me and told me to bathe my eyes with the cool and soft snow water it contained, and not to look at the fire or anything else. A fever came on, and for the first time in my life I knew what it was to be perfectly helpless in a wilderness. Coming into it in the full strength of youth and health, no idea of anything that could disable me ever came to mind. Here I was, laid up and despondent. There was no belief that youth and an iron constitution were sufficient to cure my ills; all I knew was that I was a wreck and a hindrance to my partner.

"I'll tole you dat make no dif'," said Antoine; "you doan min' a-me; keep-a still. I'll get some bark an' stop dat feve', an' you come 'long all rite. I'll tole you, you lie down an' doan min' noding. Keep-a eye shut—dat snow blin' he make no dif'; I'll tole you he'll be all right in ten day."

This was consoling, and might be true. Antoine cared for me like a mother. He steeped some bark—perhaps white oak, I knew at the time—and my fever left me in a few days, but my eyes could not even bear the fire light. Ah-se-bun came into the cabin. He was hungry, as usual, for I never saw an Indian that wasn't, and after filling himself with bear meat he rested, and Antoine said: "Ole Miss'r 'Coon, he says he stay here an' take care you, an' I'll run my trap. Ba gosh, day hain't been run in long tam, I'll guess. I'll tole you der is plenty for heat, and Miss'r 'Coon, he mus' cook w'en he got hunger. All you got for do is keep-a eye shut an' wash heem in snow water. I'll be back in t'ree day, an' here is plenty for heat, an' you eye he make no dif'; he come good w'en you doan' go on de snow."

The Ojibway tongue had seemed very easy to use with Antoine, who could translate what I did not understand. It seemed to be merely to learn another name for a thing, and I had only learned some nouns. To talk with a native was another thing. Ah-se-bun wanted the axe, and came to me and said: "Au-gua-kwet?" I answered: "Au-gua-kwet is over behind the pa-que-shi-gun," but in my mixture of English he failed to understand the last word to mean wheat flour, bread or anything else. That kind of talk did first rate with Antoine, but the Raccoon did not understand his own language. That was very queer.

The light in the cabin was very dim when the fire was not bright, for our "windows" consisted of two holes, one in the door and one opposite, over which were stretched the dried "caul," or what surgeons know as the *periton-*

cum, of a deer. When the fire was not bright this gave "a dim, religious light," such as steals into some silent crypt through stained glass in an old cathedral, and my eyes improved daily. After some days I could get about the room and do a few things, such as washing out my rifle and oiling it, and it was a surprise to see the Indian eat and sleep. He would rouse up and get wood to cook. The provisions were unlimited, as part of the bear was left, and Antoine had buried a deer in the snow. So it was a picnic for our friend, and he did not even have to hunt nor fish.

When Antoine came he whittled a huge pair of spectacles for me out of dry spruce. They were solid except a small longitudinal slit for each eye, through which one could see all that was necessary, and all lights from points outside the range of vision were excluded. They were fitted to my eyes with exactness, and where glasses would be in ordinary spectacles there were hollows which were blackened with charcoal, and with these I could venture out even in strong sunlight, and next day I ran my line of traps with them, seeing perfectly everything that I wished to see, unharmed by the light of the snow. The only unusual event on this trip was seeing where several deer had crossed my trail on the jump, followed by some wolves, as shown in the snow. As the deer were yarded up during such deep snow, the wolves must have stampeded some of them; but we had not seen nor heard a wolf in our part of the woods all winter.

Returning to the cabin the day afterward, Antoine said: "I'll tole you, Chris'mas he come to-morrow, and we stop home an' heat good Chris'mas dinner; what you say, hey?" and he showed me where he had kept a record of the days on a stick. I had not given a thought to the matter further than to note that it was midwinter by the sun being at its southern limit, but my partner was a more devout man, and told his beads at proper times, kept count of the days, and knew that this was Christmas Eve. And so it was settled that we should not hunt nor fish on the morrow, but would observe the day in a civilized manner, just as the folks at home were doing. Antoine had hung some evergreens over the fireplace and over the bed, and with thoughts of those at home we crawled under our blankets, and morning came.

ANTOINE GARDAPEE.

THE Christmas sun was not too bright for a winter day, and there was no wind. I was roused by the loud tapping of the great northern woodpecker on one of the logs of our house. This large bird is almost extinct to-day, and few young men have seen it alive. Its length was eighteen inches, and its tappings were in proportion. Antoine had been up some time, and was smoking his pipe by the fire, for he was one of those who can smoke before breakfast. When he saw me up he rose, and with a hearty shake said: "Merry C'ris'mas; I'll hope you'll be all well," and he prepared the breakfast. As I went to the spring to wash I looked at my unshaven face in its glassy surface, and wondered what the good people at home would say if such an apparition should walk in on them, for we had no razors nor mirrors, and had been all winter in the wilds of Wisconsin, with only an occasional Indian visitor to look at us.

The spring near our cabin was the head of a bit of marshy ground which was so filled with springs that it never froze nor was even covered with snow, as it soon melted and drained off into a tributary of the Bad Ax. But on this Christmas morning of 1855 there was a woodcock feeding in that marsh. I saw it plainly, flushed it, and know that it was a woodcock. Those who have followed these sketches will credit me with knowing this bird when I see it. Why it was there is a question. It could fly well.

After breakfast, and the meditative smoking which

seemed part of Antoine's religion, I thought of fleshing some skins, but Antoine said: "Let da skin res' to-day; all res', all man he res' on C'ris'mas; you doan' do no work w'en he come in you' home; no, sare, you doan' do not'ing but res', all a peep' da res'. W'at you say, hey?"

"I say that I can't sit by this fire all day just because it's Christmas; I wouldn't sit down that way if I was home among my people; I'd walk around, and if I'd been at hard work all the week I might go and spear eels through the ice. A live man can't sit like a lump on a log all day. There's no place to go here, and these last skins want fleshing and I want something to do, that's all."

"You go spear da heel on C'ris'mas, hey? Well, he's all right in da hafternoon, but I go in da church on a C'ris'mas mornin', and mebbe I'll got drunk in a hafternoon; I'll doan' work on no ole skin an' I'll doan' spear no heel; on'y res'."

"Do you ever go to church any other day in the year, Antoine? I'll bet fifty mink skins you don't, and the chances are that you go to a dance on Christmas Eve and sleep all the next morning and don't get to church at all."

"W'at you talk? Did you say some prayer w'en you got hup dis mornin? No! I'll bet nine or 'leven mink you ha'n't said prayer all da wint'. I'll count all a-my bead 'fore you'll git hup. I'll tole you I'll got s'prise wot make you' eye bung hout. Dat make no dif' w'en I'll go in da church, I'll show you some C'ris'mas dinna till you bu'st you' belt, you bet. I'll been look hout all-a wint' for see da day come w'en we res' an' heat jess lak' da peep' way down da riv' by Potosi."

Our food had been simple, but always in plenty. Venison, 'coon, bear, rabbit, partridge and fish prepared in several ways, as boiled, fried, broiled or roasted; and we had good bread, coffee, sugar and an occasional bean soup. The fat of the bear and the 'coon was as good as lard, and often our stale bread was soaked and fried. So we had a good substitute for butter and lard, and the only thing that might have been lacking was the potato, which would be difficult to keep, and was too bulky to carry. Surely this was good living for healthy men in a wilderness in winter. But from hints which Antoine dropped from time to time this profusion might not last. This was the first idle day of the winter, and as my partner had intimated that he was going to surprise me with a Christmas dinner I left him to arrange it, and wandered out with my snowshoes and snow-blinders.

Heretofore I had always gone up the several little streams which formed the east and west branches of the Bad Ax River, where our traps were set. To-day I would go down the stream, which I had not seen since we brought our provisions up its valley in the fall. I had gone about about two miles when a log invited me to rest. The winter landscape was beautiful; the bluish tints of the twigs against the sky and along the stream relieved the whiteness, and the day was perfect. A rabbit came slowly jumping along, and passed within twenty feet of my log, and soon a fox appeared following its track, but took the alarm at several times twenty feet and trotted off over the hill, with an occasional glance over his shoulder to make sure that the man on the log was not following. I fell to thinking how animals differ, just as men do—one dull and unperceiving, and another alert and watchful. A child could have shot the rabbit, but only a rifleman could have touched reynard.

Then came a thought that food might be scarce with us, as what Antoine had said was recalled. As I understood the case, the deer were in "yards," where they had trampled the snow so that the crust did not cut their legs, and as they could not forage far they were getting poor. And these yards were some distance off, so that a special trip of twenty miles or more would have to be made to get venison. Bears had gone into winter quarters, and would not stir out for a couple of months. Partridges found food scarce, were poor, and were eating bitter buds, which made them unpalatable. 'Coons were laid up, like the bears, and there was a prospect of scant rations. Antoine said that some trappers ate the flesh of the pine marten, or sable, and the related species called pekan, fisher, black cat, etc.; but Antoine wouldn't eat them, and very naturally I refused them. I should think that a man would have to be very hungry to eat any of the tribe to which the mink and weasel belong. We do not care to eat the animals whose diet is exclusively flesh —such as the cats and dogs—whether we call them tigers or wolves, but the deer and the sheep are vegetarians, while the bear and the hog eat similar food, and we eat them. It looked as though we must live on rabbit and our present store of venison and bear the rest of the winter, and rabbits were not plenty.

While engaged in such thoughts a gray squirrel came in sight, and I watched it run up a tree and jump into another, and then it stopped at a hole in a tall tree and seemed to want to enter it, and then appeared afraid and would draw back and then peer in again. The tree was an oak, and the hole was small, like a woodpecker's. I noted that the bark on it was torn, and as the sun was high I went back home.

"Hello!" said Antoine, "I'll t'ink you go got los', an' I mus' heat a C'ris'mas din' all 'lone. Jess in tam, an' glad for see you! *Bon jour!*"

We shook hands like old friends long parted, and he
motioned me to my seat at table with courtly grace, and
it began to dawn upon me that I was, for this occasion,
not his partner, but his guest. He had prepared the dinner alone, as he had intimated he would, and he was host,
chef, *garcon* and companion all in one on this Christmas
Day in the wilds of Wisconsin. The first course was a
soup of deer shanks with the marrow-bones cracked; but
I will try to put that memorable dinner in the shape that
some *chef* of to-day would put it, when it would be like
this, with my translation:

MENU.

POTAGE.

Consommé du bois. (Deer shank soup.)

POISSON.

Saumon du font, au naturel. (Brook trout fried.)

RELEVE.

Tranches d'agneau montebello. (Venison steak, sweet sauce.)

Aqua pura. (Bad Ax water.)

ENTREES.

Poularde á la chevreuse. (Boiled partridge.)

Haricots. (Baked beans.)

Vin du Bad Ax.

ENTREMETS DE DOUCEUR.

Pouding de ris au fruites. (Rice pudding with raisins.)

Café. Tobac.

Now I ask you—I mean you sportsmen, old and
young—how does that seem to you for a Christmas dinner either in the woods or in the wildest restaurants of
New York city?

Most of these things we had cooked in one shape or
another, but never such a lay-out as that at one feed.
The great surprise came with the rice pudding with
raisins, for I had no idea that these things were in camp;
but Antoine had smuggled a handful of rice and a few

raisins among the things bought at Prairie du Chien for just such a treat, and the old man enjoyed my surprise. The whole dinner was a surprise, for that matter; but the rice and raisins—well, they more than filled the bill. The "tobac" was burned by the fire, and after such a gorge we laid ourselves down and slept until dark.

We were awakened by the entrance of Ah-se-bun, the Raccoon, who accepted the invitation to dinner, and he not only cleaned up what we had left, but he put a polish on every bone until he could work no more. There was a big lot of the rice pudding left, but when he finished the last of it he grunted, "Nish-ish-shin," and curled up to sleep.

As Antoine and I sat by the fire while the Indian snored I told him about the oak tree and the squirrel which I had seen in the morning. I might not have thought of it again but for the fact that the tree was so scarred, as by some large animal climbing it.

"Ba gar," said he, "ole pard, I'll tole you what. Shake! You done foun' a bee tree an' we got da honey. Whoop! I'll tole you we'll got no bear meat no mo' w'en de las' one he all heat up, an' da deer he all in da yard an' poor, I'll tole you da honey he come in good an' I'll cut da bee tree w'en da day come. You do good t'ing w'en you go down da riv'. Shake!"

I was curious to know why Ah-se-bun was the only Indian who visited us except the party which once came with him, and why he seemed to be wandering up and down, and never carried a gun. Antoine told me that there was an encampment of Indians about 150 miles north on the Flambeau River, a branch of the Chippewa; another some sixty miles due east on the Wisconsin River, and a third one thirty miles southeast on the same stream. Our friend was a sort of messenger between the three camps, and our cabin was a convenient point for him to stop, eat and rest. As Antoine put it, our guest did not carry a rifle because he always started with some "grub," but would prefer to go hungry for a few days, if necessary, to carrying a rifle and such game as he might kill. Then it was all plain. Ah-se-bun could go hungry for two or three days, eat enough to last a week and go on, and he was too lazy to hunt and carry his gun and game. Afterward I learned that he was not peculiar in all this, but that they were the common traits of his race. As near as I can make out from the map of Wisconsin in a school atlas of to-day we were on the fork of the Bad Ax River in what is now Vernon county, and just north of Readstown; but there was no town, village or settlement on the river that we saw or heard of when we went up it in 1855. At any rate, we were near the main forks of the river, and our cabin was between the streams.

Our Christmas festival was ended. The morrow would bring the regular routine work, only varied by the conditions of weather.

> "We ring the bells and we raise the strain,
> We hang up garlands ev'rywhere
> And bid the tapers twinkle fair,
> And feast and frolic—and then we go
>   Back to the same old lives again."

It was a happy Christmas, because all our simple wants were filled. We were warm and well fed; every wish had been gratified as far as we had wishes, for we could say with Biron, in "Love's Labor's Lost:"

> "At Christmas I no more desire a rose
> Than wish a snow in May's new-fangled shows."

And so with minds at peace and bodies prepared for

rest we stepped over the sleeping Indian by the fire and crawled into our own blankets, and if there were any visions they were of the loved ones at home.

In the morning Antoine used a file on his axe while I prepared the breakfast, and then Ah-se-bun went down the stream with us as far as the bee tree, and continued . his journey without even a goodby grunt or the slightest expression of interest in our work. This sort of thing had ceased to exasperate me, and I was getting used to what Antoine termed "Injun unpoliteness," for said he: "Dem Injun he t'ink it smart to be unpolite, but he lak you an' he doan lak you, an' he doan tole you how much. Hit make no dif'. Ole Ah-se-bun, he say, 'Kego-e-kay nish-ish-shin,' an' he mean you good man."

"That may be all right, Antoine; but when the hungry cuss comes into camp he is polite, and gives us the *bon jour*, which he learned from your people; but when he's got his belly full he goes off, and never gives us a grunt—which is the salutation of his people. It may be all right, but I don't like it. Your people and mine give as warm a shake at parting as they do at meeting, and when we have been entertained we say 'goodby,' if no more."

"W'en you know Injun better you fine heem hout more, an' you doan mind. You know w'at make da , scratch all-a bark f'um da bee tree an' roun da hole? I'll tole you. He's a bear, an' he'll clam hup for getta da hun' an' fine da hole too small. Da bee he on'y come las' year, 'cause da bark on'y scratch hoff dis a-wint'."

Antoine cut down the big oak without help. I was fully as strong as he was, but when it came to handling an axe my wild blows counted but little, while not one of his was wasted. I could strike once in a place, but Antoine's stump was a level one; and the tree, if straight, would be weakened to the proper point on the side he wished it to fall before the other side was touched. An expert axeman is a mechanic in a broad sense. I never was an expert with the axe like Gladstone, Len Jewell, Antoine and other great men.

The great oak fell, and limbs which kept the trunk from the ground were cut, and then the question was: Is the store of honey above or below the small hole, which was not large enough to admit a man's hand? A careful examination of the hole showed that a dead limb had left a place which woodpeckers had followed into the heart of the tree, and the rains and the frosts had helped them to enlarge their excavations in the decayed heart, but the yearly growth of sap-wood had kept the outer hole small. The bees had so closed the hole with wax that the rain was shed outwardly, and when we cut off a section two feet above and a like distance below the hole, and split it, we found a store of honey that made us cut poles in order to carry it home in a roll of bark. It not only helped us out through the season of scant game, but we took some honey home to Potosi. What's that? You want to know what became of the poor bees which had laid up this store to keep them through the winter? In the name of man, what do you think? They simply died from cold and hunger; what's that to us? You fellows who think that because a bee had laid up a store for the winter by hard work he is entitled to use it to preserve his life make me tired. What is the suffering or death of any animal to man, if he wants the product of its labor to tickle his palate, or its fur to supply the demands of fashion? What is the suffering of his fellow man to him if he fills his coffers? Yet this spirit of selfishness exists throughout all nature; the fox eats the rabbit, but there are men who have sacrificed self for principle, a motive beyond anything that is possible for one of the "lower animals" to do, and after all there are men who are really honest as the world goes who will rob a hard-working bee of the fruits of its summer labor and leave it to perish in the winter.

A month later there was a thaw, and I got caught in it. The thongs in the snowshoes softened and stretched, and in places where the shade of hills or trees preserved the temperature the snow packed and froze on the thongs until it was severe work to lift a foot. Frequent recourse to the stream removed the snow, but it was only a temporary relief, and progress was slow and painful. The crust had softened, and without snowshoes a man would sink down at least twenty inches, which was knee-deep for me, and in snow packed by laying all winter this made travel impossible without snowshoes, while with them a thaw like this clogged them so that they were of little use. It was evident that I must make a camp for the night before the regular camping place could be reached, and before nightfall I had a shelter constructed against a huge log by means of poles and brush, and a bed of balsam boughs kept my blankets from the snow. I was out three nights on this trip, and was lame and sore on reaching the cabin. The stream was so high and rapid that it would have involved some extra miles of travel to find a crossing place if Antoine had not felled a great oak across the swollen brook at the point where he knew I would reach it.

Antoine had a severe toothache. It had troubled him a little for some weeks, but now it was raging. Tobacco had no effect upon it, and he suffered in silence except when an extra twinge forced a *sacre* or a big D from him. He ate little, but sat by the fire and thought. Pipe after pipe was filled and emptied, and still he thought. My sore muscles kept me still until it was about time to turn in, and as I moved Antoine looked up and said: "I'll tole you. You gat pull dis toot'. I can't stan' heem no mo'; you mus' pull a-heem. W'at you say, hey? I'll t'ink I'll wait till you come back; but he hurt lak da dev'."

Here was a strange job indeed. In the course of my short experience I could remember going down the Greenbush bank to Dr. Getty and seeing him wrap a handkerchief around what he called a "turnkey," and then I nearly fainted when he told me to open my mouth while he applied that villainous thing, which was like a "cant hook," which lumbermen use to roll logs, or like a stump puller, and twisted a molar out of my jaw by turning such a handle as a corkscrew has. Later, Dr. Fris--bee had used the more modern forceps on one of my incisors, and these recollections were vivid, as they called up the sensation of nerves pulled until they snapped like a harp string. I ran these things over rapidly and said:

"Antoine, I haven't got a tool to pull a tooth with, and wouldn't know how to pull it if I had. I've seen the loose teeth of children pulled with a thread, but that tooth of yours is solid in your jaw. I can't do it; no use talking about it."

"I'll gat da t'ing all plan," said he, "I'll tole you. 'Fore you come I'll run up all da lead in bullet for you' big gun an' mine. Dan we gat no use for da mole. You'll tak da mole an' pull da toot', hey?"

"Antoine, I can't pull that tooth with a bullet mould; it isn't the right shape, and it won't hold. I'll only torture you, and you'd better wait until we get back to civilization. The tooth may be better in a few days. Try and bear it; we'll be home in a few weeks, and then if it troubles you there will be a chance to have it pulled by some dentist; I can't do it, and that is all there is about it."

"Now look-a here. See how I'll fix da mole for pull-a toot'." And he showed me how he had ruined a good bullet mould to make a poor pair of forceps. He had taken one of the files which we brought to sharpen our axes, and had filed off the outsides of the mould into the cavity until the thing resembled a blacksmith's pincers. Then he had roughened the tips to make a grip for them, and had actually hollowed the edges to fit his tooth. I looked the thing over with conflicting emotions. Here was an instrument of torture which in expert hands might relieve suffering, but in mine seemed sure to increase it. One thing was certain, Antoine was in earnest; he was desperate; no suicide was ever more so. He watched my face, and after a while said: "W'at you say, hey?"

"I say that I want to help you out of your agony, but I don't believe I can do it."

"You 'fraid you hurt me, hey?"

"Yes, Antoine, that's just it; I'm afraid I will hurt you, and not do you any good."

"I'll tole you, he mak' no dif'. I'll gat all da hurt. W'at for you 'fraid? You no getta hurt; come on, I'll tak' da chance; you tole how you want me for set down so you pull da bes'."

Putting fresh logs on the fire, and bringing in some brush to make a bright light, for the old man would not wait until morning, I looked at the offending tooth. For the benefit of my dentist friends, who have given me the most exquisite form of torture applied to man in modern days, I will say that the offending tooth was a pre-molar on the right side of the lower jaw.

Antoine laid himself on the floor, and I sat with my

back to the logs of the cabin. If they did not give way I was all right. I pulled him up to me, put a wooden plug between his molars to keep his mouth open, planted both feet on his shoulders, put the improvised forceps on the tooth and pulled. There was a howl as I pulled with arms and pushed with legs, but the "pullicans" slipped from my hands. They were all right as far as a grip on the tooth went, but they were not made for a strong pull on their handles.

Let us pass over, in a spirit of charity, any remarks that Antoine made. No doubt the recording angel blotted them from the book, as he did the one made by "my Uncle Toby," and I have no desire to go behind the record further than to say that Antoine really did say something when his tooth was started from its socket, but still throbbed with violence.

Antoine arose and looked at me, "more in sorrow than in anger," and I hastened to say: "The mould slipped in my hand; there is no grip on the handles, but if you can stand another go of this I will fix the thing so that the tooth or the bullet mould will break, or I will bring out the tooth or your jawbone. What you say, hey?"

Antoine merely nodded assent, and I put the handles of the bullet mould in the fire and then turned them outward so that they could not slip through my hands. Something must come now if Antoine had not had enough. I was not sure that I could have stood another such a trial if our positions had been reversed, but it is easy to stand it when the other fellow does the suffering. When the handles were cool and all was ready I looked at Antoine, who had resumed his seat by the fire with his jaw in his hand. He arose and said:

"W'en you ready I'll come one odder tam. Mebbe

you'll t'ink da ole Frenchman got no game an' he no stan' da gaff.* Come on; I'll be all a-ready." And he lay on the floor in the proper place. His nerve gave me confidence, and again I put the plug in his mouth, braced my back against the logs and my moccasins on his shoulders. Carefully pushing the "pullicans" down as far as I could get them, I gripped the handles, straightened my legs, and with a snap the tooth came out and my head made a tunk on the log behind that seemed hard enough to have left a dent in either head or log. Antoine jumped up and yelled with joy. He took the tooth and threw it in the fire, saying a verse in his French patois which I did not understand, and after a comforting pipe we went to bed.

Spring came. The melting snows filled the streams. The drumming call of the woodpeckers on a dead tree sounded frequently, and the thunder of the cock partridge or ruffed grouse was frequent. Ducks flew up and down the stream, and the snow in places was not a foot deep. Antoine said: "I'll tole you. W'en you go on you' line it's las' time to-morrer, an' you bring in all-a steel trap an' let down all-a dead-fall. Da fur he get loose an' begin to shed, an' it's no use to stay here longer w'en you no get da prime skin. We go home. I t'ink; yes?"

I ran my line for the last time, and came in and packed up for the home trip. Our packs were arranged, and were not as heavy as on the up trip. The provisions were about gone, and the furs were dry and light, so we only had to make two trips instead of four from our cabin to the boat.

---

*The expression "stand the gaff" was a relic of Antoine's cock-fighting days in Canada, and when he wished to imply that a man had no grit he would say, "He no stan' da gaff."

Our provisions and cooking utensils with one rifle were taken on the first trip, and the furs on the second. The otter skins had been stretched on long "shakes" split by Antoine's axe; the other skins, except those of the two wolverines, the deer and bear skins, were "cased" and had been stretched on forked twigs, and therefore the flat hides made a large, broad pack, which was more difficult to get through the forest than the more valuable furs, which were cased. Just here it has occurred to me that there are technical terms used in the above that a small boy in the back seats might not understand, and for his benefit I will say that a "flat hide" is one that is split on the belly as a butcher skins an animal. Fine furs are "cased," *i. c.*, only cut on the hinder edge of the hindlegs, and the skin drawn off over the head, leaving it like a mitten without a thumb and wrong side out—that is, with the fur inside.

There was a feeling of regret at leaving the cabin, even though it was for home. It had been a home to us, and Antoine fastened up the door, saying: "S'pose we'll come nex' wint'. Who knows? W'en we come we gotta da good ole shanty. Come on." And we turned our backs to our winter home. We stopped a day at the boat to soak it up and swell the seams, and stowed our furs and provisions under the two tarpaulins, and cast loose. The Bad Ax was swollen, and the current was swift. There was no expenditure of muscle in rowing, but there was an anxiety lest pole or paddle should fail and wreck us on a bend or a riffle. Some of the latter, which we had to make a portage round in the fall, we could shoot now, with more or less risk. When we reached the Wisconsin River we camped, and felt that all danger was over. It was plain sailing after this. We killed five mallards with our rifles, and that gave us plenty of fresh duck, and we caught a large pike by trolling a minnow. Next day we merely guided our boat down the river and into the Mississippi, and after one more night out the Father of Waters brought us to Dubuque, some eighteen miles below Potosi, where Antoine had a bachelor's cabin and I had dearer ties.

When we tied up at the wharf at Dubuque and went ashore we met Frank Neaville, and learned that all our loved ones were well. Frank went home that night, and carried the news of our arrival. There were serveral fur buyers about Dubuque, and they came to see us. I was for selling to the first one, but Antoine would not have it. The buyers came down, and handled our furs and bid on them, and finally they were sold for cash one morning. There was a steamer to go up in the afternoon which would run up the Grant River to Potosi. I would go on that, but Antoine had struck some Canuck friends and had got drunk, and I did not want to leave him with the chance of his being robbed by those thieves which then infested the river towns, and I went in search of him. I got him on board the boat with one of his friends and gave the steward a good tip to entertain them, and before Antoine knew where he was he found himself ashore at La Fayette, the landing for Potosi, with the major portion of his winter's earnings in his pocket.

Once during the next summer Antoine came to me, and made me a proposition to go down in Louisiana and trap next winter. He said that fur was plenty there, and in the spring we would take our skins to St. Paul and sell them to some green fur buyers, who would think they were Northern furs. I did not do it, but will tell you where I went the next winter later on.

My good friend, Hon. J. W. Seaton, of Potosi, Wis., whom I knew in the days of which I am writing, sends me this note in response to a question: "I can give you but little information about Antoine Gardapee, the French trapper you went North with the winter you write about. I remember you both very well, and the fact of your going up on the Bad Ax the year before Tom Davies, and you went with the surveying party when Henry Neaville froze his feet; but I can't recall what became of Gardapee further than this: He ran a private ferry on the Mississippi River from Cassville, Wis., to the mouth of Turkey River, Ia., some years after you left Potosi. The generation in which he lived has passed away—the trapper, hunter and Indian have gone to the happy hunting grounds, and have left scarce a trace behind them; their names, places, kindred and friends are alike forgotten, and the pall of oblivion hangs over their resting-place."

There seems to be nothing to be added .to the very good obituary note of Judge Seaton.

SERGEANT FRANK NEAVILLE.

FISH, 'COONS AND PAWPAWS.

THE snow had left the south side of the hills, and there were evidences of spring overhead and underfoot when I parted with Antoine, he to visit some friends up the river and I to settle down in Potosi to civilized life. To get shaved again, to sleep in a bed and renew acquaintance with a potato after a winter in the woods, was an agreeable change. Few men who have once lived the life of a hunter and trapper ever care more for civilization than to keep on its outside edge, and they move on as it drives them to seek new fields. I imagine such men find it dull in summer, for they are seldom reading men, and when fur is not in season their lives must be monotonous. I soon dropped into my old way of life in the quaint little mining village of Potosi.

"Goin' a-fishin?" asked Frank Neaville, as he saw me selecting some fishing tackle in one of the stores. "Henry has a new boat, and he's goin' to take it down to the landing soon; maybe you can get him to go to-morrow; you know he's always ready for a fish or a hunt, no matter what's goin' on."

We walked down to the hotel kept by the father of these boys, and found Henry in the backyard putting a painter into a ring in the bow of a new boat and making a neat eye-splice in it, for Henry could do many such things when he chose. "Hello, Henry!" said I, "you've got a nice sharpie there, but in our talks since I came down from the Bad Ax you haven't mentioned it."

"What's that name you called the boat?"

"A sharpie. What do you call it?"

"I call it a skiff, and it is a skiff; sharpie is some of your New York language, I suppose; did you ever hear of a skiff?"

"Yes, and they are two different boats in the New York language, but we won't fight about that. I want to go fishing to-morrow, and if you want to try the new shar—skiff, I mean, just fill her full of water to swell the seams and get her on the wagon in the morning; that's all."

Frank called attention to the fact that there was room for three, and intimated that he would go if his company was earnestly desired.

"Frank," replied his brother, "you know that you're the durn'dest fool in a boat that lives in Wisconsin. Last year you upset us when we were coming down Swift Sloo by grabbing a branch to look after some wounded bird, and we had to stop all night on the island and be eaten by mosquitoes because Fred's rifle was in the bottom of the sloo. We don't want any more of that funny business, and you had better stay home." Then turning to me, Henry explained: "Frank's all right to weigh out sugar and coffee in a grocery, and he can figure up how many papers of tacks would balance a pound of nails; but you had a sample of him last year; he hasn't got good, sound sense, like a mule, for a mule can take care of himself any time, and wouldn't dump us all in the drink to look at a pelican. If you can stand him, all right; I won't object."

Then it was Frank's innings. He was the younger but larger of the two, and he replied: "Henry is the bright boy of the family, and very few families have more than one bright boy, if they're so fortunate as to have even one. He is the oldest, and there are several little fellows growing up, and if I'm not as brilliant as Henry I can't help it; but I hope some of the little fellows may come near his high standard. I don't want to go if I'm not wanted." And he turned off, and went into the house.

This was the first time that I had seen Frank resent Henry's good-natured chaff, and I hurried after him and brought him back. Said I: "Henry, I want Frank to go with us, and, confound you, you want him to go, but your temptation to roast him over that upset is fun for you; but Frank doesn't like it. As a student of Shakespeare, you will remember that somewhere he says that a joke requires a good listener, or something of the kind, to make it go. Frank thinks you are bearing too hard on him for his mistake, and it's time to let up."

Henry laughed and said: "Frank never knows a joke when he hears it; he wouldn't know one if he found it in his soup. What Shakespeare said was: 'A jest's prosperity lies in the ear of him who hears it, never in the tongue of him that makes it,' but if Frank wants to go fishing with us, all right; I've no objection, and in fact would like to have him go; but since the time when we slept out on the island I have gone fishing a dozen times, and he has never asked to go. I think he likes your company. Come along, Frank; I only wanted to knock a little fun out of you, and you go off mad." Frank winked at me; he was not angry the least bit, but this was his joke on his brother.

In the morning we walked behind the wagon which carried the boat to the river, for it had a load of lead. I took my rifle along, because I wanted some meat, either of duck or hog, or both. As related in my sketch of Henry, there were hogs on the islands, and I had bought an interest in them. I also had several cane "poles," as we called them, and loaned one to each of the boys. I was inclined to be a "dude" sportsman in that early day, if we interpret that abused term to mean a man who likes to own the best things that he can get, and who will pay a quarter of a dollar for a light natural cane in preference to using a heavy sapling cut in the woods to be thrown away after using. In fact, I would to-day, if not then, rather be a "Sunberry Fisher" than his opposite. In these days of game hogs and of men who fish for count and brag, I say with due deliberation and with full knowledge of the ridicule to which a man with fine fishing tackle is subjected if he is unsuccessful in a day's fishing, that I would rather be in his place and own tackle to be proud of than to be the proverbial boy with an alder pole, a "letter in the post-office," and a big string of trout; but the fact is that a good angler with good tackle can beat the boy, if he knows the stream well.

With the man who loves fishing for itself and not for the fish, the capture of a record-breaking string is of no consequence. The old story of the "funny man" catches the popular fancy. To-day when I fish for trout I use a rod which cost $35, and it is worth every cent of it. My reel, line and book of flies cost as much more, and on a trout stream there is no bare-footed farmer's boy with his alder pole and worm who can, day after day, take more trout than I or thousands of other anglers can. He might on an odd day, where he knew all the trout holes— but not as a rule. And if he did? Still I say: I would prefer to be the Sunberry Fisher who "caught nothing at all," for why do we prefer a gold watch to a silver one? It may keep no better time. We like elegant harness on our horses, but they pull the carriage no better than if tied to it with bits of rope. Now you young anglers can see just what I mean. There is pleasure to the sportsman in cleaning and caring for his rod and gun; he has a feeling of companionship for it—he gets to love it for the memories it brings, and to throw it aside after a fishing or shooting trip would be base ingratitude. There is a high and noble affection for old companions in the forest and on the stream, and the man who truly loves the sport for sport's sake, and not for the amount of meat he gets, cherishes the implements which aided him. Even a savage will ornament his pipe and his war club—but my pen is straying again, and has led me off from the story of this particular fishing trip. Let it go; the editor will probably "blue pencil" all the extraneous matter, and so we get back to the mouth of Grant River, Wis., in the spring of 1856, with the Neaville boys.

Henry watched the boat after it was launched and seemed satisfied with its balance in the water, and we rowed off to one of the islands which are so numerous along the great Mississippi at this point. When we pulled up on the island Henry asked: "Where do you want to fish? Here you can get swift water or still water, just as you want it." A bend where water plants were just struggling to get to the top of the water caught my eye, and it looked like a good spot for pike, so I replied: "I've got some small minnow hooks, and if we stop right here and get about fifty small fish, we may get some good pike over in that bend among the weeds." The result was similar to that recorded in the sketch entitled, "The Brockway Boys." Skittering for pike or pickerel was a new thing, and all new methods are distrusted. The old woman who saw a patent machine for milking cows looked at it and declared, "The old-fashioned way is the best;" and in this case she was right. Henry did not say a word against it, but, like

William Brockway, he thought there might be a thing or two that he had not learned, but Frank said:

"When you put one of these little fish on your hook, and let it down in the water where the big fish live, you may get one; but to 'skitter' a little fish over the surface and scare all the big ones below looks like foolishness, but if you say it's a good plan we'll try it. Mother will expect some fish for breakfast, and I want to go over in a tree top and get some crappies. I don't want to go back without a thing."

Henry had listened to all this, and after some deliberation said: "Let's land Frank in a tree top, and then go over and try for the pike. Mother can't have any of our fish for breakfast to-morrow, because we've got provisions for two days, and we propose to stay and eat 'em up, if Frank doesn't see another wounded pelican and upset the boat. Yes, Frank, you get in that tree top and fish for crappies, and we'll stop and get you day after to-morrow. We'll leave you grub enough, and there's a good big limb to straddle, so you'll be comfortable until we come back. The mosquitoes are not out yet, and you'll be very happy. If the limb gets to be uncomfortable, you can change and sit on it side-saddle fashion."

Frank looked at me and asked: "Are you going to stay out to-night and not go home until Saturday morning?"

"That was our arrangement, and I thought you understood it; when the axe was put in the wagon you asked what it was for, and Henry told you it was to cut wood for camp, and we would not need a fire if we were going home to-night; I'm sorry if——"

"No, don't be sorry about me; I'll stay out as long as any of you if you'll only make Henry let up about that accident last summer. If he doesn't stop it I'll duck him again, when I can do it without wetting you. Every man, woman and child in Potosi knows about that upset of the boat, and that's enough. I don't care about it since I said I was sorry, but all winter, while you were away, he would grin as he passed me and quote from Byron:

'Then rose from sea to sky the wild farewell—
  Then shriek'd the timid, and stood still the brave;
Then some leap'd overboard with fearful yell,
  As eager to anticipate their grave.'

"He used to spout that in school, and he thought it would annoy me, but it didn't—well, not as much as he thought it did."

Frank was more sensitive to Henry's exasperating nagging than he would own. It was not so much Henry's quotation from "Don Juan" as the "grin" which accompanied it, and by constant repetition Frank had become sensitive, as "the touched needle trembles at the pole," and this sort of thing is not conducive to congenial fishing. I told Frank that Henry would find some other outlet for his humor. When Henry came back with some minnows, after we had landed, I took him one side, and Frank's peace of mind about the upset was undisturbed afterward.

We caught some minnows and skittered for pike, or "pickerel," as we called them in New York, and took six or seven that day—fish that would weigh from three to six pounds. We had no reels—we weren't up to that in those days—but we had a ring on the top of the rod, and gave line or hauled in through it. Once Frank struck a big one. He yelled: "Come and help me! He'll get away! The line is cutting my hand," etc., and

I took his coat-tail in my palm and checked the fish. When it was safe in the boat Frank drew a long breath and said: "Well, I'll be durned if that fish won't weigh twenty pounds. If you hadn't helped me he would have broken something, or I would have been pulled overboard. Yes, by jing! He'll weigh twenty-five pounds."

My own estimate was that the pike might weigh about ten pounds, but what was the use of putting a damper on the boy's enthusiasm? My new mode of skittering a minnow on the surface had won; his skepticism had vanished, and it was a triumph for both. We went ashore, rolled a log down to the water, and dug out a basin behind it, where our fish could be kept alive, their splashings in the water serving to circulate it through the small openings at each end of the log; for we didn't want to kill our game until we started for home.

The day was a fine one, and the fishing was fair for those days; it would be called excellent, grand, to-day, and considering the high state of the river we did well. The bend where we fished was comparatively still water, just the place for pike, which prefer quiet nooks and ponds and avoid the quick waters. The geese had passed north, and so had the great bodies of swans and pelicans; but to our surprise a small flock of sandhill cranes went over us, high in the air and glistening in the sun. Most likely the last flock of the season. Frank called attention to them and wondered what they were.

"Sandhill cranes," said Henry.

Frank grinned and replied: "I never saw such a fellow to know everything as Henry is. That flock of birds are too high up to see their shape, and he'll tell you just what they are. He thinks he can play anything on me. What do you think they are?"

"Just as Henry named them. Henry is more of a

hunter, naturalist, or whatever you are a mind to call him," said I. "He notices things which you don't see. Watch the flight of that flock. See! They all flap their wings in unison, and then all stop at once and sail, seeming to follow the 'stroke oar.' Did you ever see any other birds do that?"

"I never noticed them. It is queer, though, how they all work together that way. Don't geese fly like that?"

"Oh, no; a goose is a heavy-bodied bird that couldn't sail a minute up there; it's hard work for a goose from the time it starts until it stops. If you watch the flight of different kinds of ducks and the way they flock you will soon be able to tell what they are. There goes a dozen mallards; see how differently they fly from the bluebills coming up behind them. I can't tell you the difference, but you can see it."

"Well, by jing! That's so. I thought all ducks flew alike. I can tell ducks from crows by the way they fly, but never noticed them as close as that. Henry, old boy, you know a heap more than people think you do; they haven't found you out yet."

Henry made no reply to this, but suggested that it was time to go ashore and make camp. It was quite a job to find a camping spot on the island. It had been well soaked in the spring freshets, and the lower leaves of the underbrush were covered with dried sediment, where they had been submerged. Henry knew these islands well, and led us to a knoll near a pond which was dry in summer, but was filled now, and afforded a good feeding place for ducks. We had hauled the boat well up, and tied it fast in case the river should rise in the night. We made a little bough house and a bed of dry leaves, made a pot of coffee and ate supper before dark.

As I remember the geography after an absence of

forty years, it is some five or six miles from shore to shore near Potosi, the main channel of the river being on the Iowa side. On the Wisconsin shore the Grant River came in, and there was a lot of wooded islands along there with channels of all degrees of swiftness between them. In the days of which I write the ducks congregated here in great numbers in spring and fall. We were well out, and preferred to stay on the island than to row over to the mainland. After supper I told Henry that I had never slept on any of these islands in duck time, and if he did not object we would not light our night fire until after dark, so that we could see the ducks come in. It was about half an hour before sundown, and some of the flocks began to arrive, and such a babel! The heavy mallards would come in, back wind with their wings and drop down with a splash, and then the loud-voiced females would raise a din. Swift bluebills and butterballs would rush over our heads, circle around and settle down. The swiftest of all ducks, the little green-winged teal, would suddenly appear from nowhere, and splash down into the water without circling about, coming into it much as a stone would. The high-voiced widgeon, the bass of the frogs, the heavy quack of the mallard and the lighter one of the bluewing, which sounded like an echo, and the curious *burr!* of the bluebill made a concert to be remembered. The pond might have covered three acres, and two thousand ducks, at least, rested on it that night. We did not try to shoot any, for we thought we could get what we wanted any time. After dark we lighted our fire, but it did not seem to disturb the ducks. Our talk was not heard in the racket they kept up, and we turned in on our bed of leaves. Frank said that several birds or flocks flew around our fire in the night, but Henry and I slept too soundly to hear them. Such life was new to Frank, and he didn't sleep much.

A rifle shot awoke me in the morning, and there was a thundering sound of rising ducks. Henry had killed a mallard, and then the problem was to get the bird. The shore was soft black mud, deep and treacherous, and although the duck was not over thirty feet away, and stone dead, it was no easy matter to get it. Frank and I advised him not to attempt it, but he vowed he'd have that duck "if it took a leg." He began to gather driftwood, brush and limbs and threw them in to make a bridge, and as he was in earnest we helped him. When he thought his bridge was long enough, so that from its end he could reach the duck with a pole, he started. I whispered to Frank a caution not to speak to him, and we watched. The passage was a success; he reached his pole for the duck, something rolled, and he was floundering in the mud. There was only a couple of inches of water where he was, and as he struggled he sank to his waist. We could not tell how much further he might sink if he struggled.

I called to him: "Don't move or you may go deeper; keep perfectly still, and we'll get you out. Is there a grapevine on this island?"

"Not a vine," said he, cool as a cucumber. "Take your time; I won't stir."

He was over twenty feet from sound footing, and we cut a sapling and shoved the end to him and pulled until he could hold on no longer. He let go so suddenly that we sat down. He had bent forward so that the mud covered his breast. Frank began to fear for his brother, but I had another plan. I cut a green cottonwood, or perhaps it was an aspen, which had a fork at about twenty-five feet, and these two limbs were of an inch or more in diameter. These limbs I crossed and twisted, making a loop big enough to go over Henry's shoulders, and lashed them firmly together with strips of bark at several points. With this around him and the grip of his hands, together with the use of his legs, we pulled him to solid ground, the mud being plowed up by his shirt collar so that his clothing was filled inside and out. I remained to get breakfast, while Frank went with Henry over to the cleaner waters of the sloo, where he washed himself and his clothes, while Frank returned for breakfast for himself and brother. When we reached him his garments were all hung in the sun, but he was shivering, for the morning was cool. Frank gave him his trousers and sat in his drawers, and I loaned a coat.

After he had some hot coffee and breakfast he said: "The hogs gobbled all our fish last night, Frank's big pike and all," and we found it to be so. Hogs' tracks were numerous in and about our pool, and portions of fish were scattered about. Frank said: "Well, I'll be durned! That pike would weigh about forty pounds, and was bigger than one Bill Patterson shot up in Grant River last fall."

"Yes," said Henry, "Bill's fish weighed eleven and a half pounds on Mallet's scales; I saw it weighed, and if yours weighed forty pounds there was a little difference of twenty-eight and a half pounds; not much, to be sure, but still a difference."

"Don't you think my fish was as big as Bill's?"

"Not quite," said Henry. "I think your pike would weigh nearly as much as his if you fed him half a dozen pounds of shot when no one was looking."

Frank appealed to me. I replied: "I am not as good a judge of the weights of fish as Henry is, and I didn't see Bill Patterson's pike. I am of the opinion, however, that if your fish was bigger than Bill's the scales would show that it weighed more, but as the hogs have eaten it there is nothing left but the memory of it, and you know that we can't weigh memory. Still I remember thinking at the time that your fish would go full twenty pounds if he had been left to grow for a few years."

"I see," said Frank; "if Henry was as wise as Daniel Webster he would know just as much. All right! We are three great sportsmen, and have fished one day and shot a duck the next morning, and have only our memories to show for it. Not a scale nor a feather; 'though I's'pose Henry will count the duck he shot and the duck he had in the mud as two ducks, and both were lost. No; I'll be durned if we don't take home that mallard, for Henry said he'd get it or lose a leg. How's that, Henry; which leg will we take off if you don't get that duck?"

Henry was busy getting into his half-dried clothes and said: "Frank, you may have that duck."

We fished that day, and shot ducks with my rifle in the evening, slept out next night, and took home in the morning eight mallards and all the pike and crappies we could carry.

I regret that we cannot print portraits of these boys. I have daguerreotypes of them, taken in 1860, sent me by their younger brother, Carlos E. Neaville, now living at Brodhead, Wis. The photo-engraver says that they cannot be reproduced with any effect because of the lack of shadows. Henry was about five feet six inches, broad-shouldered; a long, oval face, with a profuse head of dark hair, which came down to a point in the middle of his forehead. Frank, the younger, was larger. His forehead was broader and his ears were lower. What I mean by this is that my frequent comment on the picture of a man is: "There is much (or little) of his head above his ears." Just what ethnological value this has let others say. Frank did show evidences of the mercantile instinct, for Judge Seaton, now living in Potosi, speaks highly of him as an employee of his during the few years that he was a merchant. But Henry, he was the companionable fellow; no business for him if he could help it. He and I were alike in this respect. The woods and the streams were good enough for us, and the habits of their denizens were of more importance than dollars. What poet has ever written in praise of the slave to lucre? There I go again—off the track. A dollar is a big thing when you don't own one. The boy said: "Salt makes your potatoes taste bad when you don't put any on."

Once a drunken miner lost his purse in the streets of Potosi, and Frank found it. Henry, John Nicholas, Frank and I were talking about it with the old postmaster, Mr. Kaltenbach, when the miner came up asking if anyone had found his money. "Yes," said Henry; "we found it. How much was there in it?" The man called Henry a thief and struck him. About the same instant Frank handed the miner one under the left jaw that paralyzed him. We took the man into Jo. Hall's livery stable, and it took Dr. Gibson over an hour to bring him around. Henry scared Frank into thinking he had killed a man, and Frank went over to Constable Darcy and gave himself up.

As the summer waned and the first chill days of September approached Frank asked me: "Did you ever eat a pawpaw?"

"No; what is a pawpaw?"

"They are a fine fruit, and grow on a small tree. They are shaped like a cucumber and are like custard. There is a pawpaw grove down by the river. They'll be ripe now in a few days, and we'll make up a party and go 'coon hunting. 'Coons like 'em, and you can always start one in the pawpaws when they're ripe."

I had seen the trees when out after wild plums, which were plenty in that part of Wisconsin, and were large and excellent, but the pawpaws were merely wondered at and passed. I think there was a dozen in our party when we started for 'coons on a moonlight night. Except Frank and Henry, Charley Guyon, John Clark and Bill Patterson, the names are forgotten. Half a dozen dogs, some of no particular breed and others that seemed to be of all breeds mixed without regard to proportion, went along as a necessary part of the outfit.

I tasted my first pawpaw, but have yet to taste the second one. The others ate them with a relish. All I remember is that the fruit was shaped something like a banana, but shorter, and had the taste of a raw potato ground into a paste; its seeds were as large as a lima bean. Of course I might learn to like them, but Potosi boys acquired the taste in infancy.

Soon the dogs remarked that a 'coon had gone off, because it did not care to eat pawpaws while such a noisy crowd invaded the woods; for in hunting 'coons the more noise the better, as it puts them afoot, while if you are still they will squat on a limb at your approach. The 'coon soon treed, and hid so that it could not be shot. John Clark's axe on one side and Henry Neaville's on the other soon dropped the tree, and the dogs made a rush. We had a fire started to light up the conflict, but couldn't see a thing in that tree top but a mass of fighting dogs. Cheers and yells from the men encouraged the dogs. "Go in, Tige!" "Shake him up, Skip!" "Hang to him, Buster!" and such cries cheered on the dogs.

"There's two of 'em!" yelled John Clark, as two knots of dogs were seen, but it turned out that one knot was merely a little scrapping of a couple of dogs among themselves, perhaps occasioned by one dog's jealousy of the other fellow. The 'coon broke away and ran up a limb, and a rifle ball dropped him. And then such a row! Every dog had hold of him, and a man had hold of every dog's tail, and each dog got a kick in the ribs to admonish him that a fallen foe should be respected. I thought of the old story: "Never strike a man when he is down," said Mulcahy. "Never," replied O'Hooligan; "just sock the boots to him."

The 'coon was not badly mangled after all this; the dogs were chewed up much worse. It reminded me of Corny Lannigan, one of my father's ship carpenters, when father said to him one morning: "Cornelius, you must have had some trouble last night; your eyes are blacked, and your nose is all plastered over."

"Yes, Captain," said Corny; "there was a little misunderstanding, but you ought to go up to the hospital and see the other fellow;" and I then remembered reading that the great General, Pyrrhus, once said: "Another such a victory and I am ruined."

Another 'coon was started, and was finally found in a tree by the water, whose base had been so washed that it leaned out over Grant River. After lighting a fire and consulting as to the mode of attack, Frank offered to go up the leaning tree and shake the 'coon off, while the dogs were to be held so as to see him drop, and then be loosed to tackle him in the water. The plan worked well. The 'coon dropped at the first shake, and so did Frank. The dogs rushed in, but no man dared shoot, and after a short fight in the water and on the other shore the dogs came back, and we went home.

"I tell you," said John Clark, "it takes an almighty good dog to whip an old he 'coon, and not one in a thousand can do it. Sometimes a little she 'coon will give a dozen such ornery dogs as we've got a good tussle and get away."

"Look a-here, John Clark," said Charley Guyon to his brother-in-law; "do you call my dog ornery?" And so we talked on the way home.

"Ornery" is Wisconsinese for "ordinary," but has no such meaning. It implies baseness; it is a term of reproach. An "ornery cuss" means a low-down fellow, and an "ornery dog" is one of no possible account. If a man in New York should describe me as an ordinary man, he would hit it right; an every-day sort of man, not distinguished for anything in particular; but if a Wisconsin man stigmatizes you as "ornery" he means another thing, and if he is not a corn-fed fellow you should "let go your left and follow it up with your right."

I have already told how Frank and Henry went out with the Second Wisconsin Infantry, and both were killed in Virginia.

> "Sound, sound the clarion, fill the fife!
>   To all the sensual world proclaim,
> One crowded hour of glorious life
>   Is worth an age without a name."

TAY-BUN-ANE-JE-GAY.

WE named him—Henry Neaville and I. We had to call him something to distinguish him from other Indians who begged about our camp, and we did not think the name he gave as his own, Ah-mik-wash, "a beaver house," described him as well as the one we concocted, which means: "He-who-takes-so-much-at-a-mouthful." Ours was a perfect fit, and before long I'll tell you how he got it.

Mr. James McBride, then living in Potosi, Wis., but who lived in Washington, D. C., for the past thirty years, until his death, which occurred last March, had a contract to subdivide some townships in what is now Crow Wing county, Minn. The township lines had been run, each township being six miles square, and these were to be crossed by lines a mile apart into square miles, with the half miles marked on both north and east lines. The northern line was near where Brainerd now stands, the Mississippi River was the west boundary, and the survey took in the village of Crow Wing, which was then an Indian trading post.

The party included Thomas Davies, now living at British Hollow, Wis.; Pierre Gibbs, of Dubuque, Ia.; —— Crosby, I think originally from Boston; Henry R. Neaville, and the writer, both of Potosi. We started by steamboat from Dubuque, in September, 1856—I forget the day, but Tom Davies thinks it was the 12th—with two horses, wagon, pack saddles, tent and camp equipage and a supply of provisions that surprised me: Half a dozen barrels of flour, three barrels of pork, a ten-gallon keg of molasses, one-gallon keg of vinegar, sugar, beans, rice, grain for the horses, and all in profusion. At St. Paul half the provisions were stored, and we took a wagon load, all but the driver walking up the big military road that led to Fort Ripley, about one hundred miles north of St. Paul. Our first night out we camped on Rum River, and Henry Neaville tasted it and said: "Hum! it's nothing but water." From Fort Ripley to Crow Wing the road was not so good. Making a base of supplies at the trading post, we struck into the woods, and afterward Tom Davies drove back to St. Paul for the food left there. We took camp and grub on our backs. At the place to begin work I made camp, and Neaville went back for more supplies. There was about four inches of snow, and this lay without thaw or addition until we left the woods late in December.

I had expected to furnish game for camp, and took my rifle, naturally thinking that this far-off region abounded in game as the Bad Ax country did, where I spent the previous winter. I lugged that rifle for two months, and only killed four ruffed grouse. I saw one deer and two rabbits, but did not get a shot at them. The country was destitute of game. Indians swarmed all over it. At Crow Wing the great trail from Lake Superior crossed the one coming down from the Red River of the North, and the trading post was visited by scores of Indians every day from each of the four branches of the trails.

It was on the second day out. Henry had returned quickly, as we were not yet far from our base, and I was baking bread and getting dinner for two, as the linemen had theirs with them, and would not return until night, when in walked the American whose name heads this chapter. As before stated, that was not his name then, but he didn't know it. He squatted by the fire and grunted: *"Bon jour,* Nidgee," a salutation of mixed French and Ojibway that all those Indians used. Henry returned his salute, and said to him in Ojibway that he was welcome.

"Where did you learn to speak that?" I asked.

"Off up the Wisconsin River with a logging party one winter. Why?"

"Nothing, only I was surprised, that's all. If I'd known you spoke it we could have knocked lots of fun out of your brother Frank on our fishing trips. But you have made this man welcome, and that he will interpret to mean free feeding, perhaps all winter, and as I am camp keeper, McBride will ask questions if we feed too many. He doesn't like an Indian, and told me not to have them hanging around camp, so don't do this any more."

"All right," said Henry; "I spoke without thinking. If there's lots of pork boiled let's fill this fellow up and see how much he can hold."

I told him that I had boiled enough pork for all hands to have cold to-night, but if his guest ate half of it I would boil more.

I made all ready, and our aboriginal American announced himself as Ah-mik-wash, or "Beaver House." Henry remarked: "He differs somewhat from a beaver house, and as to the last part of his name I'll bet he hasn't washed in ten years."

"Henry, keep quiet!" Then tapping my breast I said: "Kego-e-kay," and then touching Henry, introduced him as Ke-tim-ish-ke (He-is-lazy). Old Beaver House grunted, and I served an equal portion of bread, baked beans and pork to each. There was enough for

Henry and me at the first serving, and long before we had finished I piled another big chunk on the plate of our guest.

"Henry," said I, "your friend's doctor has recommended him to take something for his appetite, and he's struck the place to get the prescription put up. Just see what he takes at a mouthful, and how he swallows it without sticking a tooth in it! I'll limit him to the pork and bread, for I'll be dingswizzled if I'll boil and bake any more beans!"

Henry thought a minute—he was a meditative man and therefore a born angler—and said: "He is filling his beaver house for the winter, but he can swallow chunks of pork that would choke a deerhound. He must have a new name. These Injuns don't get a name early in life as we do, and when they get one it never sticks through as ours do, and we must name him anew. See that last chunk go down! Give him what there is left of the pork and put the rest away, and let's see him get away with what you had provided for six men to-night, in addition to what he has eaten."

I will publicly confess to being a sinner if that Ojibway, or "Chippewa," as his name has been corrupted, did not clean up every bit of the pork. There was no such discrimination between the component parts as was made by Jack Spratt and his wife. He removed the plate from his lap and said: "Koo-koosh, nish-ish-shin," or "Pork very good."

While our guest sat by the fire in full enjoyment of physical comfort Henry and I concocted the new name for him, and this is the way we christened him. I said, leaving out as much of his tongue as possible: "You no Beaver House no more, you Tay-bun-ane-je-gay" (He-who-takes-so-much-at-a-mouthful). This name, which we evolved in a spirit of ridicule, was accepted by our simple-minded friend as a tribute to his prowess after he had scanned our faces and found no trace of levity, and he was so known, not only by us, but by his tribe.

He had caught Henry's name, and smiled as much as an Indian can smile, but seemed in doubt about mine. Perhaps my pronunciation was at fault, for "kego" means fish, and also is a negative, as "do not," "never," "beware of saying," etc. Henry said: "We have many words which mean the same thing, and so have they. Old Swallow-'em-slick is in doubt. Show him your fish lines and he will know that you are a fisherman."

When our guest had seen my tackle he pointed to me in pride at his understanding and touched my shoulder, saying: "Kego-e-kay." Then he proceeded to tell what great pike, "kinoje," could be caught in a small lake a short distance away, and we arranged to try it next day after the men had gone on the line.

The ice was not thick, but would bear us well, for it was about the last of September or the first of October in that cold country, and this reminds me that McBride wanted to know about the winters in that region and asked a half-breed who spoke English how the weather was likely to be. He replied: "October, he pooty cole; November he cole as de dev'; and December, he col'er 'an ——." I had heard the name mentioned as a comparison for heat frequently, and wondered what kind of a place the half-breed thought it might be. The snow had fallen since the lake froze, and we could not see the depth. I asked old Mouthful where there were springs and he showed us one, where we caught a lot of minnows.

We cut holes and rigged about a dozen lines with tip-ups and waited. The holes froze over, and we cut them open, but no fish came to our lures. It was noon, and not a pike, big or little, had sampled our minnows. We were like "Ye Sunberrye Fysher," our tackle was correct, but the fish were either absent or—something else. It was time to eat.

I asked Henry: "Do you think that old Mouthful, as you call him in shorthand, has brought us out here on a fool's errand? This lake should contain pike, lake trout, brook trout or perch, but we get no bites. The water is not very cold, or the ice would be thicker; the springs below keep the ice from getting too thick. Perhaps our friend is only playing it on us for his grub."

"If I was sure of that," said Henry, "I would advise that we leave him, and go back and eat ours at camp, or sit down here and eat, and only give a little bite, so that he could not take so much at a mouthful."

The luncheon was fairly divided. One of the tip-ups showed the flag, and Henry jumped and ran for it. The hook was bare; a minnow had been taken. Old Mouthful had probably divined our thoughts, for he arose and said: "Kego-e-kay-e-mah," there are fish there. We let our lines lower down, but got no fish. It was time to go back to camp to prepare for the hungry linemen. Our new friend went with us; it was evident that he was fond of our company—or our pork—it was not easy to tell which. He saw the men come in and eat their dinner, but got no invitation to join, for our chief did not wish to encourage Indians to hang round the camp. Two such men as He-who-takes-so-much-at-a-mouthful would breed a famine in our commissary in a short time. They would eat more than our six healthy white men, who had the abnormal appetite that comes with a life in the woods and active exercise in cold weather. The farmer's expression, "I'm as hungry as a hired man," fell short of our appetites.

We had a tin bake oven, made in flat sections for packing on a man's back, which, when set up before a camp-fire, flared out so as to reflect the heat from top and bottom on a bread pan, in which we not only baked bread, but beans, pork and 'coons. Imagine a yawning front of eighteen inches sloping to a back of five inches, in the middle of which was the pan, and you have the idea. Mixing soda and cream of tartar with the flour and then wetting it up—well! If you don't believe that I made the best bread that was ever baked on this planet just write to my *compagnon du voyage*, Thomas Davies. Mark the letter "private," because Tom has been married since that time, and he might not wish Mrs. Davies to see his reply; he is eating her biscuit now. Married men will appreciate this caution.

Four men went on the line—McBride, the chief or compass man; one axe man to clear a place for him to see through and to blaze the line, and two chain men. There was then an extra man to bring supplies from our base, and he was in camp with me a great deal. Henry Neaville did most of this work, because he was a very good woodsman, and could find me when I moved camp. Sometimes we stayed several days in a place, and lines would be run in all directions. In the morning I would get an order to "Keep camp here to-day," or to move it. If moved, it might be "two miles east and one mile north," and then before sundown I would clang the cow bell, which we sometimes used on the horses when hobbled. We used the horses to pack our camp at first while in the country of solid ground, but sent them to Crow Wing when we got into the swampy country, where the springy swamps were frozen enough to permit a man to travel safely without snowshoes, but would not hold the greater weight of a horse with its smaller foot.

It would have been almost impossible to run these lines before the swamps were frozen. I saw corner stakes set and "witness trees" marked, and when the man removed his hand from the top of the stake it fell. There were no stones to be found for markers; but the trees told the story, and the exact place of the stake could be found.

I can't say when it was that we met a train of Red River settlers on their way from Pembina—perhaps it was on our way up, but it was an event. We heard the creaking of their carts for at least ten miles before we met. There were eighteen carts in the train drawn by ponies, and not a bit of iron in the whole outfit! Not even a nail. The wheels had wooden tires held by wooden pins, and if one gave out there was the forest to furnish material. Some of the carts had a ham rind under the axle, but that was a foolish concession to the god of silence. The others shrieked and wailed like lost spirits, and miles before we met them we were wondering what could make such unearthly sounds. We halted and talked with the priest who was in charge of the expedition, and seemed to be the only man in the party who could speak English. The other men were French, Indians and half-breeds, and they spoke such a patois of mixed Ojibway and Canadian French that Crosby couldn't understand a word, and he spoke Boston French fluently. The priest was a jolly old fellow, a well-read man who, it seemed to me, was wasting his life among a very dirty lot; but if he was contented we should be. I listened to him talk of his mission work, and of his hope that there would be a weekly mail up from St. Paul into his frozen region before many years. His people had sold their furs; the Hudson Bay Company had a monopoly of the trade in British America, and they brought nothing to sell. They were going to St. Paul to buy coffee, sugar, clothing, garden seeds and other things; but why they didn't buy of the company I don't know.   His great good nature and hopefulness made him very interesting, for he was a good and lovable old man.   Ah, me!   If the camera and dry plates had been invented in those days, and I had owned an outfit, what treasures I would have to-day!

Tom Davies went to St. Paul for the rest of the provisions early in October, and was gone ten days.   Henry froze both his feet by riding on the hind end of the wagon with his feet hanging out after he had met Tom at Crow Wing, for we were still in a country where the wagon could be used.   It was night and Henry had told Tom that Crosby was lost in the woods, and he hurried on at once because there were but three men on the line.   They reached camp while we were breakfasting, but Henry could not stand.   He had foolishly worn leather boots, while the rest had shoe-packs of elk-skin, soft and warm in dry weather.   This reminds me to say that the Indians about us wore moccasins of buffalo, which cost one dollar a pair at Crow Wing, but did not wear well.   After the men were gone on the line I took Henry's boots off, and put his feet into snow and by chafing them got the blood started.   He joked about my cutting his feet off, and his missing the dancing that winter, as they swelled so that there seemed to be danger; but in a week he was able to walk, and by cutting one boot for a favorite toe he was soon ready for duty.

I kept up half-hourly rifle shots and cow-bell ringing for Crosby, and he came into camp, having been out one night without matches or blankets.   He had kept from freezing by walking, and had got turned around and followed the blazed lines the wrong way.   Hunger had made him colder, and he had thrown a stick at a bird, probably a Canada jay, hoping to kill it and eat it raw. He had an appetite of great length, breadth and thickness, one worthy of the man whose name heads this article.

Gibbs was very fond of staying in camp with me when Henry went on the line and he could do it. An excuse to mend his trousers or other clothing served. He was the youngest of the party and fresh from school. He knew all about Indians, for he had read about them, but was curious to study them in the woods. He was a gold mine to old Mouthful or any other Indian. When he offered a pipeful of tobacco he handed over a whole plug of Navy or such part of one as he had, and when the Indian cut a pipeful and kept the rest Gibbs thought that he didn't mean to do it, but couldn't ask for its return. He continually gave me advice on the subject of getting on with them, and I enjoyed it. Once as we sat down to a midday bite Gibbs passed the pan of hot biscuit to old Mouthful, who dumped the lot in his dirty blanket. I had frequently told him that an Indian always understood that what you handed to him was his, but there the biscuit were.

"Explain it to him," said Gibbs; "I can't speak his lingo, but we've got to have some bread for our dinner, and I don't really fancy getting it back after he has handled it and had it in that blanket."

"Gibbs," I replied, "there is no need to explain it. You gave them to him; of course, you didn't intend to give him the whole output of the bakery, but you did. Now the only thing to do is to go and take what you want without any more ceremony; replevin them; use force if necessary, but get back our biscuit. We need not eat the outside of them; there's a lot of good bread inside which his dirty hands haven't touched."

He looked at the bread and then said: "I don't like to be impolite to him. Why can't you tell him that it's all a mistake; what's the word for mistake in his patter?"

"Oh, just say to him: 'Nidgee, pungee iskoodah wabo,' and it will be all right." This was an invitation to old Mouthful to have some whiskey, an article which we did not have, but this was my joke on Gibbs.

The red man had not paid much attention to our talk, which he could not understand, but my last words must have had a familiar sound, for he turned his head and looked at me.

Gibbs arose and repeated the words in his purest Chippewa. Old Mouthful also arose, as befitted such an important occasion, grunted, shook hands and replied in fairly good Ojibway that he "didn't care if he did."

"What's that he says?" asked Gibbs.

"He says that he begs your pardon, and hopes that he has not offended; and he begs that you will take the bread, and give him such a portion as will not rob your-self." The situation was growing interesting. As the interpreter I had the game in my hands.

Gibbs struck an attitude and exclaimed: "Now, by my halidome! Our guest is a gentleman of right courtly manners. I tell you, Fred, you don't know these people if you have been around a few of them long enough to pick up some of their talk. I've read up on 'em, Scool-craft, Cooper and these authors; have studied 'em, and the noble red man has all the high-bred instincts of the most chivalrous knight, but these men who come among them to trade are not sufficiently educated to see and appre-ciate it." He then took up the bread, broke off a third of it and gave it to our guest.

Old Mouthful looked surprised. Evidently he didn't mind the bread as long as there was whiskey in prospect.

After a pause he looked at Gibbs in a way that the Governor of North Carolina might have done at that historic meeting with the Governor of South Carolina, and merely remarked: "Pungee 'scutah wabo?"

"What's that he says?" asked Gibbs.

He asked you for some whiskey, and he thinks you promised him some in exchange for the bread. I begin to think so myself, since I compare your pronunciation of Ojibway with his and mine. There are some very nice shades of inflection in Ojibway which make a word mean several things. You have told me how revengeful an Indian is, and you have mortally offended this man, and unless you give him what you have promised it may go hard with you—and, in fact, with all our party, for we are only six."

"What will I do? I haven't any whiskey, and there's none in camp."

"He won't believe that. He has seen a ten-gallon keg of molasses, but you don't suppose for a moment he believes it to be molasses? The kegs he has seen with white men have always contained whiskey. I don't know how you can square it with him. You've got yourself into this scrape, but I'll help you out if I can."

I told our guest that Gibbs had not understood, "gowin kendun," but that instead of whiskey he meant to offer tobacco. That was satisfactory—it had to be—and Gibbs gave up a whole plug of Navy, and there was peace in the land. Gibbs felt that I had successfully arbitrated the case and averted a calamity. What our guest thought was impossible to tell, but Henry and I enjoyed the thing by ourselves, and afterward Henry guyed Gibbs about it at every chance.

We had left civilization early in a Presidential campaign. The Democratic party had nominated James

Buchanan, and the newly-formed Republican party had named John C. Fremont as its candidate.   Our little party of six was divided in its choice, and in the evenings the argument waxed warm, but always in respectful shape.   The date for the election had passed, but we knew nothing of the result.   But what hundreds of bushels of oysters were bet!   It would have required several smacks to have carried all these oysters if the stews, fries and raws had all been eaten.   The fact is that no record of bets was kept, and each night the old score was forgotten and new bets were made.   When we got back in the vicinity of Crow Wing—about December 20—we first heard the result, and the Buchanan men were jubilant.   It served us well as a topic of interest, for it was not a jolly crowd, and what it would have done for amusement without the election is a question.

Unless Henry or Gibbs was in camp I did not dare leave it.   These Indians might be honest enough, but in our case it was well not to take any risks on our provisions.   One day, while out with my rifle, I came to a lake of which I had a glimpse through the trees.   Standing awhile, there came a faint whining sound, which I at once diagnosed as the talk of a bear.   Here was a chance to get a shot at bruin, and perhaps some fresh meat.   Carefully looking at the cap on the rifle, I cautiously worked down into the marshy ground and underbrush in the direction of the sound.   The marsh was frozen, or the passage would have been impossible.   The sound came from one direction, but did not seem to increase as I advanced; but it was a bear, sure.   Getting near the edge of the lake, as could be seen off to the right, the game must be close, and that creepy, trembling feeling came on.   I halted and listened; it was but a few feet away.   Through the brush a dark object could be seen on a log, and the whining kept up. If it was a bear I wanted to see how it stood in order to plant the bullet right; but in stepping one side I made a slight noise, and an Indian boy about six years old turned around. He dropped, crawled behind the log, and then jumped into the brush and out of sight. Probably it was the first white man he had ever seen. Then I knew that what I mistook for the whining of a bear was the boy's low singing. The story he told his mother would be interesting, if we knew it.

Getting back to the higher land again, I sat awhile on a log enjoying the clear, cold air and the glimpse of the frozen lake. After awhile there was another sound of life, and I saw a sight which I never have seen recorded by any writer of the woods. Below, in an open spot in the underbrush, perhaps of twenty feet diameter, and not over twenty feet away, came a troop of about thirty ruffed grouse or partridges of the Eastern States, and they were clucking and chattering at a great rate. The males were strutting with tails spread out like turkey cocks, or more like tame pigeons. I was in plain sight, and tried not to breathe for fear of disturbing them, for it was the treat of a lifetime. Among these birds was a male, I had no doubt the same species, which was black. Of course I can't at this late day, and in view of my very slight knowledge of such things at that time, be certain that this was a case of melanism in Bonasa, but I believe it.

Later I saw several ptarmigan, which I then thought to be white ruffed grouse, but did not kill any. Something alarmed the partridges, and they flew into the trees, and I picked off three. The shots brought an Indian, a stranger, who begged for a bird, and I gave him one. These men were persistent beggars; they thought every white man was wealthy. They seemed to roam the woods without either gun or bows, and I afterward learned that they lived mainly on fish, which they dried for winter. No doubt they knew how scarce game was, and that it was useless to hunt for it. I was greatly disappointed; I had left the East two years before because of the scarcity of game, and here I was in a primeval forest where there was no game, hardly a rabbit. Disappointed hardly expresses it. Why, we could go out from Albany in that day, in most any direction during the winter, and bag a few ruffed grouse, some rabbits and a squirrel or two; I began to think the far West a fraud; Minnesota was then "far West." The biggest lot of game I saw in northern Minnesota that winter was four young 'coons that Tom Davies killed with an axe as they huddled near a tree on an extra cold morning. I parboiled and baked them, and—oh, my!

Our friend, who possibly might bite off more than he could chew, but never more than he could swallow, had ceased to be interesting. He found our camp at every move, and seemed to regard himself as part of it, or at least one of the volunteer staff. Neaville and I paid little attention to him, but his eyes brightened when he found Gibbs in camp. Gibbs was curious about him, wanted to learn his language, and would touch objects and ask their names by looking up and saying, "Ojibwa?" Then, of course, he could do no less than "divvy" on pork and tobacco—a very good arrangement for his friend. Speaking of tobacco, we once found old Mouthful with the native article, the "killi-ki-nic," or inner bark of the red willow. Henry and I tried once. It was most pungent, and I can only compare it to smoking rattan and elm root, which we schoolboys used before we aspired to tobacco, and it almost burned our tongues off. I think some of the old boys, and perhaps some of the younger ones, will recall their brave attempts to smoke things, no matter how pungent, which did not upset and invert their youthful stomachs. Fifty years ago most boys in America thought it smart to chew tobacco, and they acquired the disgusting habit; but the younger ones would get licorice ball, and spit in imitation of a tobacco chewer, and then some unbeliever would challenge him with, "That ain't tobacco you're a-chewin'; it's on'y lickorish!" Yes, I was a boy once.

These Northern Indians must smoke, but tobacco was an exotic which positively declined to grow so far North, and, like the boys, they found a substitute. After they found the Southern weed it was too costly to use alone, and they mixed it with killi-ki-nic merely for economy; but preferred pure tobacco when they could get it.

"This reminds me." In my young days, when I was particularly fond of negro minstrelsy and burlesquing things, and shortly after the time of which I write, Longfellow published "Hiawatha," a poem which I never tire of reading, but one whose meter urgently invites burlesque; and with hundreds of others I essayed it. Elsewhere I have said that some people seemed shocked at seeing a thing which they love burlesqued. That means that their sense of humor is only partially developed. Then and to-day I regard "Hiawatha" as the great American epic, but I wrote:

> "Should you ask me whence I got them,
> Got these yarns of old James River;
> With their flavor of tobacco,
> Of the stinkweed, the mundungus,
> And the pipe of Old Virginny,
> And the twangle of the banjo;
> Of the banjo, the goatskinnit,

> 'And the fiddle, the catgutta,
> And the noisy marrow-bonum,
> I should answer, I should tell you:
> By one John-smith they were written.
> John-smith, soldier, sailor and explorer,
> Editor of his own adventures
> In the land of Po-ca-hon-tas,
> In the realm of Pow-ha-tan,
> Where old John-smith had a big time,
> Filled the red man full of whisky,
> Stole his daughter and sailed eastward
> To the far-off land of John-bull," etc.

There were yards and yards of this stuff, but we will content ourselves with that. It's easy to write—any boy can do it—and the grandest of themes are the easiest to burlesque. That is a fact that human owls fail to understand. What is easier to travesty than "Chronicles?" And it is often done without intending irreverence; the humor of the thing is the only thought of the writer; but "a jest's prosperity," etc.

Here you see the evil effect of tobacco, how it will lead a man off the track to talk about Pocahontas and other irrelevant things. It's fortunate for some one that my pen did not go off after Sir Walter Raleigh and the story of his weighing the smoke which came from Queen Elizabeth's pipe, but every schoolboy knows all about that.

We found another thing that the Indians used; it was the "man-o-min," or wild rice. This is mighty good feed for wild ducks or Indians, but, as they ate it, there was a grit in it which detracted from its value to men who don't like to eat the hulls of grain. Hardly a night but half a dozen Indians slept by our fire and cooked their wild rice over it, but if they could get our Southern rice they were glad. It's many a day since I ate the man-o-min, but the impression now is that if it had been properly hulled it would have been good.

Along the streams we saw where the wild rice had been tied up in bunches to keep it from bending over and being eaten by wild ducks while it was in the milky state or after. Then, later in the year, the women paddled up the stream, bent the heads of rice over, and with a light stick threshed them into a canoe.

Gibbs was always curious to taste their food; he had the true instincts of an investigator, and got more information in that line than we, who were more cautious of getting too intimate with the aborigines, for fear of our stock of provisions.

We came out all right on the rations, and had all we wished to use; but the story of the winter is too long for one telling.

WE-NEN-GWAY.

AFTER a while we got into a swampy region which was frozen, or we couldn't have run lines through it. Lakes were frequent, and we saw many wigwams where there were high frames for drying fish. Crotches about ten feet high held poles, and across these were laid others, forming a rude platform, on which the fish were dried for winter use. As near as I can remember the fish were whitefish, lake trout and either pike or mascalonge, for I then knew as little of the differences between the two latter species as an Adirondack guide or the average fish dealer does. Now I could trade bread, flour, pork or sugar for an occasional fish, but McBride always wanted to be assured that they had been thoroughly scrubbed, for he was a little shy of eating anything which an Indian had handled.

Our old friend, whom we had named He-who-takes-so-much-at-a-mouthful, still followed us up, and I had become more than tired of him, and was wondering how he could "be shook." Some little things had been missed, such as forks and spoons; there was no evidence that he had taken them, but when I once left a jackknife sticking in a log where I had been using it and it was gone an hour afterward, I suspected Mouthful, because he was the only man around camp beside myself. I said nothing about it, but resolved to keep an eye out for him. If, after feeding him for over a month, and sharing my tobacco with him, he would steal from me, I wanted to know it. I began to hate him, and he soon saw that he was not welcome; but he rejoiced when Gibbs was in camp.   One day when Gibbs stayed in I put a new handle in a little belt axe, and then began sandpapering a handle for the larger camp axe, for we had extra ones. The little axe lay by the fire and I was sitting in the door of the tent, when old Mouthful came up and grunted his salute, and sat down so that his blanket covered the axe. I noted the fact, and said to Gibbs: "Go talk to him; give him a pipeful of tobacco, anything to keep his mind off his appetite, and when I smooth up this axe helve I'll play you a game of euchre."

While we were playing cards old Mouthful arose, wrapped his blanket about him, and walked off.   The belt axe was gone.   I called after him, "Nidgee!" several times, but he didn't look around, and I grabbed the axe helve and started after him.   He was in a well-worn path, bordered with prickly ash, and when he found me close behind him he sprang into the bush, but not in time to escape a whack on the shoulders with the hickory helve, and he dropped the hatchet.   When I returned to camp Gibbs was indignant.   Said he: "If I was where I could get out of these woods I'd go.   You are always knocking the Indians around, shoving them out of the way if they crowd around the fire, and now you've struck one of them, and we may all be murdered.   These Indians are revengeful, and that man will remember you if he meets you ten years from now."

"You think he will remember me as long as that?"

"Yes, he will; he'll treasure that up against you as long as he lives, for their memories are long, and they never forgive an injury."

"Well, Gibbs," said I, "when I ask him to forgive me it will be time for him to do it.   Just now I'm not asking any favors of him, and, as for his remembering me, that's all right.   I hope he will, and I'll remember him, and if he ever comes to this camp or I meet him in the woods I'll lick him again. I'm just as mad as he is, and I've suspected him of stealing from us all winter, and now I've caught him in the act. I don't want to argue this case, but what I've told you is just what I'll do, and you can bet on it."

"Suppose a dozen of his friends take this thing up, and come down on us in the night and kill us all. What can six men do in such a case?"

"I tell you," said I, "the case is not a supposable one. You know that their head chief, Hole-in-the-day, lives near Crow Wing, and that he told McBride, through an interpreter, that if any of his men molested us in any way he would punish them, and every Indian from this place to Lake Superior has been notified of this. There is a whole mass of stuff in your head about Indians that I don't suppose you could get out with a fine-toothed comb; but you will never find that fellow around our camp again; he is a lazy, thieving beggar, who can't have any standing among his people."

Just how far this satisfied Gibbs is a question. His mind was filled with romantic ideas of the red man which he had obtained from books, and he had no idea of the degraded ones who hang around a trading post, too lazy to hunt, trap or fish. I saw many Indians that winter who were too proud to beg, and this only proves that the red man is human and differs in mental make-up as other men differ. A very different man was We-nen-gway, whom I met on the border of one of those immense cranberry marshes, which were common where we then were. Some of these marshes might have contained a thousand acres, and were red with frozen berries. As we had sugar in plenty, you may imagine what an agreeable sauce we had with our boiled pork, roast pork, baked beans, etc. His name meant Dirty-face, and he looked it. I wondered if he took pride in his name, and kept his face in that condition by some vow to abstain from washing, but on closer acquaintance it was evident that the dark spots were birth marks, for which he was not responsible. He watched me gather a quart of berries, and accepted a piece of tobacco in a dignified sort of way. He was evidently a superior man to Mouthful, and one not disposed to look too favorably on the invasion of his ancestral domain by the white man, but his tribe had sold this land to the Long Knives, and that settled it. I took a fancy to this man; here was the ideal man that Gibbs had read of.

Some days afterward he visited our camp, which was moved a few miles most every day to one of the cardinal points of the compass, and he brought me a fine lake trout. It was a fresh one, and I was interested at once. There was no game in the country, and my rifle was a useless burden in moving camp, but there must be fish near by.

I asked Dirty-face to eat, and set out some cold boiled pork and beans, as well as hot coffee. This was a treat to him, but it was evident that he had eaten during the previous week, and was not filling up for the week to come. We naturally talked about the fish, and he told me that over by his wigwam was a lake with plenty of fish; and as our move next day would bring our camp near his, he would show me where and how to catch some o-gah. This was a new name, and after drawing pictures of fish as well as I could on a piece of birch bark I drew a pike or pickerel and said, "Ken-o-shah;" he said it was the same. "O-gah" I never met before as a name for pike; but kenosha, kenoje or kenozha was the more common name for the fish. If those who wish to trace the derivation of the names of fish as used in popular nomenclature will take down their volumes of *Forest and Stream,* and look at the articles on the name of mascalonge, maskinonje, etc., they will find all that is known of the Indian name from which the various spellings are derived. See Vol. XXVI., page 149, March 18, 1886; and Vol. XXVI., page 268, October 28, 1886.

From our new camp on the shore of a nameless lake I could see the wigwam of my new friend on the other side, about half a mile off, and after getting things in shape I went over to him. His wigwam was a typical Ojibway residence, made of skins laid over many poles, which came together at the top, where there was an opening for the smoke to go out. It was circular in form, much like the cumbrous Sibley tent which some of our troops used in 1862. On the outside there were records of hunts or fights in black and red pigments, which could be read by those versed in their pictorial histories, but which were a huckleberry beyond my persimmon. A skin flap kept out the cold; a small fire in the middle diffused all the heat it had to spare, and a goodly portion of it went out with the smoke. They made small fires of twigs and squatted over them, freezing one side while warming the other, and said that ours were so hot that a man could not get near them to warm himself; but I noticed that many nights our big fires were patronized by travelling Indians to sleep by, instead of making small ones for themselves. Did you ever notice that man is the only animal which lies with his feet to the fire? If you haven't observed this, just look at your dog bake his head under the stove.

I was invited inside. Besides the flavor of smoke from burning wood there were several other perfumes which you never smelled in a barber's shop. Mentally

I quote a couplet from Tennyson's "Maud" as I recall the combined odors:

"The woodbine spices are wafted abroad
And the musk of the roses blown."

The family consisted of Mme. Dirty-face and two girls of sixteen and eighteen, and three young boys. By a most convenient arrangement the parlor, sitting-room, bedroom, dining-room and kitchen were all on one floor, with no partition nor stairs to climb when the head of the house came home with a load. I took this all in at a glance—the architectural beauties, I mean—the odors came in through a different sense. When I described it to Henry Neaville I could only compare it to a flavor met in boyhood days when I dug up a nest of young woodchucks.

"Yes," said Henry, "I've been in a wigwam in winter, but the flavor, as I remember it, was more of an ornithological character, and seemed to resemble that of a nest of young woodpeckers."

Dirty-face took down a couple of spears and an axe, and we went up the lake to an open air-hole, where it was probable that a spring boiled up from the bottom and kept the ice from forming over its warmer waters. He advanced cautiously, and sounded the ice with the poll of his axe until it broke; he chipped off the edge which would not bear us, and we had firm footing at the margin of the water. His spears were not like the gig which Guyon and I used, but were made with a single point with two barbs, like an arrow-head; they appeared to be made from saw blades, and were fastened in clefts in the handles, which were of some heavy wood. Our ice cutting had scared away any fish which might be near, so we waited and smoked. The snow on the ice prevented our seeing into the water except where it was open, and it also shielded us from being seen by the fish. Once I stamped a foot and my friend said "Kego," and, as the word means both "fish" and "don't," it was a caution either way. Soon we could see an occasional fish of good size in the clear water, but too deep to be reached with a spear.

His patience exceeded mine, and it began to be monotonous to see the fish swimming below out of range in the clear water, and I said to him: "Kego-de-me," the fish are very deep. He grunted an assent, and pulled out a thin white stone not unlike a fish in general shape, and tied it to his spear with a few feet of string. This he moved gently about, and several fish gave it respectful attention without being impertinent, and then a large lake trout rose and I struck and missed it; its tail was toward me, and my spear went on one side. I knew that my friend must be more expert, and I took his spear and played the lure in the water, drawing it near the surface if a fish arose. Soon he plunged his spear into a fish which stood broadside and was about to seize the decoy. The cord ran out rapidly, but the flight was soon checked and a fine nay-may-goos lay upon the snow. I spell the name as I learned to speak it. Scientists call the lake trout *Salvelinus namaycush*, softening the original word. Dirty-face insisted that I should try it again, and I did, for I wanted to learn how to handle this new kind of spear. A large pike came up to the lure, and I sent the steel into it and secured it. We took three more fish, and then it was time for me to go to camp to get things in shape for the return of the linemen. I went back by way of the wigwam, and stopped awhile and gave Mrs. Dirty-face some tobacco, and she ordered the girls to clean the fish for me. I took two—enough for our sup-

per, with the rice and beans—and would take no more.
I have always been in doubt whether her action was
genuinely generous or not, for the whole party visited
me next day, and again when we moved to the upper end
of the lake, and if a balance was struck between those
two fish (which may have weighed twelve pounds) and
an unknown quantity of bread, beans, rice, coffee and
sugar—really, I don't know if there would be any balance.

I have remarked on the absence of game and other
animal life. The snow which fell in September, and had
lain without addition or melting, had become too hard
to record the passing of small animals, such as mink,
rabbits or even the heavier 'coons, but I saw a mink and
a fox, and heard the great gray timber wolf several times.
The Canada jay and the raven were the most common
birds, and I saw the little chickadee and a bird which I
did not know, but now think might have been the shrike,
or butcher bird. I never ceased to be surprised at the
absence of life in this wilderness.

December came and the cold increased. One morning the trees were bursting with a sound like rifles, and
Gibbs thought we were attacked. He and Crosby
jumped up out of bed before daylight, but soon returned
when the rest of the party laughed at them, for we knew
what the noise meant, having heard it before. After
reaching Crow Wing we learned that the thermometer
had been 40° below zero on several occasions. There
was no wind in the heavy timber, and we were warmly
clad and could hardly realize how cold it was. Coats
were discarded, but no man knew how many flannel
shirts he had on; and as long as the body part of a pair
of trousers held together the legs of them were reinforced
by cylinders made of bed ticking fastened at top and bot-

tom; these were not removed when worn out, but other reinforcements were added outside them until a cross section of a leg might have shown half a dozen strata of bed tick above the original deposit of trousering.

We had now reached the northern line of our survey at its eastern end, over by Mille-lacs, and were working the upper tier of townships toward the Mississippi. One day I was out with my rifle in the hope of finding game when I came across a wigwam by a small stream. I entered without ceremony, in accordance with Indian etiquette, and found a party of perhaps a dozen bucks and squaws, seated on the ground around a small fire in the centre, over which a sheet iron camp kettle was boiling and sending forth a savory odor. I was hungry after the tramp, although I had bread, pork and beans in plenty, but had not eaten. After giving the mixed French and Indian salute which they commonly used, I invited myself to sit down, and this was also correct Ojibway form. There was an oppressive silence—oppressive to me, at least.

> "The silence of the place was like a sleep,
>   So full of rest it seemed; each passing tread
> Was a reverberation from the deep
>   Recesses of the ages that are dead."

How different these people were from a party of white men waiting for a feast. There was no chat, jest, song or story. For idle men they take life seriously, and yet they are like children in many of their moods. I could never learn to live their way; that impassive, self-contained manner seems to be a continual sort of dress parade, so to speak, for they can be roused to enthusiasm by war or the hunt. I can't say that I like such people; they are not cordial, and seem to be sitting in cold and unsympathetic judgment on not only you, but every other thing on earth. During the winter it had been evident that I was not a favorite with the native American. He-who-takes-so-much-at-a-mouthful evidently preferred Gibbs to me, and some others whom I had bounced out of camp because of persistent begging had no great love for me, and so there was no amount of love lost between us. I stood, as the commissary of our party, the custodian of its supplies, which would have melted away in a week if all-comers had been regaled as our friend Gibbs would have entertained them. They would have stayed by him as long as the provisions lasted; they liked Gibbs.

In this party in the wigwam I recognized Dirty-face and others who had been at our camp and had eaten of our pork, their great dainty, which they called koo-koosh; but there was no cordial handshake—only a nod and a grunt, which is their limit of welcome. A squaw arose, thrust a stick into the kettle and brought up meat; she was satisfied that it was sufficiently cooked, and took the kettle from the fire and went outside with it. I had curiosity enough to get up and follow. She put the kettle in the snow, and scraped up snow about it to cool it. I asked her what meat she was about to serve to her guests, at the same time giving her what pork I had. We were friends. Pork was good, and she had only muskrat to offer. Muskrat was not fat like pork and bear meat, but it was warm, and she hoped I would like it.

Away back in the fourth article of this series I told of Bill Fairchild's experience with the muskrat as food, as he related it at a seance in Port Tyler's cabin, in Green-bush. If you remember, Bill could follow the French-man's advice—could "skin da mus'rat, bile him a leetle, den fry a-heem an' eat him, an' oh!" Right here I wish to record my first experience with the musquash as an epicurean dish.   I ate it years afterward from choice while camping with Mort. Locke, John Fish and Wm. Downey on Cayuga Lake, N. Y., as the two last named, now living at Honeoye Falls, N. Y., will testify, if they have any regard for the truth; but that is another story, and there's no use telling how we played it on one of the party for something else in the way of game.

When the contents of the camp kettle were cool the squaw brought it in, and a group formed around it on one side of the fire.   I was not only hungry, but was curious to taste muskrat, which is a very clean feeder; but somehow the cook and the surroundings were not conducive to much appetite; but they asked me to join, and I joined.   They dipped their hands in the kettle, and it is doubtful if they had been manicured recently. Dirty-face handed me a piece, and I wondered if any in the party might be named Dirty-hand.   I wasn't hungry now, and said so, but felt a delicacy about refusing to eat with these friendly folk, and also felt a delicacy about eating food served in this manner.   They omitted napkins and finger bowls, and somehow didn't seem to miss them.   I ate a little, very little; said it was good, but I wasn't hungry just then, and went out.   The air outside was excellent.

I could have said with Petruchio:

> "Where is the rascal cook?
> How durst you, villains, bring it from the dresser,
> And serve it thus to me that love it not?"

Gratiano, in "The Merchant of Venice," asks a question to which he evidently expects no answer:

> "Who riseth from a feast
> With that keen appetite that he sits down?"

I pungled off, and ate my little cold luncheon beside a spring on the lake side. There were no napkins nor finger bowls there, but there was that satisfying knowledge that the hands which handled the food had been bathed since they skinned the last muskrat. On relating this to Henry Neaville he remarked:

"I don't care what any of these writers on health say about too frequent bathing being injurious; I believe that a man ought to wash his hands once a month, whether they need it or not."

Our surveys were nearly finished, and nothing was left to be done but to meander the river and figure the fractional sections which it cut, and to do a little work around Crow Wing. Henry Neaville and I were to pack up, and get back to the trading post and meet the party there. An Indian, a stranger, came to camp and begged for whiskey. I told him we had none, but he saw the molasses keg, and kept on begging until Henry said: "Give him some pepper sauce." I had put the liquor from several of the bottles into one and had thrown away the peppers, and taking up the bottle, Henry and I pretended to drink, and then he was wild for some. I showed him with my thumb on the bottle how much or how little he must drink, and he grunted assent, seized the bottle with both hands, and such swallows as he took before it burned him I never saw. If one swallow doesn't make a summer, those he took made it hot enough for him. He drew a long breath and snorted "woof," like a bear, and started for the river. Three times he stopped and snorted, and then ran out of sight. Henry roared, rolled over and roared. When he got his speech he said, between spasms: "Golly, but that Injun thinks there was more fire than water in that 'scutah-wawba; oh, dear! he's gone for a doctor; he thinks you've poisoned him. Oh, if Gibbs was only here to tell you how Mr. Lo will remember that drink!"

We stopped a couple of days at Crow Wing, and I became acquainted with the brothers who kept the trading post. I think their name was McDonald, but am not sure, and Mr. Davies isn't. They told of an Indian who died there some winters before when the ground was frozen too hard to bury him, and how they stood him up all winter against the north side of the house and buried him in the spring, and some other cheerful stories of dead Indians. A Mr. Morrison lived there, one of the leading men of northern Minnesota, for whom the county below Crow Wing is named. He had married an Ojibway woman, and had two grown-up daughters, who had been educated in St. Louis, and they played the piano for us, and our visit was an event in Crow Wing life. Bishop McElvaney was there, and preached on the birth of Christ in Morrison's house, while Davies and others sang. I didn't sing; when I sing the police always pull the house, thinking there must be a dog fight in the back room.

I went up to see Hole-in-the-day, and he showed me a Colt's rifle, made like a revolver, inlaid with gold, which was given him by President Franklin Pierce a year or two before. I understood that it was taken from the Patent Office by consent of Colonel Colt. He talked about trading it for my rifle, if I added enough dollars to suit him. He was poor, or pretended to be, and I wanted that rifle very much, but thought best to consult with the brothers at the post. One of them said: "It's against the law to trade with these people without a license, and if you trade with him for the gun he can send a man after it, and you will lose both rifles and all you've paid, and then may have some trouble with the law."

That settled the trading, but when I saw the old chief again he wanted to know, in confidence, if we had any whiskey left. I doubt if a single Indian believed that six white men, who had so many things they thought to be luxuries, spent half the winter in the woods without whiskey. To them it seemed an absurd proposition. The Indians who hung around trading posts were not of the best class, and had readily copied all the vices of the white man from a class whose virtues were not so apparent. They had not then adopted the white man's dress except the calico or the flannel shirt. They wore the breech-clout and leggings, a shirt and the invariable blanket.

When we were up along the river we were near the great northern trail from the Red River of the North, and Henry said that the mail was due in a day or two, so he had heard from a half-breed. "This mail," said he, "comes down in a dog sledge, and if we can put out some pieces of pork in the snow you'll see some fun."

That did seem the proper thing to do, and in fact it was the only way possible to extract any fun out of a dog train, and we planted pieces of pork at intervals of one hundred feet, more or less, and waited. It was next morning before we heard the driver calling to his dogs a long way off, for sound travels far in the cold and over snow. On he came, with five wolfish-looking dogs harnessed tandem, with rawhides traces and soft collars, to a flat-bottomed sledge made of thin birch boards turned up in front, and lashed together with thongs and covered with a skin tied over all, and without runners. The driver ran beside the team, touching a dog here and there with a long lash fastened to a handle about one foot long. The leader struck a piece of pork, and in a moment four dogs were on him fighting for it, and the harness was all tied up. He plied the whip, and made appropriate re-marks while doing it. Some dog bolted the meat, and the fighting stopped, for there was no pork in sight. The half-breed muttered something, evidently not a prayer, while he put each dog in its place, and on he went in no pleasant mood, and the scene was soon repeated.   He was near us this time, and we could see that the second dog won the prize, while the rest had to be contented with a bite of or from his neighbor. It was fun for the dogs and for us, but from what the half-breed said I doubt if he enjoyed it. If he had seen us he might have in-dulged in more oratory, but he had to waste his elo-quence on the dogs. It was fun to do this at that time, because we thought it fun. To-day we wouldn't do it, because there would be no fun in it.   Thus we view things at different periods of life. The fire-crackers we shot off half a century ago don't sound as joyful as they did, and we go into the country to avoid them; so we go.

McBride sold our provisions—I think there were two barrels of flour and one of pork left—and if memory serves he got about $20 per barrel for the flour, and twice that for the pork. Long prices; but transportation from St. Paul, over one hundred miles away, over a winter road, and no way of getting from St. Louis to St. Paul except by teams when the river was frozen, made things come high.   The wagon was sold and a bob sleigh bought, the box filled with straw and blankets, and on December 22 we started for home. Two days later we stopped just outside St. Paul. It did seem good to get in a bed again, but we couldn't stand a room with win-dows closed. We had slept in the pure, cold air too long for that. We left the river at Red Wing, and took the west side, avoiding the hotels in the large towns, stop-ping at country taverns, and we had what Henry called "dead loads of fun." At these rural hostelries we struck a dance nearly every night. At a small place not far from Rochester, Minn., the fiddler didn't show up, and some country roughs proposed to wreck the hotel, and the landlord appealed to us for protection. We were at a late supper, and Tom Davies finished first, and went out and talked with the turbulent spirits; but he was only one man, and he came back for reinforcements. We went out in a body at the landlord's suggestion, and after he had said a few words in a conciliatory way I winked to Henry and he came; we took the leader of the gang one side, and I said to him:

"This party of ours has just come out of the woods, and they're peaceable enough if there isn't any fighting going on; but if there's any fighting you can't keep 'em out. We don't know any of the people here, but the landlord is a white man, and if a fight is started we're with him. Do you see that dark man over there? Well, he's a Welshman; look at the build of him; he can kill a steer with one blow of his fist," and I pointed to Tom Davies.

"I've seen him do it three times down in Wisconsin," said Henry.

"It's just here," said I. "There isn't going to be any fighting in this house to-night unless we all take a hand in it, and if we do I tell you as a friend to keep away from that Welshman."

> "Buried was the bloody hatchet;
> Buried was the fearful war club;
> Buried were all warlike weapons,
> And the war cry was forgotten;
> Then was peace among the nations."

Just what delayed the fiddler is lost in memory's fog,

but the lads and lassies were impatient; a thought struck my old bosom-block, Henry. Could the landlord get a fiddle?   The landlord could, and did.   Behold Henry seated on a chair on top of a table, tuning up! Such tuning and such playing! He was not Ole Bull, but he came as near to him as he could. I can see him now, beating time with his boot—which had been cut open to allow his frozen toe to expand—and calling off: "First two forward!" etc.   After a while the missing fiddler arrived, and relieved Henry without any perceptible improvement in the music, but there was an era of good feeling, and it was

> "On with the dance!
> Let joy be unconfined!
> No sleep till morn,
> When Youth and Pleasure meet."

We went through Pleasant Grove, where me met Hiram Gilmore, of Potosi, who gave us late news of our families, and on the 28th we stopped at Decorah, Ia.; we struck the Mississippi at Clayton City with sick horses; they would neither eat nor drink, and what the matter was I don't know, only that we were delayed.   From there we took the ice to Cassville, Wis., where we stopped all night, and then struck out for home, which we reached just after sundown on the last day of the year, and, as the King says in "Hamlet:"

> "At night we'll feast together:
> Most welcome home."

SERGEANT WILLIAM PATTERSON.

THERE is some reason for believing that his name was William, although I do not know it. The reason is entirely from analogy; he was always known as "Bill" Patterson, and I had known other men to be called "Bill" whose real name was William. Further than this I find upon the rolls of Company H, Twenty-fifth Wisconsin Infantry, the name of Sergeant William Patterson, of Potosi; and my old friend, Judge Seaton, who has kindly posted me on affairs in the village since I left it, says: "Bill Patterson went out with the Twenty-fifth Wisconsin Infantry." Therefore, as I have said, there is reason for believing his name to be William. If living, he is near Portland, Ore., but letters to him have been returned to me after being opened by another William Patterson.

On that New Year Eve, when our surveying party returned to Potosi from northern Minnesota, there was quite a little visiting done by neighbors, who were anxious to learn of adventures among the Indians, and as I lived in the middle one of three cottages, all under one roof, owned by a Mr. Knight, who lived on one side, and Bill Patterson on the other, both neighbors called. Bill was then, I think, about thirty-three years old, I was twenty-three, and "Old Poppy Knight," the only name that memory recalls him by, was probably sixty; but little, weazened and dried up, and "meaner 'an pusley," as

farmers say. Bill was a strapping, broad-shouldered fellow, who had been on the West Coast in that early day,
perhaps with the "Argonauts" who went to the gold-
fields of California in 1849; a rough, swaggering fellow,
just the opposite of Old Poppy Knight, whom he seemed
to dislike in a superlative degree.

Mrs. Patterson and Miss Rowena Knight, daughter
of O. P. K., were in the family circle. The conversation
had been general, and I had tried to reply to three or
four questions at once, when Pop asked: "Are them Injun girls good lookin'?"

"See here, Pop," said Bill, who had been where the
evening had been more bibulously observed, "what does
an old duffer like you want to talk about Injun girls for?
I've been all through Sonora, New Mexico and the whole
West Coast, and I never see a squaw that was worth a
second look. I want to find out what them Injuns live
on up in that cold country, where Fred says there's no
game. I've ast that half a dozen times, and you don't
give him a chance to answer. Now you let up for a little
till we get at this problem of eating."   Then to me:
"What can they get to eat up there?"

"Mainly fish," I answered; "they dry it for winter,
and eat it without anything except salt, of which they are
fond; but where they got salt before the white man came
is a question. The Indians on the sea coast got it in
their fish and oysters, and those about the interior salt
springs had it to trade with other tribes; but when you
look at it you will see that the dwellers in some parts
must have eaten their meat without it."

"Bill says he never saw a good-looking squaw," said
Pop. "Now there's lots o' half-breeds up there, and are
the half-breed girls better looking than the squaws?"

"Pop," said Bill, "you had better go up there and see

for yourself; this thing of beauty is a personal matter. Some o' them squaws might take a fancy to you, for they ain't got the first bit of taste. I've seen men that has married squaws, but I don't think I ever saw an ugly old squaw that would marry you. I'll be obliged if you will shut up."

Put yourself in my place! As the host, I did not fancy this sort of talk; but what could I do? Although Mr. Knight was Bill's landlord as well as mine, I knew that it would only need a word more for Bill—in violation of all rules of hospitality, in which he was not well read—to take the old man by the collar and trousers, and set him outside. I turned the tide by telling of Henry Neaville's frozen feet, and we got along harmoniously until the clock said it was time for congratulations on the new year. As the good-nights were said Bill whispered that we should have a deer hunt on the first day of the new year, and after the rest were gone we sat down over our pipes and arranged for it.

A couple of inches of snow fell early in the night on top of the old snow, which was about the same depth, but not hard. The new year of 1857 opened still and mild, without being bright; as perfect a day for a hunt as it was possible to have. Every rabbit that had ventured out since midnight left evidence of its wanderings, and we saw where the quail had huddled on the ground and had risen in the morning. The partridge left a broad trail until it tired of wading and took to a tree. All these things were noted as we went off to the northwest to strike the Grant River. Bill wanted to talk about "Old Poppy Knight," and I tried to keep him still. Two winters in the woods had the usual effect of making a fellow think more than he talks. We were on a ridge and were about one hundred feet apart.

Bill said: "Old Pop made me mad last night, bustin' in the talk to know if squaws was good-lookin'. What 'n thunder is that to him?" and then he launched out in his rough way and "swore like our army in Flanders." There was a crackling of brush, followed by several thuds, and Bill's rifle spoke. I saw nothing; the deer had been lying down on Bill's side of the ridge listening to what Bill thought of the propriety of O. P. Knight's inquiry into the physical attractions of the Ojibway maidens, and no doubt feared that Bill's indignation might take a wrong direction, and so considered it best to leave him to settle it with Mr. Knight without being a party to the row. We went to the place where the deer jumped, but found no blood. Going back to the ridge, about fifty yards, I looked the range over, and then found where the bullet had cut a twig and then raked up the snow half way to the spot where the deer jumped, no doubt when it was several rods on its journey.

"Who'd think there was a deer lyin' down in that thicket?" asked Bill. "Why, I s'posed we'd have to track 'em after we found where they'd been?"

"If they're not afoot you never know when you may jump one along a ridge," said I, "for they seldom lie in the hollows, and you can look for 'em on the sheltered side of a ridge 'most anywhere. Now let Old Poppy Knight rest, and keep still for a while. Your shot has been heard by every deer within three miles, and it may have put some of them afoot, but you will have to tramp before you see one. We're nearing the river now; the ridge forks here; you take the left hand one, and we'll come together at the river."

After going about half a mile and seeing no track I heard Bill's shot from the western ridge, stopped and cocked my rifle. A buck came dashing down the hill and I slipped behind a tree. Great bounds he took, and up the hill on my side he came, panting with the effort. Gaining the ridge, he stopped, turned to look back, and presented a full broadside view to me at not over one hundred feet. As I fired he leaped into the brush, but the great spurt of blood on the snow told the tale. I gave a whoop, and got an answer, then called, "Come over here!" and sat down on a log. It seemed hours before Bill made the journey across the valley that the buck had made in a very few minutes, if he really consumed any time at all. We took the track, and down by the river we found the deer, dead. Bill's bullet, shot on the jump, had grazed the breast just back of the shoulder, cutting the hair and marking the skin—an excellent shot at a jumping deer, for no doubt it jumped before Bill saw it.

The buck was a fair-sized four-pronged one. We dressed it, and then went to a spring, washed, and ate our luncheon, for it was far past the noon hour. As we lighted our pipes Bill remarked: "We'll divide that deer when we get up, and it's about all we will want to carry home. Under the rule that the first bullet hole takes the hide it's mine, but you can have the head if you want it."

"All right, Bill; show up the hole and take the hide; that's the rule."

"Didn't I make a hole in his belly just behind the shoulder? Do you mean to say I didn't hit him?"

"There's a scratch there that a jury might decide was made by your bullet, or might have been made by a pine knot when the deer stepped over a log. I don't want the hide; Charley Mallett wouldn't give over $1 for it, anyway. I am sure your bullet made the mark, for there was fresh blood there, and the cut was across the breast, not lengthwise, as it would have been done when the deer was on the run. Take it; I only spoke in that way because of your claiming the hide so promptly."

"Now, see here," said Bill, "I don't want that hide. I ain't no hog! All I thought of was that I didn't miss that 'deer slick and clean as I did the other one, and I wanted you to know it. I'll tell you what we'll do; let's give a quarter of the deer and the hide to old John Jamison, who has been sick all winter an' hasn't earned a dollar; send a quarter to that widow up there on the British Hollow road; I forget her name, but her husband died before you got back from the North. Then we'll keep the rest, and if Old Poppy Knight would like a steak— no, I'll feed it to Charley Guyon's 'coon dog first. Say, I wouldn't let that old pelican have a smell of it. No, sir, not by a mill privilege."

His charitable proposition was carried out; we had our hunt and all the meat we needed. It's not hard to give away what you don't need; the difficulty often occurs in deciding what it is that you don't need when your neighbor is destitute, and is in desperate need of things which you don't—here I get off the track, and go to moralizing over what struck me as a good streak in the nature of Bill Patterson, who took good care that no one should discover that he had what he would have considered a weak spot. He would have fought me for that deer skin, but you see how it went.

February had come, and Henry Neaville's feet had got over their October freeze. He drifted into my house one day on a south wind when Bill was profanely reciting his adventures in Sonora and New Mexico, and said: "There's a lot of fish in a pond hole down by the river, and they're all a-crowding up to a little spring that keeps an open place and gives 'em air. There's a lot o' bass, pike, dogfish and all the other kinds, an' you can just dip 'em up by the scoopful; what do you say about going down and getting some?"

"All right," said Bill; "we'll go in the morning. I've got a dip net that only wants a handle, and I'll put one on in the morning. Come down after breakfast and we'll go. I haven't had a fresh fish this winter, and have forgotten just how they taste."

Our outfit consisted of a dip net, or a landing net of coarse mesh strung on a fourteen-inch ring, with a rake handle attached; an axe, a spear, or "gig," and some mosquito netting, which Henry brought. What the latter was for I had no idea, but then I had not seen the place. It was snowing a little, with hardly any wind. The pool, or pond hole, as Henry called it, might have covered two acres, and had been washed out of the soft soil by the great river some time when it overflowed its banks, and in summer it was dry. A spring came in its eastern edge and kept the ice from making up to the shore. Thousands of large fish crowded to this opening for air, and I never saw such a sight before nor since. There must have been many thousands of the different fishes which inhabit the Mississippi River crowded into a small space, those in the rear pushing up to the open place and forcing the others to the shore and around to the rear, as if they said: "You have had your chance to breathe, now make way for us."

I stood in amazement at the scene. Bill took the axe, and cut the opening larger until the thin ice at the margin was gone and we could stand at the edge. I took the net and dipped up a few fish, trying to select my favorite crappies and small catfish.

"Let me take that net," said Bill, and he proceeded to lift the fish by the netful. The spear was of no use; it would only mar the fish, and we could take all we wanted with the net.

After a while, when there was about one hundred pounds of fish on the ice, I thought it time to quit, and mentioned the fact that we had all we could carry and enough for ourselves and friends. There seemed no use to kill more.

"I don't intend to stop short of a ton," said Bill. "Henry, you go back to the village, and get a team from Jo Hall and a bob-sled, and we'll take a load of the best of these to Dubuque, and if they take well we'll give 'em another load this week. Keep it still, or there'll be a big gang down here to take a share in the fish."

This was taking a commercial view of the fishing, and I said to Bill, after Henry had gone: "I never liked to see men rob the woods of game and the waters of fish to send to market, and I only thought to come down and get a few for our own use. It's this wholesale slaughter for market that has made the East barren of fish and game, and I've talked against it there and I don't want to engage in it here. Fur is a different thing from game, and I could trap for a living easy enough, but somehow it doesn't seem right to take advantage of those fish and market them, when if we take what we want and leave the rest to breed, there will always be plenty for us."

Bill's remarks, carefully expurgated, were something like this, but contained more adjectives, for in his ordinary conversation he "swore like our army in Flanders:" "Look a-here! What are you chinnin' about, anyhow? I've been all over Sonora, New Mexico and Californy, and fished in more rivers than you ever see, but these Mississippi bottoms are different. It's this way: In the spring and fall there's a heap o' water comes down this valley, an' it overflows all these bottom lands, and the fish

come up close to the bluffs to keep from being swept
down in the current.   When the water falls they get
trapped in these holes, and there they are."

"Yes; but when the spring freshet comes don't they
swim out and go to their breeding grounds, and so keep
the river stocked?"

"Not by," and he referred to a spot where a mill
might be placed. "These ponds freeze over tight and
the fish die.   They die in thousands of just such holes all
along the river, and they have died in this hole year after
year.   This spring water coming in here is a new thing;
it wasn't here last winter, and it may stop or cold weather
may close it; I don't care whether it does or not, there's
a chance to send a sleigh load of fish to Dubuque, and
that's all there is of it."

I saw it was as he said.   I cut into some of these pond
holes later in the winter, and found a stench of decaying
fish.   Within the past few years the United States Fish
Commission, through the urgent requests of Colonel S.
P. Bartlett, of the Illinois Commission, has sent a car up
the river, and seined the imprisoned fish from these holes
and returned them to the river—as good a work as hatch-
ing millions of fish eggs; perhaps better, for it saves the
parents, and allows them to breed next spring.

Henry came with the team, and found us on the shore
cooking fish and frying sausages for dinner. Bill thought
he was as good a camp cook as I, but we differed on that
point.   Without discussing the question, I feel impelled
to go off the track to say: Our open-air appetites, whether
in the woods or on the waters, make camp cooking seem
superlative.   Benedick says in "Much Ado About Nothing:" "But doth not the appetite alter?   A man loves the
meat in his youth that he cannot endure in his age."

This leads me to say that after many years' experience

in all kinds of dining—strike me if you will—it is now my mature judgment that taking a dinner in the abstract, without any of the poetical surroundings of the chase, and the sentiment which hovers about game killed and cooked by yourself, a grand dinner served by a competent *chef* to gentlemen in evening dress has a charm for me that increases with age. Not that I have lost all taste for an *al fresco* feast in camp style; but there are pleasures of many kinds, and they are not always comparable. I only draw the line at those messes called clam chowders, fish chowders and the nightmare provoking clambake. These may be classed as coarse feeding, but I have had as delicious trout, venison and other game served in camp as ever tickled a tongue. Yet a service in courses, the varied products of the vineyards, the fruits and desserts—I like all good things, but the best of all is good company, whether in evening dress or flannel shirt; yet I can't admit that camp cookery excels the best hotel cookery, taking each on its merits outside of sentiment. We deceive ourselves in this; we come in hungry enough to eat a bear before his skin is off, and "hunger is the best of sauce."

You have often come into camp with a string of trout and had to clean and cook them before you could eat supper. You stuck a stick in the gills with a bit of pork in the mouth, and stood them up before the fire and turned them when necessary. When you thought they were done you sat down, and ate them half raw and half burned, and your hunger prompted you to say that you never ate such trout before in your life. If trout cooked in that same way were set before you in a restaurant you would reject them as unfit to eat. But the memory of a camp dinner with an appetite only six hours old, but very large for its age, has a halo around it that should properly encircle the appetite. Though not a taxidermist, I have stuffed several thousand first-class appetites, but never could preserve one.

Henry sat down and helped us out on the dinner, and told how he had thrown the villagers off the track by saying that we had killed two deer and a bear, and needed a sleigh to bring them in. A mink trotted down along the shore to the hole where he usually fished, stopped short of it, looked over at us and took the back track. Henry said: "That mink made a mistake, and thought it was Friday. When he saw us eating sausage the fact that it was Thursday dawned on him, and he left for the landing and Chapman's chicken house."

We sorted the fish, throwing all gars, dogfish, red-horse and other poor kinds aside, and loaded the sleigh-box with bass, pike and crappie, and my two companions started down the river on the ice for Dubuque, Ia., some dozen miles below, and after waiting a while I got a team which had brought pig lead to the landing to take up a good lot of fish and our traps to the village. Besides these things there was a bag with about a bushel of young fish of many kinds, which had been seined out of the spring by the mosquito netting which Henry had brought. None of these were over two inches long, and I was in doubt what they were intended for until Bill said: "You spread these little fish out so that they don't heat nor freeze, and when we get back I'll have 'em cooked as the Mexicans used to cook 'em down in Sonora. I've seen lots of things out there that you fellows never dreamed of, and here I am wasting my time in these old lead mines. What's lead worth? Thirty dollars a thousand! I mined for gold worth $20 an ounce. Say, when you get them fish to Potosi and go to dividin' 'em, just lay out some o' the best for old John Jamison and the widow on the British Hollow road. We'll be back to-night or to-morrow, and if this trip pays we'll do her again. Goodby."

The team I found at the landing was from British Hollow, and the driver gladly went over to the fishing place. I told him to pick out all the fish he wanted, and put them in front so that they couldn't be given away. I had the fish assorted for the different people, and delivered all but the last two lots. We stopped at Jamison's, and at my call a man came out to know what I wanted.

"I've a lot of fish for John that Bill Patterson has sent up to him; Bill knows John well, and here they are; I s'pose you're John, and you will remember that we sent you up some venison about the New Year."

The man took the fish and said: "John died early this morning, but his children may use them, and no doubt will be glad of them, for John left nothing; he's been an invalid so long. As a friend of the family, I thank Mr. Patterson and you——" but I had started the horses on, saying to the driver: "Get out of this quick! We can't do any good and—let the horses go."

A few rods brought us to the cabin of the widow. She came to the door in response to a knock, and I stepped in and explained my errand. Something in her manner made me lower my voice, and she began to cry. By the light of a tallow candle I saw that she was a poor, thin, careworn woman, and I fumbled the cap in my hands awkwardly, hardly knowing how to get out of the house without indecent haste. She was prematurely old, and it was doubtful if she had ever been even passably good-looking. Poverty and care were stamped in every line of her face. She might have been thirty, but looked to be twice as old. Her little girl, an only child, was very ill. Would I look at it?

I followed her to a back room, and found a child of about six years lying on a bed and apparently asleep, but twitching violently. Then came a muscular spasm which doubled the little sufferer up, and I was alarmed.

"Has a doctor seen the child?"

"No; I thought she'd get over it without the expense of a doctor, for I am very poor. My husband was hurt a year ago by a fall down a shaft, and died last October. I've worked when I could get work, but have not been strong enough to do much. It's a hard world for the poor and weak, and if my little girl goes from me I want to go, too."

I don't know that it did any good, but I took the girl in my arms, and walked the floor with her, trying to help her unconscious struggles. When the spasm passed I laid her on the bed, and went out to find some one to go for a doctor. I found a man going to Potosi on foot, and told him to send Dr. Gibson out at the earliest moment, and returned to the house. If the doctor would only come, and let me get out! The time passed so slowly. I was not fitted by nature to be either a doctor or an undertaker, and suffering which I could not relieve was a thing to be left to itself; but I could not leave it. The child had several spasms, and the night passed over a little cabin with sorrowing mother and a dying child in the arms of a rough, untrained fellow, who would help both if he only knew how to do it, but who wished himself a thousand miles away.

It had never occurred to me that I would be missed, so busy was my mind with the misery in the cabin, and when a jangle of sleigh bells stopped in front of the cabin long after midnight I mentally said: "There comes the doctor."

I was walking the floor with the child in my arms,

when the door opened and the doctor came in, followed by Bill Patterson, Henry Neaville, Mrs. Patterson and a dozen other men and women.

"What had kept me so long?" "Why didn't you come home?" Bill said: "When we sold them fish in Dubuque for less than we've got to pay Jo Hall for the team, I said: 'I'll be blessed if I ever take another load of fish to Dubuque.' If you've got them little fish all in good order we'll have 'em fried at Johnny Nicholas' restaurant to-morrow night, and I tell you they'll be fine. Hello! What's the matter?"

While he was talking to me the mother of the child dropped fainting to the floor, for she had seen the women take the child from my arms—dead!

WILLIAM WARREN.

IT is a blessed privilege to be past the meridian of life to-day. What a store we white-headed fellows have of things which a younger generation of men can never attain! In the charmed recesses of remembrance lie the vast flocks of wild pigeons, and of game to be had in an hour's walk, where now there is naught of life save the abominable imported sparrow. And then there was the grand and glorious Civil War—but I must not write of that further than to say to the young men who were born too late to take part in it that I am sorry for them. Still they have the compensations of youth, and if they are fortunate enough to live where there is still some game left, or if they have the means to travel to the far-off places, they will, after they get past the noon of life, have the same feeling of commiseration for the boys who are forty years in the rear of them which I have expressed.

There are two reasons for writing the above paragraph; one was because I accompanied Warren on my first and only buffalo hunt, and the other was because while taking "a cold bottle and a hot bird" with my old army companion, Baron Berthold Fernow, once of Poland, but later Major of United States Volunteers and of the Topographical Corps of Sherman's army, last winter, the Major, in response to a question if he was still living in Albany, said: "No, I am now living at 151 West Sixty-first street, in this city, a place where I used to shoot rabbits when I first came to America, and where I once got lost in the underbrush and strayed away off to the northeast, where the Astoria ferry now is." Think of it! The street is near the lower end of Central Park, and right in the middle of the city. The late ex-President Chester A. Arthur told me that he had shot woodcock where the Fifth Avenue Hotel now stands, and that is only at Twenty-third street. All this has nothing whatever to do with my fishing with William Warren further than to show what changes take place in our rapidly growing country. As a historian, in a feeble way I record it. As an American and a naturalist, I regret it. Emigration has been encouraged to build great cities where the buffalo should still range over territories which ought to have been left for Americans who will be born a century hence. These sentiments prove to you that I am an "old fogy," but one who believes that we should not give away our great farm when we have children growing; but that is "politics," and so we will go on to tell about this man with whom I fished in Kansas in the year 1857.

I was boarding with a man named Serrine, on the Cottonwood, while looking up a suitable place to claim a quarter-section, and Warren came there often. He was from Chicago, and had a claim over on the Neosho.

He was a big, strong fellow, about twenty-five years old, with a dark, pleasant face and a habit of clipping his words. A favorite way to begin a sentence was with the word "Betcher," which stood in his vocabulary for "I'll bet you." So one day in the spring he said to me:

"Betcher da'sent take a day off o' land-lookin' an' go shootin' buffler fish; they're just comin' up on the riffles now and a-wallerin'. They're thicker 'n hair on a dog; 'f you never shot 'em you'll like it. What yer say?"

My rifle had been packed in a chest and sent by

freight from Potosi, Wis., and the chest had been stolen somewhere on the rivers or at St. Louis, and I had only a Colt's navy revolver to shoot with. From what I had seen of these big, unwieldy buffalo fish on the riffles it was certain that the revolver was good enough for such work. The fish were very plenty, and were mating and spawning on every riffle, but at the least alarm would dodge down into the pools below. The Cottonwood was a series of deep pools and gravelly riffles, over which the water flowed swiftly, and sometimes these were so shallow as to leave the hump-backed buffalo partly out of water. The river may have averaged sixty feet across, and it cut through a deep alluvial soil, forming high banks in most places, except at the inside of curves, where the current had made a gentle slope to the water. The riffles were at these points, and we could get near them by approaching the fish from the low side. It was not a particle of sport, but Warren thought it fun, and wanted to go on killing after we had more than we could carry; but I said no, and we strung our fish and went home.

"Betcher I c'ld kill a thousand buffler in half a day an' not go over two mile on the river. What's the reason you wouldn't kill any more? Don't yer like the fun?"

"No; there's no fun in killing things that you don't want to use, unless they're rats or other vermin which annoy you. My idea of sport is to hunt something which is hard to find, and is some use after you have found it. Shooting these fish is good enough when you want a change of diet from ham and salt pork, but they're too easy for sport. As you say, you could probably kill a thousand in half a day, but shooting at a mark is just as much fun; in fact, it would be more fun for me than to kill things for the mere sake of killing."

This buffalo fish is a coarse thing, a relative of the sucker tribe, with a similar mouth; perhaps it is as good as the carp, but then we had not the carp, and the taste of the buffalo has faded too much in forty years for comparison. My present notion is that both are worthless as food, but a residence by salt water may have spoiled me for enjoying most fresh-water fish, especially carp and suckers.

Warren sold his claim and took another while I was still undecided, and we put up a little cabin on the bank of the river and "batched" together. Within a few miles several town sites were laid out with pegs, each with grand parks, court house squares and grand avenues—on paper.

> "Behind the squaw's light birch canoe
>   The steamer rocks and raves,
> And city lots are staked for sale
>   Above old Indian graves."—*Whittier.*

The genius of speculation was abroad, and within a radius of five miles there were at least a dozen "future railroad centres" laid out. I only remember "Columbia" on the Cottonwood, where there was a grocery and gin-mill combined, kept by a man named Jeff Thompson. He had maps, and sold lots in the Eastern cities and took in what he could gather. He offered me ten lots in the heart of his "city" for my revolver, but somehow I thought I needed the pistol more than I did town lots. Then there was "Chicago," on top of a bluff, where I shot sandhill cranes later on, which never got beyond the peg and map stage. Warren had a big interest in this, and traded some lots for a yoke of cattle and a wagon. I doubt if there is even a farm house there to-day. Emporia was laid out high on the open prairie, between the Cottonwood and Neosho, with no water in sight. It was not a promising place for a town, but when my father offered to send me his double fowling-piece I traded the revolver for a block of lots in Emporia.

Warren said: "Betcher your revolver is gone, lost, vanished, an' vamoosed. Why, that place will never amount to a hill o' beans, but if you'd invested in Chicago you'd have been O. K. They've dug over one hundred feet for water there in Emporia, and didn't get it. Whatter they goin' to do without water? Just dry up, that's all. Betcher'll wish that revolver back 'fore long, for that was worth something."

There was a big push behind Emporia. A lot of Eastern capitalists spent money to find water, and they found it. As soon as it was struck I was offered $150 for my lots, and I shook the money under my friend's nose. That find of water after nearly a year's digging made a great railroad centre, and the neighboring "peg" towns were heard of no more.

Meanwhile I had located a claim, and filed it at the land office. This gave me the privilege, as an actual settler, of pre-empting or buying the quarter-section of 160 acres at the Government price of $1.25 per acre before the tract in which it was situated was offered at public sale. That spring there had been discoveries of great deposits of lead in the Ozark Mountains, and among the miners of Potosi, Wis., there was much excitement and considerable emigration. I had written father that I would go to the mines in Missouri. That shirt of Nessus which causes the restlessness of border life impelled me to go somewhere. I had tired of life as it was lived in the mines and woods of Wisconsin and Minnesota, and a new field of adventure was opened. With the average miner, who is a born gambler, there was the prospect of gain. I was not an average miner, nor a born gambler, and only wanted change and adventure. I had read all about Daniel Boone, Davy Crockett, Kit Carson and Cooper's men of fiction, and dollars cut no figure in my calculations. I was young; old age and its needs seemed to be centuries away, if indeed it was ever thought of. I revelled in my youth and strength, and thought they would last forever. The quarter of a century that I had lived seemed to comprise the whole existence of the world, and all that had gone before my recollection was merely a fairy tale.

When I left Albany, in 1854, my father had exacted a promise that I would not join an expedition against the Indians. He knew that I loved a fight of most any kind, and when he learned that I proposed to go to the Ozarks he wrote me that he wanted me to go to Kansas and select a farm on which he could pass his declining years. This was not funny then, but it is to-day. My father was reared on a farm, but left it when eighteen years old, and always looked to getting back on one. Now, when I am six years older than he was then, I know that his nervous organization, after years of absence from farm life, was no more fitted to it than my very different temperament was. But he wrote me that he had a land warrant from the War of 1812 (not his own by right of service, for he was born in 1800), and that he wanted me to select the place in Kansas.

The newspapers had been filled with accounts of "bleeding Kansas," and the troubles were not entirely over when our surveying party came out of the Minnesota woods in the last month of 1856. There was a fight there over the slavery question—a matter that I had paid no attention to, but there was a fight. I looked around and got letters of introduction to General Jim Lane, the "Free State" leader, and went to Kansas; we spelled it

Kanzas in those days, and my tongue has never been able to accommodate itself to the modern soft way of speaking the name.

I put up a log cabin on a good quarter-section which had a stream running through it, and also had several acres of timber—two valuable things in that prairie country. Warren helped me in this, and also in splitting enough black walnut and mulberry rails to fence in ten acres. The land cost $1.25 per acre, but it cost $3 per acre to break the heavy prairie sod. I was playing farmer!

> "One man in his time plays many parts,
> His acts being seven ages. * * *"

Warren and I kept bachelor's hall until past midsummer, when my house was in order for business, and my little family came on from Wisconsin. Our work was at a distance, and we took turns at cooking, and on Sundays we cleaned up and washed the dishes. A very good housekeeper to whom I told this asked in undisguised astonishment: "Didn't you wash your dishes every day? Why, how did you get along?"

"My dear madam," I replied, "you are a most excellent housekeeper here in the effete East, but know little how to manage a bachelor establishment in Kansas in that early day. If we had washed our tin plates after every meal, as is the custom in some places, the microbes set free from the newly-turned sod would have attached themselves to the tin, and our lives would have been in danger from *tintinambulacra*. No, my dear madam, we did not dare risk it; so we turned our plates over after each meal to protect them, and only dared to wash them once a week. This was a fearful risk, but we did it; I now think it would be safer not to have exposed the plates to the influence of hot water and soap at all, but fortunately we escaped all harm—perhaps because we had youth on our side."

She paused a moment, drew a long breath and said: "You don't tell me——. Oh, men are horrid, anyway! I don't believe a word of it!"

Warren said: "When you take the ox team up to Emporia after the mail and provisions, see if you can't get some vegetables. The cows got into my garden, and cleaned up what the 'coons, bugs and other things left, and we want some green stuff; see if you can get some onions, beets, cucumbers, or anything."

Among the things which I brought was a fine bunch of early beets, and we promised ourselves a treat. We peeled and sliced them, and put them in vinegar. Next day they were set out for the evening meal, when we talked about them.

"Betcher," said Warren, "them beets is more'n a hundred years old. I've seen lots o' beets, but they wuz allers tender an' good."

"They can't be old. They don't keep beets over a year like dried beans; besides, didn't you see the tops were green? I think they're a new kind, or else the soil here is not good for beets."

"Betcher they ain't cut thin enough for the vinegar to sof'en 'em. These cukes are all right; they're cut thin, and the vinegar goes right through 'em and they're tender."

"Yes, the cucumbers are good enough, but what ails the beets I don't know. I've often eaten 'em at home when mother cut 'em up in vinegar; perhaps they want to be soaked in vinegar longer to make 'em tender; I don't know just how long they have to stay in vinegar before they're fit to eat."

"Betcher right! Let 'em soak awhile an' they'll get tender, an' beets is a mighty good relish, too; they're good for what ails you; for a man can't live on salt pork, ham and all that stuff, salt codfish and mackerel and sich like, without a little vegetable food, or he will go to the bad; betcher life he wants a change. Just put them beets away until they get tender; that's all they want."

The beets were set aside in vinegar until such time as they might be fit to eat. We sampled them daily, but there was no perceptible improvement, and Sunday came. After cleaning house, or kitchen and dining-room—for our 10x12 cabin was not only these, but also our grand *salon*—we brushed ourselves up, and walked up to Serrine's ranch, where Mrs. S. and Mrs. Judge Howell were discussing some abstruse question, of which we were ignorant, when they both turned and in the same breath asked how we were getting along with our "batching." Warren went into details about the biscuit, pancakes, roasts, fries and stews, and finally mentioned the difficulty with the beets.

There was an instantaneous duet of soprano and contralto: "Didn't you boil 'em first?"

I sneaked outside at once, and have no idea of how Warren stood off the two women; but the logs of the house were not chinked tightly enough to keep out a whole mess of laughter, which came through in ripples at first, then in waves, and finally in shrieks that toppled the barrel from the chimney, and then the cabin filled with smoke.

On our way down the Cottonwood we said little until we got to the door of our castle, when Warren turned and said: "Did you know that beets should be boiled before they were sliced and cut up in vinegar?"

"Well, no; not exactly boiled, but I knew that something ought to be done to them like baking or frying or——"

"Betcher didn't know but what they were just cut up in vinegar like cucumbers, just as I thought. Betcher Mrs. Howell will spread that story, an' every woman up both rivers will know the beet story before a week. Well, let 'em. There's a whole mess of things that they don't know. How in Gibraltar do they s'pose a fellow is to know that the tender beets that he finds on the table have been boiled, any more than the cucumbers have been boiled?"

The slavery troubles, which had partly subsided, began to break out afresh, and it was evident that another great effort to make Kansas a slave State would be made. Congress had already abrogated the Missouri Compromise, and this opened the Territories of Kansas and Nebraska to the slave power, as it left the question to be decided by the actual settlers. Two conflicting Territorial governments had been established. Blood had been shed at the first election, when armed invaders had taken possession of the polls and elected a lot of non-resident pro-slavery men as a Legislature, which passed a law making it a capital offence to harbor or assist runaway slaves; and they had the backing of President Buchanan, and the support of General Harney, then in command at Fort Leavenworth. But against this was a great majority, who had determined that Kansas should enter the Union as a free State or not at all.

Our section was comparatively quiet. We were running short on provisions, and, as the staple articles were costly owing to the long haul by teams, we would take our teams to Fort Leavenworth, lay in half a dozen bags of flour—it came in one hundred pound bags—sugar, coffee, pork, bacon and other things, saving the transportation and the profit of the local trader. The prairie roads were good in June, and at the frequent streams good camping places were always found with the three prime requisites—wood, water and grass. At Lawrence we fished in the Kaw River, and caught seven catfish, one of which weighed nine pounds; we ate the smaller ones, and gave the big one to a passing family in a prairie schooner.

There was a municipal election while we were in Leavenworth. The Free State men won, but there was a lot of beautiful fights. A border ruffian named Lyle, who had murdered several men, provoked a fight with an old man, and was killed by a Free State man named Hallen, who was arrested.

The excitement was intense and contagious. Few slept that night. Warren and I volunteered, with others, to guard Hallen; but there was no attempt made to lynch him. Next morning Hallen was refused bail, and was committed to Fort Leavenworth for safe-keeping, and only our respect for the uniform of Uncle Sam allowed a sergeant and a squad to remove him; but Hallen bribed a guard and escaped, went to Lawrence and was never disturbed.

The buffalo country was west of us, but there remained a few deer and antelope, as well as wild turkeys, along the Cottonwood and Neosho, and Warren and I each had a Sharps rifle, which had been sent from the East to help make Kansas a free State, and which had been issued to us at Leavenworth while guarding Hallen. October had come, and one morning there was a light fall of snow, and Warren came to my cabin. "Hurry up," he called, "there's a deer's track going straight for that bunch of willows in the buffalo wallow over there to the west, where we shot the prairie chickens a week ago."

We struck the track in the fast melting snow, and came up to within one hundred yards of the wallow, which was a small one not over fifty feet in diameter, and then consulted in a whisper how we should form for the attack. We had come up against the wind, and there seemed ample time to consult, when—a flash of gray bounded out on the prairie from the other side of the wallow, gathered its legs and leaped again as two rifles called "Halt!" The buck halted and never went again. One bullet nearly severed a hind hoof, and one plowed up from below through his heart. Both rifles were of the same calibre, and who it was that killed that deer remains as obscure as "the mystery of Gilgal."

We bought Indian ponies, cheap but serviceable, and accustomed to any amount of abuse, for an Indian never has a particle of regard for a saddle sore, but claps on the saddle in the same old place in perfect indifference to the suffering of an animal, and this trait has hardened my heart against the red man; he has no sympathy for suffering—not even his own. He has served the purpose for which he was placed here just as other created things have, and he dies out before civilization and must go, as we must when we have exhausted the coal which was stored up for our advent, and our planet falls in line with the dead worlds which—have no Indian ponies.

A little castile soap and water, with tallow afterward, soon put our ponies in shape for travel, and as the winter came on the troubled times increased. The bogus Legislature of Lecompton had authorized a convention to form a State constitution during the summer, and things were getting red hot. Warren and I decided to go to Lawrence, and offer our services to General Jim Lane. At that time we thought Lane to be the best and greatest living American. He could sway men by his impassioned oratory, to which his profanity added the charm of emphasis. We had met old John Brown down at Osawatomie, and would have none of him. Brown was sitting by the roadside singing "Blow ye the trumpet, blow," through his nose, and Warren said:

"Betcher he's an ole feller that turns his camp into a Sunday-school half a dozen times a day; I don't want any of him; if you want to go with him, all right; Jim Lane is good enough for me."

Said I: "Billy, I've got no more use for old Osawatomie than you have. There wouldn't be a bit of fun with him. He's a religious fanatic, and says that the Lord has sent him here to do things. I don't object to his doing things, but he won't get me to serve under him. I don't like him, and that's all there is of it. He's in dead earnest; but so is Jim Lane, and Jim is the man to make things hump."

We went back home. To-day the fame of John Brown, who freely gave his life for a cause, is sung all over the North, while my hero, General Jim Lane, is remembered by a few as a political trickster, who killed a man that contested his claim to land, was tried and acquitted (for that was a frontier custom), and then for six years represented Kansas in the United States Senate. Then, following the lead of President Andrew Johnson, he received the indignant reproval of his constituents, and died by his own hand. How differently we look at men and things when they are as widely separated as then and now, when the cool judgment of sixty-three sits upon the rash impulses of the boy forty years ago.

It was in the southeastern portion where things were hottest, and where there was more or less desultory fighting, but party feeling ran high up the Cottonwood, and several Free State men had notices pinned on their doors warning them to leave the territory, or they would be killed. I had a Sharps rifle and a double shotgun, and bought a revolver from a soldier who had come down our way on some business and had no money to get back. It was a Colt's army, big of bore and not very accurate. Every man carried a revolver, and I would as soon think of going to the spring for water without a pail as without a pistol in my belt. I destroyed the notice found on my door; it wasn't just the thing for a woman to see; you know how they are about such things; so I closed my castle, and left the little family in Emporia, giving as a reason that Warren and I wanted to examine some land further west, and might be away a month, and so smoothed it over while we started for Lawrence to consult General Jim Lane. James W. Denver had superseded Walker as Governor in December, and he struck a snag on the start. About a year before this the proslavery officials had seized a wagon containing 150 muskets and carbines from an emigrant train, and had stored them in the cellar under the Governor's residence in Lecompton.

"Boys," said Lane, "you are just in time. Colonel Eldridge is going to start with a battalion to get a lot of rifles that belong to us, and he may have to fight to get 'em; but we'll have 'em, sure. Do you want to go?"

"Betcher," said Warren; "we came up to take a hand in anything that's going on; didn't we, pard?"

"Yes," I answered, "and down our way they're threatening us, and we've got to do some cleaning out down there or abandon our homes and be cleaned out. So far they only threaten, but we know how every man stands in the whole valley, and if they kill one of us the cleaning out will begin at once, and will be thorough."

We went to Lecompton, a motley crowd, some on

foot and others, like Warren and I, on ponies; I should think the "battalion" numbered about one hundred. "Colonel" Eldridge made a demand for the guns as private property, and wound up by saying: "Governor, we merely demand our own, and are fully armed and determined to have those arms. Whether there will be a fight for them rests with you to say." That was an argument that decided the case in our favor. The history of Kansas shows that it was only by illegal voting—"repeating," as it was called—that the Lecompton constitution was adopted; but I can't dwell on this.

A peculiar state of affairs existed. The Territorial Legislature was now under a Free State majority, and it declared the last election to be fraudulent and ordered the Lecompton constitution to be submitted to the people on January 4, 1858, which somehow happened to be the same day named by the pro-slavery authorities for the election of officers under that constitution.

Said Warren: "This thing has got to be fought out. Voting is no use. For every man our side can get here from Boston or Chicago the 'Border Ruffians' can pour in twenty from Missouri. If Congress admits Kansas in as a State, it will be under the Lecompton constitution, which permits men to be held as slaves. If we don't vote for officers we can claim our rights and fight for them; but if you take part in the election you must abide by it."

I favored voting, and we discussed this in our feeble way until Warren said: "Betcher da'sent go up to Lawrence and see what Lane says." We went and found a convention in session that was as divided as we were, and that Lane had a body of men down near Fort Scott. Colonel Eldridge told me that Lane was prepared to fight the United States troops if necessary if the Lecompton men called them out to assist them, and that he thought it best to vote. Again the volcano subsided, and a peaceful victory was won at the polls, the Free State men winning every office under the hated Lecompton constitution. The officers elected promptly petitioned Congress not to admit Kansas as a State under the present constitution, and the petition being granted it put them all out of office from Governor down. Times were not dull there at that time.

Warren sold his second claim, and came to live with me. Game was plenty, and from the ridge pole away from the fireplace there was always a turkey or two, some part of a deer and as many prairie chickens as could be used before spoiling. Antelope were plenty, but I killed only one; we preferred venison. Near the timber rabbits abounded, but we rarely shot them. In summer flocks of screaming paroquets went swiftly through the woods, but boys have been raised since and have no doubt stopped all that. The mourning dove was too common for comfort if one was splitting rails in the woods; its melancholy note only ceased at night. A graceful species of kite sailed over the prairie looking for snakes, and there is a doubt if one of these is left. The only snakes I can remember seeing was a striped one, perhaps the "garter snake," a "blue racer," which, I think, is a form of our common blacksnake, and the small rattlesnake called *massasauga*, which inhabits prairies, and seldom exceeds two feet in length.

Occasionally a train of a dozen wagons would pass our cabin going to and from the buffalo ranges, and often left us a quarter of beef, but neither Warren nor I had any desire to go on these hunts. Perhaps it was because everybody else went, and we did not want for fresh meat. In the summer the little prairie wolves could

be heard running deer or antelope most every night.
No one called them prairie wolves there; they have
another name, perhaps Mexican or Indian, but people
in the East make such a mess of pronouncing it that the
name ought not to be printed. I'll tell you: the name is
ki-o-ty, but, confound 'em, the scholars spell it "coyote,"
and that leads a man to make only two syllables of it.
He lives in the ground, like a fox, and, if not as cunning
as reynard, is as fleet and tireless, and it is said that he
hunts deer in relays, one gang resting till the other brings
the quarry back on the circle. He doesn't hunt rabbits;
just picks 'em up.

One day Warren came in with four little pups in his
coat. I didn't need a "dog" just then, but somebody
said they were "just the cutest little things this side of
the Santa Fe trail," and one was left for us. The young
c—— grew on a liberal diet of milk and table scraps, but
when the first setting hen came off with a brood he
realized his place in nature. He was the fittest and
survived.

The old hen protested, but he ignored the protest, and ate her as a *picce de resistance*, to which the
chickens had been merely an entrée. I also protested—
with a switch, but Lupus could not be made to understand that chickens were not proper things to eat. At
my advanced age I don't understand why chickens should
not be eaten, and yet I tried to force that opinion on my
protegé. He disliked discipline in all its abhorrent forms
of switch, club or boot, and before long, perhaps the time
required to set several chicks free from their imprison-
ment in the shell, it was apparent that there was an absence of cordiality in our intercourse. Lupus was kind
to all but me after I put a chain on him and fenced the
chickens from his domain. He preferred to chew my

hand when I set a saucer of milk before him, and only touched the milk when my hand was no longer available as food. Perhaps, poor fellow, his epicurean palate longed for live chicken, and resented the offer of their bones after his master had taken the choice parts. Gurth, the swineherd, had some such feeling toward Cedric, the Saxon.

We passed the summer, and the corn had nearly passed the roasting-ear stage; I had learned to guard myself from the carnivorous dentition of Lupus, but one day Warren called out: "The cattle are in the corn!" and surely they were.

I was a farmer. Ten acres had been put in sod corn and there was a crop. The crop may have been due to the richness of the soil—or to my excellent farming, if you will. But the fence was down, and half a dozen steers and some cows were doing to that corn what Lupus did to the chickens. Perhaps they were right, but it was no time for argument. I rushed out, and the nearest way was past the kennel of Lupus. He was lying quietly within until I passed, when he suddenly decided to see if my leg might not have a better flavor than my hand, and he acted on the impulse of the moment, and took a piece of it, just above the boot leg, where I kept a favorite muscle well trained for running and another for kicking. He tackled the wrong muscle, and the kicking one came to the relief of its neighbor and projected a boot under his chin with such force that·he was a-weary. Other leg muscles took up the argument, and somehow the same boot that lifted him one under the jaw cracked his skull, and his hide was drying on the fence an hour afterward.

I was sorry, very sorry; so was my leg. It was too bad to kill the poor c——, and it was too bad to kill the poor little chickens. I was a brutal fellow, and I knew it.

Warren said: "You stood it longer'n I would. Them durned kiotys 's got two kinds o' teeth—one for chickens and wild animals, and another for human flesh. Betcher never try to tame another one. Say, them devils runs down a wounded deer or buffler when they find one, and they get him. S'pose we go down on a buffler hunt some time. What d'ye say?"

AMOS DECKER.

AMOS was a raw-boned six-footer, about fifty years old when I met him, bronzed with exposure, and tough as a pine knot. He had drifted ahead of civilization for over a quarter of a century, clearing timber in Michigan, breaking prairie in Illinois, taking up claims and selling out when the neighborhood became too thickly settled; one of those restless men that were always found on the best quarter-section within a township awaiting a customer for his betterments. Unlike his class, he was a man of fair education, whose memory retained much of what had evidently been an extensive course of reading in his youth; but his associations had sadly impaired any grammatical rules he might once have known.

Amos may or may not have been a bachelor. He lived alone in a well-built log house on a bank of the Neosho, near where Burlington now stands; and it was not good form in Kansas in those days to be curious about the past of such men as you chanced to meet. What little I knew of his early life I gathered from stories that he related in the intimacy of camp life. Warren and I had been down the Verdigris River as far as Independence, and then struck off northeast to the Neosho and up that stream. We were looking for land for several Eastern men who wanted to settle together if certain conditions of wood, water, etc., could be found on Government land, for they would not buy claims.

When we got up as far as the cabin of Amos my pony was lame, and we stopped and asked if we could rest and see to our critters. We spoke enough of the Missouri language, which largely prevailed in that part—although occasionally mixed with and diluted by the vocabulary of Posey county, Ind.—to know that a horse was a "critter," and a cow was a "creetur."

After the usual question, "Whar ye from?" and the answer being satisfactory, he looked at my pony's foot and pulled out a cactus thorn that had somehow got in it, although no Indian pony would go near a bed of that plant. He said: "I wouldn't ride him any more to-day; stop over with me to-night, and the pony 'll be better in the mawnin'." In the last sketch I referred to the troubles that disturbed the Territory of Kansas, and strangers were cautious, judging one to be "free State" or "pro-slavery" by his nativity. Amos probably sized us up long before we had him figured down, but it did not take long to decide that he was to be trusted, because he could pronounce his r's, that shibboleth of the man reared south of Mason and Dixon's line—in those days at least.

Warren and I had been camping and living on small game tempered with salt pork and the occasional purchase of corn bread, and when Amos suggested that if the water was not so muddy after the rain he would shoot a pike for dinner, Warren suggested catching one. Amos had no fish hooks, but we had a few and some lines. I watched him rig for skittering, and remarked that he had fished before.

"Yes," said he, "we used to ketch pike in the Wabash an' Massaseep by puttin' on a killy an' slingin' 'em out."

I caught the word "killy," and said: "I s'pose it's a long time since you left New York."

"Never lived in New York," and he gave me a look of inquiry. "What made ye think that?"

"I meant New Jersey. They're close together, and I made a mistake. I can always tell a man that comes from New Jersey, no matter how long he's been away from it."

"See here, stranger! I was a boy in New Jersey once, but you don't know it; you only guessed at it. You may be good at guessin'; guess ag'in."

"Well, you lived down along the salt water, about Raritan Bay or Staten Island Sound. I only want to look into a man's eye to tell where he comes from, and didn't have to ask where you came from."

Then I mystified him with some old sleight-of-hand tricks; passed a half dollar through his hat, let him draw a card from the pack, and then after putting it back with the rest told him to feel in his coat pocket and find it, and several such simple tricks, which puzzled him.

Said he: "Look a-here, stranger, that's the best I ever seed. Oncet, on the old Massaseep, I seed a feller do sich tricks, but he had a show on a boat an' a stage, an' we wus so fur off we c'u'dn't see how he dun 'em; but I'll be durned ef you don't do 'em right here with my own keerds. Say, do 'em over agin', will ye? I want to see how ye do 'em. Say, stranger, ef you'll stay here with me I'll keep ye six months an' show ye the bes' claims about yere."

I declined to repeat the tricks; all great magicians resist such entreaties. I had puzzled this shrewd frontiersman by some simple things, and didn't care to lose my prestige, just as you never wish to make a second rifle or pistol shot after a very lucky first one.

When we were alone Warren said: "Them tricks was all right; I don't know just how you do 'em, but that business of locating the old man in New Jersey is what bothers me, and it bothers him.   How did you do it?"

"If I tell you will you keep it?"

"Betcher!   Wouldn't tell him, but it's workin' on the old man an' it's workin' on me."

"Well, it's all based on a word.   He called a little bait fish a 'killy,' and that name is one left by the Dutch settlers along the salt waters of New York and New Jersey, and is used in no other part of the country.   You noticed that I guessed New York first, but corrected it on the second guessing."

Amos had turned his back to put some wood on the fire, and I carelessly opened a book on a shelf and saw his name in it.   Quickly closing it, I resumed conversation, and afterward laboriously spelled out his name from the lines in his hand.

"Stranger," said he, slowly, "you ar' suttenly a gifted man.   To look at yer no one would ever mistrust it, but I've read about how these things could be done, but never put no faith in it; but now I'm convinced. Stranger, put it thar!"

"Amos," said I, "I'm a greenhorn from the East, but I object to being called 'stranger' by every stranger that I meet.   I'm no more a stranger to a man I never saw before than he is to me, and I won't stand it.   If you'll drop that word we'll be friends and go a-fishing.   What d'ye say?"

Warren had caught some minnows in a little stream, and we went down to the edge of the river to fish with some heavy pecan poles, which our host pronounced "pecawn;" this is a species of hickory which bears the nut of commerce and is very strong and elastic, but heavy.   The water appeared to be so muddy that there seemed but little chance of a fish seeing our bait, but we kept casting and skittering until I got a rise that took the bait off the hook. This was encouraging. Then Amos got a strike that was a savage one; it pulled the line through the ring on the tip of his hickory switch, and scorched his hand in checking the rush. We had no reels; I had probably seen them in Eastern stores, but had no knowledge of them in practical fishing. It was evident that Amos knew as much about fishing as I did, and that was considerable, I thought. He soon checked the fish and landed it, a pike of some kind that may have weighed five pounds. Warren struck something, wet his foot and lost his line, because it was short and was not fastened to the butt.

"Betcher," said he, "that fish would weigh fifty pounds. It was the biggest one I ever hooked. No man c'd 'a' stopped him. Did you see how he took that line out? Why, lightnin' 'ud a' been left away behind in that race."

Amos suggested that the pike would make our dinner, and we let the minnows go and went up to his cabin. While he prepared dinner I looked after the ponies, which were staked out on the prairie; led them down to water, and gave them some salt. I wonder if an Indian ever wasted salt on a pony? It's doubtful. About the only thing that I ever saw them give a pony freely was a club. My tough little fellow, which I had named "Jimsey," a sort of pet form of "Jim," had become greatly attached to me through the agency of salt and sugar. Warren came out and put a hobble on his pony, and I turned mine loose. I urged him to do likewise, but he said:

"That's all right; Jimsey will stay here with Pete because he's hobbled, but, betcher, you let 'em both loose an' you'll never see 'em ag'in."

"Let Pete loose, an' if he goes away I'll give you my claim. The ponies will get better feed if they can range, and a stranger can't catch 'em. We're goin' to stop here all night, and if our ponies go off you can have my claim and its betterments."

"It's a go; Pete wouldn't fetch more'n $30, an' your claim, with house, well and ten acres of broken prairie all fenced is wuth more'n ten times that."

His pony was relieved from the hobble, and we went in to dinner. The pike had been boiled, and had a dressing of drawn butter, a most unusual thing in that region of plain living and high thinking. But Amos had cows, which are well enough in their way, but have a habit of giving milk as a raw material and leaving its manufacture into cheese and butter to other hands. The question was: Whose hands? If I had puzzled Amos with a few simple tricks of legerdemain, such as are published in many books on the subject, he presented the problem: "Who milked the cows and made the butter?" Of course he could do it, but he was often gone for weeks, and cows must be milked twice each day. He had butter, and that is all we knew.

After dinner and pipes Warren went out, and reported that our ponies were not in sight. "Gone down in the timber to browse on the mulberry bark," said Amos. "I'll tell you what it is, you fellers make a mistake in thinking them animiles 'ud druther have corn shelled or on the cob than to browse. They'd druther git down in that bottom timber, an' eat hazel brush an' young mulberry an inch thick 'an to have all the corn 'at you c'd set afore 'em. Let 'em go; they'll look out fer you ef you give 'em salt an' sugar, es Fred says he's done. Don't you worry."

Morning came, and after breakfast we went to the

edge of the woods; I gave the shrill whistle with the fingers, and called my pony's name. Soon he answered, and both animals followed us back to the cabin. Here I will say that I am not a horseman, and have no liking for horses. Few men like horses. They will tell you that they "like a good horse." That means that they like him while he is young and stylish, but when all that is past he may be sold to pull an ash cart. Out on such love! Compare it with the love that the sportsman has for his dog, that has worked the fields with him in heat and cold, his skin torn by briers in summer and his feet frozen in the winter's snows. Is the old dog sold into drudgery in his old days? "Not on your life!" as the phrase of the day goes. Therefore I do not believe that the average man loves the horse for more than he can get out of him. I have a regard for the horse as a most useful animal, just as I have a regard for a locomotive as a bit of useful machinery; but I think, with Charles Dickens, that the head of a horse, at its best, is not a handsome thing, admitting that some horses may have comparatively handsome heads by some modification of that long nose. I am wondering what Dickens would have thought of the head of a moose! There is no doubt but Mr. Moose sees most delicate lines of beauty in the facial contour of Mrs. Moose, but we are not educated up to their standard— that's the trouble, and a moose is the homeliest animal that my eyes ever gazed upon, take head, body or legs, or in "the altogether."

Before we left the breakfast table Amos had arranged a buffalo hunt for the next week, and we agreed to go with him. His idea and that of his neighbors was to take ox teams, and bring back loads of beef for present use and for salting for winter, as well as to get the skins for robes to use or to sell.

The week rolled around, and our arms were cleaned and oiled, knives sharpened, the covered wagon packed with camping necessities and all ready to hitch the cattle to long before the train of ten wagons hove in sight. By the time they reached my cabin we had the ponies haltered and tied behind, and the two yoke of oxen hitched and ready to fall in the rear of the procession when it passed. We went off to the southwest, and in a few miles struck a well-broken trail near the head of the Verdigris, which they had left some distance back to go out of the way to pick us up. We were out four nights before we reached the Arkansas River, some eighty miles from our place. The country was rolling prairie, with timber along the frequent streams, and on the third day out I saw the first live buffalo, a herd of several hundred, which pungled off like porpoises when we came in sight. I wondered why the men did not chase them, but learned that they were not going to kill a buffalo until there was a chance to camp and go at it with some sort of system. Warren counted heads, and said that the other ten wagons contained twenty-five men, and with ours there were thirty ponies in the party.

Amos seemed to be the leader and directed the movements. We camped near the mouth of a small stream on the north bank of the river; the wagons were arranged so as to form a corral to keep the live stock in at night to prevent a stampede by wolves or buffalo, but we had to enlarge the circle with logs. The oxen and ponies had been feeding while we were doing this, and then we gathered them in for the night; three guards were appointed to keep watch, one at a time, for fear of accident that might stampede our stock in spite of the corral, and leave us in bad shape. There was danger that some prowling band of Osages, Kaws or other Indians might do this, so an armed man patroled outside the corral while we slept.

It rained in the night, but the morning was fair, and leaving ten men to see that the stock did not wander and to keep camp, we saddled our ponies, and started to look for the game. To a question Amos replied: "No, we had our guard all picked afore we started, and we don't expect you boys to do any of it. Them ten men will take care o' things night an' day. I ast ye to come an' hunt, didn't I? Then what ye talkin' 'bout? There ain't even an ole bull in sight, but you can see where the herd went north toward the Smoky Hill Fork, an' mebbe gone on to the Saline or way up to Solomon Fork. But there's more—a heap more—an' if we don't strike 'em to-day, why, to-morrer's comin'. If it was dry ground we might see where there was a herd by the dust; there's an old bull now off by hisself, but we don't want him. There's nothin' good about him but his overcoat, an' that's on'y good for buckskin. Them old bulls get druv out by the young ones, an' just herd by theirselves."

We went north to the divide that separates the waters flowing into the Arkansas from those of the Smoky Hill Fork of Kaw River, which feeds the Missouri as far north as Kansas City. The Kaw River is spelled "Kansas" on the maps, but nobody called it anything but Kaw, after the tribe of degraded Indians who lived along its waters. Why this was so may be classed in Lord Dundreary's catalogue of "things no fellow can find out." It was near noon when our ponies were hobbled, and given a couple of hours to graze and drink, while we ate, smoked and talked. There had been no introductions; such things were superfluous in those days among such men, and we had scraped acquaintance, and knew a few Johns, Jims, Bills and Joes. They were rough, ignorant men, frontier farmers, and, as I was in that class, we got along; but it was evident that Amos had exploited me as a magician, for they were curious about me after we made camp at night. They were satisfied that I was a Free State man, for that was the first thing that a man wished to satisfy himself on in those days—are you friend or foe?

This curiosity became too strong to be controlled, and Joe broke out with: "Amos says you can see through a pack of cards and tell how they will deal; is that so?"

"No; Amos says many things besides his prayers. Sometimes I make a guess at what cards a man holds, and if I guess anywhere near right he thinks it wonderful. Hand me that pack, and I'll make a guess on the hand you have after you have cut the cards."

This was a rash statement, for the pack was well worn and dirty; but my fame was at stake. Running them over in shuffling, I got the four aces and a king at the bottom of the pack, and then laid it on the blanket. "Now you cut the cards anywhere you like," said I, and he cut near the middle. Catching the eyes of the crowd, I put the "cut" back on top, and played the old trick of dealing from the end of the pack, giving him a card from the bottom and myself one from the top. When the deal was finished I said: "It's hard to see through these cards, they're so dirty; but your hand beats mine. Keep 'em all together; don't spread 'em out; I can guess better when they're bunched. Let's see! I guess you've got four aces and a queen; no, it's a king, the king of spades, I think; it's a black one; no, it's the king of clubs."

He showed down the hand as I called it, and those simple men were astounded. Both Warren and Amos told me that the hand was dealt from the bottom, but they had seen more of such things than the others. The company of these men was no pleasure; they were men shrewd enough at a bargain, but children in everything else; they had read nothing, could talk of nothing but their own uneventful lives.   Yet it was necessary that something should be done to relieve the monotony of sitting around a camp-fire and listening to the talk of men who could not talk.   Therefore, to relieve myself from the dreadful situation, ten times more lonsome than if no human being had been within one hundred miles, I "opened my box of tricks," learned in the idle moments of schoolboy life, and amused myself and companions with the few simple bits of legerdemain which I could call to mind.   Later in life many such situations have occurred, when if you wanted any fun you must make it yourself, and it is my mature opinion that such a crowd have so little humor that they don't appreciate anything except practical jokes or the wonders of the magician. The humorous story or the witty repartee is wasted on them as much as it would be on a Digger Indian.   Yet that is the state of mind of over half of the people of the United States, taking them "by and large."   It is safe to say that outside what may be called the educated classes few appreciate a joke unless it is in its roughest costume. Refine it, put it in evening dress, and it "is caviare to the general;" but the few who can and do enjoy it are those for whom it was intended.   Jests are of so many kinds that some are offensive.   Bacon, in his "Essays," says: "As for jest, there be certain things which ought to be privileged from it—namely, religion, matters of state, great persons, any man's present business of importance, any case that deserveth pity."   This definition is "funny" —to this generation.

It is funny because "matters of state" are the subject of political cartoons in almost every illustrated paper of to-day, and as for "great persons"—they are the fellows who get it! A young friend at my elbow, who is fully abreast of the current idioms of the day, says: "Yes, an' they git it frequent, right where Alice wears her pearls."

"Johnny," I asked, "what do you mean? What has Alice and her pearls——"

"Why, they get it in the neck! See? Oh, I forget, you wasn't alive last week. Say, that was a big scald on Senator —— in last week's *Scalder*. Did you see it?"

This is the sort of interruption that comes to a man who writes of old times when his surroundings are not congenial. After removing Johnny I tried to get back by a jump of forty years from the present to the day when the buffalo grazed from Oregon to Texas.

On our way back to camp we saw a few solitary bulls, and some time in the night there was an alarm that turned us all out with our rifles ready for action. One of the herders had gone off to the eastward, and struck a small bunch of buffalo and had killed a calf. He had brought the dressed carcass and the skin back, and had stretched the latter between two trees just outside the camp, and some wolves had torn it down and were fighting over it. A few fire brands settled the dispute, and the torn skin was brought in the corral in the interest of harmony.

The next morning was rainy, but the ponies had their corn and we our buffalo veal, and off we went. In less than an hour we saw the whole prairie covered with buffalo, grazing and going south. From a knoll the entire earth seemed covered with them as far as we could see. There might have been a million, or a hundred million, or as many figures as you please to add to the guess. I tell you in sober truth, and I ask you to believe me, I don't know how many buffalo were in that herd. War-

ren said: "Betcher there's more'n ten hundred millions!"
You may take Warren's estimate or mine, as you prefer,
or you may go there and try to count the tracks of that
great herd, I don't care; but I will assert that—that—
there was a big lot of buffalo out there in the open air of
that Kansas prairie one day in the fall of 1858.   That
herd was too big for a few men on ponies to stampede,
and we put in the spurs and got alongside.   Those on
the outside took the alarm, and pressed on without other
effect than to cause the others next them to think they
were pressing for better forage.   Amos had told me to
pick a barren cow if I could find one, a fat young cow
that had no calf near her, and to keep a sharp eye in the
rear, and not get mixed in the herd, or there would be
a dead man and a dead pony.

There was then the spice of danger in this hunt!   It
began to be more interesting.   I had thought it would be
sufficient to make the trip and study the types of men,
see a herd of buffalo with its flankers and rear-guard of
wolves ready to capture a weak straggler, or a calf that
strayed too far; but now that there was danger there was
a promise of sport.   Hotspur truly says:

> "The blood more stirs
> To rouse a lion than to start a hare."

Our party had stretched out over two miles on the
flank of the herd, which was moving slowly in the mass,
but more swiftly near the hunters, and an occasional shot
was heard.   My pony would not take me too near; he
had evidently seen a herd of buffalo before, and I only
feared danger in the rear.   It was getting to be interesting, and after I had singled out my game and tried to get
alongside it, with no other buffalo intervening, it was
exciting.

Unconsciously I gave a whoop as the picked animal came in plain view, and the pony didn't need spur nor whip to quicken his pace to get alongside; he understood it all. Once alongside the galloping beast, a new difficulty appeared; she was at my right hand, and I feared to twist in the saddle, not knowing how the pony would act, and I had never shot from my left shoulder. I did, however, shift the rifle to my left arm and fired. The pony never swerved, and the huge beast dropped. The shot caused the animals near me to crowd away, and I circled about and shot again as the animal was about to rise; a few struggles and I had killed a buffalo.

"Come on! Kill some more!" yelled Warren as he passed, seeking a fresh victim; but I had cooled down, and was content to watch the herd as it turned off to the right up the river, looking more like a sea covered with rolling porpoises than anything I can liken it to. I sat on my pony gazing on the wonderful sight while my companions followed the herd and thought only of killing. To-day it seems like a dream. Where we rode beside that great herd the locomotive shrieks, and a generation of men has been born who may occasionally plow up a bone or a horn that tells of an extinct race of great animals.

It was well along in the afternoon before all had gathered at the camp, and the rain still fell. The guards fed the ponies, and we made a big fire to dry ourselves by, and by the time supper was over there was a rainbow in the east. Amos came over to our wagon, and wanted to know how I liked buffalo hunting.

"Well, Amos," I replied, "it's a good deal like goin' into a barnyard an' shooting cattle; just galloping alongside of a steer, an' pluggin' him with lead until he drops. I'd a heap sight rather shoot woodcock."

"Woodcock!   What's them?   Them air big wood-pickers 'at drums on trees fur grub?   Why, they ain't good to eat, an' it takes as much powder an' lead to kill one on 'em as it does to kill a buffler that weighs over a quarter of a ton.   Wal, that's all right; you can shoot woodpickers ef you like, but when I shoot I want to see something worth shooting at."

I hadn't the courage to explain what a woodcock was; it wouldn't have helped the matter in the least, nor the disposition to argue the case of sport *versus* meat; that would have been equally hopeless.   So I said: "Won't the wolves spoil the skins and the meat to-night before we can save both in the morning?"

"Yes, some on 'em," said he; "but it's the best we could do, an' if we're short we'll kill some more.   We allers kill enough for ourselves an' the wolves, too; there's plenty of 'em."

After Amos left us Warren said: "Betcher didn't kill any more buffler 'an I did.   Honest, now, how many?"

"One."

"Is that all?   Why, what joo do all day?   Betcher I killed half a dozen, and put my mark on a lot more; I come out here for fun, I did, an' now the gang's goin' back as soon as they skin an' load up the meat."

There was no use in talking to this man.   I began to feel myself out of touch with the rest, holding opinions which I did not care to expose to ridicule by expressing them, so I turned the talk in another direction.   We could hear the wolves howl and fight as long as we heard anything, and when silence came morning came with it.

Camp was broken, and the oxen were hitched up and the wagons scattered to do their work.   Guards and all hands went to the labor of skinning, and from inquiry afterward I learned that nearly one hundred buffaloes had been killed by seventeen men! But they were not all choice beeves, and then only the forequarters with the hump rib were to be taken back, for those and the tongues were the choice parts. If time permitted, they would all be skinned, and the wolves would put a polish on the bones.

I had been greatly impressed by that pigeon slaughter which Cooper relates in one of the "Leather Stocking" tales, where the people loaded a cannon and brought down hundreds at a shot, while Natty protested, killed one pigeon for his own use and went his way. That's a good thing for a boy to read; it had its effect on me all through life. It's the fashion to sneer at Cooper, and say that there never were any such Indians as his. That may be so, but it's the fault of the Indians. I like Cooper's Indians, but the real thing, with the dirt and vermin-laden blanket, "Faugh! an ounce of civet, good apothecary, to sweeten my imagination."

We will pass over the disgusting detail of skinning and loading up. Six skins fell to Warren and me, and several forequarters and tongues. That's all there is of our hunt. The party was a most uninteresting one, devoid of intelligence and consequently of humor. Amos and Warren were the only two whose company was endurable on this, my first and only buffalo hunt. If my friend of later years, old Nessmuk, had been there he would have agreed with me, and in his fondness for parody might have said:

> "Better fifty shots at woodcock
> Than ten tons of buffalo."

I learned that the hide of a buffalo bull was not worth taking, because the hair was thin or absent on the hindquarters, and that their beef was worthless; but that the fine robes came from the cows, and that the hump rib of a two-year-old heifer was a fine bit of beef.

On the wall of my den hangs a pair of buffalo horns saved from the slaughter of that day. Below them are a pair of snowshoes, and the sword of an officer of the line. Sometimes an old man rests his eyes upon these relics until the present is forgotten; the rushing bison with their thundering tramp and grunting snort go by in countless herds, which somehow change into battalions of armed men with glistening bayonets and ragged colors, which afterward fade into the brown of the forest and the stillness only broken by the fall of the snowshoe, until he is aroused by a soft hand on his shoulder, and a soft voice by his side says: "Hadn't you better get ready for dinner? You've been asleep."

FRED MATHER.

A CHRISTMAS WITH "OLD PORT."

IT was not a bottle of "crusty Oporto," that celebrated promoter of gout, that made this particular Christmas a day to be remembered; but the "Old Port" was none other than my dear old friend, Porter Tyler, who figures frequently in this book; the same old bachelor, market gunner and trapper of Greenbush, N. Y., whom I had left something over five years before to seek sport in the West.

It was the old story: A boy had spurned the parental roof, and longed for adventure; had found it, and came back under the ancestral shingles. Many weeks before this I had gone the rounds of old friends, and shaken hands; but I was not in physical shape to engage in our usual sports of winter. The freshly-turned prairie sod with its decaying vegetation had left more than what some of the Kansas settlers called "a leetle tech o' ager." But one day the mail at West Albany brought the following:

"GREENBUSH, December 18, 1859.

"YOU OLD JAYHAWKER: Old Port will serve a 'coon, with all the trimmings, one week from to-night, the same being

Christmas. He will get up this dinner in honor of your return to civilization. A few of your old-time friends will be there—not many, for there is only one 'coon; but what they lack in numbers they will make up in quality. Tobi Teller has seen the list, and pronounced it 'a small party, but intensely respectable.' Jim Lansing said: 'Port has killed the fatted 'coon; the calf has returned.' Don't fail to be with us, for Old Port will not be able to skin a muskrat in a month if you disappoint him. It isn't often he gets a 'coon about here, and yesterday he brought one in and said: 'This is just the thing to get up a dinner for Fred.' So never mind your liver nor your ague, but come. Let me know at once, but don't refuse.

MARTIN MILLER."

Dr. Jones said that if I wished to shake off the accumulated malaria of years I must be very careful in the matter of diet, and that a roast 'coon might do a lot of things which I can't now recall, but to which I gave respectful attention. There is no possible use in employing a doctor unless you put yourself in his hands and obey his orders. That is merely common sense. Yet I went to the dinner. How true it is that "all the good things have been said," and that when we read a good book it seems as if the author had somehow forestalled our thoughts before we got to the point of writing them. Honore de Balzac said: "I can resist anything but temptation." I had often acted on this saying, but could never have formulated it. I acted on it in the case of this invitation. Away with Dr. Jones and his hygienic treatment of a disordered liver! Was I to become a slave to a disgruntled gland? Never! "Enslave a man and you destroy his ambition, his enterprise, his capacity."

Climbing the hill which is now Mechanic street, but then was known as the road between the woods, the cottage where that modern Natty Bumpo lived was entered, and there was General Martin Miller. Said he: "Port will want to know that you are here, and I'll go tell him; I've sent down for old Billy Bishop to come up here, and help serve the dinner, for we want Port to sit down and keep down."

While General Miller—Mat we called him, for we were not too stiff in our intercourse—was gone in came Billy Bishop. The old fellow shook hands and said: "I don'd like to get this hill up by Fred Aiken's ole spook house when der nide coom, but by der day he was all ride." Then in came Tobias Teller, a bachelor of some fifty summers and no one knew how many hard winters, who lived down on the banks of the classic stream which we called the Popskinny, the spelling of which is disputed by Colonel Teller and Mr. Stott. He was a delightful old fellow, with a flavor of cognac and madeira about him that mellowed the atmosphere in his vicinity. He was called Tobi among his intimates. His worthy nephew (my army comrade), Colonel David A. Teller, resembles him in many respects, especially in being a bachelor. Then came Low Dearstyne, pilot and captain of the railroad ferry. His name was Lawrence, but the Albany Dutch shortened it to Low; please rhyme this with "now," and not with the negative. The Irish call the name Larrence, and abbreviate to Larry, and, as the old Dutch have gone, this explanation may be necessary: Larry is Irish, and Low is Dutch for Lawrence. Then came Jim Lansing, a man of about forty-five years, who kept a hotel at Clinton Heights, but had been a hotel man in several places. He also was from one of the old Dutch families.

The dinner came on. There was no printed nor written menu, but, as I remember it, the feed was in this order:

MENU.

Soup de snapping turtle.

       Coutlettes de snapper, braisee.

POISSON.

Brook pike au naturel.   Pommes de terre.

RELEVE.

Roast coon, entire. Motto: "Whole hog or none."
Sweet potatoes.

ENTREES.
Grouse au Port Tyler.

ENTREMETS.
Mat Miller's cheese.
Punch.

As master of ceremonies, General Miller took his share of the good things without flinching, and destroyed a goodly portion of the succulent 'coon, and wrecked a grouse so that no anatomist could have identified the remnants; and when the punch came on he arose and remarked: "There doesn't seem much to be said after this grand gorge that our host has got up in honor of the wayward youth who went to the great West with 'Excelsior' as his motto, and has returned like the Biblical hero from herding with swine to the paternal mansion, without the motto on the linen which fluttered in the rear, and looked for all the world like a 'letter in the post-office.' As he is a Shakespearean scholar, I can say to you in the words of the melancholy Jaques: 'Bid him welcome. This is the motley-minded gentleman that I have so often met in the forest.' Let us pledge, standing: The return of the calf—I mean the return of the prodigal."

Tobi turned his off eye in my direction, and Low Dearstyne nudged me to get up. Never had I spoken at a dinner in a formal manner. Miller's quotation from "As You Like It" suggested another saying of Jaque's, beginning, "I met a fool in the forest," but it was evident that it was very inappropriate; but, as I got up in a bewildered way, I somehow blundered through some thanks, and finished by saying: "Somewhere between the lids of the volume that Mat quotes you will find these words, 'I hold your dainties cheap, sir, and your welcome dear.'"

OLD PORT'S YARN.

General Miller then called on Port to rise, and tell how he came by the 'coon which we had eaten. The old man would not get up, but said:

"Y' see, it was this way. I was off, over beyond, away back of Teller's, an' a-makin' toward the hell-hole to pick up a few pa'tridges, 'cause Mat and Tobi said they wanted to have Fred come over here on Christmas. As I watched the snow, I see what looked like a funny track. The snow was soft, an' it had been a-thawin', an' the surface was all spotted with fallin' leaves and dropping snow; but there was a kind o' regularity in these marks that made me look closer, an' sez I to myself, sez I, that's some kind of an animile that's been a-runnin' here, an' I don't know what it is. It was a long track, as near like what a baby could make if it walked through the snow; for there was a heel to it, and it wasn't a bit like the tracks of dogs, foxes, cats, minks or other animals that can be read on sight; but I was bound to know what the thing was. I had no dog—I never hunt with a dog if I can help it—and after tracking it a few miles I found the thing in a tree and shot it. When it came down, I knew by the bushy-ringed tail what it was. It's the only 'coon that I ever heard of being killed around Greenbush, and that's all there is about it. My father, who lived up in Vermont, used to tell of a hunter who had no bullet for his Queen Anne musket, and rammed down a peach-pit on top of the powder and shot at a deer, but thought he missed. Three years later he saw a commotion in the bushes, and fired into it and killed a big buck which had a peach tree growing out of his back; and the hunter not only got a great lot of venison, but took home three bushels of peaches."

Tobi Teller said: "I rise to a question of privilege. This story of the deer and the peaches appears in the sagas of the Norsemen, and is coeval with the sun myths, with the story of the man who cut off the dog's tail, ate the meat and gave the dog the bone. It is just as good, however, as the day it was told by the lamented Baron Munchausen, and I would be the last man to take a shaving off it. But, as every man must contribute his mite of unwritten history, I will ask General Martin Miller to tell our guest what has happened in Greenbush since he left us to seek fame and fortune in the wild West half a dozen years ago."

MAT MILLER'S STORY.

The General looked the party over as he arose and said: "In this quiet village there is little change from year to year, and the only thing which I can recall that might interest you is the stealing of Mrs. Parsons' geese. You all know that this old lady, who lived down on Columbia street, raised great numbers of geese, and derived quite a revenue from the sale of feathers and dressed birds. A neighbor, on a back street, used to help dress these fowls; his name was Gordonier; you all knew him, and he stuttered awfully. When he was drunk he didn't stutter, and so we knew just what his spiritual condition was. When there was a revival in the church there was no penitent louder than old Gordonier, nor one so ready to backslide when the revival was over.

"One morning, when the early birds of Greenbush had gathered about the two bar-rooms which guarded the approach to the Albany ferry, for their morning bitters, old Gordonier entered. Said he: 'D-d-d ye hear the n-n-news?'

" 'No,' said John Pulver; 'what is it?'

" 'S-s-s-som'b'dy s-s-stole all Mrs. P-p-parsons'es g-g-geese. It co-co-couldn't ha' been me, for I was in S-s-s-schenectady.'

"Then he crossed to the other bar-room, and the crowd followed him, and he told the same story, winding up with: 'It c-c-c-couldn't 'a' b-b-been me, for I was in S-s-s-schenectady.' Afterward he went down to Ike Fryer's bar, and the story was retold. John Pearl had heard the yarn three times, and went off and told Pop Huyler. Pop thought a minute and said: 'Let's go 'round to old Gordonier's house, and see if he's got the geese.' So they went and knocked on the door, and when the ole woman opened it Pop said: 'Good morning, Mrs. Gordonier; we just bought a couple o' geese of the ole man, an' he sent us around here for 'em.' The ole woman hesitated a moment and then said: 'All right; just wait here a second, and I'll bring 'em to you; we didn't raise but a few this year, an' I didn't think he'd sell any.' She was very deaf, and didn't hear the men follow her into the house, but just as she pulled a couple of geese from under the bed John Pearl raised the curtain, and he and Pop Huyler saw a great pile of geese, and John remarked that she had a great many. 'Land sakes,' said she, 'you don't call half a dozen many, do ye? Why, they're jest thrown in there on top of a pile o' 'taters, an' that makes 'em loom up.'

"They took the two geese up to Mrs. Parsons, who had just discovered her loss, and told her where she would find the rest of the stolen geese, and then found Gordonier, who by this time had absorbed so many ante-breakfast nips that he stuttered very little.

"The old man, long and lank, was leaning against the bar as they entered, and said: 'It's too bad, but I dunno who done it.'

" 'You're sure you didn't get any of 'em?" asked Pop.

" 'Sure? How c'u'd I when I was in S-s-s-schenectady all night? Just came in on the train.'

" 'All right, but we found the geese under your bed, and you've got to go down with us to Squire Hogeboom's until Mrs. Parsons makes a complaint; come along!'

"He begged and protested, said that some of the boys had put the geese under his bed, if there were any geese there, and the excitement loosened his stuttering valve, which the nips had cemented down, and away they went to the Squire's; but on reaching the corner he broke away, and ran to the dock and jumped off, with a crowd at his heels. John Stranahan jumped into a boat and fished him out. Mrs. Parsons refused to make a charge, but the old fellow picked and returned to her thirty-nine geese. When Pop Huyler met him and asked: 'When have you been over to S-s-s-schenectady?' the old man replied: 'I on'y w-w-wish I'd a d-d-died the day I j-j-jumped the d-d-dock off.'

"There was a time, not over a dozen years ago, when if Bate Hayden's troughs for feeding horses were all found on top the little schoolhouse there was a suspicion that our guest had a hand in it, but, as he has been absent a number of years, he can prove an alibi, like old Gordonier, and say he was in S-s-s-schenectady."

Billy Bishop, who had been waiting on the table during the dinner, and was now serving the punch with frequent regularity, remarked: "Der old Gordonier was a ole hicocric, so he was."

"Now, Billy," said Tobi, "you are a little jealous because he got several jobs of hog-killing that you wanted. There are worse men than old Gordonier."

"Yes," replied Billy; "dere's meny wus as ole Gordonier; dey keep 'em chained, but——"

The master of ceremonies looked at Mr. Teller.

TOBIAS TELLER'S STORY.

"You all knew Bill Fairchild, big-hearted, generous Bill, who'd give the shirt off his back to any one who needed it. Well, one Sunday morning in May a poor clam peddler's horse drew his wagon to the ferry with its owner lying flat on the load. It was early, and people looked and remarked that the man was drunk, and passed on. Colonel Mike Bryan wanted some clams, and came out and selected what he wished and tried to rouse the man, and found that he was dead. Some one happened to know him, and also knew where he lived, and sent for his wife. In about an hour she came over from Albany, and about that time Bill dropped down that way. She was bemoaning her fate, and the fact that no clams had been sold. The fact was, the man had intended to reach some of the river towns before Monday morning, and peddle his stock on the homestretch, but had died from some cause; and the old horse, finding no controlling hand on the lines, had turned around somewhere, and started for home with his load and his dead master on its top. The crowd stood around idly looking at the dead man and the sorrowing woman, who really hadn't money enough to pay ferriage for the horse and wagon, when Bill pushed through and learned the situation.

"The man had been taken into Charley Bradbury's livery stable, and with only a word to the wife Bill mounted the wagon and started down street singing that old song, but in better voice than it was usually sung:

> 'Here's clams, prime clams I have to-day;
> They're fat and fresh from Rockaway;
> They're good for to roast, they're good for to fry,
> And they're good for to make a clam pot-pie.'

"The church-going people looked, and some thought Bill must be drunk, for everybody knew him; but if people didn't come out he knocked at the doors and told them all about the case, and before noon he was back, all sold out.   He asked the woman how much the load ought to bring, and she said it had cost $6, and at retail prices ought to bring $15.

" 'Well,' said Bill, 'I don't know much about selling clams, and here's all I've got for 'em,' and he emptied a lot of silver and bills in her lap, and went out.   The pile counted out nearly $40, and it was suspected that Bill had put in all that was left of his month's salary from the railroad.   When we asked Bill about it he would curl his lip and say:

" 'I'm a good clam peddler, an' can get the prices. Clams, ma'am?   Johnny, open the lady a nice fat one. Fresh?   Yes, m'm.   See 'em kick.   I think they spoiled a good clam peddler when they made me a bookkeeper. Yes, sis; they're fresh; how many?'

" 'How do you sell 'em?'

" 'Thirty cents a peck.'

" 'Mother says she'll give twenty-five.'

" 'Tell your mother to go to heaven.   Does she think

I stole 'em? Whoa! back, Jake! Here's another customer. Yes'm, just up by lightning express from Rockaway; caught last night. Ah, see how the juice runs out of his shell, thinking how you'll enjoy him.'

"Poor Bill! When he was burned to death trying to rescue the books from the office of the Boston & Albany Railroad, when the station burned at East Albany, and an appeal was made in behalf of his widow, the board of directors said: 'He did no more than his duty.'

"It is true that corporations have no souls, but Bill Fairchild had one, and when I think of his sacrifice for the widow of an unknown clam peddler and his heroic sacrifice of his life for a soulless corporation, I recognize the hero. Gentlemen: To the memory of Bill Fairchild!"

We had all known the reckless dare-devil, Bill, who in a good cause would cry "clams!" in a quiet village on a Sunday morning, and whose tragic death was fresh in the memory of all present; so when the next speaker began telling of him we were surprised. General Miller had selected his victim, and we heard

LOW DEARSTYNE'S STORY.

"Talking about Bill Fairchild reminds me of a winter night when my boat had been frozen up for months, and the ice in the Hudson had begun to get tender in spots. No teams had crossed the river for a fortnight, and where the foot passengers crossed there were boards placed in the most dangerous spots. Although there was a man in charge of the boat, who slept on board, I kept watch of the river to see that everything was safe. We usually wintered the boat in the Albany basin, but this time she was moored in the canal between the two big freight houses of the B. & A. R. R.

"On this particular night there was a heavy fog in which a man could easily get lost, and the ice was getting weaker every hour. I had looked in at the railroad office, and found Bill at work on his books, and sat down by the stove. After a while he looked up, and remarked: 'It's a bad night on the ice. Some people crossed the river just before dark, but you wouldn't get me on it. No, sir! I wouldn't try to cross that river for a thousand dollars.'

" 'Listen!' said I. 'What was that?'

" 'Somebody singing,' suggested he.

"A wail came from the river, distinctly this time, for the night was still. Bill grabbed a lantern, and we rushed out on the dock. The feeble light did not show an object ten feet away, but we heard a splash and a groan, apparently not far out in the river.

" 'Hang on!' cried Bill; 'I'll be with you soon,' and in spite of protest he dashed down the slope by Dandaraw's, where people took the ice to cross. He shouted, and soon I heard this dialogue:

" 'Oh, Lord! Help me out! I'm a respectable colored man, and live over in Nigger Hollow, an' my name's Stephen Baker. Oh, do please send someone quick!'

"Then Bill said: 'You're respectable, are you? What did you say your name was?'

" 'It's Stephen Baker, an' I'm a respectable colored man. Oh, do send some one quick, for I'll drown sure!'

" 'Are you Steve Baker that stole Sim Diamond's chickens?'

" 'No, Lord, no! I never took no chickens; it was my brother Jim. Oh, come quick!'

" 'What you got hold of?'

" 'A board. Oh, do come!'

"All the while Bill was looking for the edge of the

hole and taking off his clothes. In he went, and towed
the board and the darkey to the sound ice; but both were
too chilled to get out. I had alarmed the men in Dandaraw's bar, and they pushed out boards and rescued
both men. Bill had an attack of pneumonia and rheumatism, and lost a month's work. And that's the kind of
man Bill Fairchild was, and you all know how he died."

As I write this, thirty-seven years later, Whittier's
verse comes to mind:

> "Dream not helm and harness
>   The sign of valor true;
> Peace hath higher tests of manhood
>   Than battle ever knew."

When Low had finished Billy Bishop said: "Yes, Pill
Fairchild vos a goot fayler; we should trink punch mit
him." And

> "They drank to one saint more."

General Mat arose, and suggested that a representa-
tive Jayhawker from Bleeding Kansas was anxious and
willing to tell something about the human fruit which
the trees bore in that sanguinary region, or perhaps a
story of Osawatomie Brown, who had been hanged to
a tree in Virginia some three weeks before, would be
acceptable.

THE LOST HAT.

I had expected to be called on, and had laid out what
I thought to be a good story, but Miller's remarks sent
the whole thing out of mind. I was nervous and self-

conscious to a degree, and so with some remarks about the newspapers having told the whole Kansas story, and perhaps a little more, I said:

"Our host, Porter, would, I know, rather hear of my hunting and trapping experiences than about jayhawking, as they call it, so I will tell him how I lost a hat on a hunting trip. It was not a valuable hat; just one of the kind that you see in rural villages—a hat that under no conditions could ever have been a new one. You know the kind; they were never created by man, but have the air of having always existed. If I cared to paraphrase Byron I would say:

> 'I had a hat which was not all a hat,
> Part of the brim was gone, etc.'

"These details are necessary when you tell about a hat, for its shape, texture and color are all that comprise individuality in a hat. Its texture was felt, and its shape was not like the shiny 'nail keg' which adorns the brow of a member of Assembly when he comes to Albany; its color, if it had any, is beyond my power to describe. The sun had toyed with its hues until it had attained that delicate shade of old-mown hay seen on the chin whiskers of the member from Sqeedunk.

"That's the best description I can give of the hat. It was a rare day in autumn; you know how the hills and the maples looked; I won't go into that because I didn't lose them; they get around every year.

"I had a new turkey call, a sort of small box with a thin cover that said 'keouk' when you tickled it, and the turkeys were wild in Kansas, wilder than deer, and an old gobbler that had been shot at once or twice took no chances. I found a place to lie in the leaves behind a huge pine log; laid my rifle handy, and at intervals worked the new call. After a while a distant gobble was heard. More call and nearer gobble, and I began to feel very good. Soon a fine gobbler came in sight, strutting and feeling his way. I had learned not to overdo the calling trick, and kept silent as he advanced. I wanted to get him to come within thirty yards, and then try to take him in the head or neck, and utilize him for a dinner; so I watched under a limb that I had laid on top of the log. He was probably fifty yards away, and my heart was pumping more than was really necessary, when I dropped the call, and began to scratch leaves like a hen turkey looking for beech nuts, and shoved my hat up on a stick to represent a turkey's back, when ——! Lightning couldn't have been quicker! Something hit that hat and cut my head. Feel the scar! The fact was that I had called up a turkey gobbler and a wildcat or catamount at the same time, and fooled 'em both.. I didn't get the turkey, and I didn't get the hat. It can't be lost, for science says that nothing is lost—it only changes its form. Content with that assurance, I know that my hat is still somewhere in this universe; perhaps a portion of it has been taken up, as it decomposed, by the roots of trees and plants, and so it lives in other lives, or like

> 'Imperious Cæsar, dead and turned to clay,
> May stop a hole to keep the wind away.'

"But my hat was gone, taken without so much as 'by your leave,' and I only regret that I have neither the hide of the catamount nor the fragments of the hat to decorate my den. I can only say with Pope:

> 'A heap of dust alone remains of thee,
> 'Tis all thou art, and all the proud shall be.'

Billy Bishop by this time was beginning to feel very numerous, although Port had tried to keep the punch under his own eye, for Porter was a man who seldom looked upon the wine when it was rosy; but Billy paid no attention to the color of it; the white schnapps of Holland was as welcome to Billy as any. He wasn't anywhere near being "over his head," but just felt his oats, and wanted to talk.

BILLY BISHOP'S ADVENTURE.

"I'll yust tole you 'bout de hell-hole w'at Port had gone by for pa'tridges. John Pulver he always tell 'bout it, an' how spooks set 'round de edge in de dark of de moon an' work all kinds o' harm to people who come by der hole. I was a-choppin' in Glen Van Rensselaer's, when I dinks I co by Mr. Teller's for my ole axe to split de trees, an' it was so warm I lie down by myself to rest, an' I fall asleep by a nice shady place. W'en I wake it was all dark, an' I see a light down in a deep hole, an' den some stumps he roll up f'um der hole an' dey all get me around. Den I knowed dat was de hell-hole w'at John Pulver telled aboud. Was I schared? Vell, you bet you was some schared, too, ven you find yourself in de mittel von some stumps, an' dey all choin hants an' tance you aboud like some chilld'n w'en dey sing 'Ring Around Rosy.'

"Pooty soon dey stop, an' one big stump he say, 'Billy Bishop, did you got some schnapps? If you got some, yust put der pottle on my head an' go home.' I find der pottle in my coat, an' I put him on dat stump, an' by Chimminy, dey open der ring an' I nefer stop runnin' till

I reach Ike Fryer's tafern. Dey can all chop around dot hell-hole, but I know when I got a blenty."

JIM LANSING'S STORY.

"Gentlemen," said Jim, "I think that if Billy's bottle had not been so near empty he would not have seen so many stumps all dancing in one set. Just what might have happened if Billy had finished the bottle, and had none to leave for the spooks, will never be known; but that remarkable hole has a great many stories clustered about it. Men who call themselves geologists say it is only a 'sink,' but there is a foundation for the dread which some people have of it.

"During the Revolutionary War a portion of the American army were in barracks on what is now the McCulloch farm, just opposite my place on Clinton Heights. Almost every night the sentinel on the post at the southeast corner of the encampment, just in the edge of the woods, deserted. It was singular that all the desertions were from that one post, and 'most all the men were soldiers with good records. The officers were puzzled, and the men had all kinds of theories about it. My grandfather was a private in one of the regiments stationed there, and he, like the others, was perplexed by the singular state of affairs. This is what he told us boys in later years.

"It came grandfather's turn to be detailed for guard duty. A sentinel had deserted from that post the night before, and grandfather went to his captain and asked to be put on the same post. Said he, 'Captain, I don't believe all these men deserted. Some of 'em were as good men as can be found in the army, and wouldn't desert any more than you or I would. If you'll get me assigned to that post I'd like it.'

" 'How's this, Jim?' said the captain, for grandfather's name was Jim, same as mine; 'surely you don't want to desert like the rest, do ye?'

" 'Cap'n,' said my grandfather, 'they didn't desert. There's —— and ——,' naming two of his chums; 'they've gone, and I want to know where. Put me on that post on the relief that goes on past midnight, and if there's anything to find out I'll find it.'

"When he went to his post after midnight he picked his flint, and put fresh powder in the pan of his musket, and made up his mind that no matter about the rules against making an alarm, he would shoot the first thing that came near him. A 'coon whickered close by, but he could not see to shoot it. A hog feeding on beech nuts grunted satisfaction occasionally, and soon came in sight. When it came within twenty feet grandfather fired at it, and an Indian rose and yelled. When the corporal of the guard came there was a dead Indian and a hog skin. That told the story. Searching parties were sent out, and found a hole in which the bodies of ten soldiers lay. Its bottom could only be reached by jumping into a tree and descending. Six Indians were encamped in the hole, but they never got out alive. It's no wonder that the place has a bad name."

"Jim," said Tobi, "I read that story in my school history when I was a boy."

"That proves it," said Jim; "but no matter where you read it, my grandfather was the man who killed the Indian in the hog skin that had murdered all the sentinels on that post by the corner of the woods."

Tobi Teller rose to a point of order and remarked: "As there is a peep of daylight coming through the shutters, I now move that we adjourn."

A feeling of sadness comes over me when I recall the

fact that all these old friends are dead; but, in fact, most of the men I have fished with have gone over to the majority, and while in this train of thought up comes the old verse:

> And Jennie is wed and Annie is dead,
>   And Alice she fled in the auld lang syne;
> And I sit here at sixty year,
>   Dipping my nose in the Gascon wine.

THE END.

www.ingramcontent.com/pod-product-compliance
Lightning Source LLC
Chambersburg PA
CBHW032016120726
47902CB00013B/981